Dean Winternitz

Yale Medical School's Passionate Humanist

Priscilla Waters Norton

and

Howard Spiro, MD

The Program for Humanities in Medicine
Yale University
New Haven, Connecticut

ISBN: 1453718494
ISBN-13: 9781453718490
Library of Congress Control Number: 2010914637

Dedications

Priscilla Waters Norton:
To Levin and our sons, Quint and Jonathan

Howard Spiro:
In memory of my parents, Thomas and Martha Spiro

Contents

PREFACE

Over the entrance to the Sterling Hall of Medicine, just to the left of the entrance to the Yale School of Medicine, are incised the words "The Institute of Human Relations." That phrase summarizes Milton Charles Winternitz's concept of a medical institution in which mind and body, individual and society, are alike objects of clinical attention. Guided by that grand vision, he set out in 1920 first to save, and then to recreate, the Yale Medical School. Fifteen years later, he lost his position as dean, though he remained chairman of the Pathology Department. Today, many of Winternitz's colleagues and peers are commemorated in plaques, professorships, lectureships, laboratories, and buildings at the Medical School, while only a single prize is named for "Winter," as he liked to be called (and even that misidentifies him as "C. Winternitz"). Oh yes, a new "society" named for him can be joined by those who contribute money to an alumni fund! Yet Winter's influence, however unrecognized, can be found everywhere.

The grand entryway to the Institute of Human Relations reflects Winter's lofty dreams in words and architecture. Inside, the visitor passes under a pediment on which is painted a Greek phase translated as, "Will horsemen carry torches and pass them one to another during the race?" In the ancient Greek torch races, a torch was passed from hand to hand, as in the modern Olympics; here, the torch of knowledge is handed from one generation to the next.[1] Across Cedar Street, as medical students and patients make their way to the Dana Clinic and the Yale Physicians Building of the Yale-New Haven Medical Center on Howard Avenue, they come upon a courtyard with a fountain and Corinthian columns supporting what once was the elegant entrance to the old New Haven Hospital, a "state of the art" facility now used for offices. The building dates from the Winternitz era, and its philosophical foundations still underlie the "Yale Plan" of medical education that Winternitz created.

Photographs of Cedar Street about 1920, when Winternitz began what can justly be called his reign, show bustling city streets lined with shops and other businesses, activity now banished from the sprawling hospital complex that has taken over the neighborhood. The center of the Medical School is gradually tipping in an easterly direction, with the huge edifice for research and teaching, the Anlyan Center, erected on the city block that once held the nurses' dormitory, several drinking establishments, and a gas station frequented by mid-century medical faculty.

People either thought highly of Winternitz or they hated him. To some he was a pioneer and an inspired administrator, a great man whom they found compassionate, thoughtful, and kind. Others, probably the majority, described him as arrogant, unreasonable, and unmercifully cruel. Those who valued his intellect accepted his arrogance as something that neither he nor they could change.

Winternitz's career can be divided into four periods. The first includes his early childhood and education. He was bright enough to enter college at age fourteen and medical school at seventeen. Later, he joined the pathology staff at the Johns Hopkins Medical School, where he remained for fourteen years. The second and most important period began when he took over Yale's Pathology Department in 1917. Three years later, his appointment as dean of the Medical School enabled him to put into play his ideas about medical education, research, and clinical practice; in partnership with President James Angell, he rebuilt the school. The third period began when he was forced from the deanship in 1935, only to be rescued by World War II, which provided a timely focus for his talents and energies. Given the task of masterminding the national program for research and training in chemical warfare, he became a key figure on the National Research Council in the postwar years. The fourth and last period of his life was irresolute: he chaired committees and looked in vain for more spotlights.

Winternitz was an important figure in the history of American medical education in the 1920s and 1930s. Although more gifted as an administrator and teacher than as a scientist, he played a pivotal role in transforming the Yale Medical School from a third-rate appendage of the university into the prototype of the modern, research-oriented American medical school. As the catalyst for a renaissance in medical education at Yale, he set an example that may have led foundations in New York and elsewhere to apply pressure on other medical institutions to make similar changes.

Sadly, there have been no extensive historical studies of Winternitz's life and accomplishments, although certain aspects of his work have been described in some detail. Among other things, historians have yet to investigate his role in helping President Angell fight the forces of conservatism that were holding the university back. Many "Old Blues" resented the change from a private institution that prepared children of the wealthy Protestant elite for professional and financial careers into a more open and, by the standards of the time, "diverse" university accepting, if not welcoming, students of less exalted parentage.

Our account of Winternitz's personal saga falls somewhere between a memoir and a biography. Priscilla Norton was long married to Winternitz's protégé, Levin Waters, a 1937 graduate of the Yale School of Medicine and from 1937 to 1976 a member of the Department of Pathology. As a result, she knew Winternitz quite well during the last fifteen years of his life. Howard Spiro, a quondam professor of medicine and a gastroenterologist who worked at the Yale Medical School for forty-five years, muses that he resembles Winternitz in many ways. At the very least, he claims, "Every good idea for changing medicine that came to me was one that Winternitz had tried out during his time as dean." (Many of Winternitz's early ideas, which seemed radical in the 1920s, are commonplace today—for example, that medical professionals should try to keep people healthy, that nurses should be professional partners and members of the medical team, and that medical students should be treated as junior colleagues.) It is impossible for us to dissect our individual contributions. Priscilla wrote several entire chapters and Howard rewrote them all. Priscilla conducted most of the interviews, collected an amazing amount of material, and is the chief author of the book.

Winternitz destroyed many of his personal and professional papers, presumably sparing only those that he expected to enhance his reputation. When Levin and Priscilla Waters visited him during the last months of his life, he would often point to a few tidy cartons that contained "all I own in the world." This small archive, now at the Yale University Library, is the principal source for our book. One of Winternitz's children told us about a "locked cabinet" in his study, the contents of which were destroyed—to safeguard his secrets, some speculate--by his second wife, Polly Whitney Winternitz. In any event, the dearth of personal materials has led us to search elsewhere to fill in missing links. For example, personal opinions gleaned in interviews with people who knew

Winternitz served to balance the somewhat unflattering portrait that has taken shape over the years.

In addition to talking with Winternitz's children, friends, and former students, we have read through collateral files of many of his colleagues, including President Angell, who was his chief supporter. Yet we have taken considerable freedom in writing our narrative, in a way that professional historians will abhor. In extenuation, we take refuge in George Kennan's observation that those who write history must try to put themselves in the situations and emotional states of the protagonists, to imagine why they felt and acted as they did.[2]

Throughout our research and writing, we have repeatedly asked ourselves how many of Winternitz's ideas were original and how many were in the air or part of the zeitgeist. In search of answers, we have consulted the literature of the time—selectively, to be sure, for we are not historians. Fortunately, like so many other academic endeavors at the turn of the twenty-first century, history has turned to narrative for its perspectives, as eagerly as it has turned to psychoanalysis for explanations. A good story is worth a thousand facts, in medicine as in other fields. In constructing what Plato called a "likely story," we have necessarily relied heavily on memories--our own as well as others'—and on informed supposition based upon the available material.

In a mere fifteen years, Winternitz raised the Yale School of Medicine from respectable mediocrity to the top ranks. A man of the mid-twentieth century, he had little of the grace of the nineteenth, but all of the drive of the entrepreneur so praised today, coupled with a well-developed social conscience. How does it happen that an individual who did so much for Yale University, and had every reason to expect that the Medical School would be his monument, is almost totally forgotten some sixty years after his death? We offer our informal memoir as the first step toward a re-estimation of this great man.

The year 2010 marks the two-hundredth anniversary of the founding of the Yale School of Medicine, observed as its "bicentennial." It seemed appropriate, therefore, to celebrate also the life and works of one of its greatest leaders, and so we are delighted that our work appears at this time. We hope that it will prove a fitting tribute to the school and its dean so long forgotten.

Author's Note

Where there is friction, progress eventuates was one of Dr. Winternitz's favorite themes, which may explain the long gestation period of this book. His spirit has been hovering over our manuscript for a decade. I knew Winter as one would know a domineering, charismatic, and possessive mother-in-law. Although Howard Spiro never met him, he shares my fascination with the pioneering quality of Winter's mind and what he was able to accomplish.

Winter did not identify with his background or agonize about his heritage; he cared about the future and progress. He suffered from a loneliness of the mind, for few people could soar with his vision. I hope someone will be inspired to write about him from a historical point of view. His World War II experiences and postwar career round out his professional career on a high note.

I intend to place my interview notes and observations with the Archives at Yale.

Priscilla Waters Norton
October 13, 2010
Stony Creek, Connecticut

ACKNOWLEDGMENTS

We have many to thank. Foremost among them are three Winternitz children, Tom, Mary, and Bill. Priscilla Norton interviewed each of them, including two intensive days spent with Bill and his wife, Madeline, in Alabama. She also contacted Winternitz relatives in Maryland, two of whom had vivid memories of "Milton." She interviewed Eugenia Whitney Hotchkiss early on in the project, and corresponded with Steven Whitney. Elizabeth Harvey heads the list of surviving colleagues and students who have been generous with their comments and recollections.

In New Haven we interviewed friends of the Winternitz children, as well as several of Winter's junior colleagues and students. Dr. Max Taffel, a medical student when Winternitz was dean, offered valuable insights into those shining years. We owe another special debt of gratitude to Dr. William Wedemeyer, a student and member of the Pathology Department, who generously shared information about the department in the Winternitz era. Helen O. Heard astutely enlightened us with her unique knowledge of the Whitney family. Priscilla was able to draw on her own recollections from 1945 on, as well as on unpublished memoirs of Levin Waters.

Where would any project such as ours be without libraries? To Judith A. Schiff and the staff of Manuscripts and Archives at Yale's Sterling Memorial Library; to Toby Appel, librarian of the Medical History Library at the Yale Medical School; and to the staff of the Johns Hopkins Medical School Library we express our thanks and appreciation for their help, courtesy, and patience. The archives staff of the National Academy of Science couldn't have been more accommodating or cordial. We thank Pamela Spiro Wagner for her help early in this writing.

Finally, we owe a huge debt to Harry Haskell, master copyeditor, who clarified our thoughts, aligned our sentences with grace if not glory, and made this manuscript readable. He could not overcome, however, our disdain for scholarly paraphernalia.

Part 1.

Before Yale

Chapter 1. The Early Years

The story of Milton Winternitz began in the waning years of nineteenth century in the largely Jewish section of East Baltimore, Maryland. A plodding horse pulled an old black fiacre, making its way slowly along the cobbled streets. In it, ten-year-old Milton Charles Winternitz carried on a conversation with his father, Carl Winternitz, an insurance physician, as they made house calls among the neighborhood's immigrant tailors, cigar makers, vendors of pots and pans and furniture, clothing salesmen, and junk dealers. In the East Baltimore of Winternitz's time there were teeming tenements, but also, for the more prosperous, comfortable apartments, cozy delicatessens, movie houses, and small homes with yards and barns, like the one Milton's parents owned.[1]

Dr. Winternitz knew that his son had a brilliant mind and a good memory, and early on began teaching him--among other things--how to formulate drugs and how to recognize symptoms of typhus among the new arrivals from Eastern Europe. After school, Milton rolled pills and put them in vials; sometimes he did simple urine and sputum tests. More important, on those trips through East Baltimore, the boy must have seen that his father, usually so remote and autocratic, had another side to his personality, one he rarely revealed.[2]

Carl was a major influence on Milton. Later on, when Milton's own children showed an aptitude for science or medicine, he reminisced happily about what his father had taught him. He rarely mentioned Carl's autocratic rule, nor how this might have shaped his boyish ambitions. It was, however, no secret that father and son shared a terrible temper, one that Milton could rarely subdue. Many years later, when he was dean of the Yale Medical School, Winternitz seldom looked back on those days or told students about his father. True, he may have been too proud to deny his Jewish roots in a world where they might have stood in his way, but he seemed to find it hard to reckon with a difficult childhood, especially one that did not fit his vision of himself or where he was going.

Milton's parents, Carl Winternitz and Jennie Kittner, were Austro-Hungarian immigrants who had married in Europe and settled in the German-Jewish neighborhood of East Baltimore. Carl was by all accounts a self-important but respected insurance doctor. Germanic, demanding, domineering, and harsh, he was given to scant words of encouragement. (The legend that Carl sent his collars to Paris to be washed and ironed seems to have been transferred from the surgeon Halsted to Dr. Winternitz. It is doubtful that the family had either the money, or the pretensions, for that kind of luxury.) The property he bought on the corner of Lombard

Street and Broadway, more imposing than a row house, displayed a tidy front yard and a backyard where Jennie kept a garden and a few chickens. It had, in addition, a barn for one or two horses and a carriage.

Carl and Jennie's first child was a girl they named Irene. Carl looked upon females as inferior, so whatever her true temperament or capacities, Irene was banished to the kitchen with her mother. While Carl was alive, Jennie kept her spirits up reading French novels, something she may have had to do more or less secretly, as such books were considered racy at the turn of the century.

After Carl died, Jennie lived with Irene, who had married into the Bachrach family of Baltimore. The Winternitz children remember their grandmother as a small, shadowy person dressed in black, a dutiful cook and housekeeper. By contrast, the warm, loving, and religious in-laws found her fun-loving and easy to be with. Living with the Bachrachs, the drab old woman whom the Winternitz children only dimly recall seemed to become almost youthful again.[3]

EARLY LIFE AND EDUCATION

Carl and Jennie's first son was born on February 19, 1885. Family tradition holds that he was named Milton after John Milton and Charles after Carl. It was soon apparent that he was very bright. When he was first able to talk, his father started his training by teaching him to memorize poetry. Soon Milton could recite reams of *Paradise Lost*, much of which he remembered to the end of his life. He attended Baltimore's Public School Number 3, graduating at age fourteen. In high school, he taught himself both Latin and Greek. An added benefit, the family was bilingual at home, so he spoke German as well as English. Their private library was comprised of the books his parents had collected, including his mother's French novels. These no doubt broadened his outlook.

Milton does not seem to have found much joy in childhood. Before school each day he had to feed and groom the horse, then hitch it up to the carriage, bringing it around to the front of the house to wait for his father. But he didn't like horses, or dogs either, preferring the aloof, free spirit of cats--good company for a boy who had little time for play. The few leisure activities he truly enjoyed as a child he would continue to pursue as a man: berry picking, reading, gardening. As an adult he understood the importance of fresh food and became a highly skilled gardener. All the same, he sometimes regretted his lack of interest in music. Occasionally, he would play chess with his father, but he gave it up when chess became a distraction from his work at Johns Hopkins. Milton could never just play. His early years may have built a strong foundation for work and a medical career, but they most certainly failed to equip him with the ability to relax and have fun. For that Milton needed a childhood, and, in a very real sense, he never had one.

Milton's German-Jewish neighborhood was orthodox, blessed by several synagogues. The Winternitzes were not particularly observant, however, and their Jewish heritage seemed to mean little. Jennie's only nod to Passover seems to have been to put out a plate of matzo. There is no clear evidence that Milton had a bar mitzvah.

Because of the early tutelage his father had provided, Milton, ahead in school, was always younger than the rest of his schoolmates. Feisty enough to protect himself, he had acquaintances, but no friends--a lifelong trait--and while often solitary, hated being alone. He learned social interaction not through sports or gamesmanship but by observation, through books, theater, and the movies. He was intellectually competitive and took pride in besting others in argument, yet he valued people who had something to teach him, or at least with whom he could converse on an equal footing. Many years later, when the microbiologist Hans Zinsser spent a night at 210 Prospect Street, the two men talked long into the night and continued their conversation at breakfast. Winter called his office at nine a.m. to tell them that he would not come in until after Zinsser's train had left. The message was clear: nothing could come before this conversation, so enjoyable did he find a true meeting of minds.

JOHNS HOPKINS COLLEGE AND MEDICAL SCHOOL

At fourteen, Milton went off to John Hopkins College, from which he graduated with a B.A. degree after a three-year course. Little is recorded about those years. He may have lived at home, commuting to college by trolley car or bicycle. Surprisingly for such a small man, he played guard on the Hopkins football team. Traditionally, football at Hopkins was not taken seriously, but was played strictly for entertainment; many years later, Bill Winternitz gleefully chortled that his father would "spit tobacco juice at the opponents." In later years, he always bought season tickets for the Yale football games, to give to his weekend houseguests, but rarely attended them himself

On June 6, 1903, in his one-page application to the Johns Hopkins Medical School, Milton related that he'd read the Latin of "Caesar, Cicero, Virgil, and Ovid," the French of "Racine, Moliere etc.," and, in German, *Faust* and Wallenstein. He noted that he had taken undergraduate courses in physics, chemistry, and biology. The application asked nothing about his ability to pay; he worked his way through medical school by selling penny insurance.

Given the job of planning for the Johns Hopkins Hospital in 1879, physician John Shaw Billings helped pick the faculty, designed the buildings in which they would work, and planned the curriculum they would teach. A military surgeon in the surgeon general's office, after the Civil War he was responsible for a small library that was the predecessor of the National Library of Medicine. There he developed the first volume of the *Index Medicus,* which in its computerized form remains indispensable to academic physicians. In 1895, as the first director of the New York Public Library, Billings helped plan the great edifice on Fifth Avenue with its famed lions, "Patience" and "Fortitude." He died in 1913, these two monuments his memorial.

A private, nonsectarian university founded in 1876 according to the will of Johns Hopkins, a Baltimore businessman, Johns Hopkins University was the first to emphasize graduate education (although the Ph.D. degree was first granted at Yale). Its Nurses' Training School opened very early in 1889, but the launching of the hospital, which Hopkins had stipulated was to be an integral part of the Medical School, had to be postponed owing to a reduction in the dividends intended to pay for its construction and endowment. Fortunately, the women of Baltimore raised the needed money in 1890: the Women's Fund Committee stipulated that that women were to be admitted on equal terms with men, a step that other medical schools delayed taking for many, many years.

Billings got Hopkins's first president, Daniel Gilman from Yale, to appoint William Welch to the Hopkins faculty on the recommendation of Prof. Julius Cohnheim of Germany, with whom Welch had worked. Welch was delighted by the chance to go to the new school in Baltimore, where he would have a full-time salaried position in the Pathology Department and work under the famed William T. Councilman. Later, Welch was joined by William Osler, surgeon William Halsted, and gynecologist Howard Kelly. These four clinical chiefs were immortalized by their achievements and writing, even more than by the famous painting of Thomas Eakins.

THE PATHOLOGY DEPARTMENT

Winternitz quickly fell under the spell of Welch, a man large in mind and body, a visionary teacher, and a scientist. Endowed with a genial personality that made him much beloved, Welch embodied qualities that young Winternitz most craved and lacked. As its first dean, Welch had encouraged the growth of the Johns Hopkins Medical School. By 1903 a master of the politics of medicine, he planned to remake American medical education; he also played a large role in the saga of the Yale Medical School.

Welch had studied in Germany and admired Rudolf Virchow, one of the founders of the discipline of pathology. Virchow was convinced that human disease had its origin in the cell, but recognized that men and women are the product of their environmental influences, occupation, heredity, and even social class, all of which generate the pathological changes doctors call disease. As Sherwin Nuland has written, he "recognized the primacy of the whole person if disease is to be prevented."

During his studies in Germany, Welch had been fascinated by laboratory research, but his interest was mainly intellectual. He did little hands-on research himself; the cheerleader, he had enough understanding to discuss what his students were doing, but never directed their research. Nicknamed "Popsy," a name that expressed his unique place in the hearts of his colleagues, he was an absent father much of the time, leaving the "family" in the care of older children. H.L. Mencken, a good friend and fellow Baltimorean, called Welch an opportunist and "one of the laziest men alive."

Welch had "class"--another quality that Winternitz greatly admired—as well as money. He was comfortable with himself and treated everyone with charm and consideration. He told good stories and enjoyed good food and wines. He had been a natural leader at Yale, where he was a "Bones" man, a club that even today is said to guarantee success in life after Yale.

Winternitz was twenty-two when he joined the staff of the Pathology Department at Hopkins. The more senior investigators were otherwise engaged and handed many of their duties over to him. George Whipple was in Panama and William McCallum was "flirting with several offers of professorships," leaving the department to be run by four junior men.

The resident staff lived in the hospital and loved the camaraderie as much as the stimulation of sharing ideas. Those were happy, stimulating times and Winternitz found the Hopkins nurses the prettiest of all. And what did those pretty nurses see in Winternitz? At his tallest, he stood five feet six inches, and his hair was thick and black. His passport says he had dark skin, an oval face, and dark eyes. To many, they seemed like one-way mirrors through which he could see without being seen. Occasionally, his eyes would twinkle with amusement, flash with anger, or soften with sympathy, but most of the time they gave away little more than the entrance to a tunnel. His dark, olive skin was the sort that never seemed to burn, only darken.

Fire and ice--Winternitz could be both. One of his students described him as "like a mirrored ball reflecting light in all directions," for that is the way he talked when he was inspired. In a dark mood, he was more like a thunderhead ready to strike--lightning followed by a cold wind. To the Hopkins nurses he was meticulous, demanding, and very masculine, with a smoldering magnetism that some women found fascinating and others repulsive. His male colleagues agreed that he was brilliant. Some found him brash and insufferable, in others he engendered unqualified loyalty, but no one could keep up with him.

Welch's delegating was wonderful training and no hardship for Winternitz, who loved work as the best way to gain experience. Ten years later, in welcoming the entering class at the Yale School of Medicine, he would tell them that they were "here to learn rather than to be taught." Winternitz made himself indispensable to Welch, working his way up from fellow to associate pathologist and pathologist to the City Hospital. More and more, Welch relied on young Winternitz, now indisputably one of Welch's "Rabbits," to go out into the world and spread the gospel of "the Hopkins."

Welch was happy to make his own life easier by taking advantage of his juniors in the most jovial and polite way.

March 11, 1911
Maryland Club

Dear Dr. Winternitz--

I find that I shall not be able to meet the class tomorrow—Friday--afternoon, as I had expected.

Will you or one of the others on the staff give the lecture at two o'clock?

Yours sincerely,
William H. Welch

At twenty-six, four years after receiving his degree, Winternitz was able to give the lecture for Dr. Welch on a moment's notice. He was proud enough of the ensuing praise to save the notes of thanks. One in Dr. Welch's hand, dated April 28, 1916, congratulates Winternitz on having "all your papers" included in the final "programme" of the "Pathologists and Bacteriologists." Filling in for the boss was wonderful training, but not reward enough for a man who saw his destiny as a leader in medical education. The first annual report of the Department of Pathology in 1916 contained five reports bearing Winter's name--three written by him alone and two others by him with an associate or two.[4]

HELEN WATSON WINTERNITZ

Winternitz fell in love with a student named Helen Watson, daughter of Thomas Watson, the legendary "Come here, Mr. Watson" who had worked with Alexander Graham Bell on the telephone and other inventions. Lovely and spirited, Helen was both older and taller--at five feet nine inches--than Winternitz. She was an independent young woman: when her father would not send her to college, with her mother's connivance she ran away to Wellesley. After a while, Thomas Watson became as proud of his daughter's graduating Phi Beta Kappa as he might have been of any son, and when she was accepted at the Johns Hopkins Medical School, he sent her on, secretly pleased. Family legend tells how she took an extra year with William Osler after receiving her M.D., but in that case she must have gone to Oxford, because Osler left for Oxford in 1905. It is difficult to accept that she would have done that, but it is not impossible.

Helen's brothers, Tom and Ralph, both died before reaching maturity, sad events that most likely motivated her to become a doctor. She was more interested in doing than recording what she did, but a thoroughly nice person, modest and intelligent, speaks to us from the pages of her schoolgirl diary.[5]

When Milton Winternitz was promoted to associate pathologist in 1913, he finally could afford to get married. According to his daughter, Mary Cheever, the Watsons were very much against their daughter's marriage to a Jew. Regardless, Helen Watson and Milton Charles Winternitz were married on March 20, 1913. We have no record of what was probably a simple home wedding, if they followed the custom of the time.

The marriage was never listed in the Watson family Bible, we have been told. There are no pictures of the bridal couple, but a photograph survives of Helen wearing a handsome blue-velvet suit and a dashing blue hat with a long white ostrich plume trailing gracefully; it is said to be her wedding outfit. Whatever resentment the Jewish son-in-law may have caused, the arrival of grandchildren tied everyone together as a family. And as with many families, summer became a bonding time when the grandparents wanted to be with the children. Mrs. Watson and Winter quickly developed a bond that lasted as long as she lived, and Thomas Watson couldn't help being proud of Winter.

The Watsons were the Winternitz children's real grandparents; they hardly knew their Grandmother Winternitz. The Watsons were reconciled enough to build a summer house for their son-in-law and his family later on--the legendary Treetops that was to play so large a role in their family life. The dream of acquiring acreage on a lake where the children could run barefoot, and they could raise most of their food, was a natural progression from the Watsons' summers on Lake Champlain. Helen particularly wanted her children to observe the natural world at first hand. The Watsons could afford to make these dreams materialize. Every indication is that

Treetops was a joint project from the beginning, a family project, a shared enthusiasm.

The Winternitzes' honeymoon was a year's sabbatical visiting universities, studying new techniques, and just traveling around the world. As the bridegroom carried along his black bag equipped for emergencies, his family believes that he treated people along the way as the need arose. We know very little about that year. There are no snapshots and no letters have been saved, most likely because upon their return Winternitz scooped up all their letters home to use as notes for his report. A few blank postcards in the Winternitz family archives may date from that trip; there is a lone image of the Jewish Cemetery in Prague, looking very much as it does today, dated only by the paper and photography. A few old-style postcards of European buildings from the 1920s are mute reminders of other unrecorded events.

We know that Helen and Milton went to France and then Germany, where they studied for a few months. Then they moved on to Lebanon, Turkey, Persia, Russia, and China via the Trans-Siberian Railway. By then Helen was pregnant with their first child, who would be born after their return to Baltimore. In later years, Winternitz rarely talked about the trip to his children. In the Winternitz archives at Yale we found a letter from a Persian doctor whom they met and who consulted with Winternitz about a young man suffering from "neurasthenia." The doctor and his patient went to England, where the diagnosis was "dementia praecox," or schizophrenia, as it is called today. The Persian doctor saw Osler at Oxford and the two of them spoke about the Winternitzes; this is almost the only evidence that they stopped in Persia long enough to connect with at least one person.

Upon their return, Winternitz took over running the Pathology Department at Hopkins. Stanhope Bayne-Jones, later to succeed Winternitz as dean at Yale, joined the department the following year, 1915, to get extra training as a pathologist. Bayne-Jones worshiped Welch, but he got Winternitz! Their careers were to touch and interweave for the rest of their lives.

Winternitz first demonstrated his gift for administration in trying to help Bayne-Jones get started. Routine service work in the department was often delayed because laboratory work for the hospital was sent out to a commercial lab, where there was no quality control. Winternitz figured that if he could raise enough money to build and equip an in-house laboratory, it should be self-supporting in a year. He raised the money and offered the job of running the lab to Bayne-Jones, who hesitated, explaining that he lacked the necessary training. Winternitz sent him to New York to work with Hans Zinsser, a well-known microbiologist best remembered for his autobiography. Bayne-Jones regarded that year with Zinsser as particularly fortunate, for he found not only his career in microbiology but a friendship with Zinsser that would last the length of his career.

Yale people who trained under Winternitz never forgot his teaching methods, which came from his time at Hopkins.

He learned from Halsted both to use sarcasm to make his point, which was already in his nature, and to "[n]ever do anything to a patient without understanding the why and the wherefore," a lesson he drummed into his own students' heads. Nevertheless, his quiet, respectful ways of doing an autopsy, explaining and observing as he proceeded, had about it the spirit of Halsted at the operating table.

From exposure to Osler, Winternitz learned compassion for patients and the importance of the home environment in their treatment. Osler deemed the hospital the equivalent of the laboratories for the third and fourth years of medical school, emphasizing that the whole art of medicine lies in observation. Before the Johns Hopkins Medical School set the example, a physician could, and usually did, graduate from an American medical school without having spent any time at the bedside. Nor did most American medical schools of that era have any requirements for admission; one simply had to be able to do the written work and assimilate the textbooks and lectures.

Among the Winternitz papers is this letter from Dr. Welch:

> 807 Saint Paul Street
> Baltimore, April 28, 1916
>
> Dear Winternitz--
>
> You and Councilman seem to have had a fine time together, and he is very enthusiastic about you and

> the laboratory. I am so glad that you have had the opportunity of getting well acquainted with him, and realizing what an original and inspiring man he is in the laboratory. When he left I felt that the underpinning had dropped out, but no one has ever had such good fortune with the succession of assistants as I have had. Everyone seems to appreciate the splendid work which you are doing in developing and improving the department as much as I do.

Winternitz was hard put to assess his future at Hopkins. On March 28, 1917, he received a letter from his father-in-law in Boston, who wrote that he had met Dr. Welch at the railroad station and discussed his prospects at Hopkins:

> McCallum may not accept and in that case you will stand an exceedingly good chance to get the position you are entirely capable of filling, but you are so young that your contributions to your science, although most excellent, are not as voluminous as need be in one filling so prominent a place. Age, he intimated, was the only objection against your election. . . . [H]e said you had a genius for organization. He said you are the same type of a man as Simon Flexner. . . . [H]e asked me what I thought of your going to China. . . . [H]e did not want you to go and thought they could not spare you here.[6]

As it turned out, McCallum was offered the professorship at the Hopkins. The General Education Board--founded by John D. Rockefeller to improve educational institutions--offered Winternitz the chair in Peking, and he was also approached by Albany Medical School.

LOOKING FOR A JOB

Even though Winternitz hoped that he might succeed Welch as chairman of Pathology, he must have realized how slim his chances really were. "Dr. Welch always told us he hoped we would become good enough so that someone else would want us, and that we could not look forward to a permanent position in Baltimore," he wrote to Simon Flexner in March 15, 1937.

He knew he was "good enough" and that his time had come, but the offers from China and Albany were not what Winternitz had in mind. Then he received a confidential, long-hand letter from J. Morris Slemons, professor in the Department of Obstetrics and Gynecology at Yale. It is worth recording in its entirety because of its content and because it is our earliest record of the name "Winter" by which he was known to his friends and which we shall use from now on.[7]

March 24, 1917
My Dear Winter,

For some time, as you know, the medicine faculty has been ambitious to reorganize the department of pathology. This has been delayed because when the reorganization took place they wished it might be thorough and complete. Naturally in these circumstances, provision would have to be made for the present professor of pathology, Doctor Charles Bartlett, so that he would no longer be connected with that department. Thus far the way to accomplish that object has not been clear; but the completion of the new laboratory has put a new face on the problem, and, it seems one accomplished result is that the authorities now realize the need for an immediate settlement of the problem. I have reason to believe we shall know within two weeks what this solution will be.

Naturally, I have thought of you and in my own mind have been wondering what your reaction would be, if there were an opportunity to join us. Are you going to be at the New York meeting of laboratory men in April? If so, would you care to meet with me about the situation? I would be glad to go down to see you.

Sincerely,
(signed) Slemmons

Please regard this letter as absolutely confidential.
JMS

Winter's reply is dated March 29: "Your letter interests me personally more than anything that has happened during this eventful past year." He informed Slemmons that Mrs. Winternitz would be with him in New York and that he was eager to talk over the situation.

The next letter from Slemmons, dated April 22, 1917, related that the Yale Corporation had voted to keep the clinical years of medical instruction. "They decided to place all branches on a full-time basis as soon as funds were available; and appointed a committee to make sure that the Rockefeller gift would be secured, and, finally, they decided to make the changes in the Department of Pathology about which I have talked to you. I believe, therefore, that within a few days now you will be authoritatively approached regarding this matter." Slemmons closed by saying that he was sending two slides of uterine scrapings for Winternitz's opinion.

Winter's appointment as head of Pathology was held up because of widespread public indignation about the dismissal of the very popular Dr. C. J. Bartlett, who had long been head of the department. Bartlett was recognized as a practical pathologist, the "second best professor" at the Yale Medical School, and an excellent teacher. But the new dean, George Blumer, was intent upon replacing "practical physicians" with "scientific research experts." In his effort to keep up with the new spirit in medicine, he had come in for criticism, even in the newspapers of January 1917.

After much private negotiation, matters gradually eased, with Bartlett becoming chief pathologist at the Grace Hospital, down the road on Orchard Street. There he continued to work until he was more than eighty years old, supervising the merger of that hospital with the New Haven Hospital in the 1940s and 1950s. After all that acrimony, he took considerable pleasure in the much later assistance of Levin Waters in the Pathology Department at the Grace Hospital. Levin had been the assistant to Winternitz, and here he was helping Bartlett, who had been dispossessed so many years earlier. Waters did not want rival laboratories on either side of the soon-to-be Grace-New Haven Community Hospital, so he gave the job in the Grace Hospital (soon to become the Memorial Unit of the new merged hospitals) to Barry McAllister, the nephew of Lewis Weed, who had been Waters's boss in the wartime laboratories in Washington.

Winter was offered the job of head of Pathology at Yale on April 17, 1917, at a salary of $4,000; he accepted on June 14. Three years later, on May 7, 1920, he was unanimously voted dean for five years at $8,000 a year.

Chapter 2. The Yale, Hopkins, and Harvard Medical Schools

In the first two decades of the last century, the Yale Medical School was of little or no national consequence. To put Winternitz's accomplishments into context, we will consider the state of American medicine in the early twentieth century, with particular reference to Yale's modern rivals, the antipodes of Harvard and Johns Hopkins. In doing so, we rely on information provided by G.W. Pierson, Wilbur Cross, K.M. Ludmerer, and others.[1]

Doubtless, education at Johns Hopkins shaped Winternitz's ideas, but to put them into action he needed financial support from New York foundations. Fortunately, such support was forthcoming, thanks to Yale alumni, notably Dr. William Welch. Abraham Flexner of the General Education Board was certainly indirectly responsible for much of the Medical School's success, though George Blumer and Milton Winternitz were the catalysts.

THE JOHNS HOPKINS MEDICAL SCHOOL

Throughout the first half of the nineteenth century, the French influence on medical practice in the United States was dominant. American physicians who could went to Paris to complete their training. However, during the latter half of the century in Germany, the growing emphasis on science provided a rational basis for practice in the application of experimental physiology to clinical practice. This new approach to science led many American physicians to choose central Europe for advanced medical education, instead of studying with the excellent French clinicians.

After the Civil War, local medical schools and medical education at American universities slowly improved thanks to the new emphasis on science. The Johns Hopkins Medical School served as the model for the Flexner Report of 1910, which led to the recreation of American medical education, as both the symbol of this revolution and its beacon. By the time Winternitz came to Yale in 1917, Hopkins boasted full-time salaried faculty, having brought the German approach to medical research to America. Moreover, the four eminent physicians we have already mentioned (Halsted, Welch, Osler, and Kelly) provided its clinical foundation for years to come.

By 1920 Johns Hopkins had become the very model of a modern teaching hospital, its Medical School a home for scientific investigation. Osler insisted that students should learn directly from patients, using books and lectures as supplements. One physician was in charge of both the Medical School department and the corresponding clinical department in the hospital. Residents in clinical medicine and research fellows in the preclinical sciences brought to the hospital a notably new group hitherto unknown in the United States.

Coincidentally, and most important to the ensuing changes, were the foundations set up by millionaire industrialists like John D. Rockefeller and Andrew Carnegie to help erase their reputations as "robber barons." These foundations supporting education were run by men like Frederick Gates, chairman of the board of Rockefeller's General Education Board, and Dr. William Welch.[2]

Harvard's rejection of the full-time system disturbed the New York foundations, which were run, as it happened, by many loyal Yale alumni. Doubtless, they were not disappointed to have the chance to reframe the provincial Yale Medical School as another Johns Hopkins. Winternitz would prove its "steam engine" once Welch had put him there.

The American Medical Association had created a Council on American Education in 1904. In its first report in 1905, the council recorded that only 5 of 155 medical schools in the United States and Canada required at least two years of college training; Johns Hopkins was one of the very few that required a college degree for medical training.

ABRAHAM FLEXNER.

The Flexner Report focused the direction of American medicine by highlighting the Johns Hopkins Medical School. Sponsored by the Carnegie Foundation for the Advancement of Teaching, the report has been taken as the apotheosis of a reform movement that was already well on its way by 1910. It encouraged the reorganization of American medical schools on the model of German-speaking schools. Generous grants from the New York foundations made changes happen far more quickly than might have been expected. Money speaks—and people obey.

Flexner had graduated from Johns Hopkins in 1886, at age nineteen. He ran a private school in his home state of Kentucky for a few years before going on to study at Harvard and in Germany. His book *The American College*, published in 1908, attracted a lot of attention, most importantly from Henry Prichett, the head of the Carnegie Foundation, who was setting standards for a number of professions, including medicine. Impressed by Flexner's observations about American colleges, Prichett asked him to evaluate the medical schools of the United States.[3]

Flexner first traveled to Europe to see what was going on there. Like his more scientific physician brother, Simon, who later became director of the Rockefeller Institute, he admired the German system of medical education. Not unexpectedly, therefore, Flexner took that tradition of medical study and research as the model for American schools. His admiration for Yale must have come mainly from his associates rather than from his own experience. Yet by classifying the Medical School at Yale as "of the better type," and urging its parent university to mount "a vigorous campaign" for an endowment, the Flexner Report stimulated the school's rebirth.

The impression is hard to resist that the hierarchy knew how to prepare the way for what they deemed desirable changes. When Frederick Gates of the Rockefeller Foundation famously asked Flexner the best way to spend a million dollars to reorganize medical education, he could not have been ignorant of Flexner's earlier association with Hopkins. Nor was it surprising that Flexner gave the possibly apocryphal response that the support ought to go to Welch at Johns Hopkins. Young Flexner could not have been unaware that Gates was a friend of "Popsy" Welch, then dean of the Hopkins Medical School, but that is how myths are made. The choice, however foreordained, was a wise one. By 1913 the Rockefeller Foundation was providing $65,000 a year for Johns Hopkins to set up a "full-time" clinical teaching staff.

Flexner went on to join Rockefeller's General Education Board, which he is credited with steering toward its role in medical education. Flexner was to play a large, if sometimes behind-the-scenes, role in the expansion and improvement of the Yale Medical School. Partly, this was the result of his connections with Col. Abraham Ullman, president of the New Haven Hospital, and of his growing friendship with Winternitz. That all three were Jews making their way in a Christian society could not have weakened their bond. For a long time Flexner was so close to Winternitz that it seems almost as if Winternitz had only to ask and funds would flow—until the development of the Institute for Human Relations strained that bond..

Welch exemplifies the deep connections between the Medical Schools of Yale and Hopkins. The very first president of Johns Hopkins University, Daniel C. Gilman, was a native of Norwich, Connecticut, a graduate of Yale College, and a former professor of geography at its Sheffield Scientific School. After being passed over by Yale, he took on the presidency of the University of California for four years before moving on to Baltimore.

The academic world of those times was small and inbred. Pathology was the preeminent basic science of medicine in the 1880s, and the focus of most academic physicians who had studied in Germany until experimental physiology gradually took its place. Pathology was truly the mother of clinical practice in the twentieth century, for it helped physicians to understand the diseases in their patients, especially those that the "images" from the new field of radiology would depict. In the early 1900s, almost anybody who was to be somebody had had special training in pathology, either in central Europe or at Hopkins.

The prospect of a full-time salaried faculty alarmed physicians everywhere, even at Hopkins. Lewellys Barker, who was to succeed Osler as professor of medicine at Hopkins, is credited with being the first, in 1902, to bring up in public the idea of well-paid but full-time clinical faculty who would teach and do research. Any patient fees would redound to a general fund. Welch and Gates were in agreement, but others were not.

William Osler had been much against a salaried system, fulminating in his letters against the proposal that Dean Welch was pushing; in 1905 he left Hopkins for Oxford partly for that reason. (Later he came to recognize the virtues of the full-time system, at least when he did not suffer its consequences.) But Barker, its onetime proponent, for reasons never fully disclosed, left his position as chairman of Medicine to go into private practice, and so Theodore Janeway, another Yale graduate, took his job.[4]

It was not until 1914 that the General Education Board and Johns Hopkins finally agreed on the full-time system. Even then, it was limited to the Departments of Medicine, Surgery, and Pediatrics. Kelly, the chief of Gynecology, opposed it; and presumably his generosity with the money he had earned at Hopkins bought the exemption of his department. Nor was Psychiatry included, which may account for its later exemption from the full-time strictures at Yale.

Thanks to the financial backing of the General Education Board, full professors gradually became full-time, while the rest of the faculty remained only partly salaried. This development split the Hopkins faculty into university staff and clinical staff, the latter defined as "such instructors as are engaged in private practice." The clinical staff were segregated by title as "professor of clinical medicine," a distinction later adopted at Yale and other medical schools. That division may not have been to the Medical School's advantage in New Haven, where town-gown relationships remained troubled into the 1990s.

WILLIAM HENRY WELCH: WINTERNITZ'S MENTOR

William Welch had an extraordinary influence on the rebirth of the Yale Medical School as well.[5] Like John Fulton of Yale later, he was not at heart a scientist, but a director and a thinker, and a medical politician with estimable goals. He was quite disorganized, according to his lifelong friend and critic, the acerbic essayist H.L. Mencken. Even though Welch founded the *Johns Hopkins Bulletin* and the *Journal of Experimental Medicine*, stories tell of how he would pile up letters and manuscripts on chairs and on the floor, without ever opening them. It is said that periodically Welch would spread a layer of newspaper over his desk, figuring that the layers below would take care of themselves!

Welch had a suite of rooms in a boarding house at 935 St. Paul's Street, then a good address in Baltimore. The good doctor spent much of his leisure time at the

University Club or the Maryland Club, the latter famous for its food, gentlemanly entertainment, and atmosphere. His quarters at home were said to be so messy that he usually held dinner parties at the Maryland, where tradition still ruled. Winternitz's successor as dean at Yale, Stanhope Bayne-Jones, so it is said, took rooms on the floor above Welch, placing his bed directly over Dr. Welch's in case some wisdom drifted up through the cracks.

Welch deserves this interlude in the life of Winternitz, for everywhere in those years his influence was evident. More than anyone else, he was responsible for bringing the German model of medical education to America. According to his associate and acolyte, Simon Flexner, and Flexner's son, Thomas, he was truly the "Dean of American Medicine." Almost anyone of any consequence at the Yale Medical School had worked with him at Hopkins. Unlike Winternitz, whose records are sparse, Welch left "an amazingly full collection of original documents."

Simon Flexner, the physician brother of Abraham, described Welch as "a short heavy man whose bright blue eyes twinkled over a dark beard. . . . Stocky rather than stout . . . his clothes were dark and inconspicuous . . . and his manner was very quiet and comforting." Welch's strengths lay in his geniality; his relaxed, even lazy approach to life, and doubtless also his appearance in an era when a van Dyke beard and a "portly" profile conjured up images of a grandfather. Yet the Flexners labeled him a "battler," and Welch certainly worked to get his way and, as Mencken caustically observed, serve his own interests as well.

In a later memoir, Winternitz's faculty colleague, Prof. John Paul, a graduate of the Johns Hopkins Medical School and a professor of epidemiology and public health at Yale, marveled, "It has never ceased to be a mystery to me that Welch tolerated him [Winternitz] as a member of his department, for even as long as a decade. 'Popsy' Welch was to us students a kindly and infinitely wise old gentleman who always did his best to help and encourage medical students in the learning process, whereas Winternitz was cocky in his younger days, almost a martinet. He taught by the method of terrorism." Welch always had a positive point of view, and his laissez-faire method of letting people who worked with him do whatever they wanted must have been enticing. A letter to C.J. Bartlett (the pathologist whom Winternitz would later replace at Yale), who was inquiring about postgraduate training, sets the tone:

> With the training which you have already had I infer that you may not care for a regular course, but prefer to follow the work of the laboratory and to work under general supervision. This I should be glad to have you do and should endeavor to see that you had such advantages as the laboratory offers. You can have free access to the autopsies and can become familiar with the methods, working upon such subjects as you

> desire. —You can remain on as long as you desire in the summer. The charge will be twenty-five dollars.

Welch had no preconceived plan of research, but looked at whatever his staff brought to him. He often failed to turn up in the laboratory, was late for lectures, and was "imperfect" in his autopsy work. His inability to complete any project was well known. As the Flexners put it, "Success depended entirely on one thing: the personality of the teacher." People just naturally wanted to win his approval, to be like him, and to be liked by him. Welch had no system, but he had good manners and an attractive disposition, he liked good food and wine, and he was the right man in the right place at the right time, with the connections to make American medicine strictly scientific.

In response to Simon Flexner's request for a personal memoir of Welch many years later, Winternitz was candid in his remarks:

> Dr. Welch certainly never suggested specific problems of research to any of us while I was in the department. As a matter of fact, I think it may be said that he never suggested anything concerning the conduct of the department to us. This, of course, I realize is important from the standpoint of his general attitude towards the training of his pupils, although at the time many of us felt that some parts of the work of the department required reinforcement.

> Dr. Welch of course was idealized by the students. I remembered that we wondered how he could spare the time to conduct the weekly quiz on Monday; how he would ask a very simple question and nod approval at the answer, whether it was right or wrong and then go on to elaborate the answer from his vast personal experience that lent such an intimacy to the rapidly evolving field of science. . . .
> We saw Dr. Welch very rarely and we rather resented the time that he spent with the students during the brief periods he was in the laboratory. It hardly gave us an opportunity to discuss even the most important occurrences with him. They were his busiest years, and later after Whipple went to California, when the staff clinical pathologic conferences were organized, Dr. Welch made it a point to attend. I think I saw more of him during those next two or three years at the clinical pathological conferences than at any other time.

Welch had the greatest influence of all on Winternitz, and it seems no exaggeration to suggest that he made Winter's career possible. An advocate for medical science, Welch gave addresses all over the country. But more than his oratorical ability, his connections with Gates and Rockefeller much enhanced his influence. In 1901, the Advisory Board of the Rockefeller Institute was established, with Welch as its president. Grants were given out the very next year. In 1904 Simon Flexner headed the parent Rockefeller Institute, and by 1907 Rockefeller had given it enough money to fund the Hospital of the Rockefeller Institute, which opened in 1910 with full-time clinicians on its staff.

In 1912 Welch proposed that General Education Board fund a full-time salaried system at Hopkins, doubtless like that at Rockefeller. The board agreed, with the pleasant suggestion that the fund be called the "William H. Welch Endowment for Clinical Education and Research." One hand washed the other without embarrassment even in those days.

Welch resigned his professorship of pathology in 1917 to head the School of Hygiene and Public Health at Hopkins. He plumped for an improved sewer system and is said to have changed the city of Baltimore from a city of cesspools to one with a modern sanitary system. He gets credit as well for introducing pasteurized milk, and for getting the Rockefeller Institute to abolish hookworm in the South. Of interest, given the pertinence of Welch to Winternitz's career, he regarded the mental hygiene movement as extraordinarily important. After reading Clifford Beers's autobiography, *A Mind That Found Itself,* Welch got Phipps to establish the Psychiatric Hospital at Hopkins.

In 1934, Welch died of cancer. The Flexners' last sentence says it all: "Popsy, a physician who had been so greatly beloved, died as he had lived, keeping his own counsel, essentially alone."

Welch was the éminence grise in the resurgence of the Yale Medical School and a model for Winternitz, who loyally developed many of his ideas Curiously, in the Flexners' biography of Welch, we found only one reference to Winternitz among the "brilliant men" who worked in Welch's laboratory, even though he is listed twice–and no more–in their index. Social medicine did not rank high in either of the elder Flexners' agendas, as Abraham Flexner's oft-repeated disdain for the Institute of Human Relations suggests. With it, Winternitz lost their confidence and their praise.[6]

THE HARVARD MEDICAL SCHOOL

At the other pole of the small academic world of the Northeast, matters were different. Writing of the first three hundred years of medicine at the Harvard Medical School, with pardonably parochial pride, Henry Beecher and Mark Altschule, two mid- twentieth-century Harvard physicians, credit Charles Eliot, an earlier president of Harvard, with revising medical education at the Medical School.[7] Harvard had no good reason to want a "full-time" system, as it enjoyed a unique federation of several Boston hospitals, each of which considered itself the equal if not the superior of the others. Moreover, in practice Harvard had already adopted the requirement for a college degree; in the Medical School's 1909 class, sixty out of sixty-two men already had bachelor's degrees. In the early part of the twentieth century the list of eminent professors at Harvard was far longer than at Yale.

The Harvard Medical School was also expanding thanks to five new marble buildings for its central campus. Its clinicians had fended off the threat of full-time salaried medical practice, and despite its new Peter Bent Brigham Hospital, captained by Hopkins surgeon Harvey Cushing, the faculty had also refused to consider making any one hospital *the* University Hospital. Ironically, years before, Osler had urged Cushing, a Yale alumnus, not to return to Yale as chief of Surgery, because of that very absence of a university hospital!

In any event, Harvard rejected any offer from the Carnegie or Rockefeller Foundations to support a full-time system that would allow members of the faculty to double their academic salaries in private practice. Full-time teaching was opposed by almost all the important people at Harvard, from Henry Christian, chief of Medicine at the Brigham, to Harvey Cushing. Harvard was loath to choose one hospital as its sole university hospital, in the belief that a number of affiliated hospitals would have varying interests and prejudices.

Beecher and Altschule claimed that the Flexner Report had almost no effect on their school and was hardly mentioned in reports. In favoring a scientific education, Flexner differed sharply from President Abbott Lawrence Lowell of Harvard, who supported classical education as the best preparation for medical practice.

Nor did Harvard need the foundation support that was so essential at Yale. Grand new buildings were being erected all around the Harvard Medical School. By 1906 it had acquired a huge new quadrangle, jocularly known to its early faculty as the "Great White Whale" because of the white-marble exterior. Nineteen-twelve saw the erection of the Peter Bent Brigham Hospital, with Harvey Cushing as its head of Surgery, and shortly thereafter the Children's Hospital was built.

We should not overemphasize the glories of Harvard, however much one of us might be so tempted. When Yale was beginning to ride the wave of success, many of the senior staff at Harvard were dissatisfied and depressed, as Dean David Edsall of Harvard lamented in his 1927-28 report. While this may have represented only a disguised plea for more funds, Edsall raised the question as to whether the school would "not go downhill rather than forward."

Given its opposition to his ideas, Flexner lost interest in Harvard. He wanted to promote excellence in three areas: preclinical research and human biology; sophisticated clinical research; and better teaching and training for clinical medicine. He was convinced that full-time clinicians, like full-time basic scientists, could not teach and do research well in their spare time and with only "left-over" energy. The faculty at Harvard countered that so-called full-time professors were still only part-time clinicians because of their committee meetings and travel–

"the full-time absences of the full-time faculty." And that was before the advent of jet airplanes!

A rising tide floats all ships, fills all bays: medical schools would come to resemble each other. The freedom that Winter brought to Yale was also to be found in Boston. Students had two free afternoons a week, as well as Saturdays entirely free. "Institutes" for special fields were built at Harvard, where they never incited the huge opposition that persisted at Yale until the present century.

HARVEY CUSHING

A graduate of the Harvard Medical School, Harvey Cushing gained his worldwide reputation at the Peter Bent Brigham Hospital in Boston. His career began at Yale College and ended, many years later, at the Yale Medical School, which he helped to shape over the years. Of parenthetical interest, Cushing originally applied to work with William Osler; but, not hearing from him, trained in surgery instead. In 1906, after a visit to Yale at the invitation of President Hadley, who hoped to convince him to take on the job of chief of Surgery, Cushing wrote:

> The one pressing need of the school is a hospital with a continuous service for those occupying the clinical chairs.... [W]ithout such a hospital, a medical school

> can hardly be expected to develop. Then from a hospital point of view nothing so certainly assures its growth and reputation as such an alliance, for unless it be primarily a teaching institution and issue publications, it can hardly have more than a local reputation.

Growing widespread was the need for a university to have a medical school where original research required a hospital under university control.

Cushing turned down the invitation to become professor of surgery at Yale. Despite the move to give the Medical School a quarter of the beds of the New Haven Hospital, he pointed out that the arrangements were still not those of a university hospital, "in an institution not under the control of the school, with far too few public patients at its disposal, and with its students as yet not recognized as a necessary part of the hospital organization." Hadley went on to recruit Joseph Flint as professor of surgery, but relations between the hospital and the Medical School remained tortuous. Controversies about medical fees paid to academic physicians and those closely associated with the Medical School continued into the late twentieth century.

At age sixty-five, after his required retirement from Harvard, Cushing returned to Yale as Sterling Professor of the History of Medicine, and is now memorialized in the renamed Cushing-Whitney Medical Library. His bust is on view in the Historical Library.[8]

Chapter 3. The Yale Medical School Before 1920

Early History

Founded in 1701 in Old Saybrook, Connecticut, and later removed to New Haven, Yale was the first American university to confer the degree of doctor of philosophy. It remained a school run largely by clergymen until 1899, when a professor of political science, Arthur Vining Hadley, was elected its president. His appointment was greeted with much enthusiasm. Twenty years later, when Hadley resigned, the Yale Corporation again wanted someone without church connections. Abraham Flexner of the General Education Board recommended James Rowland Angell, enthusiastically seconded by Yale alumni at the University of Chicago, where Angell had been the dean.

PRESIDENT JAMES ROWLAND ANGELL

Even though he had worked in physiological psychology, Angell had studied philosophy and metaphysics under John Dewey and William James. After a stint as acting president of the University of Chicago, Angell held the Carnegie Corporation presidency and served as chairman of the National Research Council and on the board of the Rockefeller Foundation and the Alora Spelman Rockefeller Fund. Members of this coterie were eager to improve higher education, especially in medical schools. Doubtless with enthusiasm, Angell accepted the Yale job.

Arriving in New Haven in 1921, eager to turn Yale College into a full university, Angell found the faculty, who controlled matters, unhappy with his proposed changes. An outsider, Angell felt more than a little uncomfortable with his conservative colleagues. In fact, frustration may well explain his enthusiastic collaboration with Winternitz, his ambitious new medical dean with revolutionary ideas.

Eager to get the humanities experts to work together with the scientists, Angell was ready to form new departments or even new schools in the university where borders were fuzzy, for, as he pointed out, "Knowledge after all is one, and life is one." Although he wanted to expand university scientific research, historians have pointed out that his native diffidence kept him from exercising authority to get the Yale professors do what he required.

President Hadley had appointed new deans before Angel took over, and they were trying to improve matters. But the Law School, like its medical counterpart, was "less than second-rate," and the Graduate School little better. Winternitz was lucky in that Robert Hutchins at the Law School was trying to incorporate elements of the social sciences into legal education.

THE NEW HAVEN HOSPITAL AND THE YALE MEDICAL SCHOOL

The Yale Medical School was an old school. In 1810, Yale College and the Connecticut Medical Society received a charter for medical education in the state, and in 1812, the Medical Institution of Yale College admitted its first class of thirty-seven men. But the school sank into financial difficulties for a hundred years, remaining generally as "mediocre and undistinguished" as most other American medical schools before the founding of Johns Hopkins.

A medical school needs a hospital and so money was raised for one in a former hotel on Howard Avenue. For a long while, "State Hospital," erected in 1833, ran an operating deficit, supported mainly as a kind of a prepaid health plan, with income coming largely from the Seamen's Hospital Fund.[1]

During the Civil War, "State" was requisitioned as a military hospital and renamed the Knight Hospital, honoring Prof. Jonathan Knight. Only in 1884, when Yale finally took on some responsibility, was it rewarded by the city it served with the designation of the New Haven Hospital. Nevertheless, the name itself suggests a fundamental separation from the Medical School that would plague both for a century. For most of its history, which will not concern us here, the hospital was to have a tenuous intertwining, but never a union, with the Yale Medical School.[2]

As the importance of clinical education grew in the early twentieth century, there were several attempts to move Yale's Medical School to the neighborhood of the New Haven Hospital. At the time, the hospital was the direct beneficiary of fundraising at Yale and entirely dependent on the Medical School and the university for leadership and financial support. Practicing physicians, however, then as now suspicious of the university, were unhappy with that arrangement. "Turf battles" grew bitter and in the early 1900s community physicians began to boycott the New Haven Hospital, moving their private practices and patients over to the new Hospital of St. Raphael, which led to a financial crisis at the New Haven Hospital.

Because it lacked a university hospital, early in his career Harvey Cushing turned down a position at the Yale Medical School. Changes began when the Flexner Report of 1910 brought about crucial improvements at the school.[3] Although deeply critical of some aspects of the school, Flexner was pleased by its general "tone," and by its professors and some of its laboratories. He noted its proximity to the New Haven Hospital, which promised a close university connection, and felt certain that he could shape the Medical School at Yale in the image of Johns Hopkins.[4]

A quasi-union of Medical School and hospital was one result of the Flexner Report, which highlighted the potential of the Yale Medical School as "one of a very few in New England so circumstanced as to have a clear duty and opportunity." At the same time, Flexner advised a "more intimate relationship with the present hospital," something the medical faculty had wanted for a long time. His report encouraged the Yale Corporation to seek an endowment to improve the school. George Blumer, who was appointed dean in 1910, proved the catalyst for a more academic approach to medicine, centered around the New Haven Hospital as its primary teaching site, if not its "university" hospital.

GEORGE BLUMER

Blumer, who had come from San Francisco in 1905, had married into a New Haven family.[5] As professor of the theory and practice of medicine from 1907 to 1920, like almost everyone else he had earlier worked with Welch. Blumer's portrait outside the dean's office in the Sterling

Hall of Medicine reveals a tall, grayish man. That he had never gone to college must have contributed to a sense of inferiority. A letter dated June 9, 1931, gives a poignant example of his self-effacement. Declining Welch's invitation to celebrate some anniversary at Hopkins, Blumer responded, "Traveling about is a labor. I like the status quo wherever I may find myself. Besides, I have no international reputation in medicine, and would be nobody except in your immediate presence."

Three years later, in 1934, Blumer advised Welch that he came "from a family more celebrated for taciturnity then loquacity" and had inherited "a truly British horror of 'stepping over.'" The contrast with Winternitz could not have been greater. Blumer deserves far more credit than he has received, for he truly prepared the way for Winter's success. It was in his time that the Department of Public Health got its start and Charles-Edward Winslow, who was to prove such a help to Winternitz, was appointed its chairman.

The Medical School administration had been moving, however glacially, toward a close relationship with the hospital. In 1908, after the hospital opened its beds to practitioners and let them charge fees, the university won the right to nominate a professor of medicine and a professor of surgery, each to control a quarter of the hospital beds for teaching purposes. At a meeting of Yale's Board of Permanent Officers on April 17, 1912, the new dean was urged to emphasize to the Yale Corporation the "importance of gaining control of the hospital." That was fine with Blumer, who had preferred to have the university control the New Haven Hospital, rather than construct a new and divisive university hospital. Building a separate university hospital, he wrote,

> in a town of New Haven's size would result in cutthroat competition which would certainly have a very serious effect on the relationships of the University to the profession in general. . . . The most desirable plan would be for the authorities of Yale University to enter into a contract with the authorities of New Haven Hospital, whereby the University authorities would have the power of nomination of all the medical attendants of the hospital, and should also probably have the power to exercise some control over the policy of the administration of the hospital.

Meanwhile, students were protesting their poor clinical education; one of their leaders, Samuel Harvey, was later to become the chairman of Surgery under Winternitz. In 1913, the hospital trustees finally accepted Blumer's proposals. An agreement, signed by Hadley for Yale and by Eli Whitney for the hospital, provided for a closed medical staff, with full-time chiefs of service appointed by the university. It also made hospital beds and patients fully available to Yale medical students for teaching purposes in return for the university's concentrating its new Medical School buildings around the hospital, as Flexner had wanted.

Surprisingly, in 1914 a college degree was not yet deemed necessary for admission to the Medical School. Two years later, the Board of Permanent Officers voted to admit a certain number of female college graduates to the Medical School, if the buildings could be suitably altered and bathrooms fitted for women. Since Alice Farnam, daughter of a Yale benefactor, was eager to attend, her father paid for the changes at a cost of less than a thousand dollars.

That new era of Medical School-hospital cooperation was quickly enhanced by more generous financial support. In a donation later singled out as "the turning point of the medical school," the New Haven Hospital received $600,000 for the Brady Memorial Laboratory. To strengthen university control over the hospital, the General Education Board in 1918 gave $2 million to put the Yale clinical Departments of Medicine, Surgery, and Obstetrics and Gynecology on a full-time basis. In 1920, the board pledged another $1 million toward a Medical School endowment of $3 million, the balance to be raised by the university.

In the interval, the New Haven Hospital completed its own drive to cover a growing deficit: bonds were issued for $1 million to rehabilitate the hospital with new construction. Although community leaders reluctantly agreed that both hospital and Medical School should be improved, confidential notes in the Yale files suggest the community leaders were fearful of what that might bring. Then, in 1920, the Yale Corporation took the crucial decision to develop a "medical school of the highest type."[6]

In a paean to Winter on his leaving the office of dean in 1935, Winslow depicted the truly dismaying situation that had existed in 1917.[7] There were only 88 students in the entire school, and by 1920 only 118 had registered for the M.D. degree. The School of Medicine was located at 150 York Street, close to Chapel Street and the modern college, but several blocks away from the hospital. Anatomy was taught in two "dark, gloomy, and inconvenient" buildings (now torn down), also on York Street, while classes in physiology and public health were held several blocks away on Park Street, in the remodeled former Elm City Hospital.

An army barracks on the corner of Cedar Street and Congress Avenue provided the main site for teaching. A nearby two-story "brick annex" held the only laboratory outside the hospital wards. Except for what was then a modern Isolation Pavilion for infectious diseases (demolished in the 1960s), all the buildings were quite old, some dating back a century. Indeed, the first buildings associated with the Medical School, a pair of frame houses of the Federal period on Cedar Street, were still in use as late as 1920; one held classrooms for chemistry, the other for obstetrics and gynecology. What would now be called the "basic sciences" were taught at the college, mostly at Sheffield Scientific School, half a mile or so across town on the main campus.

At the time, Yale remained the "second-rate medical school" that John Paul later described, with only a few distinguished teachers such as Yandell Henderson and Lafayette Mendell.[8] Some at the university had even considered abandoning the school as too great a financial burden, advice that was repeated several times in the first half of the twentieth century.[9] Finally, by the 1960s, the faculty began to get large grants from the new National Institutes of Health, with "overhead" in such generous amounts that the university could depend upon its contribution.

JOHNS HOPKINS AND YALE

Still, no one at Yale could ignore what was going on at the new Johns Hopkins Medical School, thanks to the people who had worked at both schools. Prof. Ross Harrison, who had done "Nobel-quality work" at Hopkins, gets credit for many of the early changes at Yale and, together with Blumer, for bringing Winternitz to New Haven at the urging of Welch.

Just to mention a few other names suggests the Hopkins influence on the coterie that was to shape the Yale Medical School. Simon Flexner, Abraham's brother, had been an associate in Pathology at Hopkins from 1892 to 1899, working with Welch on syphilis. From September 1909 to March 1913, Winternitz was an assistant resident in Pathology, a position that Blumer had held from May

1895 to September 1896. Edward A. Parks, a 1900 Yale graduate and a professor of pediatrics, spent his entire career at Hopkins except for six years at the Yale Medical School, which he left out of dissatisfaction with Winternitz's "authoritarian ways."

One important non-Hopkins graduate was Col. Isaac Ullman, president of the New Haven Hospital during these crucial years and one of the few Jews whose home Winternitz visited. In a letter of Dec. 14, 1948, Winter wrote to Flexner, "I am so glad you remember the important role Col. Ullman played in the program. One never hears of that great man in this community–but I know he got a great satisfaction in doing so well what he thought it was important to have accomplished–nothing can replace that knowledge."

In the years 1926-28, the Endowment Campaign brought $20 million to Yale University. A great deal came from devoted alumni, but much more from the Sterling and Harkness bequests and from the Commonwealth Fund, the two Rockefeller Foundations, and the General Education Board. Additions to the New Haven Hospital were built on Howard Avenue, in the same block as the Brady Memorial Laboratory. Tall stone Corinthian columns framed a row of windows where the grand entrance to the new hospital wards welcomed patients in 1928. A noble front with the Winternitz stamp of grandeur; the columns were physical symbols of his vision for the Medical Center, to be shared by Yale and the New Haven Hospital.

By 1920, when Winter became dean, university-hospital cooperation was becoming inevitable, but the extent of that cooperation has never been specified. Today's Yale-New Haven Hospital is a separate "university-type" hospital independent of the Medical School, though relying on it for administrative and teaching staff. This arrangement hobbled both institutions for most of the twentieth century, as their friendly rivalry often gave way to fierce competition. By the end of the century, some regarded the partnership as having become unequal, the Yale-New Haven Hospital far outdistancing the Medical School in "profit" from the care of patients, its financial experts astute in wringing money from many sources.

The relationship with the New Haven Hospital has never been easy for the Medical School. From the beginning the university has been more than a little wary of taking on the huge debt that charitable hospitals used to run, until they turned into profit-making enterprises hard to distinguish from any other corporation. The twentieth century saw a dance in which the hospital and the Medical School alternately grew close and then parted.

At this remove, it is difficult to tell how much Winter was influenced by Welch, by Angell, and by Robert Hutchins of the Law School There was a real partnership among the three men, who held much the same notion of physicians as urbane, articulate, educated men (and women). It was time for change, and the growing American hegemony after the First World War helped.

The world of medicine in the universities had been changing for several decades. If these men had not worked together, doubtless others would have brought about similar advances, fortified by the largess of New York foundations. Biographers usually credit the man or woman they are writing about, but we agree that Abraham Flexner, as much as Winter, deserves credit: his teaching experience, his survey of education and subsequently of medical schools, together with his close relationships with so many powerful administrators, prepared the way for fundamental improvements. Winternitz would prove that he was the right man for the time, but Flexner was the catalyst for Winternitz's victories.

Part 2.

Winter at Yale

Chapter 4. Professor of Pathology

When the Winternitz family arrived in New Haven in the summer of 1917, the United States was mobilizing for the First World War. The dean's report for 1917-1918 recorded that "Professor Winternitz will begin work with a new and thoroughly equipped laboratory and with an amount of assistance that for financial reasons we were never able to give Dr. Bartlett [the previous head of Pathology]." Winternitz had appointed Dr. Leroy Upson Gardner assistant professor of pathology, but the war made it impossible to complete the reorganization of the department.

When the United States entered the war, William Welch urged Winternitz to go with the Johns Hopkins unit to France. George Blumer, however, was much against his leaving New Haven, so Winternitz prudently stayed home. He had a staff of five in pathology, headed by George H. Smith and Gardner. The head of Histology was Adah Baird, "a woman of unusual experience." Another woman, Marion McNamara, a graduate of Smith College on a fellowship in bacteriology, probably worked for nothing. In the histology laboratory, Alice Thing replaced an assistant after only a few months.[1] All the secretarial work of the department was done by one woman, who made carbon copies on a single typewriter.

Winter's first annual report in 1919 reads like a handbook for a model department of pathology. Outlining the essentials and leaving nothing to chance, Yale's new professor of pathology could have been the inspiration for the definition of a pathologist as "a person who, when asked the time of day, explains how to make a watch." This remarkable document reveals much about Winternitz's first two years at the university, his general plans for the department, and his attitude toward teaching and research. (The report also illustrates his somewhat cavalier attitude toward grammar and syntax—a trait shared with many in the medical profession.)

> One of the country's foremost financiers, interested in the welfare of a university laboratory, arrived unexpectedly at the Department of Pathology one day, and bluntly asked the question, What are your assets? The answer, not so readily found, may be in part: First, the training of men—students, assistants, and colleagues; they learn methods –and by correlation of anatomical and bacteriological facts with the clinical findings, their efficiency in diagnosis and in the accumulation of records –. This material, efficiently and accessibly compiled, offers a substantial basis for the investigation of specific conditions.

Third, the advancement of science–this is reflected through research.

In his report, Winternitz described how to set up an autopsy room, how to perform the procedure, how to care for the surgical instruments, and how to clean up and disinfect them afterwards. He offered detailed comments on histology, bacteriology, and serology. There was even a chapter on preserving and displaying teaching specimens in the departmental museum. As always, Winter was precise about what he wanted.

One thing the report did not say is that Winter collected photographs of each member of the incoming class.[2] He memorized all of the students' names and bestowed nicknames on most of them, changing Taffel to Tolliver and Longo to Long Ago, or sometimes Auld Lang Syne.[3] Unaccountably, names like Bloomer and Waters, which seem ripe for levity, remained unchanged. Winternitz probably called Levin Waters by his first name because he found it amusingly incongruous for a white Anglo-Saxon Protestant. Indeed, Mory's—the private dining club patronized by generations of Yalies—initially refused to admit Levin Lyttleton Waters IV as a member under the misapprehension that he was of Jewish origin. (Winter joined Mory's when he became dean of the Medical School.; it was de rigueur.)

THE WAR YEARS

From that first dean's report, one might think that Winternitz was given a beautiful, new, well-equipped laboratory and a full staff. In reality, the war forced him to put his ambitious plans for the department on hold. Gardner was soon called up to the Army's Medical Reserve Corps at Fort Devens, Massachusetts; he contracted tuberculosis and was transferred to the Trudeau Sanatorium in Saranac, New York. Dr. Frank McNamara (no relation to Marion) was hired in February 1918, and the following summer Dr. Isabel Wason, a 1917 graduate of Johns Hopkins, and Kathleen Greely, a bacteriologist, joined the staff. This handful of people had to do all the work of the department–teaching, performing autopsies, and carrying out original research suggested by the Boss. They set up a museum of specimens and started a departmental library. Winternitz did more than his share, but his zeal and energy were nearly superhuman. Those who couldn't keep up with him fell ill, left, or were fired.

With publications in mind, Winter hired Flora Schaeffer, a medical illustrator who had trained in Baltimore under the renowned Max Brödel, as well as a photographer named Miss Jewell (whom Winternitz whimsically nicknamed Miss Ruby). Armin Hemberger, another of Brödel's protégés, also came to New Haven and spent the rest of his professional life in the Pathology Department, where he held his own against "upstart" techniques like microphotography and color photography, at least as long as the trolley cars ran along Congress Avenue. (The photographers had to wait to snap their microphotographs until a trolley had gone by and the building stopped shaking.) It was well known that Hemberger worked best under the inspiration of an attractive young female assistant. Winternitz remained loyal to his quirky colleague, although his references to "our darling Mr. Hemburger" had a sarcastic twist.

In the beginning autopsies were done at the rate of one every two weeks, far fewer than were needed for the purposes of research and teaching. Within a year, Winter had increased the number to three or four a week by offering Yale's services both to the local sanatorium and to the New Haven County coroner's office. When local undertakers objected that autopsies delayed and complicated the embalming of the bodies, Winter offered to take the task off their hands. This arrangement naturally pleased the undertakers, since they could now charge families the same fee for work that was merely cosmetic.[4]

During Winternitz's tenure as dean of the Medical School (1920-1935), the autopsy room was run like an operating room. The atmosphere was professional, even reverent, the face and genitals of the deceased being kept covered with a clean towel in a show of respect. The Latin inscription on the wall, borrowed from one Winternitz had seen in Florence, Italy, set the decorous tone: HIC LOCUS EST UBI MORS GAUDET SUCCURRERE VITAE (This is the place where death rejoices to be of aid to life).

The Pathology Department has preserved the motto to this day, although owing to a remodeling of the autopsy room it is now bifurcated on the walls of two basement offices.

Oddly enough, after Winternitz was commissioned as a major in the U.S. Army in 1918, he proposed that Yale establish a military medical school in tandem with the civilian one. The surgeon-general agreed, but the idea faded after the war. Winter reportedly was photographed in uniform with his arm in a sling; he liked to quip that he had been "wounded at the Front–the front of a Ford." In the days before cars had automatic ignitions, he broke his arm while starting his car with a crank!

WAR GAS STUDIES

The widespread use of poison gas on First World War battlefields opened a new field of research that was best carried out in university laboratories. Scientists with the U.S. Bureau of Mines, who were familiar with toxic mine gases, set up an independent department of the Army known as the Chemical Warfare Service. Prof. Yandell Henderson of Yale, an expert in the physiology of mine gases, was chosen to organize the service's Medical Science Section. In June 1917 the section was established at Yale, with a field station housed in temporary barracks hastily constructed along Congress Avenue next to the Brady Building.

Much later, in a manuscript entitled "The Yale School of Medicine in Wartime, 1917-1941," Winter recalled a

> ponderous wire sent President Hadley, urging him to offer the facilities of the Yale School of Medicine to the Government for the training of medical personnel. . . . Within a few weeks carpenters were at work: a barracks was erected on the grounds of the New Haven Hospital adjoining the new Anthony N. Brady Memorial Laboratory, and the Yale Army Laboratory Training School became operative under the command of Col. Charles F. Craig of the class of '94 M. Another building was acquired without delay for the study of war gases here at the University and it may be said parenthetically that had it not been for these buildings, medicine at Yale would have had the questionable advantage of the great outdoors for a considerable part of its activity during more than a few of the post-war years.[5]

Never one to miss a chance, Winter began gathering material for a monograph on poison gases. The result was a major opus entitled *Collected Studies on the Pathology of War Gas Poisoning,* which Yale University Press published in 1920 with a $10,000 subvention from the Yale Corporation's Prudential Committee.[6] The title page states that the book emanated "from the Department of Pathology and Bacteriology, Medical Science Section, Chemical Warfare Service, under the direction of M.C. Winternitz,

Major, MC, USA." The volume was copiously illustrated with photographs of gross and microscopical specimens, many in full color. Winternitz discussed the pathology of poisoning by chlorine, phosgene, chloropicrin, and mustard gas, observing that the latter differed from the other "suffocating gases" because its effects were not limited to the respiratory tract.

In his Introduction to *Collected Studies on the Pathology of War Gas Poisoning,* Winter wrote that the pathology labs in New Haven had collaborated with those organized by the new "Department of Pharmacology and Toxicology at Washington." Noting that a large university situated in a small town could attract only so many patients, he went on to observe: "The fact that few gases were studied has been amply compensated for by the many subjects used, since with these it was possible to investigate the progressive lesions from those almost immediately after gassing, through the various acute periods to the residual chronic changes, which are in turn associated with more remote complications." Winternitz was confident that in-depth study of certain pathological symptoms often produced as much information as studies on a far grander scale. He pointed out that bacteria contributed significantly to the destruction of the upper respiratory tract and suggested that this might offer clues to prophylaxis against pneumonia. He also emphasized the observation of his colleague, Professor Underhill, that animals which had been bled in the course of the experiments were the least likely to die.

THE INFLUENZA EPIDEMIC

When the influenza epidemic reached New Haven in 1918, Winter quickly realized that it was of even greater scientific interest than poison gas, as a naturally occurring disease whose depredations might be correlated with the lesions of gas poisoning. There were plenty of patients to study because only the most critically ill could be admitted to the hospital, and many of them died. This gave Winter an opportunity that he could not pass up, even if it meant spending long hours at the autopsy table.

The second important monograph that Winternitz cowrote during this fertile period, *The Pathology of Influenza*, also appeared in 1920 under the imprint of Yale University Press.[7] Like *Collected Studies on the Pathology of War Gas Poisoning,* it was a compendium of finely drawn black-and-white microscopic illustrations, along with color illustrations of gross specimens. These images, together with the authors' meticulous verbal descriptions of gross and microscopic pathology, made the book an instant classic. As Dr. Edward Kilbourne, the internationally known virologist, points out, pathology had reached its apogee about that time and had not yet been eclipsed by molecular biology. So it seems likely that *The Pathology of Influenza* will serve students and scientists alike for some time to come.

The authors were listed on the title page as M.C. Winternitz, Isabel Wason, and Frank P. McNamara of "The Brady Laboratory of Pathology and Bacteriology, Yale University School of Medicine and the New Haven Hospital." A subsequent notation elaborated:

> The present volume is the fourth work published by the Yale University Press and the Anthony N. Brady Memorial Foundation, which was established June 15, 1914, by members of the family of the late Anthony N. Brady to enable the University to declare operative the agreement for an alliance between the New Haven Hospital and the Yale School of Medicine. In addition to the pledge of endowment for this purpose, the donors had erected for the University on the grounds of the Hospital a clinical and pathological laboratory, and have since, through additional gifts to supplement the income of the Memorial Foundation, made possible the publication of this and other works by members of the faculty of the School of Medicine at Yale.

This fulsome acknowledgment bears the fingerprints of the book's chief author, who had so recently become dean of the Medical School and was committed to forging a lasting alliance between it and the New Haven Hospital.

The Introduction to *The Pathology of Influenza* stated that the first cases of the disease in the United States appeared on the New England coast. "During a period of about three months, beginning with September 18, 1918, while the epidemic raged and waned in New Haven, there were approximately 1,100 cases of the disease admitted to the New Haven Hospital." Eighty-two of the 280 patients who died underwent autopsy and extensive study, along with other cases from the United States General Hospital No. 16, a military hospital in Allingtown, West Haven, about a five-minute drive from the New Haven Hospital.

Winter was usually at his best in making correlations, but, as Ray Yesner comments, his conclusion that the epidemic of influenza would lead to a surge in the incidence of lung cancer was an example of being right for the wrong reasons.[8] He called attention to the "analogous changes in the respiratory tract initiated by the inhalation of poisonous gases," observing that the "respiratory lesions are dependent primarily upon the damage produced by the true etiological agent and the systemic capacity to compensate, and only secondarily upon invasion by the bacterial flora of the mouth and inspired air." As such precise descriptions show, Winternitz stood in a long line of observational pathologists who have contributed so much to clinical medicine.

The years 1917 to 1920 set a dizzying pace. In addition to collaborating on ten scientific papers—all signed with the chairman's name first, and all typed on old, rattling typewriters by the department's two secretaries—Winternitz turned out a series of annual reports and other minor reports, to say nothing of supervising the routine business of the department. One student remembered him as looking "like an animal about to spring." The staff Winternitz assembled may not have been his dream team, but they had done a good job in laying the foundation for the future growth of the department and the Medical School.

TOWN AND GOWN

New Haven was known as the Elm City when the Winternitzes arrived in 1917.[9] Before the ravages of the Dutch elm disease, most of the streets and the Green in the center of town were shaded by the gracefully arching limbs of American elm trees. Electric trolleys shared the main arteries with cars, bicycles, and horse-drawn wagons laden with coal, ice, wood, and beer. Smaller wagons went about the neighborhoods delivering or peddling produce, meat, and fish, leaving a trail of melted ice on the pavement. Streetwise children learned to recognize the distinctive "cling-a-ling" of a bicycle bell, the clangorous "ding-ding-ding" of a trolley, and the honking "eh-u-ga, u-ga" of a Model T Ford.[10]

Despite these outward signs of modernity, New Haven had changed remarkably little since Victorian times. In its social relations, the city remained complacently provincial, a small universe with Yale very much at its center. Many middle-class New Haven families sent their sons to the university so they could move up the social ladder. Old Yankee families with deep roots in Protestant New England constituted the backbone of the local gentry. New Haven society respected and protected its own. The criteria for admission were simple: old money was preferred, but lineage would do.

On the "gown" side of the town-gown divide, Arthur Twining Hadley, Yale's popular president since 1899, was New Haven's leading citizen. Next in the social pecking order came the officers of the university—the treasurer, the provost, and the various deans. A faculty position was considered an honor for gentlemen of independent means and bachelor scholars. But Yale salaries were modest, and junior faculty with families had a hard time making ends meet unless they had private incomes. Wives who were professional women frequently stopped working to raise their children and do volunteer work, which was usually determined by their husbands' ambitions rather than their own interests.

Certain categories of people, of course, were not warmly welcomed into genteel upper-class homes. There were comparatively few African-Americans in New Haven in 1917, but Italian-Americans had created a lively subculture in the predominantly Catholic enclave around Wooster Square, while the Jewish population was concentrated along Legion Avenue. Both Jews and Catholics had to prove themselves in order to gain entrée to high society, something that could take years to achieve, or might never occur. Upper-class WASPs might accept, or even admire, Jews and Catholics as individuals, but for the most part social intimacy and intermarriage were out of the question.[11]

Winternitz's Jewish ancestry created problems on both the social and the professional levels. Like most American universities at the time, Yale didn't appoint Jews to its faculty without compelling reasons. That Dr. Welch thought highly of Winternitz was a significant, but not decisive, factor in his favor. Inevitably, there were some who sneered that he used to sneak over to Legion Avenue to buy pumpernickel bread and eat pickles.[12] (It was hardly Winternitz's style to sneak anywhere!) Winternitz chose to ignore such prejudice whenever he could. Naturally self-confident, he seems to have thought of himself first and foremost as a German–even if Germans were at least as unpopular as Jews during the First World War.

FITTING IN

Yale, in its way, was as insular and socially exclusive as New Haven. There was a formal protocol for welcoming new faculty, but once that was completed, all further socializing could end. Neighbors did not call on neighbors just because they had moved into the block, and they scarcely nodded to each other when passing on the street. The grand houses on St. Ronan Street were not always sold on the open market: if a family had to move, neighbors often bought the property in order to handpick the new owners and maintain the quality of the neighborhood.

By all accounts, Helen Winternitz was a lovely, lively, and gracious young woman in 1917. Custom dictated that she be called upon individually by the wives of ranking university officials. Mrs. Hadley would have gathered a committee to perform this duty. Such house calls were made by properly dressed ladies wearing hats, gloves, and formal street wear, and most likely carrying silver or tortoiseshell card cases in their handbags. If the newcomer was not "at home," the caller would leave three crisp calling cards–two of her husband's and one of her own. (Ladies called only upon ladies, while gentlemen called upon both the ladies and the men of the house.) One could neither issue nor accept an invitation until all such calls had been exchanged. It was like a chapter out of a Jane Austen novel.

Although most faculty members received the Winternitzes with correct formality, and even their neighbors on Prospect Street gave them the cold shoulder, they gradually made friends among his professional associates. (Winter seems to have been oblivious to anti-Semitic slights. A passing remark in a letter to his children in 1931, referring to "a house where we always felt welcomed," is the only written evidence that he noticed he was not welcome everywhere.) Each year the Pathology Department held a Christmas party at which Winter sat like Santa Claus dispensing presents from a grab-bag.

The five children—Elizabeth was born in 1915, Jane in 1915, Tom in 1916, Mary in 1918, and Bill in 1920–were enrolled in good schools where in due course they found out from their classmates that they were Jewish, but this does not seem to have influenced their friendships or their popularity.

Until they moved to Chicago in 1929, Robert Maynard Hutchins and his family were the Winternitzes' closest friends in New Haven. Professors C.E.A. Winslow and Ross Harrison also welcomed them enthusiastically. A pioneer in public health, Winslow became Winter's valued friend and colleague, their special bond being an interest in human welfare and what was then called "mental hygiene." A tall man with thick, white hair, Winslow cut an impressive figure, and his wife, also a doctor of public health, was equally tall, graceful, and reserved.

Harrison, who was particularly interested in the teaching of the sciences, had been instrumental in bringing Winter to Yale, and their friendship lasted to the end of Harrison's long life.[13] Sterling Professor of Biology and chairman of the Department of Zoology, Harrison might well have received the Nobel Prize for his work on cell culture had the prize not been canceled during the First World War. A meticulous researcher, he often allowed his work to sit unreported for years until it had been thoroughly digested and proven—a quality rarely seen today. Winter respectfully deferred to Harrison, keeping him on the Scientific Board of the Jane Coffin Childs Fund for Cancer Research even when he was in his nineties.

Despite his academic eminence, Harrison knew how it felt to be ostracized. As the husband of a German woman, he came under suspicion during the First World War and was investigated by so-called loyalists at the university. According to historian Gaddis Smith, President Hadley concluded that Harrison was a loyal American citizen, but two of his associates in the Zoology Department were arrested and charged with subversive activities. That Hadley praised the government agents for the "civility" with which they conducted their inquiries on campus speaks volumes about the strength of anti-German feeling at the time.

210 PROSPECT STREET

The Winternitzes bought a large house on Prospect Street, half a block from the stately mansions of the old New Haven elite on Hillhouse Avenue (most of which have since been converted to Yale offices). President Hadley had to vouch for his newest appointment before the deed could be signed, given the restrictive covenants against Jews then in force. (Now home to the Josef Albers Foundation, the house sits just up the hill from the Ingalls Hockey Rink, known affectionately as the "Yale Whale.") Although a convenient trolley line ran along Whitney Avenue, one block to the east, Winternitz usually preferred the brisk walk across town to the Medical School.

Probably dating from the mid- to late 1800s, 210 Prospect Street was a tall, handsome Victorian residence built around a generously proportioned central hallway. . On the first floor were a dining room, a library, and a bright living room with windows on three sides, big enough to entertain thirty or more people. Beyond the dining room was a butler's pantry that led to the kitchen and servants' quarters. A full basement, invisible from the street, looked out onto the sloping backyard. In addition to the coal bin and furnaces, it contained a root cellar, a summer kitchen with its own fireplace, and a large storage room.

Happy memories of sledding behind 210 Prospect Street live on with those who played with the Winternitz children. The grounds were neat and well maintained. Winter and Helen shared a love of gardening, and in their first year in the house he put in a large garden to produce fresh food and flowers for the table. (Winternitz regarded gardening as good practical recreation; he never learned how to play and hated wasting time.) At the foot of the garden was a small chicken house with a fenced-in yard, which supplied the family with eggs and an occasional fowl. Although such Victory Gardens were common in 1917, the neighbors may have been surprised when the Winternitzes kept their vegetables and chickens after the war.

EARLY SUMMERS

Until the Second World War, academic vacations customarily lasted all summer, but Winter took his work with him wherever he went. Because he wanted to be readily available to the Medical School that first summer, the Winternitzes and the Thomas Watsons rented twin Victorian cottages on the Branford shore, a few miles east of New Haven. They were accompanied by the Jamaican couple who "did for" the Winternitzes: Gladys cooked while Eddie cleaned house, drove the car, took care of the garden, and served as general factotum. A genteel Irish woman named Molly Cummings later joined the household staff as "upstairs maid" and helped with the children. The Winternitzes did not hire a nanny, as Helen insisted on raising the children herself. Whenever Eddie and Gladys took a month's vacation, Winter did most of the cooking, since Molly was a terrible cook.

In 1921 the Winternitzes and Watsons summered together at Pasquaney Lodge on Newfound Lake in Bristol, New Hampshire. Helen had her hands full with their fifth child, William Welch Winternitz (named after his godfather), who was less than a year old. For his part, Winter enjoyed being the doctor on the spot. He endeared himself to the other guests at the lodge by taking care of scratches, sprains, and medical emergencies. His standard treatment for abrasions was to "put a bichloride of mercury pill in a basin of water and soak the afflicted area." Once he dove into the lake to save someone from drowning. Another time he took care of a young woman who had the tip of her finger bitten off by a horse, changing the dressing every day; she wrote Winter a fifteen-page letter of gratitude.

Both families loved New Hampshire and returned the following summer, renting Idlewild on Pasquaney Bay. In 1923 they went back to Newfound Lake and found lodgings in an area where they would soon build their dream vacation home. After Grandpa Watson picked out the location, Winternitz climbed a tree and decided which ones needed to be cut to give them the best view of the lake below. Although the rustic compound existed only in their imaginations, it already had a name: Treetops. We have the impression that Helen and Winter planned it, with assistance from the Watsons. Helen only had two or three summers of feeling well and vigorous at Treetops before becoming ill, but her imprint is still there.

TREETOPS

The first summer at Treetops stood out in family memory as the year of plans. Apple would be the name of the main building, which would house the kitchen, pantries, and a large room where the two families could socialize. (At first everyone camped out in tents, and even in later years the Watsons' chauffeur sometimes slept in a tent, as did extra male guests.) On rainy days, meals were usually served on a wide porch overlooking the lake. The porch steps were a good place to gather for picture taking. Behind Apple was a barnlike structure for storing equipment, machinery, and tools, with a dormitory or "bachelor barracks" on the second floor. The chicken house was easily accessible from the kitchen as well.

Other buildings were added as the need arose, thanks to the indispensable Peter Charon. A French-Canadian who had moved to New Hampshire as a boy, Pete had little formal education but an abundance of common sense and native ability. Winter would tell him what he wanted and Pete could do it–everything from repairing machinery to building the Stone House at Treetops. With the help of a few hired men and the Winternitz boys, Pete built all the cottages at Treetops, each with a fireplace in a small living room, a deck overlooking the lake, a bedroom or bunkroom, and a bathroom with shower. In the beginning there was no hot water in the cottages, but after a few years water heaters were installed in the bathrooms and a new well was dug.

Grandma Watson's house, Balsam, stood on the lawn in front of Apple. Behind it, along a path leading into the woods, were the children's cottages, Pine for the boys and Birch for the girls. (Mary Winternitz told us proudly that the girls helped build their house.) Over the years the unfinished wood inside the cabins mellowed to a golden glow, marked by occasional footprints of all sizes.

On warm days the compound buildings had the evocative smell of camp in an evergreen wood, and after a spell of bad weather they were musty. Pete made no attempt to hide the wiring and pipes, and the exposed framing provided shelf space for small objects like flashlights, paperback books, pine cones, stones, and other toys and talismans. .

Every summer, Tom and Bill were assigned to help Pete Charon, and Bill became particularly fond of him. From Pete they learned practical skills like the elements of carpentry, how to get a heavy piece of equipment out of the mire, the relative merits of excavating a boulder or burying it deeper, when to repair machine parts or replace them, and how to prepare the soil for planting. Pete taught them to understand nature, without expecting to dictate to it. Most of all, Pete gave the boys nonjudgmental friendship. Unlike their father, who never seemed to be satisfied with himself or others, he was a man they could aspire to live up to. His even, steady pace and good humor provided much-needed balance to their lives.

Although Winter did not expect the girls to do everything the boys did, they had to pick the vegetables, gather the eggs, and do "girl's work." After Eddie and Gladys left (when Winter remarried), a country woman was hired every summer as cook, with the girls pitching in as needed. At harvest time, everyone, guests included, was pressed into service preparing the fruits and vegetables for canning. Corn was the messiest job; it had to be scraped off the cob and poured into jars to be processed in a bath of boiling water. Winter was always hovering around the big table, like Charlie Chaplin in *Modern Times*, urging the crew to speed up production. Songs and banter helped to make the work light. Every Sunday the family made ice cream behind the kitchen, using ice from their own ice house. One summer Bob Thomas, a favorite staff member from the Pathology Department, rigged a bicycle up to the hand-cranked machine, which made the tedious job easier and faster.

Peter Charon preferred building to farming, though he did both. The nearest neighbor down the hill from Treetops was Peter Wesul, who loved farming and little else. Winter hired him too. Peter Wesul was a disagreeable man, but a tireless worker. Naturally, Winter liked and understood him, and treated him with care. The two Peters didn't care for each another, but they learned to work, if not together, at least on the same property. It was typical of Winter to keep both men on because they were best at what they did. He ran his medical school, his department, and his family the same way, expecting everyone to get along or to work out problems among themselves.

In the 1940s and 1950s, when Priscilla Norton used to visit Treetops, one of the loveliest sounds of evening was the sound of Peter Wesul scything rhythmically around the Stone House. It was the time of day when the sun was setting, the dew was settling, and voices dropped to hushed tones as the fireflies came out. He knew, as farmers have known since Virgil's time, that the dew softens the stubble and makes the grass easier to cut. Two very difficult men, M.C. Winternitz and Peter Wesul, had collaborated to tame the landscape, and Winter wore a look of contentment as he surveyed his property with pride and serenity.

The work of the Medical School followed Winter even to Treetops. He spent a few hours each day on deskwork, calling the office and either dictating his correspondence over the phone or answering it in longhand. He built a little laboratory halfway between the Stone House and Apple, for simple research that needed no more sophisticated equipment than a laboratory bench, some petri dishes, and a microscope. It was a place to try out ideas, and he kept some research going all the time he was dean. The microscope he used for studying slides sent for his review to New Hampshire either in consultation or by way of keeping in touch with the work in New Haven. Bill Winternitz and Bob Thomas made a sign for the lab, a parody of the Latin inscription in the autopsy room at the Medical School. Translated, it said, "This is the place where summer finds Winter."

Chapter 5. The Glory Trail

Dean Blumer and Professor Winternitz: The Sounds of Change

Winternitz was to prove the engine of change for the Yale Medical School.[1] Deep within him was the desire to improve the whole world; medical education would be his vehicle. He favored the full-time faculty system; he had a strong interest in psychiatry, fueled in part by personal concerns; and, most important, foundation money was available to establish all kinds of new ventures at Yale. It seems probable that Winternitz was hired less for his research skills than for his administrative ability, which he exercised so vigorously once he came aboard.

Department chairmen served as an advisory board to the dean, and one can imagine Winter at one of Dean Blumer's meetings. He has been compared to one of those coruscating mirrored balls that hang in ballrooms, reflecting every light. He loved selling his ideas to a room full of people, his voice penetrating even deaf ears. According to Annie K. Goodrich, the first dean of Yale's

Nursing School, he was a master at speaking extemporaneously, a facility he had developed during his years at Hopkins, when he had to fill in by giving all those lectures for the absent Welch.

Both the future of the Medical School and Winter's own future depended on making dramatic changes in medical education. He was not reluctant to make his views known, as in a letter to the dean dated January 2, 1920:

> My dear Dr. Blumer:
> The documents recently received from you regarding the instruction provided for students in bacteriology have been given thoughtful attention and I should like to present my views on the subject. . . . For example, Prof. Rettger's statement that the attempts to develop bacteriology in connection with medical schools in this country have resulted in complete failure is quite the opposite from what I supposed was the case. . . . [T]he development of bacteriology received a tremendous impetus from its medical aspects and in recent times many of the notable contributions to the subject have come from workers connected with medical institutions. Furthermore, in this as in other sciences the proximity of a laboratory to a medical school has not prevented the carrying out of work concerned with underlying scientific principles...
> The time of life when a student intending to study medicine shall take up the subject should not be

> during the college period. Premedical work, as I understand it, is intended to serve two purposes: first, to provide a certain measure of general culture; and second, to supply the basic scientific training which will enable the student to pursue medical studies with greater facility and profit.[2]

Winternitz asserted that premedical students should study English composition, modern languages, logic, psychology, mathematics, physics, chemistry, and biology. He saw no place for bacteriology in that busy course, but made a strong argument for teaching it in medical school, rather than in graduate school or "institutes." It would, he wrote, only be a "question of time before the instruction given in the Medical School became seriously limited. Such a process of disintegration as is typified by taking bacteriology out of the Medical School will militate against the integrity of the school." He concluded by requesting that the dean give his letter the same publicity he had given his own, which suggests how far the differences between Blumer, who had hired him, and Winter, who had found his head, had progressed.

The "Meeting at Mr. Stokes'"

In the archives of the Medical School lies a faded, two-page report entitled "Memorandum of Suggestions derived from the meeting at Mr. Stokes.'" It is dated May 29, 1919, and signed by Frank Underhill, professor of experimental medicine. Anson Phelps Stokes, the secretary of the university, was a rich young man who was widely expected to become its next president. There is no list of participants in the meeting, but it seems clear that Winter not only attended but was its dominant force, for many of the ideas expressed in the report are characteristic of him and foreshadow his first few years as dean.

The memorandum lists fifteen ways to improve communication within the Medical School, as well as public perception of the school. Among the group's recommendations were "frequent informal dinners at which the affairs of the Medical School may be discussed freely and frankly," and an annual series of lectures to ensure that "the doctors in the community may be in sympathetic touch with the Medical School progress and problems."

The memorandum devoted considerable attention to other ways of generating publicity favorable to the Medical School. It was suggested that a registrar be hired to relieve the dean of routine responsibilities. The report also advised that financial aid be given to needy students, so that they could devote full time to their studies and the school could improve the quality of its students and recruit better ones from other New England colleges. The need for closer relations between town and gown doctors was recognized, as was the desirability of faculty exchanges with other schools. Finally, the group urged the president of Yale to feature the scientific work done by the Medical School faculty in his annual report. The report ends, "It was the sense of the meeting that the fundamental principle for the improvement of the morale in the Faculty is that when a majority of the members believe in a certain line of action that line of action shall be adopted and that all members of the Board shall give to it its hearty cooperation and support."

Optimism and solidarity shine through the document, but the last comment would come back to haunt Dean Winternitz years later, when his wheeling and dealing enraged his own faculty. The meeting at Anson Phelps Stokes's house was a milestone. Though the hour was late, those who attended probably found themselves on their own doorstep without being aware of how they got there, so full were they of hope and enthusiasm.

Appended to the Underhill report is a one-page "Memorandum on the Meeting at Mr. Stokes'," dated June 4, 1919, and signed by Dean Blumer.[3] He regretted that he had been unable to attend the meeting, but felt that the group's energy and enthusiasm were misdirected. "American universities are obsessed with the importance of organization," he commented, adding that "the important things in any university are . . . teaching and research. Let this idea simmer in your *brain pans* for awhile" (emphasis added). Dean Blumer's use of that arcane phrase may have reflected the backward glance of a man who was on the right track but not the fast track, a man who had done so much for the Medical School over the previous years that he was irritated by the new suggestions. And he must have been tired of all the infighting. Blumer concluded with the dismissive remark that few people read the president's report anyway.

Did Winternitz conceive the Underhill report? He believed in publicity, and the memorandum targeted its direction. Winter knew from experience that some of the most motivated and brilliant students could not afford to go to medical school; the notion of financial support put a new spin on the policy of Johns Hopkins, which as late as 1933 did not accept students who could not pay their way and granted no student aid. The last suggestion, of which Dean Blumer seemed so scornful, has very much the sound of Winternitz. He probably had his annual report already half-written for inclusion in the president's next annual report!

The tension on both sides comes through. Blumer, frustrated by the rebuffs he had received and unhappy with administrative work, was ready to resign the deanship. His last report for the year 1918-1919 is a historical account of the problems faced by the Medical School. Blumer was implicitly warning his successor that the school's very existence was in danger. He had done a great deal for Yale–fostered collaboration between hospital and Medical School, and raised much money–but he was weary and no longer felt appreciated. Blumer spent his last years in clinical practice in New Haven, where he became a much-loved physician (and the Winternitz family doctor).

It is easy to see why Winter was so enthusiastically elected dean of the Medical School in 1920.[4] Just as the columns and high ceilings of the Sterling Hall of Medicine have the Winternitz stamp, so do the suggestions for improving the Medical School. He had seen how much Welch accomplished at Hopkins over a fine meal at the Maryland Club, lubricated by the fruit of the vine.

Within months of the meeting at Mr. Stokes', the Yale Corporation held an even more important meeting, at which it was agreed:

1. That there is a clear and definite opportunity and obligation of the University to Medical Education.
2. That the Yale School of Medicine has a valuable nucleus of men and Material and sound traditions, which richly justify the development of an Institution for medical education of the highest type.
3. That the Corporation accepts as a policy the development of a Medical School of the highest type to include the pre-clinical and clinical years of instruction upon such principles of medical education as may be approved by the Corporation, after conference with the medical faculty.
4. That every effort be made to obtain at the earliest possible date the necessary funds with which to expand and develop the buildings, the

> equipment, the instruction and the research, and the service, in accordance with the best ideals of modern medical education–as an essential unit of our University Plan of Development.

Since Stokes was still widely expected to succeed President Arthur Twining Hadley, his interest in the Medical School may have been motivated by a desire to lay the groundwork for his own administration.

THE BEGINNINGS

All was in readiness for Winternitz as dean in 1920, and he was eager to take on the task. That he cultivated first the collaboration and then the friendship of Abraham Flexner and William Welch contributed to his success. In a letter of January 3, 1920, he had already expressed to Welch his dismay at the "precarious situation" of the Medical School: "The Corporation has neither decided its policy nor just how far it will support the Medical School, and the hospital, now on full-time, has been boycotted by the local physicians and has a deficit of over $10,000 a month. Needless to say, it will be unable to continue in the present year unless financial help is received." The famous cartoon of a sinking ship represented Winternitz's view of the Yale situation, and it was realistic.

Winternitz prudently invited Flexner to visit Yale and offer his advice. That must have been the beginning of their long collaboration (until the Institute for Human Relations got in their way). By June 7, 1921, Flexner was writing cheerful letters to Winternitz, basically urging him not to stew.

> Let me say once and for all that, whenever you have anything you would like to say to me, say it , and don't let it ferment inside. . . . I am delighted with your account of the way [Professor of Medicine Francis] Blake and the other fellows are forming their respective organizations. . . . Now let your mind dwell on the constructive things. Stop worrying. Let those of us who are paid to worry and carry other people's worries do that. Why, if these things were easy, I should be out of job.
>
> With affectionate good wishes . . .

Flexner reinforced Winternitz's natural confidence. As we have already observed, it is hard to separate what Winter originated from what his soon-to-be close colleagues had already thought about. Just as Flexner had been selected to make his magisterial report on the parlous state of American medical schools in anticipation that he would come up with the answers that the Carnegie Foundation expected, so too in Winter at Yale may be seen an relationship between the times and the man, between the opportunities available and those seized. Winter caught the rising tide and transformed the Medical School in ways that have lasted for more than seventy years, although his influence is not universally acknowledged today, partly owing to the animus that still surrounds his reputation.

The times were propitious. Thanks to Flexner and Welch, both the Sterling Trustees and the General Education Board agreed that the Yale Medical School, with its seemingly close affiliation with the New Haven Hospital, was the ideal place to launch another experiment to strengthen medical research and education on the German model then thriving at Hopkins. In 1920 the Yale Corporation affirmed the university's commitment to "the development of an institution for medical education of the highest type." Animated by that vision, the Sterling Trustees provided $1.3 million for the Sterling Hall of Medicine, which later, much enlarged, was to be one of Winter's enduring monuments.

THE 1920 REPORTS

All this ambition required setting explicit goals for the Medical School.[5] A committee appointed to redefine the school, and dominated by Winternitz, published its report in 1920 as *The Past, Present, and Future of the Yale University School of Medicine and Affiliated Clinical Institutions*–a grandiose title typical of the new dean. In it, the committee laid out plans for the physical expansion of the Medical School, for major changes in the way medicine was taught, and for the conversion of the Connecticut Training School for Nurses into a university school of nursing. The report fortified the officers and faculty of the Medical School. In a burst of parochial enthusiasm, Charles-Edward Winslow later called it "one of the remarkable monuments in the history of medical education," characterized by "extraordinary courage and vision." In his valedictory to Winternitz in 1935, Winslow, by then an old friend and colleague, averred that all the goals set forth in that document had been reached.

"MEMORANDUM FROM THE MEDICAL BOARD TO THE CORPORATION" (1920)

In 1920, a committee appointed by the authorities at the Medical School to study its relationship with the New Haven Hospital and the dispensary again came out strongly in favor of control of the hospital by the Medical School. The committee deplored the lack of ambition on the part of the hospital's board of trustees, "a hold-over from a time when the New Haven Hospital was purely a local institution." Not only had the hospital plant failed to become one of the best in the country, it had "not even succeeded in becoming the best in the State." Noting the hospital's yearly deficit of about $50,000 and consequent "spending down of capital," the committee concluded that "the only change of control which it deems adequate is a change whereby complete responsibility for the New Haven Hospital is taken over by the corporation of Yale

University in the same way that the University Library, for example, is a part of the University." The committee suggested that any private wards to be built should be open only "to those holding teaching positions in the school," prudently recognizing that as an aim and not a requirement. Winternitz's name was the last on the report, but his must have been its dominant voice.

ANGELL, HUTCHINS, AND WINTERNITZ: THE EARLY YEARS

One year after Winter became dean of the Medical School, the psychologist James Rowland Angell was elected president of Yale. It was a fortunate coincidence for Winternitz. Like him, Angell was an outsider. As a scientist, he was about as sympathetic a president as Winter could have wished. Angell was a firm believer in social medicine and the increasingly important field of social engineering. Even the *Harvard Crimson* was enthusiastic. "Dr. Angell will be president of Yale, but not a Yale President. In his selection Yale has emancipated herself, perhaps for all time, from dynastic control. She has made herself free to select the best men the country can afford to be her leaders: and in so doing has dedicated herself not to Yale, but to America."

Robert Hutchins, "the boy dean" of the Yale Law School (he was born in 1899), joined the duo of Angell and Winternitz in trying to change the university.

Hutchins wanted to turn law into a social science and believed with Winter that the Medical School should aim to improve society and health, more than just curing disease. All three held much the same notion of physicians as urbane, articulate, educated men (and women).[6]

Winternitz, Hutchins, and Angell quickly made huge changes in the Law School and the Medical School. In this they were guided by Wilbur Cross, whose name adorns the scenic auto route that passes through New Haven. A later governor of Connecticut, Cross was dean of the Yale Graduate School during Winter's ascendancy. In 1928 Winternitz and Hutchins would ask him to be advisory chairman of the Institute for Human Relations, which the Rockefeller Foundation had promised to support. A man of sixty-six, Cross recalled with amazement the tempestuousness of his junior colleagues.

> I felt as if I were a snowball between two balls of fire, which in an instant would consume me. . . . It was a great experience to play the part of advisor to two young men of boundless energy, who after loud and profane protests would usually heed my advice to slow down a bit. . . . The original aim of these two young men, as I understood it, was the synthesis of the biological and social sciences. . . . [T]hey started out with a declaration that both medicine and law are social sciences. . . . Had Hutchins remained at Yale instead of running away to Chicago, more might have

been accomplished in that bold attempt to integrate related sciences.

Winter was well suited to lead the effort to rebuild the Medical School. As a pathologist, he saw the big picture in microscopic detail; as an outsider, he was unmoved by the collegiality that might have made an Old Blue hesitate or compromise. Levin Waters, his associate for decades, pointed out that Winter advanced directly toward his goals. Ruthless in his demands upon himself, he was intolerant of others' attitudes and of any situation that might obstruct the path he so clearly saw. Even though his methods made colleagues unhappy, Winternitz was the right man in the right place at the right time.

BUILDING A FACULTY

The immediate problems that Winter faced were assembling a faculty, raising money, and building a new physical plant. He remained convinced that folding the Medical School into the university was the best way to attract financial resources and outstanding faculty. He wanted university to have departments of the basic biological sciences, as long as they were under his control and adjacent to the Medical School. Among them would be a department of full-time teachers and investigators who, relieved of the responsibilities of medical practice, would be free to follow their own bent, to study and develop medical science as they saw fit.

The results were impressive and quick in coming. Years later, Dr. David Hitchcock wrote Winter: "I have often recalled with pleasure a remark you made when you first offered me the opportunity of coming to work in the Department. . . . [You said] that you did not care in what field a man did his research so long as it was good research and that a member of his faculty might even work in astronomy if he wanted to."

Winter's very first dean's report announced the appointment of an impressive group of young men to important posts in the Medical School. He had spent 1920 luring the very best young faculty he could, with a chance to teach and do independent research. Francis G. Blake became chairman of the Department of Medicine, with John P. Peters and William_Stadie in the "chemical" division, James Trask and Arthur Dayton in the "biological" division. Harold S. Marvin came to direct the work in electrocardiography, which was "state of the art" in 1920. Samuel C. Harvey, who "had spent the last ten years in scientific investigation and clinical surgery," was put in charge of the Department of Surgery, succeeding Joseph Flint, who had resigned. As Winter revered Halsted, it is a tribute to Harvey's attributes that he did not look elsewhere for his new chairman of Surgery. John J. Morton became Harvey's assistant, and Arthur Morse of Baltimore was chosen as professor of obstetrics and gynecology.

Clyde Deming began a tenure in the genito-urinary division that spanned more than forty years. He was the only professor permitted to practice medicine gainfully within the Medical School, and to use the facilities free of charge. Winter thought highly enough of Deming to make these concessions to keep him at Yale. It would not be the last time private agreements were struck between deans and special interests. Notably, Howard Kelly, chief of Urology at Hopkins, also had had the same private-practice arrangements, which suggests how closely Winter was following the Hopkins model.

BECOMING DEAN

The patterns set in Winter's first year would persist throughout his tenure as dean. No one could get to work early enough to beat him. He would put on a lab coat and explore the corridors early in the morning or late at night, inspecting for cleanliness and workmanship, and generally keeping an eye on the operation of the Medical School. He was already fashioning a legend. Eminent clinicians from around the country and abroad were invited to Yale. Twenty-nine came in the first year to talk to the students and broaden their instruction while the new faculty was being assembled.

Winter may not have relied on his close colleagues, but he put a lot of trust in the personnel in his office, who were extensions of himself. Miriam Dasey, the first registrar, was mother hen to generations of students and indispensable to Winter.[7] She saw and processed every application, learning the dean's ways so well that she could answer for him without even bothering him. For years the two of them picked the next Medical School class on their own, without consulting any committee. Miss Dasey mothered her boss as much as the students. Sometimes she went home with him for Sunday dinner with the Winternitz family. In a pinch she babysat, and when Winter was ill, she came to his house to bring him important mail and take dictation. Everyone liked and admired Miss Dasey, recognized her as a character, and was careful not to test her goodwill. She made a lasting impression on a generation of doctors.

The other essential person in the dean's office was Lottie Bishop. A college graduate and a quintessential New Englander, she was both the business manager of the Medical School and its memory bank. Miss Bishop was a tidy woman with a small frame. She gave her all to the Medical School, invariably showing up at school functions to be seen and make sure that everything was being done properly. She was an extra pair of eyes and ears for Winter.

Carl Lund, the public relations man for the Medical School, served as Winter's editor. He met with the dean every Sunday morning to take voluminous notes, draft reports, and generally polish up his inspirations, not to mention writing grant applications, news releases, and in-house publications. When Winter spoke, he used body language–flashing eyes, shading of voice, and an innate sense of drama–to sway his audience, but he needed Lund to put his persuasiveness onto the written page. Lund probably knew as much as anyone about the inner workings of the Winternitz mind. We have not been able to trace any of Lund's writings, nor do we know what he did in later years.

Even after he became dean, Winter kept for himself the title of chairman of Pathology and held onto his office in the department, which he ran through a surrogate, Raymond Hussey. (Hussey would leave when Winter returned to the chairmanship full-time in 1935.)[8] Winter continued to teach his part of the pathology course, doing an occasional autopsy while dean, as an "honor" to an esteemed colleague.

GOALS AND PLANS

Winter had two major goals for the Medical School. Given his interest in what would later be called the "holistic" approach to medicine–which now rejoices in adjectives like *alternative, complementary,* or even *integrative*—the first was the education of doctors who would take care of the whole person. His second goal was the training of investigators in medical sciences who would study the pathophysiology of clinical problems. Characteristically, Winter later blurred the boundaries between these goals. Students midway in their medical course had a choice of two career paths: one, for would-be clinicians, took them on to the standard M.D. degree; the other, for those who could be enticed into investigation, consigned them to the graduate school for a Ph.D. degree and more intensive research.

Winter also distinguished the "clinician," who looked at the whole patient, from the "specialist," who looked at parts of the patients. He wanted to encourage both research and clinical care, but, unfortunately, never worked out how to achieve that goal with the faculty of a medical school who were all on salary (and hence didn't get paid for seeing patients).[9]

In the *Yale Alumni Weekly* for February 10, 1928, a commentary by Winter was headed "Medical School Now an 'Honors' College." The dean wrote that the Medical School (by which he presumably meant himself) preferred students who were interested in one or another field of biology, rather than those who, as he put it, "vaguely wanted to become a doctor." Winter went on to say that

> some post-graduate students in biology often decide to go into medicine and the elastic boundaries at Yale between the graduate school and the medical school make this possible. . . . Yale is unique in being so closely part of the university. The school of medicine now prefers to admit students primarily on account of their interest in the biological sciences,

> rather than a preconceived idea that they expect to become Doctors of Medicine.

In what seems to have been a conflation of hope and reality, Winter claimed that students were not grouped by classes; instead, each person set his own pace. He had talked a lot about that ideal, but we have found little evidence that it was ever put into practice. An undated manuscript in the archives states that "the educational program at Yale University School of Medicine is based on the belief that medicine is a social science and that its ultimate purpose, in common with other social sciences, is the promotion of human welfare. The particular avenue by which medicine approaches the general objective is that of physical health."

MEDICAL STUDENTS

In a lecture to the Alumni Board given on November 1, 1940, after he had left the deanship, Winter summarized his thoughts about medical students:

> They are considered to be the cream of the educated collegians. They are considered to be people who decided that they want to have an intellectual career. They are considered to be people who should not be marked whether they are present or absent, but that they should be given the freedom of the insti-

tution and get their enthusiasm through intimate contacts through their instructors, and they do. . . . They have the same keys we have. They can get in the front door any time at all and they can get into most of the laboratories. And we find that we do not lose things. We actually benefit by trusting them and giving them that type of freedom.

THE YALE PLAN

In the years before Winter came to Yale, the increasingly strict requirements for entrance to the Medical School had resulted in a marked decline in applications. Not unexpectedly, this trend upset the faculty, who demanded that something be done to reverse it. The "Yale Plan" had its beginnings in Winter's first year as dean .These new ideas, seemingly of Winter's own inspiration, carried the "Hopkins Experiment" a step further.

Students were to spend fewer hours on a required curriculum and more time following their own choices. The dispensary teaching of clinical medicine–what would now be called "outpatient" teaching–was emphasized, because Winter was convinced that study of clinic patients in various stages of illness was more instructive than that of the much sicker ward patients. Moreover, caring for such patients gave the students an insight into socioeconomic and environmental factors that would lead them to understand the importance of preventive medicine

Thirty years after Winter's plan for medical education was first implemented, Vernon Lippard, his successor as dean of the Medical School, described it as a success. He concluded that

> teachers and their attitudes are more important than curriculum structure and methods. There is much discussion about "integration," "comprehensive medicine," "vertical" versus "horizontal" curricula. Unless the student is given an opportunity to think for himself, is given time for pursuit of special interests and, most important, is freed from frequent course examinations and constant attention at didactic lectures and recitations, efforts at integration–vertical, horizontal, or diagonal–are wasted.

Lippard observed that "an unusually large proportion of the graduates over the life of this program have become teachers and investigators." Yale, he noted, stood third among American medical schools in the percentage of graduates holding full-time faculty appointments in the period 1925-1940. But Lippard declined to give his opinion as to whether this happy result was a function of the Medical School's instructional method or the type of student it attracted.

WHAT STUDENTS THOUGHT

Under the Yale Plan, professors treated students as junior colleagues, who were mature enough to study independently when freed from the pressure of preparing for exams. The only exams were those required by law at the end of the second year, and the final exams for the M.D. degree. Although word was already spreading that Winternitz was a great and colorful teacher, he recognized that his reputation alone would not attract first-rate students. Accordingly, he regularly visited colleges to recruit and ferret out good candidates, often making his decisions on very personal grounds. On rare occasions, so we have heard, students would be told on the spot of their acceptance.

The following memoir by Dr. Nelson Ordway is typical:

> I first met Winter (whom I never so addressed) in my last year as a Yale undergraduate, when I applied for admission to Yale Medical School. . . . I had been warned, when the Dean would ask me why I wanted to be a doctor, to avoid such reasons as wanting to do good for humanity, which might evoke his suggestion that I be a minister or social worker. So when the question came, I said that I had done well in biology. . . . I told the Dean that I would not receive credit

> for that year, and would therefore not have a bachelor's degree. "Does that bother you?" he asked. "No," I replied. . . . I was accepted on the spot, as one of the 40-odd students in the medical school's smallest class of that era.[10]

Dunham Kirkham wrote that when he appeared for an interview,"[i]t chanced that Winter was on vacation so I saw his faithful secretary, Miss Dasey, who quizzed me properly and advised me to take Physics and chemistry in Summer School and I would be accepted. I always credited Miss Dasey for accepting me under a shadow and admired Winter in trusting to her good judgment."

Winternitz could be casual about keeping applicants informed, as Bill Wedemeyer discovered when he heard nothing from Winter about his application.

> I finally told Winter that if I were not taken at Yale would he give me a recommendation for somewhere else. He replied, "Who told you you weren't accepted here?" And that was all I ever got out of him! Likewise when Winter asked if I'd be interested in joining ABCC [the Atomic Bomb Casualty Commission] when I went on active duty and I said "yes," he arranged for an interview with Dr. Weed of N.R.C. [the National Research Council] when he came to New Haven. After the interview I heard nothing until one day Winter asked me if I were going or not. I said I didn't know if

I'd been accepted. "You want it on a silver tray with a ribbon around it?" he snorted and walked away.

THE NEW BUILDINGS

Winter became dean at an auspicious moment for the Medical School. In 1921 the Laboratory for Medicine and Pediatrics was built; the Boardman Administration Building followed in 1922 and the Winchester private pavilion in 1923. In 1928, the new main hospital building, with its Corinthian columns and ward pavilions, was erected. Later the Laboratory for Medicine and Pediatrics was rebuilt, along with a new clinic building and more.

ANNUAL REPORTS

Throughout his career, Winter was always looking for, and finding, grand unifying views, not all of which could be translated into reality. A detailed recitation of each year's accomplishments would prove tedious, but the following summary of his very illuminating annual reports highlights the main themes of his fifteen-year term as dean (1920-1935). Written by Winter, though polished by Carl Lund, the reports mirror his ideas, plans, and accomplishments as he attempted to build a new Johns Hopkins in New Haven's green and pleasant land.

1921. The first report of Winter's deanship abounded with ideas. He praised the new unified records that accompanied patients from the outpatient dispensary into the hospital and back again. He highlighted the outpatient department as the place where students could learn about the natural history of disease from more than a single "snapshot" of a hospital admission. He wrote of his plan to promote group teaching along interdepartmental lines, a theme that he would sound throughout his tenure. In addition, he remarked that three years of college work should be required before admission to medical school, and he must have been thinking far ahead about raising money, because he mentioned enlarging the scope of the Alumni Association.

In a major move, Winternitz introduced his intent to implement the full-time system, which had been limping alongside the part-time system since 1915. In part because Dean Blumer had never been in favor of the full-time system, most of the clinical departments were still run by part-time faculty in 1921. Moreover, town-gown divisions had been deepened by the imposition of full-time positions, which demoted former "professors" to "clinical professors."

Harry Zimmerman much later commented that one reason he left Yale was that Winter did not want local physicians on the Medical School staff and expected Zimmerman to act as his hatchet man to "cut off [their] heads." This observation seems to fit with Winter's early academic disposition, but it is also possible that he thought the town doctors needed "updating," a polite term for educating. Aware of the many town-gown tensions, Winter concluded that the best way to attract and mollify doctors was to raise the level of medical practice in all of Connecticut, not just New Haven, by organizing clinical congresses with national and international speakers. These congresses became very popular because they made it possible for a visiting expert to lecture to the students in the morning and in the afternoon to his colleagues.

1922. Winter's second annual report shows how quickly he had come into his own: the mood at the Medical School, he boasted, was one of "pride in progress made, a feeling of cooperation." He had plans to turn Psychiatry, which was then part of the Department of Medicine, into an independent section. He took pleasure in noting that the full-time university system had recently begun to have a real trial. Again, he underlined the importance of medical students learning something of "the life history of a disease," not just the manifestations of disease. Preventive medicine was already something of a goal, as he urged that the ambulatory clinic should be "not only a disease clinic but also a health clinic, and, in part at least, a health center for its immediate environs."

Characteristically, in his gradual creation of the Yale Plan over the next decade, Winter had much to say about reducing the required time for the students, leaving free two-thirds of their time for elective courses and research activities.

1923. By the following year Winter's report brimmed with self-confidence; he wrote as if he and the Medical School were synonymous and claimed to have achieved total unanimity among the faculty on most matters. The full-time university system, the erection of new buildings, and the study of the natural history of disease all came in for repeated attention.

Winter had begun to wrestle with how to study the mind, "not only from the standpoint of the insane and pre-insane, but also with the idea of analyzing the mental factors of safety in the individual." Mental health had become a conspicuous concern in the outside world, and Winter knew how to run with any ball that he caught. In lauding psychiatry, he pointed out that specialists, then coming to the fore, were interested in one or another portion of the body only, but paid scant attention to the patient's personality. Even then newly minted internists were ignoring the mind. Once again, Winter proposed raising psychiatry to the level of the other four major divisions in the Department of Clinical Medicine, and he began to herald a "psychopathic" clinic adjacent to the hospital buildings, like the one in Massachusetts.

The School of Nursing opened its doors in April 1923. Yale's affiliation with the Connecticut Training School for Nurses dated back to March 1918, but the formal designation of a university school for nurses resulted from the joint efforts of Winter and Annie Goodrich, the school's first dean. Goodrich was very much in sympathy with Winter's interest in the whole patient and in psychiatry.

Requirements for admission to the School of Nursing were more stringent than for the Medical School: nurses had to be college graduates, while medical students had only to meet Winter's standards—and, as we have seen, he was prone to making exceptions.

The Sterling Hall of Medicine–not the grand edifice we still admire, but the more modest Georgian colonial nucleus of the later building—was also completed and occupied in 1923.

1925. In his report for 1925, Winter expressed pride in the contributions of the full-time faculty of Internal Medicine and Pediatrics. In his drive to liberate medical students from "required and stultifying" courses, and put them on an equal footing with students in the Graduate School, he warned that confining their education into separate years did not give medical students enough freedom to decide what courses to take, and when. Exposure to graduate-school education and preclinical science would, he hoped, further his old but rarely fulfilled dream of turning some students from clinical medicine to research. This seems to be the first time that Winter explicitly equated medical-school with graduate-school education in print, and he took the opportunity to praise physiology and research in that field.

Winter's mind was always working. On concluding that the dean had more than a full-time job, he proposed that a department of "medical education" be established. "It would be unfortunate to have the head of the school a mere executive who does not have the time or ability to keep in touch with the progress of the pre-clinical and clinical sciences, nor to engage in independent research." Winter wanted a staff to study, on an almost continuous basis, the curricular needs of the students. Meanwhile, he staked a claim on future building sites by installing tennis courts, recreational areas, green lawns, dogwood trees, and much more around the Medical School.

The *Yale Journal of Biology and Medicine* first appeared in 1925; in Winter's mind it was a vehicle for students to learn how to write and publish manuscripts. He never forgot that the students were the most important product of his medical school, and that they deserved as wholesome and rounded an education as possible. He was forever suggesting ways to expand the school's recreational facilities and increase social contact between faculty and students. He wanted to build a "common recreational gathering center" near the hospital and Medical School, where faculty and students could meet outside their scheduled hours.

The need for a medical-student dormitory was another recurring theme of Winter's reports. He was not to get his way until the second Sterling Hall of Medicine was built, with a gym, squash courts, and showers for men and women students. A dormitory, however, was not to be built until the 1950s, again with Harkness money.

In 1925, Winter finally obtained financial support for a Department of Psychiatry and Mental Hygiene, although it would be a long time before he found someone he considered qualified to head it. The report offers a first glimpse of the Institute of Human Relations and the Medical School as the potential coordinators of "the University's activities in the medical and biological sciences." Winter again praised physiology and student research. Even then, however, any suggestion of Medical School hegemony aroused suspicions on the part of the college faculty, who were already fearful of his motives.

1926. The following year Winter proposed bringing into the neighborhood of the Medical School, probably in a single building, "the various sciences associated with behavior, chiefly human behavior." To the discomfiture of their deans, he included in the new grouping the Divinity School and the Law School. The latter's new dean, Charles Clark, who had succeeded Hutchins, reacted furiously to a proposal that had been made without his agreement.

For the first time, there are inklings in the annual report that all was not well at the Medical School: Winter reiterated the need for more frequent and closer contact between faculty and students. At the same time, he rejoiced at the reduction of "didactic and fixed instruction, which allowed the student more freedom in selecting courses and in deciding whether to go for an M.D. or a Ph.D. degree." Winter's oft-repeated hope of training more physicians as research biologists occasioned considerable anxiety among Yale's administrators, as reflected in an unsigned letter of January 27, 1928, presumably from President Angell to Winter:

> I have a feeling that in its present form the statement will be too frequently misunderstood by the average doctor under whose eyes it might be taken–particularly in New Haven and Connecticut–as indicating that the school has entirely lost interest in training physicians. . . . [O]bviously if an appreciable part of your students go off into the biological sciences, even with the ultimate interest of medicine in mind, it cuts down the number of outright doctors that you send out into the world and if this matter is brought into context with the extremely high cost of the whole medical-scientific- educational program it gives another handle for acrimonious critiques to grasp.

Angell advised Winter to make a statement, presumably unambiguous, to reassure the community physicians.

1927. Winter's next annual report labeled the new educational reforms at Yale the "Yale Plan." Although the previous year he had mentioned an "Institute for Human Relations," he now called it the "Institute for Human Behavior," only later reverting to the former title.

Over the next few years, Winter's reports reflect his increasing focus on sociology, the Law School, and the Graduate School. He also began to display a far broader view of medicine than the application of what he was beginning to think of as mere technology. Despite his ever-grander goals, however, his later reports convey a sense of slowing down, of a loss of determination and energy. Yet Winter never forgot the medical students, advocating for a research club where they could report on their dissertations.

Up to 1927, the Medical School had followed the university's leisurely summer vacation schedule, closing down in June and opening again in late September, leaving a modern faculty envious of long trips to Europe, with returns postponed as late as October. At this time Winter proposed keeping the departments active throughout the calendar year so that students could carry on their research and clinical work during the summer.

1930. Winter's 1930 report praised the new Institute for Human Relations and its first full-time head of Psychiatry, Eugen Kahn, whom he had recruited from Vienna. His notions of occupational medicine, or "industrial medicine," as he called it, had also begun to crystallize.

1931. As the Depression brought a halt to years of growth at the Medical School, a long list of problems demanded attention. Because the Board of Permanent Officers had grown too large, an executive committee was needed to run the school. There were hitches in the application of the Yale Plan, as well as difficulties in integrating the Medical School into the university. Nevertheless, Winter proposed that a mental hospital be built next to the Institute for Human Relations. And he pressed his argument for a section of clinical sociology, a vision that continued to enrage his colleagues.

As the Depression worsened, interactions between students and faculty became more problematic. The dean's reports were increasingly taken up with administrative and educational issues, and with the Medical School's survival in difficult economic circumstances. Yet Winter continued to harbor halcyonic hopes of humanizing the medical curriculum and, one supposes, the medical students. He faced the need for reorganization squarely, listing the criticisms that had surfaced.

1935. Understandably, there is little joy in Winter's final report as dean. The major issues that came up for attention were a liberalized curriculum, full-time medicine, and the development of preventive medicine and of psychiatry. Winter was not one to go gently into the dark; he rubbed the noses of his adversaries on the faculty in his admonitions for more clinical sociology.

COMMENTS BY CONTEMPORARIES

Accounts by people who worked with him give an idea of Winter's general demeanor and reputation as dean. For example, the autumn 1932 issue of the *Yale Scientific Magazine* featured a story about Dean Winternitz under the subtitle "Worcester Sauce in the Academic Bill of Fare." Celebrating the rebirth of the school under Winternitz, the anonymous author comments: "Naturally, there are those who do not like the course or the destination. On such matters it is rather hard to have unanimity of opinion, and that is why captains rarely ask for a vote from passengers and crew." The article describes Winter as

> [a] man of many seeming contradictions. Unassuming in appearance, he has sometimes been mistaken for a student or a helper. . . . In action, whether in the classroom, on the platform, or in private conference, the effect is different, the vigor of his mind and body become apparent. For a while he may hold himself in check, but soon his expression, voice and gestures all reflect the tensions within. . . . At times the Dean will seem to put himself on terms of intimacy with students, jesting with them as he passes. But the wary student will detect a reserve beyond which it is not well to go. Dr. Winternitz is not the "hail-fellow-well-met" type. . . . The affections and recreations of the average man seem to him intolerably silly.
>
> A despiser of most sports and games, particularly golf and bridge, Winternitz is physically an outdoor type. . . . Winternitz's geniality, as we have seen, is more of an intellectual than an emotional phenomenon. He believes in social activities for students, for instance, but he thinks they should be rigidly controlled.
>
> Himself a person who has had to create his opportunities, Dr. Winternitz likes particularly those who have been highly favored by circumstance. The struggling, circumscribed lad usually finds small favor with him. This is another seeming contradiction, for

he likes to extol the virtue of poverty and struggle in which he does not believe. . . . The Dean likes independence as well as courage. . . .

Medicine, to him, is not an end in itself, but one of the means by which the greater problems of human behavior are to be approached. There are those who are afraid that such an extension of interest will mean minimizing important traditional values in medicine, but such has not proved to be the case. . . .

His personality is like a thermometer, fluid and full of seeming contradictions in its indications. It is highly sensitive to external and internal conditions. There are long periods when it is at a low mark, followed by a flare up of brilliance; brusqueness and graciousness; a biting tongue and an ingratiating manner; humbleness and pride; intellectualism and emotionalism; despair and gaiety. . . . [E]veryone who has been in contact with him knows that here is a definite personality, one that is thoroughly liked or disliked but is never colorless. Winternitz is the Worcester sauce in an academic bill of fare which otherwise often enough would be flat and uninteresting.[11]

In the *New York Times* of March 6, 1932, Winter is quoted as saying: "Medicine is not looked upon at Yale as a self-sufficient entity, set apart by man and God as an independent realm into which only a chosen few may enter: it is considered rather that medicine can become enriched and significant to the extent that it fits into the scheme of the social organism as a whole and contributes to the well-being of society." The article goes on to praise Winter's belief that man should be seen as a soul as well as a body:

> The aim of Yale University is to restore to medicine the point of view of the old family physician and at the same time to retain the benefit of concentration in special fields. . . . [E]veryone who enters medicine will be "exposed" to attitudes and knowledge which should make him aware that human beings are mental and social as well as physical organisms.

In another undated piece, Winter quotes John Shaw Billings's reports to the Johns Hopkins Trustees: "A sick man enters the hospital to have his pain relieved, his disease cured. To this end the mental influences brought to bear upon him are always important, sometimes more so than the physical. He needs sympathy and encouragement as much as medicine."

After he left the deanship, building on the study-group idea, first for neurology and the Institute of Human Relations, then for dentistry, Winter conceived the idea of a group interested in atypical growth, now called the "Atypical Study Unit." The Jane Coffin Childs Memorial Fund provided the funds.

WINTER AND THE FACULTY

Some examples of the interplay between the dean and the faculty recruited under his aegis may be pertinent. Many went on to fame: Francis Blake, John Peters, Grover Powers, and Samuel Harvey made up the nucleus of the group of full-time faculty that was transforming Yale, while others were doing the same at the University of Rochester and Vanderbilt Medical School. Although the authors are convinced, from personal experience, that hiring a full-time, salaried faculty is the best way to organize a medical school for teaching and research, such an arrangement may make the faculty overly dependent on the chairmen and the hierarchy. Men with the security of independent private practices might have taken Winternitz's need for control less emotionally than did the full-time faculty at that time.

Winter did more than treat his faculty as his children. He was forever urging them to travel abroad, learn new techniques, absorb new ideas, and, presumably, make the renascent Yale Medical School better known in Europe. This was a favorite theme of Flexner, who had urged just such a course on the dean more than once.

Edwards A. Park had returned from Baltimore as professor of pediatrics and "founding chairman" of the Department of Pediatrics, which was established on July 1, 1921. He arrived in New Haven full of enthusiasm, but was quickly disconcerted by Winter's autocratic ways.

Strong differences of opinion emerged between the two men, and on March 8, 1927, Park submitted his resignation in a letter to the dean: "I have not been satisfied that all appointments to the Board of Permanent Officers have been wise and consequently have not felt complete confidence that the early hopes concerning the future of the school could be realized or that I could play a satisfactory part in furthering the development of the school."

Under Park's successor, Grover Powers, who had given up the job of pediatrician-in-chief at the Henry Ford Hospital to come to New Haven with Park, the department developed many innovations, including the Rooming-In Project, the culmination, as Powers generously put it, of Winternitz's ideas about integration of departments. Powers was such a gentle soul that even Winter curbed his temper in his presence.

Francis Blake in 1923 received an offer to move to the University of Chicago as a professor of medicine and dean of the Medical School.[12] Impressed by the construction of a "strictly university hospital" in Chicago, and by the Medical School's liberal budget, he was tempted to accept. Ultimately, however, he remained at Yale for the rest of his life, serving for one term as part-time dean of the Medical School. In a letter to President Angell, Blake stressed that it was important for the New Haven Hospital "to continue functioning as a university teaching hospital" and urged the university to boost its support significantly. "The ultimate solution of the hospital situation lies, I believe, in its becoming a university hospital in fact, if not in name," he wrote.

Samuel Harvey, a Yale Medical School graduate, had been put in charge of the surgical service in 1923, but had grown unhappy, in part because "the administration of the surgical service and the hospital has been subject to some criticism." Although he apparently was considered ineffective in directing the staff, more important was his failure to voice unqualified approval of the full-time system. At the expiration of his term as associate professor, his dissatisfaction with the operation of the full-time system led to the appointment of a committee to find out how he really felt. On February 6, 1923, Angell wrote to Harvey Cushing that Samuel Harvey must have interpreted this action "as an attempt to force his hand, and now to the surprise of such of his friends as I have contact with, he has put in his resignation." Although the president did not think that personal bias or animosity had played any essential role, "I am told that Dr. Harvey regards the Dean of the school as responsible for the whole affair." Angell asserted that this was untrue, but later observers may wonder if it was not the reason for the long and tortuous animosity between Harvey and Winternitz.[13]

Cushing responded, in a letter date July 4, that Harvey had just come to Boston to see him, adding, "I think it would be calamitous if he should feel obliged to withdraw from the school at this juncture nor do I see how he could be replaced. Well-trained young surgeons who have academic leanings are few and far between." Cushing went on to urge that Angell see Harvey, who had the gift of reticence. Of Winternitz he commented, "The Dean, whom I know equally well, and whose good qualities I admire, has his faults like the rest of us and I doubt whether Dr. Harvey can get the moral support and encouragement from that quarter which he just now needs. Do therefore see him yourself."

Fortunately, Harvey, apparently eager to stay on as chief of Surgery, wrote a conciliatory letter to the Board of Permanent Officers. In part a metaphorical journey to Canossa, this long letter suggests how difficult it was for faculty members to differ with the dean.

> That there could be any question of lack of sympathy on my part with the principle of "full time," I had not supposed for a moment. I gather, however, that my discussion of the "clinical fund" before the Board of Permanent Officers and the Medical Board has aroused misgivings in some minds. I spoke frankly and unreservedly before these two Boards, where I supposed discussion should be carried on in such fashion. I spoke freely because I had not been consulted previously concerning the "clinical fund" and its problems, although the size of the fund and its importance in the carrying on of the Department of Surgery made this question of greater weight to me and to my staff, than to the staff of any other clinical section. I did not know that the University policy

had been virtually decided upon, so that I was unwittingly placed in the position of arguing against a "fait accompli." I felt also that the matter was being passed upon hurriedly, and that there were many phases and aspects, the effects of which possibly had not been thoroughly weighed. I did not say that I would not take care of private patients if the "clinical fund" was taken over by the University, or make any statement to that effect, and I took pains to say at that time that I would support without reserve, whatever policy was decided upon.

I wish to state that I endorse unreservedly the effort to establish the clinical branches on a basis by which ample time for teaching and productive work may be found, and this I feel to be the essential point in "full time." Necessary modifications or even encroachments on this principle may take place, and I think that everyone should feel free to discuss these and discuss them frankly without being subjected to misinterpretation of motive.

The disposition of the earnings of the members of the departments is not, I think, an essential part of the "full time" principle. It is merely one phase of a problem that should be tried out on an experimental basis with an open mind.

A second phase is the care of private patients by a physician on a "full-time basis," and there, I think, is a definite conflict of interest between the Hospital and University. If the Hospital required my per-

> sonal attention to every private case, the position would become untenable because of the absorption of my time, and if the school allowed no care of private cases, then bad feeling in the community would be engendered against the clinic. It is, I feel, of the highest importance that the relations of the University and Hospital to the community as maintained through contact with physicians and patients, be of the most cordial nature, and to my mind, the greatest danger to the successful consummation of the experiment of "full time" at Yale is the possible disastrous breach of such relations. The harmonizing of the two policies outlined above must be worked out by the University and the Hospital and definitely stated. The physician cannot be left with fairness in the position where he may be subject to criticism because of his non-conformity with the one policy or the other. I wish to state, however, in order that there may be no misapprehension, that I shall be pleased to work under any agreement that is adopted, and to set up the necessary type of organization in my staff to carry it into effect.

Harvey stayed on, but he could not have been a friend toWinter.

Chapter 6. The Winter Years: Highs and Lows

Winternitz as a Teacher

Five years after Winter became dean, he had become recognized as one of the "movers and shakers" of American medicine. Quality students were applying to the Yale Medical School in ever-larger numbers, and the brilliant young faculty he had assembled was coveted and courted by other medical schools. Even allowing for the gloss of nostalgia, stories from the graduates of this time are remarkably consistent in describing the flavor of the school and Winternitz's teaching style.

When Max Taffel, later the "surgeon's surgeon," entered the Medical School in the late twenties, Winter was in the habit of reminding each entering class that they were there to learn rather than to be taught, a basic tenet of his Yale Plan.[1] There would be no tests or exams until the end of the second and fourth years unless students asked for them. A full week was devoted to the first exam, to ensure that the students were prepared to continue into the clinical years. One part was an essay, another a written exam with open-book access to the library and journals; while oral exams in the final session could take anywhere from half an hour to three hours or more.

Although the students did not have to attend any classes during their first two years, they had to know the subjects covered. Working three jobs to pay his way through medical school, Taffel skipped the dull pharmacology lectures, which were straight from the textbook, so that he could read them at his leisure. In due course, the chairman of Pharmacology argued that since Taffel had not attended the lectures, he should not be allowed to take the exams. Winter admonished Taffel but, conceding that Pharmacology was not well taught, let him take the exam. Taffel scored the highest grade on record.

Of Winter, Taffel said, "He taught his students to think, to question, to be precise, to be observing. When he asked a question, it wasn't a question, it was a dare!" Winter used Taffel as his sparring partner for that second year. Every week he would say, "Tolliver [for Taffel] up front!" and they would discuss the organs displayed. The class knew they were lucky to have Taffel up there, for Winter—who could be pitilessly intimidating–might search in vain for someone who enjoyed matching wits with him.

According to Taffel, Winter made sure that the New Haven Hospital became state of the art, with private rooms for private patients, but he also turned the staff into "family." They lived together and ate together in their own dining room, where they were served "real meals with tablecloths and napkins." They knew one anothers' patients, and in an emergency they knew where to get all the help they needed. This sense of family spirit came through strongly: as Taffel talked about his class and his early years in the hospital, his face showed the pride they had felt in having the best equipment to go with the finest teachers. The Medical School and the hospital had provided him with a foundation for a fulfilling life.

Anatomy was a favorite source of anecdotes, none particularly unique to Yale or to Winternitz: meeting one's cadaver for the first time is usually a memory that sticks. The large dissecting room was on the top floor of Sterling Hall. Each of the dissecting tables was shielded by a curved metal cover, a larger version of the silver domes in hotel dining rooms. Students were assigned half a cadaver and usually approached the table cautiously. When T. Dennie Pratt lifted the cover, he exclaimed, "Look! It's a woman!"

It was in the gross anatomy sessions that Winter excelled as a teacher. That involved studying fresh or preserved organs so that the students could learn to recognize diseased organs as well as normal ones by their gross appearance. L.A. Chotkowski recollected,

> The great one called me up before the class during a gross pathology exercise, and handed me a grey formalin smelling slab of presumably human tissue. The interrogation went something like this:

"Chotkowski, what do you see here?"
I proceeded to struggle with a description of the size, color and structure of the specimen when interrupted with "Chotkowski, this is a specimen of human lung. Does it look like a lung to you?"
"No, sir."
"Oh?" said Winternitz.
"Well, not like any lungs I have ever seen."
"So, how many lungs have you seen?"
"Not very many."
"Chotkowski, have you ever seen a millet seed?"
"Yes, sir."
"Do you see anything in this specimen that looks like a millet seed?"
"No, sir."
"Well, you are looking at military tuberculosis named after the millet seed."

William Wedemeyer recalled,

Because I considered him the best teacher I had ever encountered I studied and imitated his technique by sitting in on his lectures–and gross sessions for the two years I was in training. He taught us how to "see" when you "look," how to describe as distinct from interpreting your observations, the "monkey wrench" approach as uncluttered by a bunch of fixed notions, like a set of "socket wrenches," none of which fits a particular problem. He never answered a student's question about something he should already have learned. Instead he asked another student to give the answer, which was intended as a real putdown, and sometimes trapped the student who hadn't paid attention. Then he would ask a third.

From William E. Bloomer came the following anecdote:

> As a medical student I came to enjoy and fear Winter's informal discussions with half of our class going over gross pathology specimens in the big room built around the autopsy table. . . . His teachings were often imprinted on one's memory because of his quick wit and sharp sarcasm. I of course enjoyed watching my fellow class-men and class-women in their discomfort as they were singled out to be mercilessly grilled by the professor. . . .
>
> I remember one time Winter asked for someone to tell the rest of the class his understanding of fat metabolism. Winter then turned a big pan upside down and sat on it to listen in rapt attention. As the student launched into his discourse, he would occasionally glance down at the professor, who would nod and smile and urge him on. The student thought he was making a big impression, but unfortunately he did not realize he was not describing fat metabolism but had gotten it mixed up with carbohydrate metabolism. When he came to the triumphant end

of his speech Dr. Winternitz turned to the rest of the class and said with a sad face, "Ain't that pitiful?"

Another anecdote from William Bloomer is perfectly pitched to the sound of Winter's speech:

> Dr. Winternitz was describing the function of the synovial fluid in a knee joint. It went something like this: "Yes, Dr. F—, the synovial fluid lubricates the surfaces of the joint, just like the oil lubricates the surfaces of the cylinders in your dad's Rolls Royce. Isn't that right? . . . What? Your dad doesn't have a Rolls Royce? . . . I thought the only reason we let you in this medical school was because we thought your dad had a Rolls Royce.

One tale tells of a different conclusion:

> Whenever he had a free half-hour between appointments, Winter would grab his lab coat, cross Cedar Street and check on the research. He blended in as if camouflaged. One day he was returning to his office for a student interview when a flashy convertible car caught his eye: in it were a very well dressed young man and his handsome dog. The man hailed Winter to ask if he would watch his dog while he went for his interview with the dean. Knowing all the shortcuts, Winter agreed, but as soon as the man's back was turned, he disappeared into a side door while the prospective student entered through the rotunda. When the student reached the dean's office,

there was his dog and a small man looking vaguely familiar wearing a dark coat and bow tie sitting behind the desk with an inscrutable look on his face. The interview went something like this:

"Where did you go to college?"

"Dartmouth, sir."

"I didn't ask you where you learned to ski, I asked you where you went to college. And why do you want to be a doctor?"

"I'd like to be a surgeon, sir."

"Oh, you like to sew."

Poor fellow, his dog had a better chance of getting into medical school. Winter was up to his old tricks.

The second year concentrated on pathology and Winter lectured at 8 a.m. Even though CPCs (Clinical Pathological Conferences) were held in the evening, everyone attended, especially when John Peters and Winternitz matched wits and witticisms. It was a show that no one wanted to miss. To present the case up front in the amphitheater was a terrifying experience for most students because both Winternitz and Peters were ready to pounce on the slightest slip-up. They quizzed the presenter and dazzled the assembly in virtuoso performances of one-upmanship.

In the quadrangle of Sterling Memorial Library on a sunny morning, Taffel talked about his early days in New Haven; remembering Winter, he became the young, idealistic student of sixty years before. Then his face clouded over, he paused a moment, and remarked, "Winter was a mix of good and evil." During the Depression, Taffel's last sixty dollars vanished with a failed bank. There was nothing for him to do but take a year off to earn the next year's tuition. But he couldn't do that without speaking to the dean. Somehow, Winter found him a loan. Sometimes, when Winter would come upon him studying late at night, he would put his arm around Taffel's shoulder and ask how it was going. Such fatherly gestures, and the concerned tone of his voice in unguarded moments, say much about Winter's character. Do they also mitigate the anti-Jewish sentiment that has been attributed to him?

"And the evil in Winter?" we asked. Taffel told of Winter's merciless treatment of timid students, then of a classmate who had a drinking problem. During Prohibition, illegal drinking was widely tolerated, but Winter did not like students drinking at the Medical School and complained about it to President Angell. One night a drunken student was evicted after harassing the nurses in the hospital, whereupon he got into a fight with a guard. In the process he lost his coat, which was brought to the dean's office, so that anyone claiming it had to speak to Winter. The student's roommate recognized the coat, but would not tell the dean to whom it belonged. This loyalty enraged Winter, who immediately suspended the roommate. He was bothered enough by the incident to mention it in a letter to his son Tom.

> Monday especially was a crowded day. The most annoying thing was a student problem which I thought involved the wrong viewpoint of a student concerning responsibilities to the School as distinct from his responsibilities to a fellow student. I think I probably was somewhat wrong myself so it worried me, I got it straightened out after a bit and without too much injustice to the student. The thing which annoys me now is that I do not seem to have the equilibrium I ought to have and get angry too easily, which in the end reacts more on the person who gets angry. . . . So it doesn't pay, is bad form, and destroys judgment.

Three weeks later Winter relented and readmitted the innocent roommate, Irving Friedman, who went on to become one of New Haven's leading obstetricians and gynecologists, one whom Winter recommended to his friends and family.

CHANGES IN THE MEDICAL SCHOOL

In September 1922, Winter sent Dr. Henry S. Pritchett of the Carnegie Corporation a two-page memorandum on the needs of the School of Medicine. After reviewing the philosophy and history of medical education, he wrote:

> The greatest need of the School at the present time is the development of the nursing field. The progress in Medicine, particularly of the clinical divisions, will soon be blocked unless there is a thorough reorganization of the nursing situation. Such reorganization cannot be effected without adequate housing, teaching, and recreational facilities, which are not available. . . . A sum of $500,000 is needed for the erection of a building for the School for nurses. An equal sum is needed for educational endowment for which we believe a successful appeal may be made if the buildings are available.

THE NURSING SCHOOL

On April 25, 1923, as another step in converting Yale from a college to a national university, President Angell announced the establishment of the Nursing School under the direction of Dean Annie K. Goodrich. The first such school in the country to enjoy equal status with the other professional schools in a university, the Yale School of Nursing later would be the first to require a bachelor's degree for entry.

Within a year of its founding, the Nursing School had demonstrated its beneficial impact on patient care. The student nurses were all college graduates with a professional mind-set. The curriculum was dedicated to patient care and hands-on nursing in a ratio of three hours of patient care to one hour of classroom instruction, largely taught by physicians. Nurses also went on medical rounds and accompanied fourth-year medical students on house calls to deliver babies, an activity they greatly loved. Sometimes neither the doctor nor the nurse got there in time, thereby weaving the stuff of great stories. Levin Waters delivered a boy with a caul on the Fourth of July as a parade marched by, the band playing "The Stars and Stripes Forever." The nervous father tried to feed the "doctor'" a slice of pizza as the baby presented himself, and the nurse arrived just in time to check mother and child. All was well. Two days later the family had gone to the beach when Waters returned to check the mother and child. They were way ahead of their time!

With the full cooperation of Dean Goodrich and Winter, as well as of Charles-Edward Winslow, who headed the epidemiology/public health section, the Child Study Center became part of a nurse's education. Winslow did everything he could to encourage more nurses to work in the community. So many years later, it is hard to imagine the visiting nurse as a concept that was met with skepticism, but Winslow, Goodrich, and Winternitz all agreed on the direction of the Nursing School, and so it was bound to succeed. These strong idealistic individuals understood, respected, and liked one another. Goodrich in particular supported all of Winter's ideas about psychiatry, and particularly about "the patient as a whole."

THE MEDICAL SCHOOL EXPANSION

The Medical School grew at an impressive pace during the years 1920-1925. Its first visible expression, the original Sterling Hall of Medicine, was going up on Cedar Street. Across the way, the New Haven Hospital, exemplifying the latest advances in hospital design, was being rebuilt and expanded. Together, the two facilities offered tangible evidence of progress, consolidation, and efficiency. Winter enjoyed all of the new building and gave as much thought to details as to the big picture. For example, he selected the trees (*Cryptomeria compacta*) in front of Sterling Hall because of their tall and spindly habit. A muted shade of evergreen, they enhance the architecture without overwhelming it; in seventy years they have hardly changed. Winter expected the forsythia to come out on Cedar Street before blooming anywhere else in New Haven, and it usually does.

NEW FACULTY

One challenge that Winternitz and Angell faced early on was to get faculty to stay on because Yale was the most stimulating place to be, not because they had the best-paying jobs. A characteristic and oft-repeated phrase of Winter's was that he wanted "brains, cheap." Raises were not given on a regular schedule, as the dean thought that everyone should pitch in together while the school was still taking shape. Winter had received an increase in salary each year at Hopkins, but that practice that was unheard of at Yale. He liked to send people abroad on sabbaticals for more training when they needed a boost, but some would take their sabbatical, then leave within a year of their return.

Finding a chairman for the Department of Physiology was almost as difficult as starting the Department of Psychiatry. First, Winter had to convince the Committee on Educational Policy and the Yale Corporation that the teaching of physiology belonged in the Medical School as a separate department, with its space included in the architectural plans. Abraham Flexner, who knew that Yale was looking for an outstanding scientist to head the new department, told President Angell that the German physician Otto Meyerhof was being seriously considered by another American university. Winter, who knew Meyerhof, was asked to make discreet inquiries and learned that he might enjoy working in America. Even though Meyerhof had won the Nobel Prize, Yale hesitated when it emerged that Meyerhof was Jewish. Angell wrote to C.A. Duniway, an American who was president of the British Division of the American University Union in Europe:

> A few years ago the German physiologist Meyerhof, now a Professor at Kiel, worked in conjunction with Professor A.V. Hill, the eminent physiologist of the

> University of London, and was accorded conjointly with him the Nobel Prize. We are considering bringing Meyerhof over here, if he is willing to come, and we desire very much to learn from Professor Hill something of his impression regarding Meyerhof's personality and the chances that he would work agreeably with academic colleagues under American conditions.

Duniway's reply was prompt and reassuring:

> I made an appointment with Professor A.V. Hill as promptly as I could. I found him very ready to give information on the points raised by you. . . . Professor Hill believes that Semitic origins and Teutonic environments have not resulted in a product showing marked difficulties for one called to work with academic colleagues under American conditions. . . . Meyerhof worked agreeably with British colleagues and has shown liberal independence not relished by many of his German colleagues.

On the strength of Duniway's letter, Winter was instructed to offer Dr. Meyerhof the job of establishing a Department of Physiology at the Yale School of Medicine. In declining the offer, Meyerhof gave the impression that he was eager to come to Yale, but could not because of his wife's poor health.

Two years later, the position still had not been filled. Winter, at a loss for what to do, wrote to Hans Zinsser at Harvard:

> What we propose is to liberalize the curriculum to permit a student as much latitude as is compatible with his ability and initiative in the choice and amount of work he should carry at any time. He will elect his curriculum, subject to the approval of instructors in charge of the courses he wishes to take. All authorized examinations will be eliminated excepting group examinations to be given at fixed intervals, enabling the student, when he thinks he is prepared for such an examination to proceed,
>
> 1) From the preclinical group of science to a particular science
> 2) From the preclinical science group to the clinic
> 3) To qualify for a degree whether a Ph.D. or an M.D.
>
> Arrangements have been made with the Graduate School, Yale College and the Sheffield Scientific School enabling us to exercise very much more liberality in the admission of students. For example, a student with a good biological training and a limited amount of chemistry may enter the school and complete his chemical work in one of the undergraduate schools. Students will be encouraged to utilize more of the year than is at present possible by our two

> term sessions, taking courses either during the summer or in the academic year in other institutions. Briefly, what we are doing is practically adopting the Continental system of education. There has not been any detailed program prepared but we are working on the arrangement of courses and making plans to meet the general suggestions embodied above. . . . We are in no way sure that this plan is good but we know the old plan is not good and anything that will offer a release of the quantitative, qualitative curricular bondage for student and instructor will be welcome.

Zinsser encouraged Winter to concentrate on youth in his search for a physiologist, but the episode suggests some of the problems, and the reason for the problems, inherent in Yale's chauvinistic inclinations.

JOHN FULTON

Winter next approached John Farquhar Fulton, a bright young American from Minnesota who had worked with Charles Sherrington at Oxford and stayed on in England. Fulton's wife, the former Lucia Wheatland, came from an old and wealthy Massachusetts family. Her native dignity and sense of fun ensured that the couple would fit in at Yale. But Fulton had found his home in England and was not ready to leave, so Winter continued searching for and interviewing promising physiologists, without success.

Two years later, in 1929, Winter traveled to Europe "to learn something about psychiatry" and suggested to President Angell that he pay Fulton a visit. This time he was able to convince the reluctant candidate that such an opportunity would never present itself again. Fulton agreed to come to Yale, where he became an international figure. Equally important to Winter was the friendship and support that developed between the two men.

The Fultons returned to England every summer, maintaining strong ties with British scientists, libraries, and book dealers. Winter prized them for adding luster to the Yale community. Lucia Fulton became a patron to the Medical School and carved a niche for herself in the social life of Yale. During Helen Winternitz's illness, she generously helped with official entertaining. Later, her interests centered around the new Cushing Library. She even contributed her own unique brand of scholarship by giving a talk on the production and enjoyment of champagne, illustrated with samples decanted from well-iced bottles. Fulton took a personal interest in the research for this particular paper and reported on it in his diary. Although his appetite for alcohol earned him the sobriquet "Four Quarts," Fulton became one of the leading professors of physiology of his time. Through his passion for collecting incunabula and old medical books, he promoted an interest in the history of medicine and was responsible for putting together the great medical-historical library at Yale, named for the donors who sponsored it.[2]

HELEN AND THE FAMILY

Well known, sought after, and consulted, Winter was riding high. In the Winternitz archives, there are few hints that his wife was very ill.[3] Others were aware, however, and commented on the problem. We found the earliest reference to Helen's illness among the paper of President Angell. At the end of a letter to Angell, Dr. Fred Murphy of Chicago, a member of the Yale Corporation, wrote:

> May I also say at this time that I am very deeply disturbed over Winternitz's problems. His wife has been desperately ill for the better part of a year and it is not at all sure whether she will recover and, even if she does, it seems likely that such recovery may be long delayed. Meantime, there are five children from six to twelve in age, who are quite without home care and there are no family connections who can be called upon to help out. Winternitz has, I fear, quite exhausted his financial resources and the mental and emotional strain is greatly undermining his strength and health. I should like to talk with you about this when you come on. I think the University must consider some method of giving him at least temporary financial assistance. He is far too valuable a person to have incapacitated.[4]

The summer of 1926 was the last in which Helen enjoyed good health, so her son Tom recalls.[5] Up to that time, she occupied herself with raising the children, although she was active in the League of Women Voters and other organizations. Elizabeth's daughter, Dr. Helen Morehouse, relates that one summer evening at Treetops the family noticed a glow in the sky coming from the direction of Bristol, New Hampshire. Suspecting a fire, they drove to Bristol and found the hardware store burning out of control. Helen caught a chill on that jaunt and developed a bacterial infection that turned into pericarditis, for which in 1926 there were no antibiotics. Dr. Betsy Harrison believes that she had a kidney infection and "too many babies too quickly," while another person we consulted is of the opinion that the original infection started in her teeth.

The Winternitz children were full of energy and high spirits. Elizabeth, known as Buff, was twelve when her mother became ill. As the eldest, she did her best to take care of her siblings and be her mother's right hand at home. She remembered doctors tapping her mother's pleural effusions. All five children loved and respected their Grandmother Watson, with whom Winter developed a deep and lasting bond during this difficult time.

The details of Helen's illness elude us, and the hospital records from those days can no longer be found, but the death certificate makes it clear that she had chronic nephritis. Obviously, any depression or psychological overlay was unlikely to have appeared in that record. Winter, using the best medicine available, fought for Helen's life for the next four years.

Gladys, Eddie, and Molly took care of the house and family. Although Mary Cheever remembered the servants as not being particularly good, by today's standards Eddie was both loyal and perceptive. With his help, Helen could run the house from her bed or chair. She wanted to keep the children at home as long as possible, so that she could be in daily touch with them. When Mary had an accident, Eddie drove her to the hospital and stayed until she fell asleep. He was equally good medicine for Helen, who depended upon him .Molly may have thought she was too good for many of the things she was hired to do. She slept in the family's part of the house, not in the servants' quarters, at a time when it was unusual for household help of different races to live and work together. Winter's only criticism of Molly was that she was a terrible cook, but he needed continuity and loyalty at home, and he got it.

The only time Helen speaks to us in her own, mature voice is through her letters to Winter when he went to Europe in 1929. These poignant letters paint a picture of a very loving family, five bright children, and a concerned community of doctors and university women, Grover Powers among them, attending to the children's medical needs.

It must have been worrisome for Winter to leave Helen for an extended time, especially when her parents were also abroad. Yet go to Europe he did, trusting Eddie and her doctors–James Trask, her primary physician, and George Blumer–to take care of her. When Helen developed German measles right after Winter left, the woman of the Yale community were most solicitous. Her heart was checked regularly and found to be "alright."

Once Helen was on the mend, she sent Winternitz almost daily reports of life at 210 Prospect Street that give us our only glimpse into their relationship Without her sense of humor, and the occasional account of a conversation with a colleague, the letters would be saccharine. Winter saved receipts, accounts, and insignificant bits of paper, but there are no copies of the letters he wrote to Helen. He used them as his notes when writing his report of the trip, disposing of the personal letters and saving the formal report. Those letters would have let us tune into the voice he used with Helen. If he was her "Daddy Boy," did he sign himself Daddy Boy? When she reported professional conversations, was it as a colleague or as his confidante? A letter from that time gives the flavor of her writing:

> Dear Daddy Boy,
> It's Sunday evening and the girls have just gone back to New York, and the boys are on the third floor and Mary down in the living room reading Silas Marner so the house seems quiet. It was a lovely summer like day, the children–Jane and Mary especially–brought me 3 kinds of tulips, lilies of the valley and lilac from

the garden for my room as it's Mother's Day.—Jane took some lilies and tulips back with her to N.Y. to brighten the apartment. Edward took them to the station as we had an April Shower just when they were ready to go, but then he would have anyway. They had duck for dinner and had used up the last of the potatoes. . . .

Ray and Edith came in for a few minutes this afternoon. They seemed very well. Ray said he heard that the Fitkin [Wing of the New Haven Hospital] was ahead of schedule and that they had already gotten the steelwork for the first floor up and it was going fast which sounded encouraging. I asked him if everything was O.K. in the medical school and he allowed as far as he knew. He isn't very communicative & I do miss knowing a little something about many things like what my Daddy Boy always tells me.

Jim Trask told me that Raymond Pearl was going to Cambridge Mass to be head of some biological Institute & that Hopkins was quite pleased by the prospect, which was news to me as I always thought Hopkins thought him a real Pearl. He also told me the excitement of the Atlantic City meetings was the discovery of the adrenal had no adrenalin in it but a ferment which had an extraordinarily curative effect on Myositis Gravis, which he opined might be the same as Addisons disease. The work was done by a man who is now in the University of Chicago but did the work before he went there. I will try to look it up & be a little more intelligent on the subject.

This ink is some Buff imported and as usual since their departure I can find neither my proper pen nor ink so must use this sloppy stuff..—I wrote your mother yesterday and sent her your itinerary as I knew she would be interested in knowing when you would be where. . . . — The rain has gone and that lovely clear light has come that comes after summer rains. If you were here we would go out together in the garden and say "howdy"to every peony and iris bud. . . .

There goes the Boston Mail Plane. I love to hear it go by. You can tell it as it is a much larger plane than most & makes a deeper sound. The robins and red winged blackbirds are singing good night so I will say goodnight and loads of love to our Daddy Boy from all of us.

Your Py

The trail of crumbs becomes a slender sheaf of Helen's touching letters to Winter at the end of her life, a peek into their life together. When we came upon them in the archives at Yale, we copied a few for Bill and Mary because they were so young when their mother died. We thought they would like to have them and they might even trigger a memory. Bill remembered "lots of hugging and tears" when his father was leaving for the trip. Neither he nor Mary could imagine anyone calling their father "Daddy Boy" or "Pie Face," which led us to wonder what endearments Winter might have used with Helen and how his off-guard voice might have sounded, what they talked about.

It is safe to say that his professional life and plans for the future were uppermost in his thoughts most of the time. Winter saved a lot of inconsequential papers, but none of his letters from the 1929 trip, our last chance to "hear" his side of their conversations. He kept quite a few letters to his second wife, Polly, but they are not deeply personal. Then, late in our work on the manuscript, Priscilla Norton was given a folder full of Winter's letters to his secretary during the 1940s. We will have more to say later about Miss Jean Barnes, who brought out Winter's playful side. Judging by his letters to her, it is reasonable to speculate that Winter had a variety of pet names for Helen and that their relationship was unique among his relationships with women. Helen was his student before she became a colleague, they were young when they met, and science, medicine, love, and children bound them closely. It is likely that Winter and Helen were a team.

Gladys cooked some very good meals. Most of their food was home-grown, the potatoes lasting until the first week of May. Eddie and Gladys suited the family well, although they may not have measured up to New Haven society's standards. Dressing late in the day, Helen came downstairs once a day and went out in the garden, when weather permitted, to admire and pick flowers. She read the *Saturday Evening Post* on her chaise or in Winter's study, where she could have a fire. She dined with the children and they played word games during dinner. Mornings, if she felt strong enough, she sewed and mended while someone read to her; otherwise she just lay in bed listening, a far cry from the rebellious active young woman she had been.

Winter dealt as best he could with the strain of caring for a chronically ill wife, dealing with adolescent children, and running the Medical School. Reducing tension at home was essential, and he put a lot of thought into selecting the right schools for his children. True to his philosophy of education, he sent the three girls to the Lincoln School in New York City—a progressive school with advanced teaching methods and a bright student body–rather than to boarding school. First Elizabeth and Jane, and then Jane and Mary, were set up in an apartment and placed in the care of a companion, whom Mary described as "an awful woman."

Tom was sent to the Avon School in Connecticut, leaving only the two youngest children, Bill and Mary, at home in the 1929-1930 school year. Tom had grown very big and gave Winter his first experience with an adolescent son. Winter didn't like to be reminded that this huge, untidy person–who had a pretty good mind, but wasn't using it–was his flesh and blood. In 1930, when Bill was only ten years old, he was sent to the International School in Geneva, Switzerland, a truly progressive school where the classes were mostly held in French and vacations were taken skiing or traveling as a group. Bill loved it so much that Mary followed him to Switzerland the following year.

The girls came home from New York every weekend, bringing their laundry, mending, and homework. Helen rallied to help them, but she was exhausted by the time they returned to school. She singled Elizabeth out for special consideration, either because Buff was fifteen or because the instability of her college years was beginning to show. To Helen, her older boy was "dear big old sloppy Tom," while Jane was already the dependable, sensible one who quietly did well and made no fuss. Mary was the artistic, imaginative, crisis kid who dramatized everything. Bill, the lovable youngest child, seemed always to have a friend in tow and a smile on his face.

Helen does not mention friends visiting in her bedroom except when she had German measles and they were "popping in." Either she would dress and go downstairs to receive guests, or she would be "unable to receive." She relied on the telephone and Eddie, who did all the errands and drove Helen in the car when she felt up to it. Once they were out, he would suggest a little drive out of town or through the park, and sometimes she invited others to go with them.

Even though she was an invalid, Helen was on a committee for the nurses' dormitory–the last committee she served on at the Medical School–but rarely attended meetings. She also remained active in the Wellesley Club of New Haven. She had been active in the woman's suffrage movement and helped establish the New Haven

Chapter of the League of Women Voters. A physician herself, she genuinely enjoyed talking with Winter's colleagues, but those opportunities grew few and far between. In those days, it was unusual for a man and a woman to have a good gossip; one always had to think of appearances, especially in New Haven.

Monday, May 27
Dear Sweetheart:
Like all Sundays when the girls are home it was a busy day. So busy that when evening came I climbed into bed with this letter unwritten. Buff had her Biology Note Book to write up and she was badly behind so she wrote nearly all the time she was here and then didn't get it all done–so Jane and I washed her undies, pressed her dresses & mended her stockings and I copied 5 elaborate drawings for her out of the book, thereby renewing my acquaintance with the internal workings of the frog, crawfish, chick etc.

It was a lovely day and we all had a hilarious time at dinner playing "I packed My Grandmother's Trunk" till we had 36 or 7 things.

After dinner all five went out on the lawn & played Blind Man's Buff. Just before dinner Billy came to me with a few enormous tears running out of his eyes & saying he had an infected finger which hurt him for a day & a half. It was slightly swollen & seemed to have something in the ball. . . . If you had been here I wouldn't have given it a thought, but you weren't. . . .

Ray wanted to know if you had written anything more about Fulton so I told him what you said after all. He was very much interested and hoped you could get him. Ray had seen Bob [Hutchins] the morning after his talk with the President & he told him all about it but asked him not to tell. Ray thinks Bob has not made such a wise decision in taking the headship of such a "heterogeneous mass" as one of those Midwestern Universities & thinks his opportunity here in the next 5 years would have been as great or greater but of course he didn't tell Bob so.

The Medical School is proceeding quietly. Ray says he hopes no one is throwing a monkey wrench into the administration of the Institute in your absence–in other words putting too much of a finger in the pie–but I said if he did you could probably get it out on your return, that he was noted more for what he did not do than for what he did do–usually.

Ray looked very well and had just had a nice ride to New London & back.

I'm to have a new reader this A.M. a friend of Mrs. King's.

The Winternitzes' only close friends were the Hutchinses, and they were moving to Chicago. One beautiful spring day, Helen wanted to drop off flowers from the garden for them and had Eddie drive her over, the first time she had ventured out since Winter left for Europe.

Bob opened the door–Maude came to the head of the stair and said hello but that she must put the baby to bed so Bob and I had the pleasantest talk. He said the only reason he didn't want to go was on account of you and that everything you had said or written had made it ten times harder. I told him you had written you were afraid you had developed a real friendship for him & he said, "Well it's reciprocated. We have worked hard together for two years and gotten awfully fond of each other." Really he was sweet about it. Then he went on to say that President Angell had been so nasty to him about it that when he got through talking with him he would have gone to Chicago if he had to start a peanut stand for a living. He said he practically called him a fool, and a Crook. A fool because he would not be able to make a go of his new job & a crook because of his immoral "letting down" of all the new men he had attracted to the Law School & the Institute and he said these new men would feel he had treated them very badly. Three days later he went back to see him about some Law School matters and told him that one of Mr. Angell's predictions had not come true because every man in the Law School had been perfectly splendid about his going. Mr. Angell sneered "Well of course they wouldn't tell you their real feelings."

My, Bob was sore and can you blame him. I told him we knew he would make good and were just going to watch him put things over in Chicago.

The spring of 1929 was the last time Winter could have left Helen for more than a few days. By July she could not leave New Haven, and he would not leave her. Tom remembers a gray cat that spent most of the time on the bed with Helen, causing Winter to wonder if she loved it more than him, and inspiring him to write a little poem as if by Helen:

> I wish you wouldn't ask me which one I prefer.
> Of course I love you dearly,
> But I love the kitty too, and he has fur.

The Watsons watched over the children at Treetops. A home movie starts with the drive up the hill to Treetops from the main road. The road looked the same twenty-five years later. Visitors are greeted by the Watsons and ushered into the house. The scene quickly shifts to a card table on the lawn in front of their house, where Mr. Watson, in white shirt and tie minus a coat, sits with one of the first telephones, explaining the invention of the telephone to his grandchildren. The last scene is of the children swimming and diving off the raft, dressed in their woolen bathing suits, all looking robust and active.

Helen was a stabilizing influence on Winter, simple and decent, moral and loving, with a well-trained mind. She was not social and did not appear to be interested in style. Winter might have wished her to be more social; had she lived and been in good health, that might have smoothed his way. Her open, honest charm and genuine goodness could well have dispelled some of the rancor Winter engendered and might have changed how colleagues found him. She had simple, down-to-earth tastes, and what little we know of her and her background leads us to believe that Winter's idealism and vision appealed to her. She was, it must not be forgotten, a physician, and his vision for the future of science and the Medical School must have been hers as well. She worshiped him and, in illness, leaned on him. There is never a hint of her caring about making an impression or a splash; in adulthood she appears to have been as modest and natural as she was as a young girl. There was only one Helen. Winter wisely did not look for someone just like her when he remarried.

HELEN'S DEATH

This is where the trail of crumbs becomes a slender sheaf of letters. Winter wrote a weekly letter to the family to keep everyone in touch. The children hated these letters, which were rarely very personal. Worse, his carbon copies to all the children let personal worries become common knowledge and led them to see themselves as satellites of the Medical School. They were supposed to write home every week. These letters often tell as much by what they omit as by what they say. Winter did not like to pour out his soul on paper, and rarely did. He did not look backward, only forward. At the time of Helen's death and afterwards, he was vulnerable, in need of feeling close to his family and letting them into his thoughts. The most open letters are to Tom, a very sweet and tolerant child. Although he was the one Winter found the most difficult to deal with face to face, he was also the one to whom his father could write the most comfortably–and honestly.

Preparations for Christmas 1929 had poignant undertones, as Winter knew it was likely to be Helen's last, and he tried hard to make it a happy one. Afterward, he wrote the children that he thought they would all remember that Christmas as special. To President Angell, who had shown him real friendship and support, he wrote:

> Dear Mr. Angell:
> Your letter of Sunday morning is just another indication of the fine sympathy and support I have always had at your hands. I fear in my more or less overwrought state it has not always been deserved. The damage that has been done to my poor wife's morale is considerable and whether the counter suggestion that has been instituted will be effective to any degree remains problematic. In the late evening and often in the long hours of the night, made longer frequently for Mrs. Winternitz by pain and discouragement, the trial seems unbearable. This must reflect itself in every other activity in which I am associated. The great opportunity the University has so generously given me is a wonderful [illegible] and I

am heart and soul bound up in this work as I think you know.

So if at times I seem petulant, radical, and intolerant please bear with me.

Faithfully,
XII 2 29
Milton C. Winternitz

We do not know what the emotional injury to Helen had been, but the letter testifies to the anguish that Winter suffered. A mid-March letter to the children tells them that a meeting at Johns Hopkins went well, although he "couldn't avoid saying some rather unpleasant things." Winter went on to remark that "self complacency is almost the worst thing that can happen to people and it is always true where one's faults are pointed out, and one becomes quite angry, progress eventuates."

Helen Watson Winternitz died on April 25, 1930, of kidney failure, it has been agreed.[21] No autopsy was done, but she had "follicular tonsillitis" in 1925, and after that she was never well again, a not unusual sequel to streptococcal infection in those days.

Winter wrote the following letter to Tom.

April 29, 1930
Dear Tom,
We got home promptly and safely after leaving you at Avon–a bit tired and cold, so after supper we had a fire in my study and read the evening paper. Miss

Dasey came to talk over student problems, and Bill came in with Charles Buell to join Miss Dasey, the girls and me. But Bill did not come for long. He had dined with Charles and wanted permission to stay at Charles' for the night. Bill looked as usual for the evening–hair disheveled, tie half down, face red where it could be seen, shirt out, knickers down to ankle length, shoe laces gone–but happy as was Charlie. I wasn't at all inclined to let him go, but I guess I am a bit soft now for I did consent after hardly a struggle. Then Miss Dasey left. Mary went to bed and I wrote just a line to Grandma and Grandpa. They have come to be so near to me that they really are my own.

Now Buff and Jane are "putting the flowers to bed'" as Mommie used to say. The flowers are so beautiful and they have come to mean so much to me–to whom they already had meant so much. During these last days they seem to offer a positive something for a negative within me–to take me outside myself so full of shadow, and with their form, color, and grace to hold me to life more promising in joy. The house is very quiet. I guess Elizabeth and Jane have gone to bed too and long, long hours of still darkness are ahead till morning.

As I have sat here these last ten days or so I have thought of you a great deal and wondered at first, as you know, whether or not to bring you home–and then when you did get here it was too late and all my fault. You see I had hoped and hoped–there was cause for my more optimistic outlook–that Mommie would get better again. So many times these last years she has neared the valley of the deep, deep shadow when only I was at her side, and so many times my hope for a favorable turn was realized, that I fear I was too sanguine. It was my mistake–an error in judgment of great moment to you. For I realize already how I have benefited through this experience heart-rending and terrible as it has been and must continue to be for me.

Understanding seems to be dependent on depth of experience, and those deep experiences of my life that have contributed to the molding of what character I have and what insight may be mine have been hard to bear–but, Tom, none was ever like this. Time after time in the years that have just gone by when the chances that mother might not withstand some new phase of her disease, I have felt the almost overpowering burden of sorrow that this parting must eventually mean. Each time it seemed almost that I could not suffer again–each time I grew, I think, to be a better man from the experience–each time it has been more terrible, and a battle thought to be won was really only a skirmish preparing me to bear the last and most devastating fight–the worst because mother this time suffered great pain and what had been an intermittently expressed desire for release now grew until during those last hours of anguish she begged for oblivion. Would that you too had

> been here so that your soul also might have been stirred to the depths and that through this you too could feel more keenly and sense more accurately so many things of life.
>
> Time can not be influenced. It goes on steadily and regularly without change of speed. . . . [I]t is all too short in retrospect: and were it not for this retrospect, perhaps too long in anticipation.
>
> What I have learned–for me more important than for you, for you are more kindly than I am, I have learned to see more good in things and in people, to be more tolerant–more anxious to give pleasure and I have had impressed upon me what I already believed–that we live after death in what we have done–our children–our work. A peculiar transference is going on for me, and I see and feel much more of Mother in you–my boys and girls–nd this is a great comfort for me for it gives me an outlet, a renewed ambition.—I want your frank friendship–as outspoken as though I were your brother and on just that plane of equality–and I am going to rely on you all to help me to attain this so I can do what is at once my duty and my greatest joy–whatever may mean the most for the development of your characters and abilities and happiness.

Winter kept his personal and professional lives quite apart. Indeed, to our loss, as we have noted, he destroyed most of his professional correspondence and personal letters in order to maintain his privacy. Here, however, in Winter's letters to Helen letters during her last illness, we get a glimpse–a hint rather–of the feelings that Winter kept so strictly out of sight.

Chapter 7. Winter, Social Medicine, and Psychiatry

Psychiatry was in the air in the 1920s, thanks to the growing influence of Freud, Jung, and their disciples, not to mention the nurturing ardor of the great New York foundations. Mental health and disease–"mental hygiene," as it was called–were a major focus of Winter's years as dean of the Medical School. The twin themes of psychiatry and social medicine, as played out in the brief history of the Institute of Human Relations, could serve as an inspiration for the current generation of "post-modern" physicians.[1]

Psychiatry at Yale

The Phipps Psychiatric Clinic, founded at the Johns Hopkins Medical School in 1914, was headed by the legendary Swiss psychiatrist Adolf Meyer. William Welch had raised the funds for a clinic dedicated to the psychiatric approach to people and their diseases, which he described as "one of the great movements of all time."

After reading Clifford Beers's autobiography, *A Mind That Found Itself,* Welch wrote, "Psychiatry is an outgrowth of psychology, which in turn has developed from metaphysics. It deals with the behavior and conduct of the individual."

Harvard had started a Department of Psychiatry in 1920 with another recruit from Hopkins, so it was not surprising for Winter, with his enthusiasm for mental hygiene and a medical practice that treated the whole person, to undertake a similar initiative at Yale. On June 25, 1920, he brought together a group at the Graduate Club to consider the "establishment of a Department of Psychiatry," emphasizing that the General Education Board was prepared to give "substantial aid" to such an endeavor.

Winter enjoyed solid support from the incoming university administration. President James Angell was a psychologist who hoped to expand psychology as a department at Yale. As head of the Carnegie Corporation before coming to New Haven, he must have helped establish the priorities that the new medical foundations applied to psychology and related fields. Doubtless the foundations' willingness to fund such endeavors fed his own predilections–and Winter's too.

Winter's enthusiasm for psychiatry might appear to be another of the passions he acquired at Hopkins. Yet deeper and more personal motives played a part as well. Most obvious is Helen's transformation from the energetic, even rebellious woman physician of Baltimore days into the docile mother of the New Haven years, who deferred to her pathologist husband even when it came to administering first aid to their children. An equally compelling motivation must have been the mental illness of their daughter Elizabeth.[2]

EARLY DIFFICULTIES

Jonathan Engel of Seton Hall University, who has reviewed the same Yale files that we have consulted, has detailed the early struggles to establish a Department of Psychiatry.[3] With his customary enthusiasm for collaboration, Winter wanted to make the planned psychiatric unit part of the New Haven Hospital rather than a freestanding "psychopathic" hospital, like the one in Boston.

For reasons that are not at all clear, it was not easy for Winter to attract financial support for his plan, either from the New York foundations or from private donors. Finally, in 1922, the State of Connecticut pledged five years of support, $15,000 per year, to establish a Psychiatric Department. Three years later additional aid came from the Commonwealth Fund, endowed by the same Harkness family that was shortly to finance the houses at Harvard and then the colleges at Yale.[4]

Even so, it was hard to find a psychiatrist who was willing to come to Yale, particularly as President Angell was fearful of enlarging Yale's budget to the "dangerous" degree considered necessary. Dr. Arthur Ruggles, then one of America's foremost psychiatrists, had come from Brown to set up a Psychiatry-Mental Hygiene Department for undergraduates in the university Health Department. Before he could develop a psychiatric liaison service in the New Haven Hospital, however, he returned to Providence at the end of the 1925-1926 year because the meager funds at Yale made his prospects at Brown more enticing.

Other senior professors turned Winternitz down, among them Stanley Cobb, who was to become chief of Psychiatry at Massachusetts General Hospital. As a result, for a long time the Medical School supplemented the teaching activities of several assistant clinical professors with lectures by well-known psychiatrists from New York and Massachusetts.

One suspects that the rather closed nature of Yale University in the 1920s, and its generally anti-Semitic aura, may have dampened the enthusiasm of any young, ambitious psychiatrist. It is equally probable that some qualified candidates were deemed a poor fit for New Haven's genteel collegiality. Of course, it may also be that astute psychiatrists recognized the potential difficulties of working with Dean Winternitz.

EUGEN KAHN

On his trip to Europe in 1929, Winter settled on Eugen Kahn, who came to Yale in 1930 as the first professor of psychiatry.[5] Winter was never very happy with his choice and came to regard Kahn as an "enemy," because he was more interested in mental disease and psychoses than in "mental hygiene" and the workings of the "normal" mind that Winter wanted medical students to study. A psychiatric clinic was established in the new Institute for Human Relations (IHR) and its Psychiatric Department. In 1932, when the Commonwealth Fund grant for psychiatry ran out, psychiatry and mental hygiene were cut off from the IHR. The clinic established for very disturbed psychiatric patients was changed to one caring for less difficult clients in "a much more inclusive study of human behavior."

Still, in his final dean's report of 1935, Winter asserted that students needed far more training in psychiatry: "All should gain enough knowledge of mental disorders and enough interest in human personalities to judge when the patient ought to be referred to the specialist in mental disorders. . . . Science needs to discover the factors upon which mental, emotional and physical health depend in the kind of society in which we live."[6] These observations stemmed from Winter's commitment to the Institute of Human Relations and his enthusiasm for "social medicine" in general.[7] A digression on social medicine and its cousin, "constitutional medicine," may place the IHR in context.

THE RISE OF SOCIAL MEDICINE

For the most part, social medicine developed as a response to nineteenth-century industrialization. It flourished with the growth of what were then called "sanitary reforms," evolving into a mixture of preventive medicine, public health, and personal medicine, as attempts were made to mitigate the effects of industrialization on the poor.

The term *social medicine* has been applied variously to the study of (1) disease in groups, (2) social factors in disease, (3) social sciences in medical practice, and (4) the effect of the environment on humans. It has even been defined as *all* the contributions to medicine which are not science, but which, as William Hobson put it, "provide a connecting link with the wider humanities." George Rosen summarized the point: "Social medicine rests equally upon the social and the medical sciences. Anthropology, social psychology, sociology and economics are as important for this field as the various branches of medicine."[8] In focusing on diseases in groups, social medicine turned away from the classical medical concern for the single patient, and that may have been its downfall.

The physicians responsible for the major advances in scientific medicine—as exemplified by Jenner's smallpox vaccination in 1796, Pasteur's rabies vaccine in 1885, and Koch's antitoxin treatment of diphtheria–relied on the objective findings of microscopy and the emerging field of bacteriology. They considered bacteria the likely cause of most diseases, an argument that has once again come to the fore in the early twenty-first century.

Other physicians, equally based in science, argued that environmental factors played an equally critical role in disease, but the excitement of bacteriology won out. In 1901, Max von Pettenkofer, one of the founders of social medicine, who had campaigned to improve the water supply in Munich, grew so depressed by the rejection of his ideas on the importance of the environment that he shot himself. Rudolf Virchow, the father of "cellular pathology," also held that, whatever the importance of bacteria, it was crowded, unsanitary conditions that had led to typhus epidemics in Silesia.[9]

The triumphs of scientific medicine over the next hundred years obscured the contributions that concern for social and environmental conditions could make to human health. In the early 1900s, as expanding scientific knowledge raised the status of physicians, along with their ability to help patients, Western doctors increasingly turned to scientific dogma to buttress their authority as experts. Some critics accuse doctors of opportunistically embracing science in order to increase their prestige and earnings. But many practicing physicians surely stood by their duty to treat the individual patient rather than society.

The tension between the particular and the universal is as old as Aesculapius and Hippocrates, but it has been heightened by the conversion of medical practice from a profession to a business. In the late 1700s, for example, Jeremy Bentham developed plans for poorhouses in which a salaried medical "curator" would care for the inhabitants. Poorhouse doctors would not charge for their services and drugs would be dispensed by the government, for Bentham wanted physicians to be paid very little, in the hope that they would feel amply rewarded by the chance to add to their experience, skill, and reputation. Bentham also wanted research–by which he meant statistical records of health and disease—to be carried on in the poorhouses. This was the way things worked in America in the first half of the twentieth century, when doctors cared for the poor in hospitals and clinics at no charge, in the expectation that the poor would offer their bodies for study and research.

Bentham and other pioneers of social medicine began by caring for the individual, but ended up relying on group outcomes. Yet they could not convince most physicians to go along with them–a familiar dilemma for the modern adherent of "outcomes." In turning their attention from the sick patients whom they knew to a sick society about which they could only theorize, they abandoned their own expertise, apparently without realizing what they were losing. To this day practicing physicians still think of the individual patients they can see, listen to, and touch, far removed from public health's focus on groups. Modern algorithms, now called "pathways," for modular patients look for outcomes in groups, not individuals. Even today, the goal of doing the greatest good for the greatest number–long the battle cry of utilitarians like Bentham–makes most practicing physicians uneasy, as they try to fix their gaze on the patient before them.

THE SPREAD OF SOCIAL MEDICINE

Germany may have been the modern birthplace of social medicine, but Great Britain was its twentieth-century home, particularly after the advent of the National Health Service in the late 1940s. Sir Farquar Buzzard, Regius Professor of Medicine at Oxford, advocated an "Institute of Social Medicine," and in 1942 his distinguished colleague, John Ryle, the Regius Professor of Physic, left his medical post in Cambridge to head the first such institute at Oxford.[10]

A quondam gastroenterologist, Ryle wrote that he had grown weary of studying and teaching clinical medicine "on the whole more and more mechanically."[11] Much like Winternitz, he pointed out that in the teaching wards of the medical schools the "less lethal diseases and the beginnings of disease" were barely discernible. Medicine had become too much a technical exercise. As he warmed to social pathology rather than individual pathology, Ryle warned that physicians were becoming less attuned "to the deeper personal needs of the individual" and paying little attention to the "broader social needs of the group or the community." To the modern ear, he sounds much like Winternitz.

In "John Ryle: Doctor of Revolution?" Dorothy Porter describes how, after abandoning his position in internal medicine, Ryle hoped to create the new discipline of social medicine to balance the dominant biomedical model.[12] For Ryle, as for Winternitz, the duty of the physician was to study the entire biology of disease, from the environment to bacteria. A "naturalist of disease," the physician would not simply view a duodenal ulcer as a hole in the duodenum, but would describe it in terms of its symptoms, associations, and origins. Agreeing with Alfred Grotjahn that "many diseases of social importance are chronic in character," Ryle argued that focusing on the laboratory had eliminated the patient from the clinical view, while doing little to help those with chronic illnesses worsened by social and economic factors. In creating what he called "social pathology," Ryle tried to wrest authority from the biochemists and assign it to the social scientists, who would wield statistics and epidemiology the way pathologists used the microscope.

It was–and is–difficult to demarcate the field of social medicine or to highlight its victories against the stupendous triumphs of scientific medicine.[13] This was—and is—the Achilles heel of social medicine. Ryle, who had earlier designed a tube to withdraw gastric juice for study from the stomach, proudly summed up his new credo: "We no longer believe that medical truths are only or chiefly to be discovered under the microscope . . . by means of the tube and the animal experiment or by clinical examination and increasingly elaborate pathological studies at the bedside. Psychological and sociological studies have as important a part to play." William Welch would have agreed with these conclusions.

WELCH AND SOCIAL MEDICINE

The split between the individual and society was quite apparent in Welch's life. He had recreated academic medicine along "Teutonic lines" and encouraged the full-time academic medical system in the United States. At the same time, he was a great supporter of psychiatry and social medicine, fighting for sewers in Baltimore with as much fervor as for a department of public health or a medical library. The time he had spent with Pettenkofer in Germany had left its mark. Writing to Daniel Coit Gilman in 1884, Welch told how impressed he was with the "Hygienic Institute" in Munich. Much later, in his enthusiasm for locating a similar institute in Baltimore, Welch overcame Abraham Flexner's objections by agreeing to head it himself. "It is a well-known fact that there are no social, no industrial, no economic problems which are not related to the problems of health," he wrote in 1915.

Viewing everything from sewers to housing as sanitary problems, Welch gave talks on how improved hygiene was the main reason why typhoid fever had so waned in Europe, particularly in Germany, just as Virchow had claimed. In Baltimore he was instrumental in ensuring that milk was delivered in clean bottles rather than being dipped from a pail into a pitcher. He advocated well-ventilated houses and workshops, shorter working hours, and a living wage to help in the control of tuberculosis. That Welch excelled as a "booster," publicist, and administrator rather than as an original thinker does not make his achievements any less impressive.

THE DECLINE OF SOCIAL MEDICINE

After the discovery of insulin in 1921, it grew ever easier for physicians to laud the accomplishments of scientific medicine, while victories in the humanitarian and intuitive aspects of medical practice proved more difficult to find. The closure of the institute that Ryle headed at Oxford and the failure of Winternitz's Institute of Human Relations at Yale illustrate how the triumphs of modern scientific medicine seemed to make social medicine superfluous. In retrospect (though neither mentions the other, curiously enough), Ryle sounded much like Winternitz in his "emphasis on man and endeavors to study him in his relation to his environment."

Another modern proponent of social medicine, the psychiatrist Iago Galston, vainly predicted that social medicine would ultimately prove the "fulfillment of the modern biological science."[14] In fact, the scientific advances of the early twentieth century far outpaced the growth of social and psychosomatic medicine. Even the classical education for physicians that Flexner and Winternitz had taken for granted was discarded as a relic of the fuzzy-headed romanticism of earlier times.

In the 1950s a scientist like Pittsburgh's Arthur Mirsky, for example, might show how emotions and stress in diabetics increased their insulin requirements, but such observations had very little influence. The mainstream remained entranced by the torrent of discoveries like vitamins, antibiotics, and steroids, and later by the even more spectacular advances of molecular biology. Yet tuberculosis had already partly yielded to sanitary improvements before the antibiotics that were to prove its quietus. The victory of Streptomycin highlighted the role of the scientist as knight, a far more dramatic hero than myrmidons digging sanitary trenches. Antibiotics seemed more important than better housing or improvement in working conditions.

Peptic ulcer, now deemed the result of bacterial forays into the stomach, offers a more recent example. Despite the victory of antibiotics over ulcers, chronic complaints like irritable bowel are still hard to treat, and the aged are still put away in retirement centers and nursing homes. Clinicians, who might have seen themselves as mediators between the complaints of the patient and the images so readily available, have learned to think of themselves as simple conduits of these other powers, holding no power in their own right.

Today's practitioners of alternative medicine, who talk of "wellness" rather than sickness, derive much of their impetus, even if they fail to recognize it, from the social medicine movement of the 1920s and 1930s. For example, in *The Meaning of Social Medicine,* Galston suggested making health rather than disease the focus of medical education. He recalled that those responsible for the Hippocratic corpus had been concerned with health and preventive medicine as much as with disease. And so he urged medical schools to emphasize "life and its fulfillment" rather than "death and disease." By replacing anatomy in the first year of studies with embryology, he hoped to get students to consider how people lived rather than how they died. Like so many others before and since, Galdston also proposed that medical students learn more about the history of medicine and about sociology, anthropology, and psychology–the same ideas that Winter and others had tried to fold into medicine. For Galston, as for Cabot, Ryle, and Winternitz , a peptic ulcer demanded that the doctor "determine and correct or amend, what ails the individual; what, in other words, impedes the individual in the fulfillment of an adventure in living." These ideas still resonate, even at a time when physicians busy themselves with eradicating bacteria in the stomach.

The abandonment of the institutes at Oxford and Yale, among other disappointments, has led many to regard social medicine as just another utopian concept. For Galston, psychiatry still reigned as "the outstanding exception" to scientific medicine, even if, as a psychiatrist, he feared that the field could be seduced by "so-called specific modalities," a premonition of the current fascination with neurobiology. "At its best, which is rare enough, psychiatry offers the best operating example of social medicine," he wrote.

The trouble, then as now, was that social medicine seemed to be taking medical practitioners away from their proper concerns with the sick by extending medicine into the community. Moreover, those good ideas were twisted into evil ends in Nazi Germany, where the re-emphasis on the medical model of politics led to the destruction of Jews as a disease. Elsewhere, those ideas could have been the force for good that Welch had promised and that Winter so much wanted. As Ryle put it, "A social science differs from a natural science in that it has other main motives besides the advancement of knowledge . . . to balance the emotional with the rational components of a developing social conscience."

Flexner's objections to the Institute of Human Relations may well have arisen from his firm foundation in "etiologic" medicine and all the diseases that were being prevented by modern medical science. An undated note in Winter's files reads: "The educational program at Yale University School of Medicine is based on the belief that medicine is a social science and that its ultimate purpose in common with other social sciences, is the promotion of human welfare. The particular avenue by which medicine approaches the general objective is that of physical health. (MCW)"

CONSTITUTIONAL MEDICINE

Almost side by side with social medicine, and somewhat before the rise of psychosomatic medicine, "constitutional medicine" had a big run in the first half of the twentieth century. Another route to holistic medicine, it focused on individuals, and particularly on their body types. This approach took into account not only the patients' organs but their "anthropometry," endocrine function, general behavior, and "diathesis," a predisposition to a particular frailty or strength. Constitutional medicine degenerated into an attempt to correlate the three body types– ectomorph, mesomorph, and endomorph–with a proclivity to different diseases as well as with certain personality types. The relationship between constitutional medicine and the notions of the German psychosomatic psychoanalyst Franz Alexander are apparent in his seven postulated psychosomatic diseases and the personalities that supposedly fueled them.

Sara H. Tracy views the convergence of social medicine, constitutional medicine, and psychosomatic medicine as a way of bringing the "sick man" back into medicine–looking at the patient as a whole rather than as a collection of organs or cells.[15] These disciplines reminded clinicians that the patient may be as important as his or her disease, and that a specific idiosyncratic response to bacteria may well account for whether the patient with meningococcus will develop meningitis. Tracy finds American constitutional medicine different from the other holistic approaches in its emphasis on heredity, as well as on its elaborate body-typing schemes derived from what George Draper called the "four panels of personality": anatomy, immunity, physiology, and psychology.

These issues grew important because foundations like the Rockefeller Institute were trying to turn psychiatry, especially psychoanalytic psychiatry, into a medical discipline, particularly at Yale. As the twentieth century progressed, constitutional medicine became associated with the eugenics movement and, tainted by the horrors of the Nazi period, was wrongly discredited and disregarded.

THE INSTITUTE OF HUMAN RELATIONS

At Yale, social medicine found its fulfillment in what was originally called the Institute of Human Behavior, a diverse collection of physicians and social scientists who hoped–or who were expected–to develop a general theory of human behavior.[16] The team of Angell, Hutchins, and Winternitz was eager to change the conservative climate of the university.[17] Frustrated by the long-delayed development of a psychiatry department, Winter began, characteristically, to let his imagination roam. He first mentioned an "Institute of Psychobiology" in 1925 as an extension of the Department of Psychiatry and

Mental Hygiene.[18] Its building was to be situated close by the New Haven Hospital, with laboratories for investigation, classrooms for graduate teaching, and outpatient clinics for therapy, as well as space for psychology, anthropology, and other social sciences.

The forerunner of the Institute of Human Relations was a creature of the times as well as of the players at Yale. In 1923, Robert Yerkes had proposed to President Angell that Yale sponsor an "academic center for psychobiological research" as part of the development of a larger "graduate" school of psychobiology. Angell responded that Flexner might well be interested in establishing such a unit at Yale, news that might have pricked Winter's imagination. Credit for conceiving the Institute for Human Behavior, for which they began to plan in 1925, belongs to all three men. The world of medicine in universities was about to change, and even if they had not worked together, others might well have tried to give body to the vision of social medicine. Nevertheless, Winter was the driving force. Determined to acquaint physicians with "modern psychiatry" and to train psychiatrists for clinical work, he sought to integrate psychiatry into the IHR.

President Angell was committed to stimulating research in the university and, like Winter, to interdisciplinary activities. In 1924, hoping to strengthen Yale's Department of Psychology (which students had recently voted the worst in the university), he established an Institute of Psychology and began to collaborate on the so-called Institute for Human Behavior. Any support for Medical School activism would have enraged his more conservative college faculty.

As newly appointed dean of the Law School, Hutchins wanted to put legal education in a broader academic and social context, and to improve the intellectual quality of students and programs at the Law School. He was the ideal man for the job: Angell and Winter were outsiders, whereas he had been appointed secretary of the university at age twenty-three, shortly after graduating from Yale in 1921. Hutchins enjoyed the advantages of an insider, but his appointment of Donald Slesinger, a political scientist, economist, and psychologist, to the Law School faculty irritated his more conservative faculty. He wrote somewhat petulantly to Angell that "the general atmosphere is (or seems) inhospitable to the intellectual development we are working for, and I feel the absence of a tradition that would carry on in the absence of any of you."

Happy to find allies in the Medical School and in the new president of the university, Hutchins persuaded Winternitz to adopt an even broader view of medicine as a social science–humans in their social as well as psychological context.

PLANS FOR THE IHR

With growing enthusiasm for studying behavior, Winter began planning new buildings without thinking it all through or considering his colleagues. A number of sketches and diagrams can be found in his papers; one for the "Human Welfare Group" shows the IHR as a star in the center, with the Law School and the Divinity School sketched in as "equal" to the Medical School. The diagram suggests Winter's usual lack of attention to practical arrangements. His grand design for the institute combined psychology, "biopsychology," and anthropology, along with psychoanalysis, psychiatry, and mental hygiene, in an effort integrate medicine and psychiatry into the university as a whole. To the consternation of his fellow deans, he even conceived the idea of bringing the Divinity School and the Law School down to the Medical School. Such proximity, he was sure, would encourage integrating the psychic well-being of patients into medical practice and foster interdisciplinary research.

Everything fell apart when Hutchins, frustrated with President Angell, left Yale after two years to become president of the University of Chicago in 1929. His successor, Dean Charles Clark, was more than a little annoyed at the proposal to move his school away from the main campus; for the rest of his life, his son told us, he remained suspicious of the deans of the Medical School. Although in December 1928 the Law School faculty voted that their new building be erected near the IHR, the Yale Corporation vetoed such a move, diplomatically expressing a desire that the Law School not be "entangled architecturally with any other unit."

When the Divinity School faculty voted not to have anything to do with the enterprise, Winter's hope of bringing the three schools together was shattered.[19] However, Dean Luther A. Weigle of the Divinity School assured him on January 9, 1929, that there would still be a close association in the working out of "educational policies." While Dean Edgar Furniss of the Graduate School praised the fusion of Divinity, Law, and Medicine under the control of the Graduate School, he remained skeptical that the IHR had ever acquired any educational function, calling it a rather a "congerie of unrelated research projects." In that regard, he quoted Flexner as telling Winter that the IHR was just another term for Yale University.

FOUNDATION SUPPORT AND STIMULUS

Despite Hutchins's defection, planning for the IHR proceeded rapidly. In 1927 the Yale Corporation approved plans for the Institute of Human Behavior, which a year later was redefined-or at least renamed–the Institute of Human Relations. In 1929 the Rockefeller Foundation, under the leadership of Alan Gregg, who was eager to integrate psychiatry into the medical schools, concluded that Yale had gone further than Rochester and Chicago in connecting research in psychology and law with work in the Medical and Graduate Schools. Accordingly, the foundation pledged $50,000 a year for ten years to fund staff salaries at the IHR.

In the end, the foundation and the General Education Board together contributed $4 million over a ten-year period to build and develop the Institute of Human Relations. The original building still stands adjacent to the Sterling Hall of Medicine, itself remodeled into the more classically impressive portal to the Medical School. The IHR was meant to give medical students a background in sociology and psychology so they could better understand the patients they would see in their third year. Winter wanted them to learn about crime, divorce, and unemployment, in order to treat patients as physical, mental, and social units.

Angell appointed twelve men in the university to the provisional institute staff. The building was completed in 1930 and in May 1931 the Institute of Human Relations was officially dedicated, with much triumphant publicity. As other buildings began to take shape, Winter's concept of the institute grew ever grander; he continued to emphasize the fusing of activities of the Medical School with those of the university. More self-assuredly than ever, he wrote in his dean's report of 1930, "The idea of the institute has so appealed to other groups of the University that they too have come to look upon it as a means of applying their intellectual resources more directly to the practical problems of human well-being." He came up with the idea of a Clinical Sociology Section to be headed by a professor of clinical sociology, who would offer courses in sociology at the Medical School, at least during the preclinical years. The IHR was to be Winter's university, where a real synthesis of knowledge could take place.

MEDIA HYPE

In bringing scholars together, Hutchins and Winternitz regarded interdisciplinary collaboration as their unique contribution. The expectation that locating faculty offices in close "propinquity" to laboratories would somehow bring about professional collaboration was characteristic of Winter's faith in social get-togethers. Over and over again, his reports emphasize the advantages of dances and dinners and sports. Many others might have been talking and even working in the same way, but Winternitz's 1929 report conveys a characteristic buoyancy that smacked of solipsism.

> We take pardonable pride in thinking that under the conditions which I have outlined no University will be able to offer similar opportunities for research and for practical work with students. Such cooperation will enable the University to undertake a third purpose, that of the correlation of knowledge for the advantage of all study groups—a purpose hardly considered of major importance among educational institutions or on a plane with teaching and the pur-

> suit of truth for truth's sake, and yet it is one that may be of untold significance for the well-being of the University itself as well as for the world it serves.

Winter's enthusiasm was matched by that of his colleagues. In a letter to the alumni, Angell wrote:

> We believe that in all this we are launching a great movement which is destined not only to achieve distinguished success within the walls of Yale, but also one which is reasonably certain to exercise an enduring influence upon the procedure of all institutions of higher learning and upon the thinking of men the world around who are concerned with the knowledge and control of human nature.

Such hubris is familiar to anyone who has passed several decades in academic life. Claims of revolutionary changes in teaching come along every decade or so, making the dreams of those in authority seem like old delusions returning through a revolving door. But, after all, it takes arrogance to make a revolution! Just as there are said to be only seven basic plots in fiction, so there are only a few ways to go about teaching. "Mark Hopkins on one end of a log and a student on the other" was closer to Winter's goal than the structured, closely organized, over-lectured Yale Medical School of the early 2000s, with so little of the leisure that President Hadley had praised as fostering contemplation.

The Institute of Human Relations began as a serious academic enterprise, but Winter had always loved publicity, and the IHR got it. Huge fundraising dinners were held at Yale Clubs around the country, where celebrities like Harry Emerson Fosdick and William Welch spoke. One big party was planned at the University Club in New York City in January 1929, but many people turned down the invitation, apparently out of distaste for the hype that preceded it. Arthur Viseltear writes that of the seventy-eight people invited, fifty-seven declined and only twenty-one came. Dean Edgar Furniss of the Graduate School wrote of his own misgivings, "We have already done considerable damage to the Institute through premature and ill-advised publicity about it." On January 31, 1931, professor of psychology Roswell Angier warned that "the Human Welfare Group presents itself as essentially a hospital and medical enterprise. . . . I am convinced that this publicity . . . should stop until real accomplishments can be emphasized."

The publicity campaign yielded some unexpected results. More "crackpots" than university faculty scientists offered help, including several musicians and Indian mystics. One man submitted five pages of ideas to be studied at the institute, while another inquired, "As a saloon keeper I know plenty about drinking habits–can I be of use to you in any way?"

How far the IHR had to cast its net is evident from a paper by Prof. Elliott Dunlap Smith published in the January 1931 issue of the *Yale Scientific Magazine*.[20]

He told how Sheffield Scientific School had begun to work with the IHR through a new "industrial unit" intended to apply scientific attitudes and methods to "the human problems of industry"—in this case, the weaving industry. They proposed to look at the "stretch-out," to save labor costs by increasing the number of industrial spinning frames and looms tended by an individual worker. This had led to layoffs, labor unrest, and strikes. To understand these "unfortunate" social consequences, Smith proposed to form a "total science" committee consisting of a sociologist, a psychologist, a psychiatrist, a lawyer, a statistician, and an industrial economist, with an industrial engineer as chairman. Bravely, he proclaimed the research to be an example of the "integrated study of human problems," adding, "As with most units of the Institute, it is undeveloped, but aware of its immaturity and anxious to develop in a way that will enable it to measure up to its possibilities."

On October 9, 1929, Winter gave one of his "boiler-plate" criticisms of specialists and their arcane interest in topics such as the big toe. He noted the importance of the family doctor to the average patient. "Your interest is not primarily in your physical well-being but in your happiness and usefulness. How can medicine go on specializing and obtaining greater knowledge of all parts of you and at the same time bring those parts together and correlate them to your happiness, to your well-being as an individual?"

Winter emphasized that outpatients in a psychiatric hospital must be understood in relation to their "environment, family, social and financial condition. . . . Here we have to add that the individual is a social mechanism. That is, we cannot understand man unless we understand his relationship with men. Conversely, we cannot understand man's relationship with men unless we understand the individual man. Therefore the problem is not a problem for the medical school nor for the law school, it is a problem involving both schools." He concluded that "all investigations travel in a circle and no problem can be considered finished unless it goes the whole gamut of the circle."

DIFFICULTIES ARISE

Winter must have been having second thoughts about all the hoopla, given the criticisms that were floating around. At a meeting of the Yale Alumni Association in New Haven, he was at pains to emphasize that "this is not a new enterprise at all . . . quite the contrary, [it is one] which will bring about a correlation of existing knowledge, the integration of activities [already] going on." Correlation was always a favorite topic with Winter, but now he began to suggest that it was all the institute was going to do. This was borne out by another talk in November 1929, at which he made broad claims that "the HSG approaches in scope the aims of the university and of life itself." His interest in the Medical School per se was flagging as his hope to find an academic career as president of a university was growing. If that was not to be, he could turn the HSG into a university.

On June 5, 1930, Angell warned Winter of the danger of "jurisdictional" disputes. "It appears to me in the interest of all concerned that you do not figure as exercising an exclusive jurisdiction over parts of the building set aside for psychology and the social sciences." About the same time Angell wrote to Henry Farnam about the fears of some of the other users of the IHR building that "Dr. W has adopted a rather dictatorial attitude and certainly an attitude of rather exclusive proprietorship in the building." Angell tried to curb Winter's enthusiasm by warning him that he was provoking "a too violent negative reaction in important quarters" in the university.

And so the IHR rolled on, with little focus and no one clearly in charge. Even the advisory board complained that it was nothing more than a grandiose plan, which Winter justified by his aim "to alter the attitude of the skeptics without embarrassing and/or unduly hurrying our educational program." Critics wanted firm plans for how the IHR was to work; instead, all they got was rhetoric. Many began to feel that the sole purpose of having their names on the letterhead was, in Winter's words, "to create a desirable public confidence in our plans."

DISAFFECTION AND DOWNFALL

Dissatisfaction dogged the IHR from the start, as Priscilla Ellis has remarked. By its dedication in May 1931, Winter's visionary enterprise had already begun to fall apart. Despite the vaunted "propinquity" between disciplines, individual researchers raised their own funds and prudently continued to work toward their own goals in their own interests. Few found any reason to collaborate with others: careers in colleges and universities have always been advanced by specialization, in 1930 as in the 2000s.

Mark May took over when the institute began to flounder, and by 1933 even he was worried. On June 21 he wrote to Angell:

> The IHR was established to stimulate and support research along well defined lines in the social and biological sciences. Among its major objectives are the correlation of investigative activities and the integration of data bearing upon selected aspects of human behavior. . . . No one can prescribe the methods by which scientific activities and activities in related fields are to be coordinated. [The institute] has therefore no set of procedures and no permanent staff. . . . Its specific fields of interest may change from year to year.

The exchanges between Flexner and Winter that ended their amity for a while ran along the same line. "A handsome building has been erected, considerable funds raised, but what will the building contain?" Flexner demanded, adding that "the name of the building and its contents do not correspond." Like many others, Flexner believed that specific departments come about to support knowledge and advances in certain areas, and that breaking down barriers in the way Winternitz wanted made no sense from a research standpoint. "Knowledge advances in the first instance by artificial simplification! Departments are set up not because life of the physical world is simple, but because no progress can be made by observation or experience unless this field is circumscribed. Once results are obtained, cautious interpretation takes place."

Flexner carped that Winter was "destroying his own handiwork" in putting the IHR at the helm of the Medical School. He went on to praise "the necessarily individualistic character of genuine thinking," asserting that "it would be as easy to write a poem or a symphony by a committee as to promote the study of human problems by physically arranged groups." Confident in the freedom of the individual to do research, upon which "in the last resort progress depends, " Flexner was convinced that too precise arrangements or "articulation" would destroy research, which he defined as "a brief, painstaking effort on the part of an individual himself, not through someone hired through him."

It is evident from the extant correspondence between Flexner and the dean that Winter's clinging to the IHR destroyed him, enraged his faculty, and severely strained his friendship with Flexner. As noted above, although Winter is listed twice in the index of the Flexners' biography of Welch, they refer to him only once among the "brilliant men" who had worked in Welch's laboratory. Neither Ryle, who came somewhat later, nor Richard Cabot, an earlier enthusiast for social medicine, is mentioned at all. Social medicine did not loom high on either of the Flexners' agendas, as Abraham Flexner's disdain for the IHR attests.

Yale's standing in the sciences had fallen alarmingly. In November 1933 the student newspaper the *Harkness Hoot* deplored that "Yale had no standing" among serious students of science, pointing out that nationally recognized research scholars in physics numbered seventy-six at Princeton and sixty-three at Harvard, but only twelve at Yale.

On September 14, 1936, May wrote to Charles Seymour, the new president of Yale, "We are not one of the taproots of the University. We are a superstructure set on top of three or four of the larger University departments–psychology, psychiatry, social science." May suggested that the IHR become a department, but by then the funds for the institute had been committed to other departments.

REASONS FOR THE FAILURE OF THE IHR

The institute set goals, so great was the confidence of its founders that proximity alone would work magic. The IHR was defined largely by what it was not: "neither a school nor a department within the University." Many of the faculty saw Winter as maneuvering to be head of the institute, a dread that remained pervasive throughout the life of the IHR. His suggestion that the Law and Divinity Schools be relocated to the Medical School area made it clear that the IHR was a predominantly medical creation designed to raise money for the Medical School. Winter's support for the Human Welfare Group, as well as his publicity maneuvers for "his" new institute, provoked criticism that increased faculty resentment. It was their fear of medical domination that underlay the flexibility, informality, and autonomy built into the enterprise.

This fear on the part of the faculty seems to explain why the IHR had no central authority. It was unlikely that an executive committee of representatives from the Graduate School, the Law School, and the Medical School, as well as from the Departments of Social Science and Psychology, Economics, Sociology and Government, could bring direction or purpose to any group. After considerable discussion in which it appeared to be the feeling of most of the members of the Executive Committee that it was not desirable to import or appoint a dictator, it was voted that the plan appended be approved as the present organization of the Institute of Human Relations.

Much later, John Dollard , who had joined the institute faculty with great enthusiasm, commented somewhat skeptically on Winter's idea that simply bringing scholars together would lead them to collaborate.[21] He pointed out that among the measures intended to facilitate collaboration was a dining room serving low-cost but good food, the so-called "Blue Room." As Dollard put it, "there risqué stories circulated faster than any new scientific theories, but nothing of moment came up."

Having been appointed by other schools in the university, the senior IHR staff felt their primary responsibility to those other schools. No one really knew–or apparently cared–what the institute was to do or how it was to function. Priscilla Ellis characterized the principal players as more "dreamers" than administrators, optimistic that erecting a building would make things work out. Only when the IHR ran into difficulties did Winter and Angell face up to the problem of encouraging collaboration. It was Winter's familiar failing: preoccupied with buildings and their architecture, he paid far too little attention to what was to go on inside them. The IHR, in Winter's words, was to "emphasize the unity of human knowledge." That was a far cry from the succinct definition of John Dollard: "The Yale Institute existed to study men's behavior and their relations to one another."

WINTER DREAMING

In 1938 Winter was still optimistic about the IHR, though by then it must have been clear how disparate its projects were. On March 22, in a letter to his longtime friend Winslow, he outlined yet another scheme that had little to do with medicine:

> The housing of a community cannot be planned without recognition of the needs of the community aside from domicile. The first and most fundamental need is the economic sufficiency of any housing community. Questions arise at once concerning the advisability of utilizing the cooperative basis for all of the needs of the housing community and then the problem arises: to what extent any housing community can be economically self-sufficient on the cooperative basis. Such fundaments are implicit in the success of any housing plan.

Winter expanded on many different ideas, among them that preventive medicine provided the "liaison" between public health and "curative" medicine. He praised the old-fashioned family doctor who knew his patients. He wanted to organize faculty interested in problems of housing "into an association with the Institute of Human Relations as its nucleus." Vainly, he cast about for a central role for his Institute: "any resources for the development of such a scheme should be in the hands of the Institute and should be allocated through a committee of the Institute, the members of which have no primary vested interest in any school of the university." He proposed many new functions for the group, including "research concerning fundamental problems associated with housing, training of managers and the education of students in the practical laboratory that housing projects offer."

May emphasized the lack of central authority: research activities dominated the IHR, but no faculty were willing to give up their interest in specific lines of research funded by grants awarded to academic departments. No one saw any reason to share anything–except, maybe, complaints.

Rebecca Lemov highlights another aspect of the institute: the emphasis on social control.[22] In discussing the psychological work done by some of Yale's luminaries, she suggests that the IHR was a somewhat malign part of the behaviorist school that led to thought control, advertising technology and techniques, and even the spying activity of federal agencies. Hers is a brilliant book, but that she does not even mention Winternitz underlines how disparate were the various activities subsumed under the mantle of "human relations."

During the Great Depression, the university was unable to offer any financial support at all to the IHR. As a result, it ended up as a loose collection of separate units housed in a single building, rather than the close-knit, interdisciplinary group that Winter and others had eagerly anticipated. Some blamed the failure on the architecture of the building, pointing out that the "rabbit warren" of offices and laboratories was more conducive to privacy than to the exchange of ideas.

Over and over again, Winter's reports suggest that he saw the IHR as his entrée into the larger educational world that he desired so strongly. The institute and its failure provide an apt paradigm for Winter's brilliance, hubris, and, ultimately, his own failure. After all, the revived Medical School was his creation and the IHR the culmination of his dreams for medicine as a social science–for bringing to bear upon medical practice all the influences that have been so thoroughly excluded from the medical curriculum since that time.

One can only conjecture what medical science and the Yale Medical School would have been like had Winter's dream come to fruition, with the Law School, the Divinity School, and all the social sciences contributing to understanding human beings as more than their molecular makeup. The building that was to house an "Institute of Social Relations" became the Yale Psychiatric Institute, a long-term-care facility for children of the rich, who could afford to pay for the two- or three-year hospitalization that psychoanalysis required. Psychoanalysis dominated the institute for many years, when schizophrenia was seen as a socially determined disease and the "schizophrenogenic mother" was seen as responsible for her child's madness.

Not all the projects that took place under the umbrella of the institute were failures. Seymour Sarason joined the Yale faculty in 1945 with a "full-time" position at the IHR, even though he had not been appointed by the Department of Psychology.[23] Later he described the work that he and others had done there as "very significant" for American psychology, as well as for anthropology and sociology. He noted, approvingly and with amazement, that half or more of the members of the department had been psychoanalyzed, which accounted for the drive to integrate psychoanalysis with learning theory.

Winter would have been delighted by Sarason's summary. It was just what he hoped the Institute for Human Relations would be–but it was not enough. Later, as psychoanalysis fell out of favor, the institute was dispossessed and dispersed.[24] Its refurbished building now houses Yale's molecular genetics laboratory, where relationships are defined by twists and turns of molecules, and the psyche is seen as the product of the brain.

Milton Winternitz 1906, Yale University, Harvey Cushing/John Hay Whitney Medical Library

Helen in wedding outfit, blue velvet with ostrich plumes on her hat.

Winter with Dr. Welch and colleagues shortly before leaving the Johns Hopkins for Yale.

Yale University, Harvey Cushing/John Hay Whitney Medical Library

Classes were held in this York Street building until 1923.

Yale University, Harvey Cushing/John Hay Whitney Medical Library

The Bacteriology Lab. Winter couldn't wait to update it.

Yale University, Harvey Cushing/John Hay Whitney Medical Library

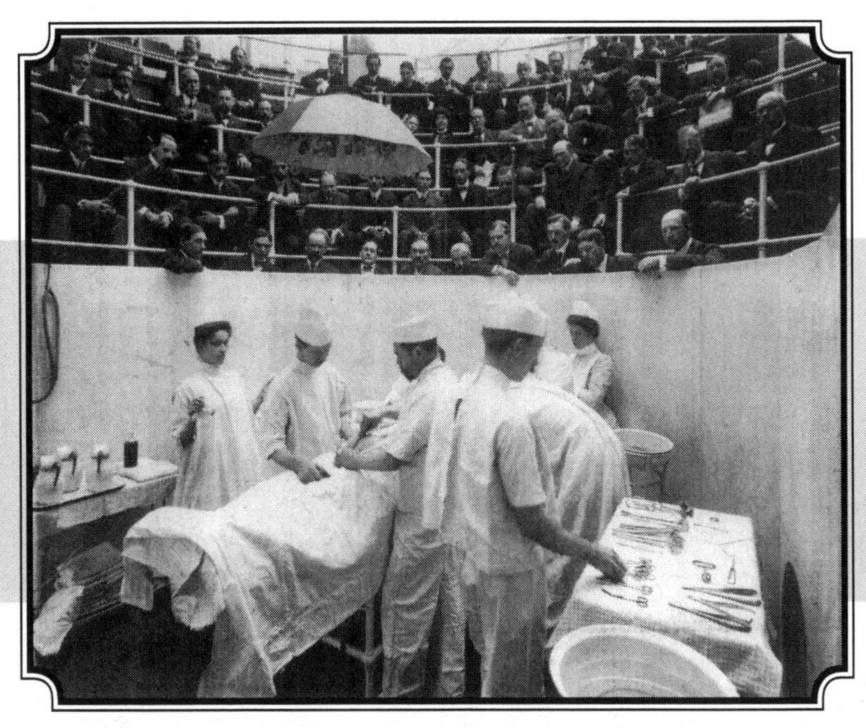

The operating theatre. "Sterile" conditions but no face masks.

Yale University, Harvey Cushing/John Hay Whitney Medical Library

Winter had Dr. Blumer to thank for this one new building, Brady, still home to the Pathology Department.

This modest-looking group of doctors were Winter's Department of Pathology, the hard-working heroes of Winter's first few years at Yale, and during World War I and the influenza epidemic. First row, R .A. Lambert, M.C. Winternitz and George H . Smith, who later became Professor of Bacteriology and Immunology and founder of the Yale Journal of Bacteriology and Medicine. Second row, Isabel Wason, F.P. McNemara, E.S. Robinson, Helen M. Scoville, E.O. Boggs and T.S. Moïse.

Samuel Harvey, Professor of Surgery

Yale University, Harvey Cushing/John Hay Whitney Medical Library

C.E.A. Winslow, Professor of Public Health, a like-minded colleague and supporter of Winternitz.

Yale University, Harvey Cushing/John Hay Whitney Medical Library

Annie W. Goodrich, first Dean of the Nursing School

Yale University, Harvey Cushing/John Hay Medical Library

CARTOON INDICATING THE SITUATION OF THE SCHOOL IN 1920

Rockefeller S.O.S. Winter commissioned Armin Hemberger to draw this cartoon illustrating the medical school's need for funds.

Yale University, Harvey Cushing/John Hay Whitney Medical Library

The Class of 1922. Front row, Doctors Blake, Morse, Winternitz, Harvey and Underhill. Underhill was one of the authors of the <u>Collected Studies on the Pathology of War Gas Poisoning</u>

Yale University, Harvey Cushing/John Hay Whitney Medical Library

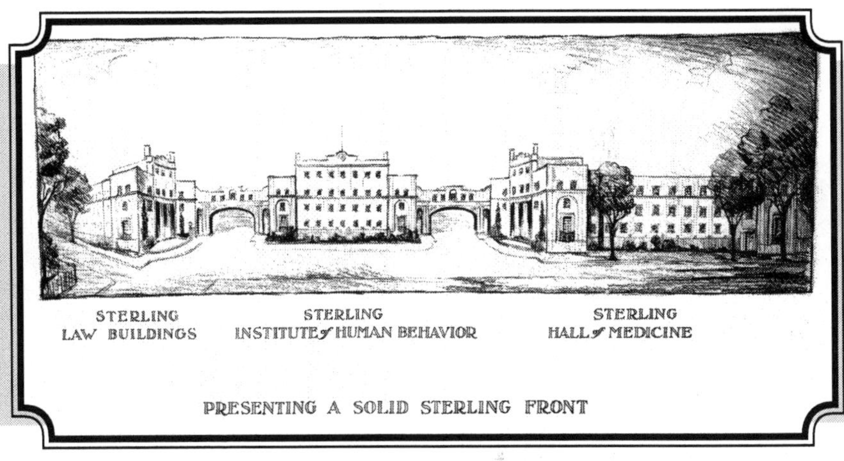

Dreams: Hutchins, the "Boy Dean" of the Law School, and Winternitz, the young Dean of the Medical School, had great plans for a Yale Graduate School campus, as this drawing illustrates.

Yale University, Harvey Cushing/John Hay Whitney Medical Library

Reality: Aerial view of the physical plant Winter put together during his fifteen years as Dean of the Medical School: New Haven Hospital, the New Haven Dispensary, more space for the Medical School, the Nursing School, the Stirling Hall of Medicine, The Institute of Human Relations, and the Clinic of Child Development. Landscaping and tennis courts laid claim to the space for future development.

Yale University, Harvey Cushing/John Hay Whitney Medical Library

Stirling Hall of Medicine with the Institute of Human Relations wing to the left.

Yale University, Harvey Cushing/John Hay Whitney Medical Library

The Dean's elegant office reflecting not only the times but the Dean's taste.

Yale University, Cushing/John Hay Whitney Medical Library

New Haven Hospital as Armin Hemberger saw it and very much the way it looked in 1945.

Yale University, Harvey Cushing/John Hay Whitney Medical Library

The Dean in his lab suit. He did very little hands-on work in the laboratory but the way he taught gross anatomy could get messy. When there was a lull he liked to cruise the corridors of the Medical School as inconspicuously as possible to pick up bits of conversation, check where maintenance was needed, or who was playing the numbers . He enjoyed the relative anonymity of his lab suit and did his best to know everything that was going on in his school .

Yale University, Harvey Cushing/John Hay Whitney Medical Library

Grandpa Watson explaining the telephone to his grandchildren in front of "Balsam," otherwise known as "Grandma's house" at Treetops. Clockwise starting with Grandpa Watson, the children are Tom, Jane (sitting on the ground,) Elizabeth, Bill, and Mary.

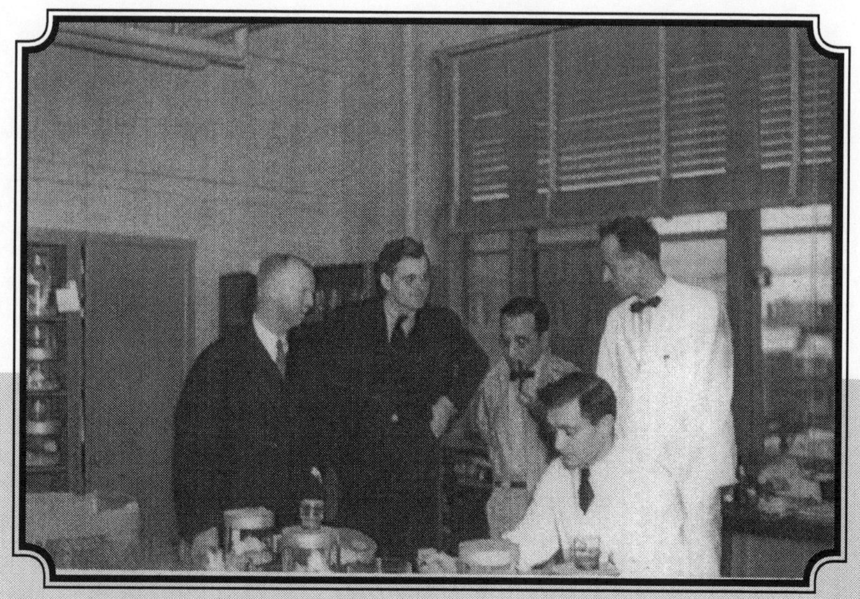

Bayne-Jones, Richard Childs, Winter, Waters, and Joe de Sopo (seated.) De Sopo is the only person who did not feature in the back story of this picture of a site visit to Levin Waters' laboratory while he was still a medical student (c. 1937). It illustrates Winter's knack for steering careers in support of his own. Bayne-Jones followed Winter to Yale after Johns Hopkins and became Dean. Soon after, he was tapped to be the first director of the Jane Coffin Childs Fund for Medical Research, and appointed Winter to his Board of Scientific Advisors. Winter suggested that Waters apply to the JCCF for a study grant and Richard Childs, a member of the Board of Managers, came with B-J and Winter to see how Waters' experiment was progressing. Thirty five years later Dick Childs was Chairman of the Board of the JCCF and Waters his Director
Yale University, Harvey Cushing/John Hay Whitney Medical Library.

The Three Deans, Dr. Stanhope Bayne-Jones, Dr. M.C. Winternitz, and Dr. George Blumer.

Yale University, Harvey Cushing/John Hay Whitney Medical Library

John Fulton, Professor of Physiology, collector of rare medical books, and loyal friend to Winter.

Yale University, Harvey Cushing/John Hay Whitney Medical Library

Dear

This is the result of Encouragement

The Thursday morn. mail is welcome astounding and delightful— So I'll write at once hoping this letter will go this P.M. when I take Marie Moreno & Ella to the movies. and then it may arrive in New Haven Friday. Please include me in the $ for Frank and give him my very sincere thanks for 25 years of superlative friendship loyalty and Service. The younger men on the Staff will never be able to repay Frank.

As for the green article by Greene – obviously you are coming definitely under his Messmer like influence if you can understand that Heteroplastic Brain by Greene.

Please –

(1) Send checks enclosed

(2) What outstanding vouchers are there from N. R. C.

(3). Acknowledge Chalkley's letter & put date on yellow pad

Winter's handwriting and a unique drawing, the first page of a letter to Miss Barnes.

4 Ask Mrs Holbrook or Miss Mestin to find out facts – Gardner will be back shortly or from George M. or Ham Meader & answer Cork letter.

You see I am lazy as ever – now lunch and its too hot even here to eat. I'll read your delightful letter again and then write more meantime many thanks & my best to the young ones in the Sun Shine of your office –

Emerston to be

Reverse side of letter.

Chapter 8. Winter and the Quota System: Discrimination at Yale

Daniel Oren's book *Joining the Club,* which discusses anti-Semitism at Yale from the early 1900s through the 1950s, emphasizes Winternitz's reputation as an anti-Semitic Jew.[1] Given the situation in the 1920s, however, most of Yale's Jewish students regarded Winter as no more anti-Semitic than they were. It was simply the way Jews had to survive amid the largely Anglo-Saxon and Protestant New Haven population at Yale. The Jewish students merely thought the dean fortunate, just as they were, to be at the Medical School. They understood his tolerance of social anti-Semitism; "going along" was, after all, one of the attitudes a Jew had to adopt in American academia of that period.

Winter did not rise above the prejudices of his time and avoided making a public show of his Jewishness.[2] Nevertheless, Dr. Raymond Gagliardi recounts a telling story of Winternitz in the men's toilet in the Sterling Hall rotunda. Unaware that Winter occupied one of the stalls, two students entered and he overheard them talking. One asked, "Is Winternitz Jewish?" The other responded, "He doesn't *look* Jewish." They heard the toilet flush and he walked out, announcing, "I am a member of the Chosen Race." Winter should be seen as a man and a Jew of an era in this country when polite anti-Semitism was the rule. Nevertheless, he never hated himself. He was too proud, too self-assured and narcissistic for that, even though he might not have chosen Jewish parents if he could have arranged matters otherwise.

AMERICAN JEWS IN THE LATE NINETEENTH AND EARLY TWENTIETH CENTURIES

Generalizations about Jews in the United States, as about many immigrant groups, must necessarily be limited. Different countries of origin, differing customs, and different responses to outside influences–intermarriage especially–make it difficult, if not impossible, to generalize. However, American chauvinism of the early 1900s—as reflected in increasing anti-Jewish prejudice–was fueled by the flight of Eastern European Jews to America, as well as to Western and Central Europe, after 1880. Before then, Jews from Central Europe, already enlisted in western society, were so few in America that they seemed exotic rather than alien. The Flexners in Kentucky, for example, became acculturated and assimilated quickly, indeed eagerly.

But New Haven was much smaller than Boston and Cambridge, where immigrants could congregate in unobtrusive areas. Yale was central to New Haven, and its faculty, like the city's "upper class," were fiercely loyal to their Puritan roots. They were more disconcerted by the mass immigration of Jews, Italians, and other groups than were citizens of larger cities, who could avoid them. The dislike of Jews, which intensified with their increasing numbers, waned in the mid-twentieth century. This may have been due to assimilation or to guilt felt by non-Jews after the Holocaust. Or perhaps it was simply a reaction to the civil rights movement: the idea that every American deserved equal rights extended even to American Jews.

In the late 1800s, there were restrictions on Jews in hotels and country clubs. For instance, Joseph Seligman, a leading American banker, was denied rooms at a hotel in Saratoga Springs in 1877 because he was a Jew. "Restrictive covenants" dictating where Jews could and could not buy houses became widespread, as the Winternitzes discovered when they moved to New Haven. These restrictions, which persisted into the 1960s, were accepted by immigrant Eastern European Jews as their lot. At any rate, the situation was far better than what they had experienced in the Pale of Settlement in Russia and Poland. At least Jews could hope that such prejudices might improve one day, as they surely have.

THE ORDEAL OF CIVILITY

In his 1974 book about the "Jewish struggle with modernity," *The Ordeal of Civility*, John Cuddihy provides a dispassionate account of the "bargain" that Jews like Winternitz had to make.[3] Raised Catholic, Cuddihy confessed that by the time he wrote his book he had left the Catholic faith, but his own experiences gave him sympathy for the dilemma of the American Jews from Eastern Europe.

The Napoleonic victories in the nineteenth century opened the wider society of Europe to Jews in large numbers. Nevertheless, if Jews wanted to join that desirable society, Cuddihy suggests, they had to buy acculturation at a "price." Rich and powerful Jews might maintain a kosher home; but to attend medical school or law school in Germany, for example, baptism was required. Once the Jews of Europe were emancipated, they could vote for members of parliament, but they were still excluded, "with varying degrees of courtesy," from the clubs and gatherings of their Christian fellow countrymen.

It took time for the Jews to learn "to be nice." Civility was a bourgeois rite, as the correspondence of the people around Winter makes clear. The worthies of Yale were experts in courteous circumlocution, employing ten words for the work of three. It was not easy for them to treat Dean Winternitz as a social equal. Cuddihy focuses on civility as face-to-face encounter: "the secularizing Jewish intellectual . . . suffered in his own person the trauma of this culture shock . . . unable to turn back, unable completely to acculturate, caught between 'his own' whom he had left behind and the Gentile 'host culture' where he felt ill at ease and alienated. Intellectual Jews and Jewish intellectuals experienced cultural shame."

According to Michael Polanyi, the scientist-philosopher and Hungarian-Jewish émigré to Britain, ghetto Judaism was "disgracefully backward"; immigrants to Western Europe and to America, both Jews and others, "were overwhelmed by the contact with a superior civilization."[4] Henry Roth's 1940 novel about early Jewish experiences in the United States, *Call It Sleep,* makes this point poignantly. As far as the young Jewish immigrants, whether German- or Yiddish-speaking, were concerned, it was attraction to the western world that led them toward assimilation. "Fiddler on the Roof" shtetl life described a world that never was. The "bargain" they made was the same one that most foreign or even rural immigrants had to make. Still, it was particularly wrenching for the Jews who had lived in a Christian Europe that had despised, expelled, and too often killed them.

Winter must have known that aggressiveness, ambition, arrogance, and contemptuousness of others' opinions were characteristics that Protestant society in the inner circles of Yale considered "Jewish." Winter despised these attributes, however much he shared them. In the eyes of some of his friends, his love of elegance was one way in which he tried to distance himself from "bad" Jewish qualities.

Still, Winter could allow himself to show these qualities only because he had likely forgotten that he was Jewish. Having submerged himself in the majority culture, he felt spiritually free to be as arrogant and single-minded as he wanted. Although he had difficulty in buying a house on Prospect Street because he was a Jew, and although he was never accepted into some of the inner-society clubs, Winter *was* dean of the Medical School and chairman of the Department of Pathology. To the observant Jews of New Haven, he was an apostate. He was largely ignored by the assimilated or assimilating Jews of Yale, while non-Jews had little to do with him outside academic life, blaming his bad manners on his "being Jewish."

Not surprisingly, Winternitz's membership in the Graduate Club was hard won. According to Oren, although he was proposed for membership in 1920, he was blackballed for election until President Hadley pointed out in a letter that he was "Dean of the Yale Medical School, and as Dean should naturally be invited to become a member of the Club, unless there is stronger objection to him than that which is based on the fact that the Hebrew element in the Club may become too large." Hadley may have been responsible for Winter's election to the club, but Winternitz was the only Jew permitted to join for the next thirty years.

A DEFENSE OF WINTER'S BEHAVIOR

Like many young Jews of the late 1800s, Winternitz and the Flexners signaled their determination to leave their culture behind by identifying with the Protestant majority. To become modern, immigrants had to accept Calvinist values as a secular goal; as Talcott Parsons has termed it, they had to become Protestant in habits if not in religion. That the children of rich Jews are Unitarians and their grandchildren Episcopalians was a trenchant observation of the time. Assimilation took more than one generation and sometimes, as the Jews of Germany and Austria were to find out, could be ripped apart even after three generations.

Charles Angoff, a protégé of Winter's fellow Baltimorean, H.L. Mencken, vividly depicts the attraction of the West to the young people of the Eastern European ghetto. In his novels about the experience of Eastern European Jews in Boston at the turn of the twentieth century, the fictional David Polonsky, a student at Harvard, finds himself entranced by that wider Christian world.[5]

> David cautiously walked into Appleton Chapel. As he smelled the mustiness of it, it made him feel good inside. . . . [H]e crossed the street to Memorial Hall. David walked deeper into the hall and was so exhilarated by the atmosphere that he had to sit down. . . .

> More and more, he said to himself, he experienced things that he could not express to others.... He was a Jew by blood and tradition, but he was an American as a result of the most powerful force in the environment of his youth.

Angoff does not deny the polite anti-Semitism of the time. A personnel manager in one of his novels writes of a Ph.D. candidate for a position in the company: "His purely academic qualifications seem satisfactory, but his family background does not seem of the sort we care to add to our business family here." On the other hand, sometimes in Angoff's fiction there is another kind of attraction. A young woman named Chasel, a socialist by conviction, is drawn to the life of old Boston in Louisburg Square, the Back Bay, and other strongholds of the Brahmins. "How much she enjoyed this atmosphere, how large a part of her being this enjoyment formed." Nevertheless, fearful of disapproval, she doesn't want to tell her family or anyone else about it.[6]

It may have been inevitable that the younger generation moved on into the American secular culture. Winter should be seen in his time, not just as an ambitious renegade, but as a young man eager to become fully American, even if it meant that all the old ores–the traditions he grew up with—were poured into the "melting pot" and lost in the process.

Jewish enlightenment, the *Haskalah*, led to a "remodeling of Jewish intellectuals in the image of America," a change facilitated by the alienation from the old traditions. As Susanne Klingenstein has pointed out in *Jews in the American Academy, 1900-1940,* the Jewish responses to "exclusionary practices" or to the wider acquaintance with western ideas culminated in Reform Judaism, secular Hebrew culture, and "ethical culture."[7] The reactions of Jewish students and academics of the time were varied. Some conceived of a mosaic in which all groups kept their own traditions, while others, like Winternitz, aimed at rapid and complete assimilation in which the Jews, like earlier immigrant groups, blended into the general population.

Today, Hillel, the Jewish student organization, sits serenely in its own building, the Slifka Center, opposite Silliman College in the center of the Yale campus. Yale's president is a Jew, as are many others in the university–officers, faculty, and students. The Yale Medical School, which even in 1950 had no Jewish full professors, virtually closes on the Jewish High Holidays. The genteel, insular, overwhelmingly Gentile New Haven of Winter's time seems to be another world.

It is difficult for the young to imagine a time when anti-Semitism belied the Hebrew letters on Yale's official seal. Those letters attest to the anti-Catholic bias of the Puritan fathers, relying as they did on the primacy of the Bible, in contrast to those they saw as their Roman Catholic antagonists. As the Puritans turned to the Hebrew Bible for revelation, a knowledge of Hebrew was essential to read the Old Testament in the original. The

Hebrew *urim v tumim* on the Yale seal may have referred to the religious regalia of the ancient high priests, but it was just as likely to have been a sign of a Bible-centered Christian college.

Klingenstein emphasizes how the Eastern European Jews began to "assail" the universities and gradually to predominate in the northeastern colleges. In 1908, 8.5 percent of male students at seventy-seven institutions were Jewish, although Jews made up only 2 percent of the American population. By 1918, 9.7 percent of American college students were Jewish, but in the northeastern colleges the figure had risen to 20.4 percent. Yale's English faculty, convinced that only proper Anglo-Saxons could appreciate English literature, didn't appoint a Jew to the department until the mid-twentieth century.[8] The process had moved ahead somewhat earlier at Harvard and in New York City, where, at Columbia, several Jews had been appointed to the Department of Anthropology well before World War I.

Winternitz, for all his self-confidence, was apparently no more prepared to take on social anti-Semitism than any other New Haven Jew. Clubs and associations, like the Daughters of the American Revolution and the Sons of the American Revolution, with their almost genetic exclusionary requirements, were unlikely to welcome any Jew, let alone a "shtetl Jew." Gentiles had a certain way of speaking about their Jewish friends, emphasizing "Jewish" in order to convey a message that was understood: *Not one of us*. In truth, many writers and others much admired by posterity had little good to say about "the Jews," despite their claims of amity with Jewish individuals. Mencken, who complained of "Jewish" foibles, still felt free to boast that he had "lots of Jewish friends."

The example of Soma Weiss of the Peter Bent Brigham Hospital, which we discuss below, personifies the problems of Jewish professors who had to choose between getting things done on their own or fighting for "equality" at a time when it was deemed unattainable, as it was. A letter written on May 1, 1930, by President Angell recommended Bill Winternitz, Winter's son, to the Loomis School with the following: "Dr. Winternitz is a Jew. His wife was not. This boy has in his physique the Jewish traits and has, I think, been something of a problem to his father because of his extraordinarily rapid physical growth unaccompanied by the type of active intellectual interests which doubtless was characteristic of the father's boyhood." Even though Angell went on to endorse the boy unreservedly, it is clear that this enlightened and friendly colleague of Winternitz was not untouched by prevailing attitudes.[9]

A PRIZE, NOT A PRICE

From the comfort of the mid-1980s, Daniel Oren found charged words to imply that the main reason Jews gave up their parochial ways of life had to do with the "price" they were willing to pay for entrance into the wider society. He may have ignored the attractiveness of western society at the turn of the century to young Jews abandoning the constraints of the ghetto. The Enlightenment, which had drawn so many Jews in Europe to identify themselves as Hungarian or Austrian or German, exerted a very strong pull. At the same time, the narrow confines of ghetto Judaism, the wretchedness of the shtetls, dismayed and even repulsed them, despite the way that midcentury legends and stories and fading photographs helped romanticize such a life.

It is not entirely fair to suggest that Jews like Winternitz, born in America of relatively secular parents, consciously or deliberately abandoned their faith. More likely, it had little relevance for them, as they chose to embrace the wider, more tolerant, and far more liberal western Christian society that surrounded them. Seymour Sarason, professor of psychology, came to Yale in 1945, ten years after Winter left the dean's office. In 1988, he recalled his own half-hearted Jewish education:

> To say that I regret that my parents did little or nothing deliberately to merge their pasts into the one I was acquiring is an egregious instance of blaming the victim. They had been severed from their pasts, near and long term, religious and otherwise. My mother had come to this country as a young child and she regarded herself (and was regarded by others) as "Americanized." It never would have occurred to her that transmitting a past was important. Family

> ties were important, [but] the past was something to be overcome, not to be passed on. She wanted "the best" for her children, and that best was in all respects in the American present and future.[10]

These questions resurfaced in Sarason's own personal and intellectual development, but the picture of his mother suggests how pervasive and persuasive was "Americanization" in the first half of the twentieth century, particularly when immigrant parents were struggling to adjust to a new culture. Winternitz's story was not unlike Sarason's, it simply happened a little earlier.

The exclusionary rites of orthodox Jews may well have evolved over time to preserve the group: strict dietary rules, for example, isolated Jews from the society around them by keeping them from participating in many social occasions. Self-exclusion as much as imposed exclusion contributed to the segregation of Jews and other newly arrived groups, a process that began to break down as a result of education in American public schools. The growth of intermarriage between Jew and Gentile over the past fifty years, together with the bewildered anxiety that has created among Jewish leaders, underlines a more positive attraction than Oren implies. The large number of half-Jews or quarter-Jews in Germany of the 1930s–the *mischlingen,* as the Nazis called them–belies the notion of inherent German anti-Semitism. Oren deserves credit, however, for bravely discussing issues that might have lain repressed for more than another generation. It is important to remember that Winternitz found his purpose and his career before the horror of the Holocaust added an element of guilt to the process of assimilation.

Oren concedes that Winternitz raised Yale's Medical School "from a dismal second-class institution to one of the finest schools in the nation." However, he also describes Winter as being "among the most vocal in denouncing Jewish practices . . . in his drive for achievement." Oren charges that in becoming an ex-Jew, Winternitz "earned for himself and Yale a great deal of resentment from the local Jewish community." At the same time, in all of Yale "no other Jew rose as high or had as much power as Winternitz. Thus to young Jews trying to leave the lower ranks of immigrant life, Milton Winternitz became evidence of the price of admission." Whether they paid the price or grasped the prize can be debated.[11]

OTHER JEWS AT YALE IN WINTER'S TIME

Winternitz's relationships with other Jews at Yale are largely unknown. We have no information about friends of his youth, or even whether he had a bar mitzvah. Oren's book describes the difficulties that Jews faced if they aspired to an academic life at Yale, thanks to a Protestant society in New Haven that was staunchly anti-Semitic. In the early part of the century, Yale had appointed an occasional Jew to the college faculty, but even the most distinguished were excluded from such social clubs as the Graduate, the Lawn, and the Faculty Club. Winter did not entirely ignore his Jewish peers, however, at least when they could help advance his goals.

Col. Abraham Ullman. Col. Abraham Ullman was a leader of the Jewish community in New Haven at that time, as both president of the Strouse-Adler Corset Company and chairman of the Board of Trustees of the New Haven Hospital. A mover and shaker, Ullman boasted of his friendship with William Howard Taft, whom he liked to drive through New Haven in his open car. Taft's files at Yale are said to contain a "thousand letters" from Ullman. The colonel was a man of great influence, though Abraham Flexner tells how President Hadley disparaged him as a "corset maker." After his term as chairman of the board, Ullman's bust was presented to the hospital, but it was later stolen and has never been returned or located. Only a few grainy pictures of him exist.

On Sept. 20, 1922, Winter wrote to Flexner that his family had remained up in New Hampshire, but "I have been adopted by Colonel and Mrs. Ullman and am living with them, which is, of course, extremely pleasant." A few weeks later, he wrote again to Flexner, "My wife and I are going to the ballgame with Colonel and Mrs. Ullman!" The exclamation point was added in pen.

Lafayette Mendel. The relatively fragmented accounts of other Jewish professors at Yale in the 1920s and 1930s, and even later, confirm an otherwise unpleasant situation. That not all of them regarded themselves as

"Jewish" does not excuse Winter's distance from men and women whom other New Haveners regarded as his co-religionists. In locating Winter in his environment, we focus more on the attractions of the wider society than on the distractions of minority status.

Lafayette Mendel (B.A., 1891) recorded that his blood was "German and that Mendelssohn the musician was his relative." After getting his Ph.D. in 1894 in physiological chemistry, under the tutelage of the Yale great, Russell Chittenden, Mendel was the first Jew to receive a regular faculty appointment at Yale. Ultimately, he became chairman of the Department of Physiological Sciences and a Sterling Professor, the only Jew of the original twenty appointed. He was praised by Dean Vernon Lippard of the Yale Medical School, who himself is credited with reviving the school once again in the 1940s, as the only real scientist there in the first quarter of the century. (Lippard forgot Ross Harrison, one of Winter's allies.)

One of the founders of the American Gastroenterological Association, Mendel had an enormous impact on the medical profession in biochemical science and nutrition. Over and over again, Winter's dean's reports singled him out for extensive praise, not only for his research but for the numbers of post-graduate students who came to work with him. Still, Mendel was never accepted socially by the insiders on the faculty. Oren quotes President Hadley, in an understatement typical of the time, acknowledging that Mendel suffered from being a Jew:

"While everybody likes him, the fact of his race has kept him in some measure apart from the life of this place."

Despite the praise so often found in the dean's reports, we find no evidence of any personal closeness between Winternitz and Mendel. Mendel regularly attended the Friday night services at the Reform Congregation of Mishkan Israel, which had been founded by German Jews in the 1840s. In public, however, he never indicated that he was a Jew, telling one friend that "he didn't object to being a Jew, but he never wore it on his coat." Mendel's role on the Committee on Undergraduate Admissions, in charge of enforcing the infamous "limitation of numbers" at Yale, remains a mystery. Perhaps in mitigation, Oren notes that "everyone of consequence" among the Yale administration and science faculty attended Mendel's funeral in Battell Chapel–presumably a testimony by a Yale faculty that ignored the irony of celebrating him in death but not in life.

Edward Sapir. An anthropologist and linguist still quoted today, Edward Sapir was another of the early Jewish professors at Yale. According to his children, Sapir often complained of anti-Jewish feelings at the college.[12] Born in Germany but brought early to America and raised in a traditional Jewish home, Sapir, like many young Jews of his time, had drifted away from Jewish traditions. But the rise of the Nazis prompted him to search for his roots, and he began to study Judaism and the Talmud.

Coming to Yale in 1939, Sapir applied for admission to the Graduate Club, which at that time had only four

Jewish members: Max Mailhouse, Lafayette Mendel, Winternitz, and IsaacWolfe. Embittered by his rejection, Sapir suffered further from a number of other perceived slights, which left him feeling a stranger in the Yale community. Although he later became the first Jewish member of the Faculty Club, he is said never to have set foot in its building.

Sapir and Winter had much the same academic and personal motives, but even though they had summer places not far from each other, they only once exchanged visits. Before moving to Armory Street, the Sapirs also lived on Prospect Street, but never visited the Winternitzes. The social milieu thwarted the natural bonds that Jews in America, like any other minority, tend to feel, at least at first meeting. The Sapirs had a Christmas tree, but no crèche, and the children were raised without any specific Jewish background. They identified closely neither with Yale nor with Jews. Yet Sapir's son, married to a Protestant, took pride in raising his children Jewish and giving them the bar mitzvahs he never had.

Harry Zimmerman. Long a much-beloved professor at Yeshiva University's Albert Einstein School of Medicine, Harry Zimmerman persuaded the scientist to lend his name to the new medical school. Later, he reportedly performed the autopsy on Einstein's body. In an interview shortly before his death, Zimmerman reminisced about Jews and Winter, describing his experience with the anti-Semitism of the Yale Medical School faculty during his many years as Winter's protégé.[13]

Although Zimmerman considered his good friend John Fulton to be the only faculty member "totally without prejudice," Fulton's private letters of that time reveal that he often referred to people as "Jews" (which is not quite the same as noting, say, that someone was a registered Republican). Although Fulton and Winter were allies and friends in academic life, in a cursory review of Fulton's diaries during those years Winter does not appear as a frequent guest at his palatial home on a hill overlooking the city.

Zimmerman called Francis Blake "a very good friend" who conducted clinical pathologic conferences with him; nevertheless they were not "too close." He described Hugh Long, who was to be dean somewhat later, as "not very nice to Jewish students or doctors," even though he was pleasant to Zimmerman. Bayne-Jones, Winter's successor in the dean's office, Zimmerman derided as "a blue-nose anti-Semite." Averill Liebow "was a Jew who . . . was handicapped by that fact."

According to Zimmerman, John Peters, a "swamp Yankee" of very liberal bent, accepted everyone. During a dinner at the Graduate Club in which the talk turned to family origins, Zimmerman recounted, Peters "deftly" steered the conversation away from "any risk" that Zimmerman would have to say, in his words, "I admit I am a Jew"–an act for which Zimmerman remained grateful.

Zimmerman was more than candid in that interview, but his memory may have grown faulty in old age. He described himself as Winter's right-hand man, or, as he put it, "white-haired boy." He ascribed his own admission to the Yale Medical School as the result of Winter's friendship with Colonel Ullman, whose support Winter needed for his own ambitious plans. Although Ullman was highly regarded for helping other Jewish boys from New Haven and Connecticut get into medical school, Zimmerman was a brilliant student and may have been admitted purely on that basis.

According to Zimmerman, Winter was always nice to bright students, regardless of their origins. When an admissions committee was finally formed, supposedly putting an end to Winter's arbitrary decisions, Zimmerman became a member; but he insisted that the committee remained tools of the dean. "He would tell us who he wanted. If they were good, we would take them in spite of the fact that they were Jewish."

Winter was not proud of the fact that he was a Jew, according to Zimmerman. Zimmerman described how Winter would periodically tell him, "I have to go visit my family," enjoining him not to tell anybody where he was going and to keep in touch by telephone. Even though he never converted to Christianity, Zimmerman claimed that Winter went to church every Sunday with his first wife, whom he described as "a lovely woman" and "smarter" than Winter. He may have misremembered, for Priscilla Norton is sure that Winter usually spent Sunday mornings with Carl Lund in more secular service to the Medical School.

To others in New Haven, of course, Winter was a Jew, though we found no records or written comments to that effect. Zimmerman quoted Samuel Harvey, chairman of Surgery and a vocal opponent of the Institute of Human Relations, saying that Winter wanted the institute "so he could get all his relatives in." Harvey, of course, had little reason to cherish Winter, given their conflicts in the 1920s. About Max Taffel, Zimmerman recalled that Harvey once remarked, "In America there is no room for a Jewish surgeon in the top category." The truth of this assertion remains in doubt, as Harvey's daughter has described Taffel as a frequent visitor in the Harvey household and a member of their extended family. In his later years, Harvey thought very highly of Taffel, who hoped to succeed him as chairman but did not, probably because of his Jewish origin.

THE QUOTA SYSTEM

Like other American medical schools in the nineteenth century, Yale's did not traditionally restrict the admission of Jews, largely because so few applied. Only later, with the growing number of applicants, did a quota system seem necessary. When "limitation of numbers" became a major issue in the 1920s, it affected African-Americans and other minorities, as well as Jews. The Jewish quota was set at 10 percent, but women were regularly admitted at a level of 5 percent, slightly higher than the quota for Italians, when they began "flocking into medicine at an alarmingly rapid rate." Yet the much larger number of Jewish applicants to the Medical School made discrimination against them quantitatively far more severe.

The Medical School's quota system for Jews was a policy that Winter followed–or did not quarrel with–rather than one he actively promulgated. In a letter of October 6, 1931, a Wall Street financier named Philip S. Manne inquired about "the possibility of restricting a scholarship fund in the School of Medicine to students of the Hebrew race." Winter replied that was indeed possible and invited him to New Haven "for any of the football games or at any other time" to discuss matters further. Yet when Fritz Redlich, dean of the Medical School in the 1940s, tried to confront anti-Semitic bias, Winter exclaimed, "Redlich, what are you trying to do? Do you want to make a synagogue out of this place?"

Winter did not encourage most Jewish students to come to the Yale Medical School, he explained, because there would be no place for them later on the Yale faculty. He chose mainly those who had qualities that he felt would be acceptable at Yale. In his descriptions of people, Winter routinely judged them by whether they were "presentable" or not. He was fascinated by John Fulton, whom he saw as eminently presentable, cultured, wealthy, and a good model for others. He was very much impressed by "breeding" and good looks, particularly Anglo-Saxon features. He liked nothing more than to march into a room followed by his tall protégé, Levin Lyttleton Waters IV.

Winter treated Jewish applicants as brusquely as he did everyone. Still, he could be kind, particularly to those who were well-mannered. The men who stood up to him, as many did, and especially those who were clean-cut, polite, and thoroughly "Americanized," were likely to be admitted to the Medical School. Of course, it is hard to imagine that in the 1920s many Jewish applicants would have had the chutzpah to stand up to this dour dean. Samuel Kushlan, a gastroenterologist and later vice chairman of the Medical Service at the Yale-New Haven Hospital, turned what might have been a rejection into an acceptance by coming back to the dean and asking to be admitted for the next year. Sam had been a basketball player and a sportsman, skills which Winter lacked and which he must have esteemed and envied.

In response to an inquiry about the limitation of numbers, Winternitz candidly wrote that "50-60% of the applicants for admission to the Yale University School of Medicine each year are Hebrews," yet "the number of Hebrews admitted to the School . . . has never been more than 10% of the total number of students admitted." He went on to state that the percentage of Jewish students admitted to the Medical School should be the same as the proportion of Jews in the population at large, which would have lowered the figure to about 5 percent.

Dr. Samuel Ritvo states that while he was a student at the Medical School, there was always a boy or two in each class from Brooklyn, which he took favorably as an example of Winter's very timorous attempt to provide an "underground railway" for his co-religionists. Zimmerman, however, related that Winter's instructions were explicit: "Never admit more than five Jews, take only two Italian Catholics, and take no Blacks at all."

WINTER AND THE "NEGROES"

Winter's views of Negroes, as they were called in his time, were little different from those of most of his American contemporaries. He often expressed racist sentiments (Zimmerman related that he habitually used the offensive N-word), but that too was characteristic of the era in which he grew up and of the Baltimore where he was born and raised. Winter's reputation of being anti-black needs to be put into the context of a time when segregation still dominated in the South. Even in New Haven, African-Americans were for the most part confined to certain areas of the city and certain lowly occupations. The first African-American students at the Yale Medical School in the modern era were not admitted until 1948. As late as the 1950s, black physicians were denied privileges to admit patients to the New Haven Hospital.

Yet Winter was capable of change. Although he excluded blacks from the Medical School when he was dean, a letter of February 28, 1936, telling of a visit to a

Negro college in Atlanta, suggests how much his early views had modified. Before leaving New Haven, Winter went to a dinner party at the Fultons' in honor of Homer Smith, a famed renal physiologist. He went home at 10 p.m. to pack and then caught the overnight train to Baltimore, where he met with his daughter Elizabeth, now in the psychiatric hospital under the care of the famed Adolf Meyer. He strolled around the eastern part of the city with Elizabeth, "seeing the places that mother and I had lived and shopped and played, etc." He had a meeting with Meyer and his wife, lunched and gossiped, and later went to see his own mother.

Then Winter went to Atlanta. There, despite some patronizing comments that might be characterized as racist today, he wrote admiringly about Spelman College for Women and Morehouse College for Men, both part of Atlanta University:

> The students one could not tell from those of the other colleges except for [skin] color. Their dress, their manners, their sports, their general activities, even their conversation was what one would hear on any large campus. The girls especially conformed to the type and dress in appearance. The men were perhaps not quite as dapper as those one would see at Yale or Harvard, more the variety that would be found in Missouri or some place of that variety.

It appears that Winter may have been learning more about prejudice between races, or at least he was discovering that there were fewer differences between them than he had been socialized to believe. Contributing to his admiration of the traditionally black colleges may have been the fine buildings at Morehouse designed by James Gamble Rodgers, the architect of Yale's new neo-Gothic campus.

JEWS AT OTHER MEDICAL SCHOOLS

Benjamin Castleman was for many years professor of pathology at the Harvard Medical School and chairman of Pathology at Massachusetts General Hospital. Winter regarded him as one of his "stars." Yet in a filmed interview, Castleman avoided any mention of anti-Jewish bias, except obliquely, and made no mention of the difficulty that he, as a Jew, though a Harvard College graduate, had in getting into medical school. Even more surprising, he failed to discuss Winternitz at all. He said nothing about the difficulty a Jewish doctor in those days had in getting postgraduate training other than in a Jewish hospital or, for that matter, in gaining any academic position. Castleman noted that he had considered becoming a gastroenterologist and had dreamed of a medical internship at Massachusetts General. As he put it without further comment, he was "not given one." For that reason, after graduating from the Yale Medical School in 1931, he went directly into pathology, where he attained great eminence. In the end, he became a bulwark of pathology for half a century at the very hospital that had not even considered him earlier.

Herrman Blumgart, too, wanted an internship at Massachusetts General, but was advised not to apply because he was Jewish. Instead, he applied to the Peter Bent Brigham Hospital, where he was the last of nine interns chosen. He went on to great achievement at the Beth Israel Hospital in Boston, now ironically, if ecumenically, united with the Deaconess Hospital down the road as the Beth Israel Deaconess Medical Center.

There were, relatively speaking, many Jews in pathology at that time–Castleman, S. Burt Wolbach, Arnold Rich, and others–though not all were identified as Jews. To have any chance of advancing in academic life, a young Jewish doctor had to train in *the* basic science at that time, which was pathology. Those who would become the teachers of medical students had studied in Austria, Germany, and elsewhere in Europe with professors of Jewish background, yet they came back to a system that systematically excluded Jews, Italians, and other immigrant groups. In his interview, Castleman never mentions this irony, nor does his interviewer, also a Jew, raise any questions. In the early 1940s. Arnold Rich was appointed head of the Department of Pathology at Johns Hopkins over the objections of the advisory board, a move that most other medical schools in the country would have found difficult to take.

Even now, quotas and anti-Semitism are matters rarely discussed in medical memoirs about that time or in histories of medical education, partly, one suspects, because of taboos among Jews and Christians alike against discussing what might now be called the elephant in the room. Yet unless such taboos are broken and the issues brought out into the open, as Daniel Oren has done so brilliantly, these evils may be forgotten.[14]

As we have noted, discrimination was not limited to Jews. In his *History of the Rise of America's Hospital System*, Charles Rosenberg described hospital "strongholds" as "a resource of the privileged" where the entrenched elite made their fortunes. William Councilman, another pathologist in Boston, unsuccessfully tried to find a place for Joseph Pratt, a Harvard graduate and a Christian for whom a later unit would be named at Tufts Medical Center. Rosenberg took that as definitive evidence of parochialism which required that one had to be a member of an inner Boston circle. Family connections, which almost no recent immigrants would have had, were all-important. To be sure, Simon and Abraham Flexner gained high positions of great influence in the medical foundations and institutes of the time, but they were native-born and from the South. In a sense, then, what to the descendants of the Jewish immigrants currently passes as anti-Semitism–as it certainly was–also was part of a much wider, anti-outsider chauvinism at its least generous.

HEALERS' TALES

The Healer's Tale by Sharon Kaufmann, consisting of eight accounts by "movers and shakers" describing how medicine was transformed between the 1920s and the 1970s, casts more light on the dilemma of ambitious young Jewish physicians and academicians.[15] Curiously, Winter, the only Jewish medical school dean in the 1920s, was never mentioned by any of Kaufmann's interviewees. This seems a remarkable omission considering how his philosophy of medical education transformed the Yale Medical School.

In Kaufmann's book, Sol Jarcho writes of choosing private practice in New York City because he knew that as a Jew he could not advance very far in academic medicine. As a Harvard undergraduate, he had thought about becoming a professor of classics, like the young Welch at Yale, until a friendly Harvard professor warned him, "But remember, you are Jewish, and the chances are against you. While I offer you my backing, I think you would be wiser to go into medical school." Jarcho added that "one could be destroyed because of anti-Semitism or caprice. At Johns Hopkins, for example, Dr. Max Wintrobe, one of the nation's leading hematologists, a Canadian Jew, found himself blocked." That was in 1934, almost at the end of Winter's decanal career.

The story of Soma Weiss, a leading professor of medicine at Harvard's Peter Bent Brigham Hospital, puts that of Winternitz in perspective. A Hungarian of Jewish origin and a brilliant academic teacher and clinician whose rounds at the Boston City Hospital attracted a huge following, Weiss succeeded the fabled Henry Christian in 1942 as the second chairman of Medicine at the Brigham

Hospital and as the Hersey Professor of the Theory and Practice of Physic at the Harvard Medical School. He understood, however, that Jews who were appointed to any position, certainly to positions of authority like his, had to be careful to play by the rules.

John Romano, whom Weiss appointed as the first psychiatrist in the Department of Medicine at the Brigham Hospital, described Weiss as "a very enthusiastic, charismatic man. . . . I remember some not very loud but distinct rumblings and questions about a Jew being chosen for their chair." Soon after he started at the Brigham, Romano proposed "the name of someone who could assist me in my new appointment, and Soma Weiss gently, but firmly, rejected his name. The candidate I had in mind was Jewish, and I've forgotten exactly what Soma Weiss said, but something to the effect that he was not quite ready to make such an appointment. As I look back on it, he probably had been warned by others not to make many Jewish appointments at the beginning. Remember, this was 1938, 1939, 1940. Later on, as his confidence grew in his job, he made several appointments of Jewish persons."

Romano worried that his remarks, if published, would hurt members of Weiss's family. Nevertheless, he let them stand. He also noted that Arthur Kornberg, the recipient of the 1959 Nobel Prize for Medicine, in the 1940s had drawn "attention to the anti-Semitism at Rochester, particularly the attitude of the Dean. . . . On one occasion, one of the department chairmen wondered whether we

(Rochester) were admitting too many 'New York arabs' (which meant Jewish students)."

Paul Beeson, chairman of the Department of Medicine at Yale from 1952 to 1965, was the first chief resident under Weiss. He related that he met Weiss, at the latter's request, at the Pierre Hotel in New York before getting his appointment at the Brigham: "I think he wanted to see whether I was a Jew." Beeson too emphasized that Weiss had been advised not to take any Jews at the Brigham or to bring any along with him when he moved over from the Boston City Hospital. "I am as sure of that as anything I could be," he remarked to Howard Spiro. Out of loyalty to Weiss, Beeson went on to bring many young Jewish doctors to Yale.

WINTERNITZ AND EUROPEAN JEWRY

Although Winter's fifteen-year tenure as dean coincided with the start of the persecution of Jews in Germany, there is no evidence that either he or Yale went out of their way to help Jewish professors who had lost their jobs in the Nazi purges.[16] Even as late as the mid-1930s, after he left the deanship, Winter never commented on what was happening to the Jews of Europe, although he had plenty to say about international affairs in general. Could he have seen a parallel between his own exile at Yale and that of the Jewish professors who had been expelled from Germany?

There were a few exceptions, Ernst Mylon (Misslowitzer), a distinguished German chemist, joined the Pathology Department to work on the treatment of burns, especially those caused by chemicals, an important credential given the widespread expectation that poison gas would be used in the next war. Winter gave him a job, a laboratory, and much of his own time. Rolf Katzenstein, another refugee who came to the department about the same time, had the dark and sinister look of a man who had "seen everything" and survived by his wits. He had already performed more than a thousand autopsies and was, as Bill Winternitz remarked, "a pretty cold fish as far as death was concerned." John Fulton and Winternitz also brought the medical historian Arturo Castiglione to Yale when he had to flee Italy because of growing anti-Semitism there.

Winter aligned himself with those who looked upon Jews as outsiders.[17] He regarded most of them as different from himself–an opinion, it must be repeated, that should be seen in the context of the early 1930s, when the "temple Jews" of Atlanta or New Orleans were more devout in their assimilation than in their adherence to ritual, and when the destruction of the Holocaust had not yet redefined Jewish identity.

We have already noted one instance of Winter recruiting a faculty member from Europe before the Nazis came to power. During the long search for Yale's first chairman of Psychiatry, Harry Solomon, later to be a chief of Psychiatry in Boston, had been mentioned, but nothing came of it. Winter therefore prepared to look for a candidate during his month-long trip in Europe in 1929. A typewritten report in his file provides a summary of Winter's travels in Germany, Austria, France, and England. In his candid comments about the medical "greats" he met, Winter describes some as Jews, often adding qualifications such as "not typical of his race," "not noticeably Jewish," or "does not have the unattractive qualities of a Jew." In 1930, he finally settled on Eugen Kahn of Vienna for chief of Yale's Psychiatry Department, even though he was aware that Kahn was Jewish.

Winter was hardly unique, of course. In the 1930s and 1940s few American leaders welcomed Jewish refugees from Nazism into the country, nor did many Ivy League schools. The issue awaits a later generation for an equitable judgment. Winter's granddaughter, Susan Cheever, seems on track in suggesting that Winter was "incapable of playing down any aspect of himself." He may never have boasted that he was a Jew, but he did not deny his background and never changed his name or shortened it, as others of his family had done. On occasion, he may even have exaggerated the "disreputable" aspects of his background. Still, as she put it, "Jewish students who looked to him for leadership were disappointed. He refused to make a cause out of his own Jewishness or anyone else's."

Winter was in the classical "double bind" of so many other Jewish professors of the time: Should he take care of himself and hew to Yale's anti-Jewish bias, or take a stand for what Yale inevitably considered "his people"? Cheever summarizes the problem in her book *Treetops:* "He was the first Jewish full-time professor at the Yale Medical School, and one of few in the University. If he stood up for Jews and his own Jewishness, he would not have survived at Yale. He wouldn't have been able to do the things he did. On the other hand, by ignoring his own Jewishness, he alienated some of New Haven's Jewish community and many Jews within the medical profession."[18]

Chapter 9. The Widower Remarries

Letters to the Children

The children spent the summer of 1930 with Grandma and Grandpa Watson at Treetops, where Winter joined them as often as possible. Winter wrote to Bill, now in Switzerland, a series of letters intended to keep the family informed about one another and, possibly deliberately, to serve as a journal of his activities. The letters have a dated and somewhat formal quality, as if he expected posterity to consult them; they became known to the children as the "weekly bores." Yet there is a subtle individuality in the way Winter addresses each child. He tried to put a cheerful spin on everything he reported, and one rarely feels he is telling us–or them–all we want to know. There are many references to projects he is working on but is not ready to talk about.[1]

The first letter to Bill illustrates Winter's style, and suggests that he was giving his son the advantages he might have wished for when he was a boy:

I shall do exactly as I have done before, i.e. send you all carbon copies of the letters I write to anyone in particular, . . . and provide a more or less continuous story. . . . Of course it has been a bit difficult and will be, but I know just the kind of fiber you are made of, and I feel sure you will go ahead and adjust yourself to your new surroundings; that you will benefit by every opportunity which comes your way. Bill I believe this decision on our part for you to go to Geneva to school is the biggest thing that could possibly have happened in your life, and that your whole viewpoint in the future will be colored desirably by the contacts and experiences which you will have during these next years. I am waiting with great interest to hear from you because I am personally so deeply interested in everything you are going to experience.

Another letter tells of Winter's impressions on his return to New Haven:

The University's building program is going on very rapidly. Really you will hardly recognize New Haven when you return in a year. So many buildings have been completed or closed in, and so many of the old ones have been torn down for sites for new ones that it is almost difficult to find one's way. More than that the street car tracks have been taken up on College, George and York Streets, and the streets have been paved so seem much wider, cleaner and better. It is remarkable how these physical changes influence the whole environment of a street.

> Over here at the School everything looks excellent. The new Sterling Wing is finished and occupied, the new Recreation Wing is all but finished–meaning it still needs a few chairs and fixtures of one kind or another put in, but all relatively unimportant. The grounds are lovely. I honestly believe it is one of the finest building groups in the whole University, and certainly one of the best I have ever seen connected with any school of medicine.

A letter to Bill dated October 6, 1931, about going to Treetops with Elizabeth before her return to Vassar mentions glorious foliage and ideal weather. Winter could wear shorts and a sleeveless jersey all day and into the crystal-clear nights, without feeling chilly. "Gladys, Edward and Molly went along and Mr. and Mrs. Shimp were there too so we had quite a party. . . .There were enough of our friends so we were by no means lonesome." Winter was riding high! Frank Fowler, a neighbor, told the most remarkable stories of bootleggers and rum runners along the Atlantic coast, which led Winter to comment, "The situation is almost intolerable. It is ridiculous to have laws of the kind we have which cause both the rum runners and the federal authorities to commit crimes such as are now consummated daily."

In a letter addressed to Elizabeth on October 12, Winter relates that Mary and Jane, home for the weekend, went to the football game, where Yale was trounced by Georgia–no disgrace, because Georgia had become "subservient to football." He took up his work with fervor:

> I had my first class this morning. It is really quite a lot of fun to teach, and I enjoy it now that I am in it again. Somehow or other I haven't been feeling very well today. Perhaps I ate something which did not agree with me. When I started work this morning I simply couldn't keep at it, but I felt better by the time I had to teach and am much better now. . . . Nothing serious–just a little burning of the candle at both ends.

Winter describes the reception celebrating the new gymnasium and recreation hall at the Medical School, preceded by a gathering at the Blakes' before dinner at the Faculty Club. Mrs. Blake loved entertaining, so the Blakes could be counted upon to help him socially. More than 800 people attended the reception, and Winter comments, "I feel quite certain everyone who was there was impressed with the service the recreation hall is going to render and–it will mark another step in the general development of education in which I have been so much interested."

The recreation hall was part of Winter's plan to make tennis courts, squash courts, and other recreational facilities available to medical faculty and students. In March 1932, the Blue Room at the Institute of Human Relations opened to serve as a lunchroom "for the exchange of ideas." It never really succeeded, any more than similar enterprises in later years, possibly because in a university the most valuable commodity is original ideas, and an in-house site could not provide the atmosphere of a relaxed social club. Whatever the reasons–and they may be parochial to the Yale Medical School–the pressure for space eventually turned the Tea Room and the Blue Room, along with the gymnasium and the big reception room, into offices and laboratories.

A COMPLEX PERSONALITY

A letter dated October 14, 1931, is for Elizabeth alone, not to be circulated among the family. (Winter kept a carbon copy for posterity, or perhaps for his biographers.) It is an important letter because, after a wordy preamble, he gives us an insight into his understanding of himself as he counsels his daughter.

> I have the greatest sympathy for you because I think your disposition and mine are so alike, and perhaps it is possible for me to be of aid to you on account of the greater experience I have had. In the first place we are both extremely impatient, and perhaps are not willing to take things in their stride. After all, the world moves slowly, and every part of the world which is dependent on human activities is likely to be disappointing to people of our dispositions. It has been a rare thing in my experience to meet anyone whose dynamic energy found sufficiently clear and prompt

> expression to meet my own expectations. . . . It is also a rare thing to find an idealistic viewpoint of service as the dominant force in the cosmos of anyone, and when you demand action and ideal in any group you are doomed to disappointments. To be fore-warned then is to be fore-armed, and it is only possible to go on conservatively with one's work by developing tolerance, patience, and equanimity. For myself it has been a bitter experience, and I am by no means adjusted because I am neither sufficiently tolerant nor sufficiently patient, and certainly have not the equanimity that the conflict of desire and opportunity requires.
> But, my dear the problem has both a negative and a positive side from our standpoint. It has been a bitter experience to me to realize my own frailties and my own faults in not attaining ideals and in seeing projects only partially completed. The very drive that you and I have may be the obstacle to the more satisfactory maturation of our plans.

This letter sheds light on the complex nature of the man. Winter laments his inability to take things in stride and the disappointingly slow pace of the world. He cherished the friends and associates who could keep up with him, hard though they were to find. Dr. John Peters was one. Although he and Winter were said not to like one another, the two men dominated any session where they were both present and had a wonderful time arguing, Peters serving and volleying words as he did tennis balls.

Peters's junior associates were careful not to beat him at tennis, but Winter was not his subordinate and loved to score points on the court as well as off.

Winter's often abrasive personality obscured the fact that idealism and service were his religion. He knew he had to strive for tolerance, patience, and equanimity, even if he was painfully aware that he was neither tolerant, nor patient, nor balanced when he most wanted to be. That discipline he could not learn. His only interest in past events was to learn from them.

On November 11, 1931, he wrote to Tom, urging and teaching at the same time.

> I think you are wise in sending mail to me here at the School, especially if it is something important you want to bring to my attention. I haven't had an opportunity yet to look up those infusions for you, but I shall be as prompt as I can in securing them. It has been a long time since I did that first chlorine experiment which you describe. I remember how pungent the odor is. You know of course that chlorine was the first one of the gasses to be used in the war. Perhaps you already have done experiments to show how it will destroy cloth and other inorganic materials. It has the same effect on tissues, and is quite dangerous to breathe in any degree of concentration. After the war chlorine chambers were advocated in the treatment of colds, but they did not succeed because the gas is destructive and it is by no means wise to

> add an agent like this to an already irritated respiratory tract. . . . Knowledge once attained can be used both destructively and constructively, and when it is destructively with this intent in mind, many questions of ethics arise in the minds of the more just.
>
> You will be delighted with chemistry as you go on. The dynamics of the thing will interest you. To see things happen always has been satisfying to me, and I gather from what you say of your work in biology and chemistry that you have a similar tendency. The whole tone of your letter gives me the greatest amount of pleasure. You are so obviously interested in your work and you are so keen, as compared to your former attitude, to make a good showing.

Explaining that he had spent a day in New York visiting foundations and fundraising, Winter added, "Yesterday among others I had a visit from Sir Thomas Lewis, a great cardiologist and probably the most outstanding clinical investigator that has ever been produced in England. He is a perfectly splendid man and I had a delightful talk with him about problems in medical education. Contact with people of such caliber is what makes the grueling kind of job I have worth while."

UPS AND DOWNS

The Stone House at Treetops was supposed to be ready by the end of 1931. In his Christmas letter that year, Winter sounded both excited and tired–frustrated that the house would not be finished on time, but looking forward to having the children home and the Watsons coming for the holiday. (Christmas was important to Winter, who liked to play Santa Claus.) His in-laws had given him an early Christmas present–the deed to Treetops—and he promised to take time off "chopping wood, resting and getting into condition." But Winter hated being alone, the weather was bad, and he never got to New Hampshire during the holiday recess.

The Depression dampened the usual frivolity of the season, and Winter's chronicle of those months suggests that he was not telling his children something. He spent New Years' Eve alone in New Haven, writing to Bill about how, for the first time as dean, he had had to cut budgets rather than increase them. "Many of the men will have hardly a penny for clothes or amusement and some will have to strain to find the funds for food. It seems unfortunate that a pretty fine fellow has to worry where his meals are coming from–each student's problem must be considered individually."

Winter's personal life was still not going well, though he never mentioned it. On January 22, 1932, he told Tom that the girls would not be coming home that weekend, as they were going to a play and a party.[2] He was "pleased with the slow evolution of our work in dentistry" and wanted to broaden the field of education in nursing. He was optimistic about the reorganization of the institute, so much so that he was thinking about pulling out of pathology. "I am feeling better all the time, and am getting more energy for my work," he wrote.

> Saturday was a rainy gloomy day. I did my work in the forenoon and after a mid-day walk around the block stayed here until late afternoon grinding out accumulations at my desk. . . .Then after dinner which I had alone at 210 I walked for several hours, and spent the rest of the evening until the small hours reading the remarkable Swedish book Kristin Lavransdatter.

The next day, he wrote to Tom again, this time from his office at the Medical School.

> I suppose this could be called an April day. Foolishly believing that the rain had subsided I walked over here after breakfast, nearly got my umbrella turned inside out at the Taft [Hotel] and got the bottoms of my trousers thoroughly wet. Moreover it was so sultry that I was steaming when I reached here. . . .When it is cold in New Haven it is bitter cold on account of the moisture, and I used to say it made one shiver to the very marrow of his bones and so agitated the red blood cells that they lost their nuclei before their time. As you know there are red blood cells in the bone marrow, and in man they lose their nuclei before they get into the circulation.
>
> Yesterday afternoon I saw Dr. Welch's grand-nephew who is a senior at Yale and who wants to study

> medicine at Johns Hopkins. I think he is going to have a pretty difficult time because he lacks some requirements and his standing is far from what it should be. Then last night Dean Furniss and Mr. May came in to dinner, and we talked until eleven about problems associated with the Institute. After they left I read some more of that remarkable book, Kristin Lavransdatter. It certainly is fascinating though somewhat horrible.

Years later, Winter admitted that he couldn't bring himself to turn down Dr. Welch's kin when he applied to medical school, and so Welch's grandnephew came to the Yale School of Medicine and did graduate.

Something happened between January 26 and February 6 to elevate Winter's mood. When the children came home for the weekend, he sounded pleased with all of them and ready to have fun. He and Tom went downtown to the Taft Hotel to get their hair cut and listen to the friendly kidding of the barbers about Tom's being so much bigger than his father. One letter mentions Tom's interest in electric motors.

> After dinner Saturday night we went to the theatre and saw Ben-Hur. It was a thriller–one of the finest moving pictures I have ever seen, in spite of the fact that it was a silent one. The picture itself was so absorbing that I was entirely unconscious of the fact that no talkie was attached to it. When we reached

> home the usual weak lemonade party was indulged in. Tom made the lemonade, and everyone seemed to think it was pretty good, but I had to put a crutch on mine to make it stand.

On Sunday morning Winter worked at his office, took time out for lunch with the children, then returned to the office, breaking only to take the girls to the train in the afternoon and Tom to the train at 7 p.m. Then he went back to the office to work with Mr. Lund until 10:30. There is no mention of Miss Dasey or Miss Weeks, one of whom was giving up her Sunday, too. But Winter was energized and happy again, so they probably didn't mind.

On February 29, Winter wrote about a visit to a certain Dr. Brown in very favorable terms:

> Dr. Brown looks, acts and is the ideal physician of this period. He is a country doctor with a broad viewpoint, and is associated intimately with the medical-political state and national organizations. He is well trained in surgery, is an extremely kind person, works hard, and perhaps is the most respected individual in his community. He is the kind of model one would like to set up as an objective in medical education.

In another letter, Winter commented on two students he had interviewed:

Perhaps the most interesting thing which happened in these two days occurred during my student interviews. I saw a chap about twenty-two who had a whole series of degrees and wishes to enter the School of Medicine. He talked extensively, admitted he was very bright, and in general affected my sensitivity very greatly. He was followed by a rather humble fellow–small, neat, and unpretentious–who I found out gradually had interested himself in philosophy and music. His father was a second hand furniture dealer, and he had gotten hold of a second hand victrola. The boy never had heard any music before then, but he grew to love it to such a degree that he is now frank to admit that it is the greatest joy of his life. He does not play to any extent, but he has a tremendous appreciation of all the better music. The thing that struck me was the way this man's whole attitude changed–how inspired he became when speaking of philosophy, but most especially music. He was quiet, self-effaced, unenthusiastic, and intelligent compared to the previous fellow who was noisy, obtrusive and only relatively intelligent. The latter made commonplace remarks in the tone one would use in announcing great discoveries. It is an interesting thing to see these various students and to judge their reactions as best one can with the limited time available.

LEVIN WATERS

Levin Waters came along at this point. The authors see him as an example of how Winter adopted some young men whom he considered ideal candidates for medical school. A letter from Miss Elizabeth Mitchell, a nurse who had trained at Johns Hopkins, asked Winter to consider a young man she had raised after his mother, Helen Waters, died when he was only three. Levin Waters had graduated from Princeton cum laude and been accepted at the Johns Hopkins Medical School. When his family lost their money in a bank failure, however, he gave up hope of attending, since Hopkins viewed medical school as a full-time job and would not allow students to work.

Miss Dasey read the letter with interest, as did Winter, who invited Waters to New Haven for an interview. Waters was conservatively dressed, in clothes of the finest cut and quality. He was tall and slender and held himself proudly, but acted modestly. His diction was flawless. Waters was an aristocrat with a very quick mind; there was no question that he could do the work and would fit in at Yale. He came from Baltimore, having grown up in Towson on one of the estates that Winter and his mother drove past when they went to pick berries. In short, he was the kind of young man Winter liked to have around him, and he never let Waters get away.

Winter encouraged Waters to come to Yale, telling him that he could live at the Faculty Club and polish floors and brass to pay for his room. Sometimes he filled in for a missing guest at table, enjoying a really good meal. He waited tables (at the Betsy Ross Tea Room) for meals, and cleaned animal cages for pocket money. When Waters asked about books, Winter told him, "That's what libraries are for."

Waters became the son Winter could keep close by. He didn't even have to make up a nickname for him: the Christian name Levin was incongruous enough for a man with Waters's WASPish looks. Winters called him "Levin," and their friendship lasted the rest of his life. Waters's only out-of-pocket expense for his medical degree was $7.50 for the parchment it was written on.

Waters waited until he was thirty-five to marry. He chose Priscilla A. Hall-Warneke, and they were persuaded to time their wedding to accommodate Winter, who was recovering from a heart attack. Polly needed to be free of worrying about Winter for the two weeks before Janie Whitney's wedding to Joseph Hotchkiss, so the Waters were married on August 4 and arrived at Treetops the following day, staying with Winter until the Hotchkisses were due to arrive for their honeymoon.

Priscilla Waters got the message. Always a people watcher and a listener, she became a Winternitz watcher, unwittingly laying down the foundation for this book.

REMARRIAGE

Winter was never one to broadcast his plans, and his seemingly sudden remarriage came as a shock to everyone, including his children. A letter to Bill dated April 5, 1932, ambles along at the usual pace, then abruptly drops a bombshell:

> Jane and Mary went back to New York Sunday afternoon, but Elizabeth decided she should stay over until Wednesday. As a matter of fact Jane and Mary are coming back here on Tuesday (today), and it is possible Tom may come, too, because we are going to have a little party tomorrow morning which will be associated with your acquiring two more brothers and two more sisters and their mother as a real friend. You probably don't know what I am talking about, so I shall clarify the situation for you. Mrs. Whitney has decided to marry me, and the ceremony will take place early tomorrow morning. We are going to Treetops to christen the stone house. I am sorry you can't be here, but we should have a great time with most of us at Treetops this summer. I am sorry too that Grandma and Grandpa cannot be here. As a matter of fact I am awfully disturbed about it because they are motoring up from Florida and I don't know just where they are or how to reach them. Edward is

> going to New York to get them there as soon as they arrive, and drive them to Boston.
>
> Now if you are a real sport you will sit right down and write Mrs. Whitney, who will be Mrs. Winternitz tomorrow, a very nice long letter. You can address it to 87 Trumbull Street because we probably shall live there until next fall or until we go to Treetops, and have had the opportunity to get 210 reorganized.
>
> I guess this is enough for one letter.

It took at least a week for the letter to reach Bill in Geneva, and he may have let it languish before reading it. He had had no idea his father was even thinking about remarriage, let alone to Mrs. Whitney, a society lady with a funny way of talking, whose four children were all beautiful, well mannered, and probably stuck up! Bill had two months to get used to the idea before going home for the summer–or to figure out a way never to go home.

The wedding was held in front of the fireplace in the living room at 87 Trumbull Street. All of Polly's children were there. Stephen gave his mother away, Freddy cranked up the Victrola to play Mendelssohn's *Wedding March,* and Eugenia was as excited as ten-year-old Helen Owsley. Louise cried, and Polly kept saying that she "had such a dreadful cold." As soon as the ceremony was over, Freddy characteristically called the society editor of the *New Haven Register,* the evening paper, and soon New Haven was buzzing with the news. "How could she?"

must have been the most frequent question. The *Waterbury Herald* headed their announcement a few days later, "DEAN WINTERNITZ QUIETLY MARRIES PAULINE WHITNEY," with the cynical subhead, "Medical Head Crashes Society by Wedding Smart Set Leader."[3]

Under the headline "MRS. WHITNEY QUIETLY WED TO DR. WINTERNITZ," the *Register* reported on April 6, 1932: "Announcement of the marriage this morning of Mrs. Pauline Webster Whitney, widow of Stephen Whitney of 87 Trumbull Street, to Dr. Milton C. Winternitz of 210 Prospect Street, dean of the Yale Medical School, comes as a surprise to society and Yale circles in New Haven. No previous announcement of the engagement or wedding plans had been made known." The newspaper erroneously listed Dr. Samuel Harvey as best man; in fact, Dr. Raymond Hussey, who ran the Pathology Department while Winter was dean, had that honor. The guests were Mrs. John Owsley, Miss Helen Owsley, and Mr. Thomas Farnam. The Rev. Howard Weir performed the ceremony. More than half the article was devoted to listing the names of their children, Polly's clubs, and Winter's curriculum vitae. It stated that after the summer months, "Dr. and Mrs. Winternitz will establish their residence at 210 Prospect Street."

THE COURTSHIP OF MRS. WHITNEY

"Polly" Webster Whitney was the widow of Stephen Whitney, a handsome and wealthy New Haven socialite.

Whitney was primarily a sportsman–good company, certainly, but not the least bit interested in causes or intellectual pursuits. When Polly would become passionate about a subject such as woman suffrage, he would say, "Oh Polly, hire a hall!"[4] Stephen Whitney died about the same time as Helen Winternitz, so Winter and Polly were both working their way through bereavement as their friendship began. After her husband's death, Polly rented a relatively small house at 87 Trumbull Street, which belonged to Yale and was directly across the street from her good friends, the Owsleys.

Mrs. Stephen (Polly) Whitney is listed among the people who attended meetings and dinners for the "New Hospital." Winter first mentioned her in a letter in September 1931. The first time they met, they quite literally ran into one another when Polly was trying to park her car. Winter gallantly parked the car for her and went on his way, but not before Mrs. Whitney said, "No wonder they made you dean. It's because you are so smaaart!" They must have met again, for in one of his weekly letters to Tom, Winter noted that after he had worked for a few hours at the Medical School, he "went out to dinner at 87."

Polly had two sons and two daughters. She tended to extend her vowels when she talked and her *th*'s were more like *d*'s. To Winter this was part of her charm. Polly was about five feet tall, with a tendency to plumpness. Her features were regular and her eyes china-blue; her lovely little manicured hands were always busy knitting, doing needlepoint, smoking cigarettes, playing bridge, or holding a glass as she kept up a bubbly banter. Self-possessed at all times, she had a way of being the gracious hostess even in someone else's house. Bright, witty, and worldly with an elegant flair, she loved flowers, which she arranged with style–all things that mattered to Winter. Polly was more passionate than warm, a survivor and a fighter. It took courage, and more than a little toughness, for her, as an Episcopalian, to marry a Jew in 1932 in New Haven.

The Owsleys were probably the only people in New Haven who knew that Dr. Winternitz was a regular caller at "87." Helen Owsley Heard remembers a number of doctors calling on "Aunt Polly" when she stayed at the Owsleys' while recuperating from an operation. Little Helen greeted Dr. Winternitz at the door and asked, "Which doctor are you?" to which he replied that he was "the doctor of the heart." There was a twinkle in his eye as he said it, and Helen and Winter had a special bond from that time forward.

Mrs. Whitney and Dean Winternitz had been seen dining at a restaurant in Cheshire, but New Haven society was discreet; one could be noticed without being "seen." When Winter and Polly were spotted walking hand in hand in East Rock Park, however, the sighting spread "all over New Haven" by tea-time. Winter was smitten, no doubt about it, and convinced that Polly needed him as much as he needed her. Winter had never known anyone like Polly; he had ambitions beyond the Medical School, and Polly was the one to have by his side.

Even in a relaxed posture, Winter stood shoulder to shoulder with Polly. He didn't need to *look* tall when he could *think* tall. His voice was loud and carried well when he wanted it to. He could modulate it tenderly, and wheedle teasingly. Sometimes he even sounded pathetic. But his words were often cutting, and he was not above outrageous flattery. Mary Winternitz Cheever wondered how people could be taken in by him. His fingers flared and curved back at the tips, the little finger darting out as he talked, but his face and words were invariably the center of attention. Always at his best speaking extemporaneously, he focused on his audience, editing or expanding his subject to fit the moment.

The courtship of Mrs. Whitney was one of the "projects" that were a recurring theme of Winter's letters during the winter of 1931-1932. Failure never figured in his scheme of things, but he didn't show his hand until he was sure of winning. Consequently, he had done nothing to prepare his family for the possibility of remarriage. It never occurred to him that something he wanted so intensely might not be seen as equally desirable by his children. Before the engagement was announced, he made them take a "ridiculous" trip to New Hampshire by way of Maine to meet the Whitneys. They got up in the middle of the night in order to be at Northeast Harbor in time for breakfast, where, according to the Whitneys,

Winter appeared "trailing all his children." That was the extent of their preparation for a blended family!

After Helen's long and tragic illness, Winter was eager to get on with his life, but the children understandably found his decision hard to accept. Winter was being true to his basic precept, "What's done is done. Look ahead." Very much in love, he was probably so bent on what he wanted that he did not consider how his actions would affect anyone else. If he could manage the faculty of a major medical school, he was sure he could run a family of eleven people, three servants, a dog, and a cat.

In fact, Polly rejected Winter's first proposal, sending him into a tailspin of depression and introspection. But she changed her mind after a beloved cousin was killed in an accident and Winter rushed over to console her. He was aware of how effective a support he could be in a crisis; people never forgot his compassion and his understanding in times of pain. By first turning Winter down, then accepting his proposal, Polly showed how much thought she gave to this man who was so unlike anyone she had ever met. Winter really cared about social issues. He not only wanted to make changes, he *did* make them. He was by far the most interesting person she had ever known—dynamic, with a lot of animal magnetism.

Winter quickly charmed Polly's friends, who came to enjoy lionizing the new couple. He made his greatest impression in times of a medical crisis with his ability to explain disease processes in layman's terms. His compassion, tenderness, and thoughtfulness are remembered as vividly as his outrageous outbursts of temper and frustration. Polly would never be bored living with Winter.

LETTERS OF CONGRATULATION

Among the letters congratulating Winter on his remarriage was one from Harvey Cushing, typed on his personal Peter Bent Brigham notepaper and dated April 8, 1932. After the usual polite note, Cushing went on,

> I understand that Sam Harvey has been approached by the Western Reserve as a possible successor to Elliot Cutler who is coming here to take my job, and I wonder how this would affect the programme which you have had in mind for me. Sam Harvey has been slowly and surely making a solid reputation for himself and is the kind of man who will continue to grow, and it seems too bad that there should be a chance of your losing him.
> Always affectionately yours,
> H.C.

Here was another man with Winter's priorities: congratulations provided the opening for the important point of the letter.

On April 29, Winter wrote to Bill:

> Your new mother is a very charming woman, and your new brothers and sisters are delightful. There are nine of you now: Steve is 20; Freddie is 19; Elizabeth is nearly 18, Jane nearly 17, Louise nearly 16, Tom nearly 15; Mary nearly 14, you nearly 12 and Janey nearly 10. —– The new house (Stone House at Treetops) is much nicer than I ever thought it would be, and I am quite sure you will be pleased and surprised. There is a shower bath, entered from outdoors, at which you, my dear son, may take ablution on occasion. There also is a large fireplace which holds five-foot logs, where you may sit and perhaps toast marshmallows on a rainy night.—
>
> Pete (Charon) is the same old sixpence. He looks well and acts well. Lady and Julia are still capable of pulling stumps and stones with a little urging.— Mrs. Hoyt is still dominant in the kitchen, Chet sits on the front steps in the sunlight, an' Filo barks and runs madly around the automobile as soon as it starts.

Winter gives the latest count of ducks, turkeys, and chicks, then reports that he has developed into an excellent cook and second maid. He was euphoric at the improvement in his social life, as his letters show.

> May 11, 1932
>
> Last night was the great event. The Board of Permanent Officers of the School of Medicine gave a reception for us, which was held in the beautiful new

recreation room at the School. The room was exquisitely decorated with lovely sprays of apple blossoms, Japanese quince, and in addition beautiful flowers were on almost every table–large masses of iris, delphinium, and snapdragon. I suppose there must have been four hundred people there between nine and eleven o'clock representing the University, town and School of Medicine, and they all seemed to enjoy it. We formed a reception line with the Provost and his wife, and Polly and me, Mr. and Mrs. Day, Mr. Farnam, and Mr. and Mrs. Lohmann, and shook hands with everyone who came in. Everyone seemed happy and pleased. I looked quite like a major-domo, dressed up in white vest, white tie, etc. and felt very much like a gentleman. I had to make the transition from busy executive to a dinner party gentleman in very short order because I was delayed at School until the last horn blew, and was a disheveled sight when I reached home with only a little time to change and to admire Polly in her exquisite gown. The Winslows and the Fultons had sent her a charming corsage of lilies-of-the-valley, yellow roses, and gardenias, and they sent me a beautiful gardenia, too. Then we went to the Fulton's where the line I mentioned above dined together, and got to the reception at nine, and back to 87 at 1:30. Today I have seen quite a few people who were at the reception and who were all raving about Polly, which will of course not make her angry. Freddy went to the reception and made

> himself generally useful. I think he probably wandered around listening to gossip which will be interesting to hear as he will detail it over an indefinite period as the occasion arises.

Freddy was handsome, amusing, and jolly; people's faces still light up when he is mentioned. Winter accepted Freddy and appreciated his considerate help to Polly; his special quality comes through in Winter's reports of their daily lives.

A letter on May 13 describes how the school is settling down and routines returning to normal. The Winters' social life is thriving: every night they either go out to dinner or entertain guests at "87." Buff is coming home for the weekend, but Winter will hardly have a chance to talk with her because he has to work and attend a soiree at the Hadleys' on Saturday. He writes at length about how he has been so preoccupied with his own life that he hasn't appreciated the impact of the Depression, noting that "uncertainty has raised the level of irritability and depreciated the usual good judgment of the average person."

Winter was regaining his focus on the world around him. On May 18, 1932, he wrote to Jane and Mary:

> The American Surgical Association has been meeting here, and there have been approximately one hundred of the outstanding surgeons of the United States in attendance. There were a good many men

> I know.— It was nice to see them again and to have the chance to gossip with them about problems associated with medicine. There have been all sorts of parties for the group. On Monday afternoon there was a tea in our recreation hall, and Polly poured.

Winter described his wife's daisy-patterned dress in detail. It wove its own daisy chain, because he wanted Polly to keep updated versions of it in her wardrobe for years afterwards.

> We stayed until about six, when we took a group of people to 87 for a little further gossip and refreshment. Then we had to dress, and went to a musical [party] given by Dr. Verdi. I wouldn't begin to detail this–it was entirely too grand.

Dr. Anthony Verdi, who founded the Hospital of St. Raphael's, was a prominent surgeon in New Haven. He was not "in" with the Yale physicians, although he was respected by his colleagues and loved by the Italian community. Winter's letter continues:

> The whole house was wide open, and the lawn was covered with a tent which was built around the trees, some of which therefore were enclosed in the tent: and the shrubbery which was in full bloom was visible and in some places projected into the tent on the sides. Dr. Verdi had three Metropolitan [Opera]

> stars who sang, beginning at ten and lasting until the party was over. There must have been five hundred people there, including doctors and their /wives from New Haven and elsewhere, University people in small numbers, and every possible group which has ever been known to exist in New Haven, it was an extremely democratic outfit.— We were glad to get away at midnight.

In another letter, Winter wrote:

> A student who had been abroad this year, came applying for admission. Among other things I asked him whether he thought it was more desirable to study abroad at this end of college, or even during secondary education. He said he had been quite convinced such study was not desirable during the period of secondary education until he reached Geneva, where he had seen Dean Winternitz's son Bill. Then he dilated about Bill, and when he finished I thanked him and told him Bill was my son. He was surprised and said he did not know who was interviewing him.

In a letter to Tom on June 1, 1932, Winter enthused about his newly energetic and busy life.

> As you know, I left early Monday morning for Washington. On the way down I had a long interview

with Dr. Gregg of the Rockefeller Foundation, which gave us a chance to discuss many matters of importance and I appreciated the opportunity. When I got to Baltimore I went to see my mother. She seemed really quite aged since I had seen her last which was a year ago. . . .

I reached Washington about ten, and by the time I was settled at the hotel and had looked over my notes, I was ready to turn in. Yesterday was a long hectic series of meetings, starting at nine and lasting until eleven in the evening. The sub-committee was in continuous session until 5:00 P.M., then I dashed off to see a social worker who we are trying to have come to New Haven. Unfortunately for me I was elected speaker for my sub-section, and was put at the speaker's table with the Secretary of State and the President of Cornell University. . . . Worse than that, I was told not to report on my section work, but to make the opening speech, and was informed concerning this about fifteen minutes before the speech had to be made. I am still alive.

Winter was glad to stretch out in his berth on the train for New York.

I arrived in time for breakfast with President Hutchins of Chicago. I hadn't seen him for nearly a year and one half, and we had a very pleasant hour together. He is a splendid fellow, and has settled

> down to the serious consideration of his obligations to the University and to life in general. It seemed like old times.— We both agreed we never had such a pleasant season as when we worked together for the development of the Institute of Human Relations.

Winter took a morning train for New Haven, arriving in time to go over the mail and write this letter before going to lunch at the Lawn Club to address a meeting of the Connecticut League for Birth Control, one of Polly's favorite projects. Ten days later he sent a letter to Bill on board the boat at Cherbourg, wishing him a happy birthday. Commencement, he wrote, was "a great success and delightful—the year ended excellently, with the appointment of Dr. Harvey Cushing as Sterling Professor of Neurology at Yale University School of Medicine–thus another plan consummated."

FAMILIES LIVING TOGETHER

Polly and Winter were still trying to decide where to live. Polly had redecorated her rented house at 87 Trumbull Street and was loath to leave it; 210 Prospect Street was larger but still needed work. In the end, they chose Prospect Street, because the yard and garden were particularly lovely, and set the end of summer 1932 as the target date for moving in.

That first summer could not have been easy, with the whole "blended" family gathered together at Treetops. Left without parental supervision for weeks at a time, the children were under strict orders to get to know one another and to plan their work and fun together. For the most part they kept their differences to themselves, bravely making the best of it, although Elizabeth was teased by the other children. When we interviewed Bill about that summer, he said, "Don't go there, it is not a pretty picture." He did not want to talk about it.

For Winter's children, his remarriage came "too soon" after their mother's death; they felt more like chattels than his own flesh and blood. They had been raised to value scholarly achievement and self-sufficiency. Their mother had been a gentle, loving, and unsophisticated person who was interested in the natural world. She was trained as a scientist and born into a family of good, simple folk with Puritan values of morality. Gentleness was important to the Watsons. It was no accident that they chose to spend their summers among their own kind in Calvin Coolidge country. Fortunately, Grandma Watson lived quite a long life and kept strong ties with Winter and the children. She expanded her family to include the Whitneys.

The Whitney children, by contrast, had been raised to be charming and entertaining. They were expected to be familiar with all sports and the most popular games–to play a good round of tennis, to have good swimming form, and to sail, row a boat, and paddle a canoe. They were trained in the social skills, including history, art, literature, and music. Being natural born story tellers, they regaled their friends with tales of their colorful home life. They were happy for their mother, and although Winter could be hard on his own children, he was nice to them.

At summer's end, all the children gladly returned to school with a minimum of fuss and bother. Bill went back to Switzerland, this time accompanied by Mary. Winter and Polly faced the ordeal of moving into 210 Prospect Street at the same time as the Clinical Congress was being held at the Medical School. By the first week in October, they needed a vacation of their own. The night they arrived at Treetops, the first frost nipped the flowers, but then they had glorious weather and enjoyed watching the fall colors intensify.

In New Hampshire they received a message that Polly's brother, Fred Webster, had committed suicide. Cutting their vacation short, the couple hurried to Boston. While Polly and her sons tended to the funeral arrangements, Winter visited the Watsons. On October 8, he wrote a long, contemplative letter to Mary and Bill:

> I was very glad indeed to see them because we had a very hard day–one calculated to cause deep thought and to question the philosophy of life.
>
> Fred Webster had been a brilliant man. He was a graduate of Harvard and Harvard Law School, had an interesting career as a lawyer and as a businessman,

> and had a remarkably good record as a captain in the Great War. He had lived alone in Boston for many years–probably ever since his days at Harvard, and had no great responsibilities, either personal or material. . . . Orderly in the minutiae of his life to the end, he had made every preparation to leave methodically and carefully, and carried out a plan after much deliberation. Why not? . . . But it seems too bad that an individual who has so much to give should find so little to encourage him to make the effort and so little compensation for it.

A year or so later, a medical student at Yale killed himself. Although the facts are unclear, his classmates seemed to hold Winternitz partly responsible for his death. In their eyes, the dean's apparent belief that the Medical School should not interfere in students' personal lives implied that he felt it was just as well to let the young man go ahead and commit suicide.

Winter took Janie to a football game and enjoyed the stir it caused to see the dean with "Mrs. Whitney's little girl." Janie, he reported, made "as much sense or more than the regulars." For the next few years, Winter relished having the house full of young people, particularly on football and prom weekends. The Whitneys called 210 Prospect Street "Bedside Manor."

Students who drank too much home brew at Medical School receptions continued to be a source of outrage to the dean.

> Unfortunately one or two students had over indulged in alcohol to the extent that it was obvious, and of course it was my ill fortune to run into these men–I had to put the men out and then police the place, and in general seem disagreeable. I assure you no one was hurt as much as I was by having to do it. We trust these men, we believe in them, we provide them with every advantage they possibly can secure not only for their immediate education in the accepted sense, but also in the social opportunity which we feel is necessary to keep a man in contact with things he should be acquainted with in order to have a rounded life. We expect these students to develop not only their characters, and to have pride in the institution of which they are a part. When they so far forget themselves and lapse into the sordid, they prove beyond all doubt in my mind that they are not fit to go out into the world of responsible physicians. On the rare occasions when I have had to make this type of decision, it has disturbed me greatly.

One Sunday, Miss Dasey and Winter worked all morning allocating aid funds to deserving students. At one o'clock, he met for lunch with Miss Wadman, a social worker who was setting up a social service department at the hospital. After supper, he conferred with President Angell until 10:30. All in all, it was a fairly typical weekend. The next weekend Winter mentions a long interview with Dr. Cushing that made him late for the football game. Peter Charon had arrived with the truck laden with "ducks, chickens, potatoes, pumpkins and produce." Winter sent him to the game with Edward, and afterwards Winter and Polly took him to the movies before they planned the next year's planting at Treetops. As usual, Winter had spent the morning at the hospital, came home for lunch, attended two teas, and visited Dr. Powers before supper. He loved to be busy, and he was.

Chapter 10. Rebellion and Defeat

Private Joy

When troubles came, Winter did not take his family into his confidence. His marriage to Polly Whitney had introduced the ambitious workaholic to an entirely different social life. His first wife had been a physician and was an invalid much of the time in New Haven, but Polly Whitney loved parties and Winter learned to love them too. On Feb. 13, 1934, he wrote to Bill and Mary:

> This is an important day in my life. Polly is taking me to New York late this afternoon where we are to stay with Mrs. Dickey and at eight tonight I am to be trotted over to Park Avenue in a tail coat and white gloves–perhaps even an opera hat, though I'm not sure–to be displayed. The Colts have invited us to dinner. You can imagine in what a flurry I am! Never having been a debutante it is impossible to know how they feel, but I'm sure my anticipation of this great event must be associated with very much the

same type of sensation. We have decided to stay in New York Wednesday and part of Thursday. I have to see a number of people, including dear old Dr. Paton, and tomorrow we are going to a show. Believe it or not a good break is very welcome. These last weeks have been extremely strenuous–bitter cold—snow–more snow–many meetings of importance–210 had larger clientele than ever–and Mr. Corning being sick in the hospital required anywhere from one hour to three hours a day of my time.

On March 12, he wrote to a stepchild:

We are still shivering. The miserable thermometer seems to be stuck somewhere around 10. . . . The broken wood-block pavement in the block from Sachem Street to Grove Street has been made convenient for vagrants and scavengers who accumulate and drag the pieces home to keep their fires burning. Yesterday at twilight as your Ma and I trudged back to 210 from Trumbull college we saw a whole gang of these poor people not only picking up the loose ones out of the street, but digging out accessory ones with crowbars.

He wrote to Jane on June 21:

Commencement is over. It was a perfectly marvelous affair concerning which you will hear a great

> deal.–We all enjoyed it tremendously and it gave us unusual inspiration. . . .The most thrilling part of the ceremony was the arrival, the presence, and the ovation which President Roosevelt received. He certainly is a magnificent personality, with a fine face, a pleasant smile, and a voice as clear as a bell and very strong. His speech was simple but very good. Then there was another surprise. When Mr. Phelps appeared on the platform as the public orator there was a huge ovation. He then proceeded with his task of the day with his usual flow of humor and enthusiasm, but just before he was about to introduce the last of two candidates for honorary degrees, old Governor Cross stood up in the last row, and in his deep throaty voice said, "Mr. President, if I may be allowed to interrupt the orator of the day in his eloquence and in his humor and in his optimism–." Poor Mr. Phelps looked around and wondered if the Governor had gone crazy, and it ran through his mind that Mr. Cross thought he was to introduce Mr. Roosevelt, so you can imagine how flabbergasted Mr. Phelps was. But then the Governor went on to present Mr. Phelps himself for an honorary degree, and as Mr. Cross said, "He loves everyone and everyone loves him. . . . The day was voted an outstanding success.

It was the last enthusiastic letter that Winter would write for a long while.

PRIVATE ANGUISH

Not unlike his few private letters that remain, the records in Winter's files are largely silent about the internal strife in the Medical School between 1930 and 1935. The faculty had grown in size and eminence, but administrative arrangements remained opaquely constrained. As the faculty saw it, Winter was treating them like children, and they resented it.

On the surface, all seemed glorious. The New Haven Hospital had been transformed physically along with the Medical School, the close, interdependent relationship between them had not yet been breached, and the Fitkin and Tompkins Buildings, which were to house the patient services for most of the next sixty years, had been erected. The Winchester Hospital for tuberculosis had found a firm foundation in West Haven that later would provide the core of the Veterans Administration Hospital. The quality of the medical student body had enormously improved, along with the sophistication of their senior theses.

All should have gone well, but Winter's way of approaching matters was destroying his relationship with his faculty. Not that his goals were unworthy, nor his ideas untimely; it was simply that the flaws in his character did not matter so much when people were all close to him and could put up with his temper tantrums and overlook even his duplicity. But when he had to lead a large group, one more disparate than his earlier ones, in which he did not allow himself to be as convivial as he sometimes was in private, matters began to fall apart.

Winter regarded the Medical School as the part of the university concerned with the broad problems of human health and welfare, a notion deplored by many of the faculty. The full-time faculty, then as now, hewed to the idea of a more conventional medical school, where they could advance the scientific and clinical aspects of their own areas.[1] They had little affection for the broad concepts of social medicine that Winter had espoused, ones celebrated in England by John Ryle and in Boston by Richard Cabot. A physiologist, for example, was far more entranced by the niceties of adrenal or gastric dysfunction than by the prospect of better housing projects. Moreover, a better understanding of organs and physiological systems would advance the state of medicine far more than improved cesspools would lessen the likelihood of disease. That was a matter for politicians and social workers–or for plumbers.

SOCIAL MEDICINE

Winter's failure to impose his ideas about social medicine on the Medical School might have been foreseen. Very rarely has anyone with such socially responsible ideas in the United States or England wielded authority comparable to Winter's at Yale in the 1920s. Yet even the support of the university's president couldn't prevent the enterprise from collapsing. The question naturally arises: Was it the field of endeavor or the characters playing on it? Welch, we have seen, had sent Winter to Yale on the strength of his potential as a pathologist and his proven ability as an administrator. Winter was expected to enhance the scientific repute of the Medical School as well as to rejuvenate it. His early work at Yale, as well as the faculty he chose, suggest that he was well on his way toward that goal, thanks to the unique conjunction of circumstances described in earlier chapters. Only after he became dean did his associates gradually come to understand that Winter was at heart a social engineer who wanted to improve the lot of humankind, and not only by biomedical advances.

The quest for Winter's true purposes can be rather like searching the Bible for answers to life's questions. True enough, much praise for science can be found in his rather casual writings, but he also wrote a great deal about the humanities and social sciences. Family members who knew him when he was young believed that Winter always had a sense of mission, and not necessarily as a scientist.

Some who worked with him have a different opinion. Winternitz liked to think of himself as a researcher: he was convinced that he directed research in the pathology labs, and grew angry whenever experimental observation led to an unexpected conclusion. After all, he had known nothing about war gases until he was inducted into the army in 1917-1918 and was told to work on gas poisoning. Even earlier, his initiative at Hopkins–starting an in-house laboratory and training Bayne-Jones to run it–made it clear that he was a "can-do" guy.

Like many scientists of his time, Winter considered all the laboratories in his department as his own (with the exception of Harry Greene's), even if he referred to the work as "Liebow's," "Bunting's," or "Waters's." He wanted to review every paper before it was submitted for publication. He would often let his name come first among the authors, claiming that it gave prominence to the work. Winter needed to regard himself as very closely involved with the research, but those who actually did the work have not always seen it that way and grew to resent his primacy as author.

Winter had free rein, or thought he did, to flesh out his ideas about social medicine. John Ryle, coming on the scene somewhat later, abandoned his position as chief of Medicine at Oxford to become a professor of social medicine there, but in doing so he moved to the sidelines. Richard Cabot, the sometimes splenetic adherent of social medicine at Harvard, was also marginalized after losing out for the job of chief of Medicine at the Massachusetts General Hospital. Winter was unique in having the responsibility of dean at a school that was looking for a mission and a reputation. Sadly, his brusque, even truculent manner gained him few true believers at Yale; nor could he have slowed the tide of scientific advance even if he had wanted to emphasize social medicine. His was the classic Greek tragedy, that of a man with brilliant ideas but with the hubris that portended failure.

WINTER'S MANNER

Evidence of how bitterly the faculty differed with their dean can be found in an informal history of those times, where the following is recorded, after Bayne-Jones took over, in relation to the succession of deans. Medicine was not merely to be considered "a division of the social sciences," as the prior administration conceived it, but was to be restored to its "ancient" place as "mother of the sciences." Dean Bayne-Jones went on to emphasize that the Medical School would remain primarily concerned with research and teaching in " biological medicine including psychiatry."

The growing rebellion against Winter was not so different from what many parents encounter as their children mature. It is one thing to give children an allowance, it is quite another to try to restrict their activities when they are away at college. While they may feel compelled to offer advice to grown sons or daughters, wise parents recognize that young adults feel under no obligation to do more than listen (if that) to their paternalistic meanderings. They are free to do whatever they please.

Winter either did not recognize, or ignored, the growing maturity of the faculty he had so carefully chosen and nurtured. He failed to acknowledge how much they needed their independence to exercise their own ideas. It has long been true in academic medicine that junior faculty have found it prudent to leave the institution where they have trained, knowing that they will always remain subordinate there until their seniors retire or die. Even those who are promoted to assistant professor may find that five years or more must pass before they will be more than "bright young persons," and that probably they will never achieve equality in the eyes of their aging mentors. Winter would have done well to ponder the admonition, "A wise father is never jealous of his children," and to recognize that, in a sense, the Yale medical faculty were his students and his children. From our distance, it seems probable that just as Winter did not easily accept his own children as independent persons who might welcome his advice but not his control, so he failed to see that the faculty, bound to him by neither blood nor law, had begun to chafe under his rule.

THE GREAT DEPRESSION

The Depression reduced funds for research, teaching, and other academic ventures; and this, in turn, destroyed any enthusiasm there may have been for Winter's goals. Lack of money aggravated the administrative problems that "had been growing as the individual departments of the school grew stronger." Winternitz's self-certainty, which must have looked like stubbornness to his colleagues, frustrated them, given the very discrete fields in which they were making their way. Social medicine and interdisciplinary activities like the proposed Institute of Human Relations were regarded with suspicion bordering on resentment by faculty members whose reputations were tied to departments of medicine, pediatrics, or surgery.

As dean, Winternitz had total control over the finances of the Medical School, allocating money and space to the several divisions as he saw fit. On Dec. 12, 1932, a 5 percent cut in the school's budget was to be carried out in a "discriminatory" fashion, depending on the activity of the departments in relation to "their primary function (teaching)." A year earlier, on Dec. 31, 1931, Winter had written to his son Bill:

> I have been seeing students for the coming year and have been going over budgets, which is a very difficult job this year. For the first time since I have been made Dean we have had to reverse our method, and instead of giving each department more money for expansion, we actually have had to give them less money because there is less money available. Everyone feels poor.

Money was obviously difficult to come by in the 1930s. The university chiefs had little time to pursue their own research interests, given their clinical and administrative responsibilities and their work on university and national committees. Winternitz asked Francis Blake to approve a request for funds to support "fellows" to carry on investigation under the direction of the department heads. After their internships, fellows with "potential ability" as investigators would be appointed for two years, each department chief to have two. Supporting fellows and their research was a pet idea of Winter's that he finally put into practice later as director of the Childs Fund. Young researchers got a two-year fellowship, with a laboratory and support for their research for at least one more year.

PATENTING IDEAS

Despite the shortage of funds, Winter never trimmed his vision of full-time academic clinical medicine and research by a full-time faculty. On Nov. 21, 1931, he wrote to Alan Gregg of the Rockefeller Foundation, who apparently had proposed that medical institutions and researchers patent new procedures or products. Winter disagreed "absolutely" with that possibility.[2]

> In the first place I think very few discoveries of any particular moment are made in one place when they are not near the threshold of discoveries somewhere else; take insulin for example. And as you so clearly put it, these are based on accumulated knowledge which comes from many different

> sources. . . . As soon as we attempt to reduce it to a commercial organization, we shall have insinuated all sorts of economic problems which are bound to bias and vitiate the present ideal conception of the institution. Everything which has come to my attention in association with education has strengthened my belief that the economic aspect should not involve either the investigator or the teacher.

FACULTY RULE

Winternitz never understood that his faculty had so grown in reputation and in experience that it was only natural for these department heads, now prominent and respected medical scientists, to resist the autocratic rule of a dean whose views seemed to them increasingly outdated. The senior faculty had a right to resent their powerlessness in allocating funds and choosing the overall policies of the school.[3] After all, the full-time faculty had taken on increased teaching and clinical responsibilities and, equally important in a time of fiscal stringency, were collecting increasing amounts of money from paying patients. Those funds went to a central Clinical Research and Teaching Fund over which they had little or no control. The dean believed himself to be all-powerful.[4]

Moreover, from the 1920s to this very day, the organization of the Yale Medical School–what since the 1960s has been called its "governance"–has given little opportunity to its faculty for discussion, dissension, or democracy. In the 1920s there were complaints about the infrequent meetings of the Board of Permanent Officers, nominally the governing body of the Medical School. The faculty had no other set time or place to discuss financial or personnel questions. They must have done so on social occasions, where cabals are more likely to coalesce and to be preserved by the alcohol that generates them.

Winter may have been stubbornly disdainful of other people's opinions, but he had to placate his opponents. The BPO had grown too large, from eight members in 1920 to twenty-six in 1930; it was not easy to get any decision there. His proposal for an executive committee to help run things looks like more an attempt to quiet faculty rebellion than to yield to it.

Winter had grown weary of those he regarded as small, querulous people with trivial concerns. Entranced by the big issues of the time, he grew lyrical about the proposal for a new Human Welfare Group. A proposed mental hospital near the Institute for Human Relations, meant to serve as "a great unifying agent," took up more of his energies than the more practical issues the faculty worried about. At a time of dissension, however subterranean, it took a lot of chutzpah to propose integrating the School of Medicine with the Law and Divinity Schools, as well as with the proposed psychiatric hospital and with the community. Winter even wanted to bring "social physicians" onto the faculty to deal with crime in the courts. To the more practical department chairmen, frantic over the realities of money and students, patients and fees, faculty and salaries, he must have seemed a mad dreamer at best.

After ten years as dean, Winter had lost touch with his faculty and their needs, and–given the times–with reality. One can well imagine the head shaking of the faculty at a dean who talked so wildly of grand but ethereal proposals for social medicine while their funding for research and education was disappearing. Winter might complain that the university administration was haphazard, that the dean of one graduate school knew nothing of events elsewhere in the university; but he seemed to ignore the mounting rebellion at his own school. Finding refuge in philosophical innovation, Winter avoided the major issues confronting him and his school. In retrospect, his view of the Medical School as the social center of the university seems to sympathetic observers logical, if unrealistic. One wonders what his faculty must have said privately in the little groups and clubs that controlled, and still very much influence, policy at Yale. After all, most of them were insiders, while he was in every way an outsider.

ACTIONS AND REACTIONS

There were more than a few attempts to give the Board of Permanent Officers greater authority to challenge and, if possible, tame Winternitz. A Committee on the Reorganization of the Medical Administration attempted to bypass the dean by excluding from membership on vital committees of the Permanent Officers any member of the board whose primary responsibility was research. That recommendation was sent to President Angell in the fall of 1932. In a letter of Oct. 4, 1932, addressed to Winternitz but clearly meant to be forwarded to others, Angell sharply criticized the proposal, noting that "subjecting the Dean to the approval of the Prudential Committee in the appointment of its own Committees is, so far as I am aware, at variance with the practice in all other parts of the University."[5]

A polite but apoplectic letter from Dr. Samuel Harvey, chairman of Surgery, to Angell on Nov. 1 made it clear that the dean was still running a one-man show:

> During the past decade of rapid expansion of plant and of educational and clinical activities in the School of Medicine, there has occurred a certain centralization of administrative action as a result of which policies have been determined, commitments made and action taken in such a manner that the approval of the Board of Permanent Officers was largely post facto. . . . The administration found it futile to bring before this board any topics which should obtain discussion and decision. In part also this centralization had been the result of the ease with which one officer might arrive at a decision as contrasted with the

> expenditure of time and effort in negotiation that was required by a group even though it be a small one and with common interests.

Harvey went on to comment on the importance of having a clinically oriented faculty. It was crucial, he argued, that a special committee be appointed to review the budget of the Medical School and that control of its affairs be turned over to "those whose major responsibility is the training of men for the MD degree." He wanted to be sure that the nonmedical faculty–the Ph.D. researchers who he feared might support the dean–would not be involved in decisions concerning the school.

Harvey quoted from an anonymous memorandum: "During the past decade or more, there has been a slow but gradual tendency toward centralization of authority and responsibility. This has been at the expense of local autonomy. The program outlined above indicates that the Medical School, as such, feels that the local control of its own problems should be returned so it that it may more effectively continue the development of the school." He then reported on a meeting with the dean on May 6, 1932.

> The opinion was expressed and discussed that a Board for the discussion of Medical School policies should be so organized that there may be free discussion in that Board of such policies. It was felt that

> the Board could accomplish nothing unless members expressed themselves frankly, agreed to disagree and to consider problems judicially, with the assurance that when a decision is reached in accord with the policies of the University an effective method of instituting it will be at hand.

Harvey had not forgotten the events of the 1920s, when he had had to recant his opinions and recommendations in order to keep his position. Indirectly criticizing Winternitz for exercising complete control over the Medical School budget, he pointed out: "It is still true that he who controls the purse-strings, controls all else. . . . The budget should be prepared by a committee of the Board of Permanent Officers as had been done antecedent to the present administration. . . . A review of the budget by the chairmen of Departments involved would provide the maximum of protection with the minimum of strife in the Board itself."

Many other matters are discussed by the protagonists, which we pass over here, concluding that Winter neither learned from his problems nor changed his behavior. John Fulton, writing to the dean on Nov. 18, 1932, conveyed his disappointment:

> I am more grieved than I care to express. After the events of last year I didn't think you could risk such a blunder as to allow Cedar Street to be disfigured by those rude signs. You have not consulted your faculty

> and it is these trifling things that turn them against you. If I didn't love you, Winter, I wouldn't write this way. You know that there are two sides to Cedar Street and there is the Prudential Committee–which might have acted favorably had you brought it to them.
>
> You gave me to understand that only one side was to be affected and I accepted the right of the Medical Board to make the decision–but the Board has no right to make a decision which affects us–nor have you. It is these trifling things that set them against you.
>
> Regretfully,
> John

There were echoes of an earlier criticism, that the Yale system was "a tutorial system without tutors and that the school was not meeting its obligations as an educational institution." And there were the usual complaints, no less justified than today, about how rarely students had a chance to talk with senior faculty about matters that concerned them. Students needed more tutorial sessions, more guidance, and more specific education than they had been getting.

By 1933, these issues had so come to the fore that Winter began to try to "create an atmosphere" that "brings out the best." Again, he expressed hope about reorganizing the BPO and the Prudential Committee. The latter, created in 1932 from the Board of Permanent

Officers, was intended to discuss policy and distribution of funds, along with other matters that "were not suitable for the discussion of the larger body." The Prudential Committee, appointed by the dean to advise him, dealt with many executive matters, but other committees were also formed, one to oversee the "Biological Sciences" and the other the School of Medicine, in both its preclinical and clinical divisions. As James Madison knew, giving equal voice to disparate opinions prevents dictatorship, and in this case progress toward Winter's announced goals was stalled, as he recorded in his annual reports.

A year after Winter's tenure as dean had ended, the problems were no less, according to notes of a meeting of the "Committee on the School of Medicine" on March 23, 1936. A letter signed by all but two of the students pointed out that "different departments had various attitudes towards examinations, grades and attendance; that the theory that examinations are entirely for the students' own benefit is contradicted by the advice of some instructors and by the fact that papers are graded and ratings given out; that students have the impression that attendance is taken in some laboratories." Nor was Winter's hope for self-directed students working out. "The students stated their wish to be offered frequent examinations to aid them in the progress of their work, but asked that papers be graded only when individual students requested for their own guidance."

The committee voted to refer the topic to yet another committee.

By 1934 Winter had to accept the need for a full reorganization of the Medical School, "with more widespread participation of faculty members in the discussion and execution of policies." He freely accepted faculty criticism that the students were not learning well enough, that the school was not meeting its obligations as an educational institution, and that students had no access to professors. In turn, Winter criticized the senior faculty for relegating teaching functions to their juniors. How much was his responsibility and how much that of the departmental chairmen is hard to discern, but the debate suggests the widespread dissatisfaction of the faculty rather than a general confession of their sins.

The dean may have regarded this "simplification" of administration as a way of placating his opponents, or of freeing himself for loftier concerns. (It may not be out of place to record another former dean's confession that he created one of the Medical School's now prominent bodies as a "couch committee," to allow discontented faculty members to let off steam by harmless catharsis.) Nevertheless, the leaders of the revolt were not much comforted by Winter's unwonted doling out of responsibility. Nor were they any happier with his conversations about erasing boundaries between sections and departments, or by his continuing emphasis on the social, economic, and psychological aspects of medicine. His actions and reflections seem, at least in part, a way of ignoring–or deflecting–the major problems that confronted him.

Winter maintained a brave front, as the letters quoted at the beginning of this chapter show.

Winter's final report for 1935, after he had lost the battle, is notable for its lack of ebullience. Although his earlier reports had all been preprinted, the last was merely reprinted from supplements of the *Yale University Bulletin*. Winter commented, even now never lamenting, that he had asked his division chiefs for reports reviewing the past fifteen years, but "this suggestion was not followed in all cases." His faculty was content to ignore the requests of a lame-duck dean. All emotions seemed drained from his report, and he records little pride in his accomplishments. He must have been very depressed.

B-J AND WINTER

As we have noted before, the careers of Bayne-Jones and Winternitz intersected intermittently from their time at Johns Hopkins, though Winter was even then senior in rank, if not in age. On June 8, 1931, Winter wrote a generous letter in support of Bayne-Jones's appointment at Yale. It attests to the respect, if not the affection, that Winter had for "B-J," as he came to be known.[6]

> I knew Bayne-Jones when he was a student in Baltimore, and I think he was in the fifth class I taught. I don't believe I remember him so well as a student, but that is my fault rather than his. He was

outstanding and secured one of the medical internships. . . . Soon after his hospital appointment in 1914 it became evident that Bayne-Jones was an unusual personality and an outstanding medical man. . . . I remember distinctly how pleased we were in Pathology when Bayne-Jones decided to join us in 1915. . . . He was not a well-known man by any means, but we felt he had the potentialities, which we deemed essential to the success of a venture of this type. . . . During the remainder of the period I was in Baltimore, Bayne-Jones went ahead rapidly, attracted good men to his laboratory, and played a major role in the department.

Then the war came. I came to New Haven and Bayne-Jones immediately buckled on his armor and went off first, I think, with the British Service, and later with the American Expeditionary Forces. Some of the more conservative army leaders decided Bayne-Jones should work in his laboratories. . . . Bayne-Jones felt this plan was not to his liking and so, I am told, he smashed up most of the glassware, freed himself of the red tape, and went into the front line trenches with the real men of the war. You never will know much about this from him because his force and ability do not lie in the exposition of his own feats, but he received all the honors the war had to offer. . . .

Bayne-Jones is in the first instance a man, clear-thinking, straightforward, and capable. He is extremely broad-minded and is interested in world

> problems as well as in the larger fields of education as these have grown out of his knowledge of medical education. He is a gentleman of the old school–delightful in work and in play. His contributions have dealt largely with problems of sera and the diagnosis and treatment of bacterial diseases. His thinking in these fields is modern, and he ranks with a small group of a half dozen outstanding men whose potentialities are all greatest in the fields of bacteriology in its relation to medicine.

After the war, Bayne-Jones returned to Hopkins as an associate in Bacteriology. He married in 1921 and, after considerable hesitation, in 1924 moved to Rochester, New York, which proved an unhappy choice. His coming to New Haven in 1933, as master of the new Trumbull College, provided purpose and prestige. B-J quickly grew popular with the Yale medical faculty, in contrast to Winter. His official portrait in the Sterling Hall of Medicine, outside the dean's office, contains a small black-and-white likeness of his wife, which is ironic in that. B-J, calm, correct, and always courteous, had a very unhappy marriage.

THE CABAL

When it came time for Winter's reappointment as dean, which he had confidently expected, a group of the faculty got together and chose Bayne-Jones as their candidate. As soon as that information was brought to the president, the end for Winter was clear.

Letters from President Angell and John Fulton suggest that even if Bayne-Jones was not the ringleader of the cabal, he did not oppose it very forcefully. Fulton's note of Dec. 21, 1934, quoted below, hints that Bayne-Jones was recognized as part of the opposition. A not-unexpected contrary opinion is offered by A.E. Cowdrey in his biography of Bayne-Jones. "B-J was not among Winter's enemies. Either out of loyalty or an acute political sense, he voted to keep the old Dean. Yet he sat on the faculty committee whose majority voted against Winternitz; the vote was taken in his office at Trumbull; and the committee at the same meeting voted B-J to become dean July 1, 1935."

In a letter of Dec. 22, 1934, Fred T. Murphy, a Detroit surgeon who had left medical practice to manage his family's fortune, wrote a confidential memo to Angell. Murphy was a member of the Yale Corporation to whom Angell turned for advice on Medical School matters, doubtless owing to their earlier acquaintance when Angell was still in Ann Arbor.

> Yours of the 20th reaches me this morning. I cannot honestly say that the news is totally unexpected for there have been from time to time waves of protest–sort of minor uprisings–against the Dean. There can be no doubt, I think, of the ability of Bayne-Jones and

> I am inclined to think that if you find the Committee really set in their conclusions it will be less destructive to accept the recommendation than to force a reappointment of Winternitz. The very fact that Winternitz has been so resourceful and forceful in his development of the school has nettled, I fear, some of his Faculty. Personally, I should question the wisdom of the proposed move but it seems to me that the decision must rest on the balance between the disadvantages of a row with the Faculty, who would never heartily cooperate with Winternitz if his appointment were forced, and a probable loss of efficiency in the administration of the school.

The detailed but somewhat ironic memorandum on the conference of Monday, Dec. 24, dictated by Angell and signed as "okay" by him, is of interest.

> The Committee of the Medical School on the appointment of the Dean, under the chairmanship of Dr. Blake called upon me at 2:30 on Monday, December 24th. Drs. Blake, Powers, Allen and Hiscock arrived promptly, Dr. Cushing (who had been appointed to succeed Dr. Bayne-Jones) somewhat later, after the conference had already gone forward for ten or fifteen minutes. Dr. Blake reported that, as a result of personal interviews with all the members of the Medical Board, with the exception of Professor

Mendel, the following expression of opinion had been informally gathered:

Ten of the Board were opposed to the reappointment of Dean Winternitz, seven favored his reappointment, and seven were neutral, with their ultimate views contingent on various factors. Of the heads of clinics and departments, seven were averse to re-appointing the present Dean, one favored his reappointment, and one was neutral. Of the men who might be supposed to have ten or more years to serve on the staff, nine favored a new appointment, four the reappointment of the Dean, and four were neutral.

At the meeting of the Board to listen to the report of the Committee, held on Wednesday, December 19th, the motion having been made to recommend Dr. Bayne-Jones as Dean of the Medical School for a period of five years, the vote was viva voce and no dissenting vote was cast. Whether it was a literally unanimous vote, or not, cannot be determined, owing to the method of voting.

After receiving a number of spontaneous suggestions that Dr. Bayne-Jones' selection would be the expedient solution of the problem, the Committee, of which he himself had been a member, consulted with Dr. Bayne-Jones on Saturday, the fifteenth and strongly urged on him to allow the use of his name. On the following Tuesday, December 18th, Dr. Bayne-Jones consented to allow his name to be presented and this was accordingly done on the next day, December 19th.

I interrogated the Committee at some length as to the grounds on which they felt the selection of Dr. Bayne-Jones would be satisfactory and learned that two major circumstances were involved: first the fact that he is personally liked by all his colleagues and that they have confidence in both his scientific and practical judgment; and second, that, as head of the Medical Division of the National Research Council and for a number of years in charge of an important division of the University of Rochester Medical School, to say nothing of his work in Trumbull College, they felt confident that he has demonstrated administrative gifts of a high order which would be particularly useful in the present situation in the School of Medicine. The Committee felt that this appointment would do much to restore morale in a group, which is at present a good deal divided. In reply to my questions as to why they wished to displace the present Dean, the statement was that given to me last year in my conferences with the heads of clinics, that they had no confidence in him and did not regard him as reliable. In response to my question whether they regarded him as morally untrustworthy, Dr. Blake, with some confusion and not actively supported by the other members of the Committee, asserted that he did not mean that he was morally not reliable, but that he could not be counted upon to carry out policies which had been agreed upon and that they were always uncertain that he would not commit the School to policies which had not been discussed and were not understood by his Board. My suggestion that this seemed to be a distinction without a difference elicited only rather embarrassed smiles. When I inquired whether these conditions have not been substantially removed by the new organization of a year and a half ago, the Committee replied that the conditions had doubtless been improved but they still felt they were not satisfactory and would not be as long as the present Dean remained in office. In all these comments, it was clear that Dr. Cushing and Dr. Hiscock largely dissented from the rest of the Committee and from the majority of the clinical members of the Board, although I carried away the impression that, with however great regret, they were both disposed to believe that the appointment of Bayne-Jones would, under all the circumstances, be wise.

It was fairly clear to me, and this was made even clearer by a very frank characterization of the situation by Dr. Cushing, that purely personal animosities and grudges were really the moving causes of the attitude of many members of the Board, and the inability to deny this made the implication still more vivid.

In reply to my question what the Committee, or the Board, proposed in relieving the Dean of the embarrassment of appearing to be kicked out of office after having for fifteen years given the most brilliant and devoted service, and after having built up from less than nothing a school of first rate quality, they had nothing to suggest, but were led to expressions of their own regret at seeing the Dean put in an embarrassing position and their hope that it would be possible in one way or another to avoid this. I did not spare their sensibilities in commenting on this phase of the matter.

Twice during the conference I made clear to them that, while their procedure had not violated any specifications of the by-laws, it had been at variance with the universal practice since the operation of the present by-laws regarding consultation with the President on the part of the Permanent Boards, in that they had voluntarily and knowingly proceeded in a manner which made their conference with me in no sense a consultation, but a mere notification of an accomplished fact. I did not hesitate to characterize this action with complete frankness and I intimated to them that, in my judgment, it would fundamentally affect the future policies of the Corporation in dealing with appointments to Deanships.

The interview was carried on in entire good temper, but I am sure that the members of the Committee were left under no illusions as to the impropriety, from my point of view, of the measure which they had pursued. They admitted that the point to which I drew their attention had been raised by Professor

Harrison in their first meeting and that, in the face of that, their Board had proceeded in the manner in which they had chosen, thus making it clear that they intended to force the issue and this in advance of consultation with the executive.

Angell wanted to keep Winternitz as dean, but it was clear to him that he had to go along with the choice of Bayne-Jones. On Jan. 2, 1935, even after the succession seemed certain, Angell felt it necessary to emphasize his support for Winternitz's policies, obviously aware that B-J would move the Medical School away from the course that Winternitz had set.

Dear Dr. Bayne-Jones:
In discussing the recommendation of the Board of Permanent Officers of the Medical School regarding the Deanship, it would be helpful to me, if I could give my colleagues of the Corporation some fairly definite impressions of your views regarding certain of the more fundamental principles relating to the policies of the School. If you could let me have a few lines regarding these matters within the next few days, I should greatly appreciate it. I think I sense your general attitude, but a brief statement would give me more confidence in the correctness of my conceptions.

While isolated acts could doubtless be cited in Dean Winternitz's administration to which exception might be taken, in general the Corporation has been highly sympathetic to his policies and would not be willing to see them essentially reversed at this time. Especially important have been such trends as these:

The effort to deal as individually as possible with the student, giving him close contact with teachers and patients, while offering the largest possible direct assurance of his mastery of his professional training.

The reduction of the rigidly required quantity of subject matter instruction in the several departments of the School of Medicine, with corresponding increase of opportunity for the exercise of individual initiative and the development of individual responsibility on the part of the student.

The integration of the several departments, in order to foster the best teaching of the student, the most intelligent care of patients and the most fruitful background for research.

The effort to knit the Medical School in as fully as possible to the general scientific and intellectual life of the university–and this with full recognition of the limit beyond which such integration cannot go without invading the obligations proper to the several constituent units.

The development through the Institute of Human Relations of opportunities for voluntary group attack upon basic human problems, whose solution inevitably transcends the boundaries of particular departments or even schools.

> The conception of the Hospital and the Institute as agencies through which the University immediately touches, and serves, the community and consequently as organizations which should be fostered with the greatest diplomacy and solicitude.
>
> There are naturally other issues of consequence, but these are particularly important in the minds of the Corporation.
>
> Believe me,
> Faithfully yours,
> Angell

Peter Dobkin Hall, who was for many years at Yale's Institute for Social and Policy Studies, suggested that deeper forces hostile to the general aims of Angell and Winternitz were at work.[7] He regarded the Institute for Human Relations as having been created "largely to insulate Yale from the contaminating influence of scholars who wanted to work across disciplinary and professional lines." He went on to comment that most of the opposition "came from people at Yale generally, in the Medical School and in the New Haven medical community, who opposed the kind of revolutionary transformation of the professions and social disciplines, W. and Angell were promoting." Hall may well be right, but sometimes institutional inertia alone may lead to the very slow way the changes come about. If Angell and Winternitz had been more politically adroit, their visions might have come to fruition, but that was not to be

C.E.A. Winslow wrote an undated letter to Winter around the time of the troubles:

> I thought until this afternoon when the surprise was sprung on us that the fight was won. Now it seems lost. But I hope you will not make any final decision until you know of the action of the Prudential Committee of the Corporation. When you have talked that over with the Provost or Tom Farnam you will know what to do.
>
> If there is anything I can do, let me know. You know how I feel I had the fortune to know three great men in my life, Sedgwick, Briggs, and Winternitz. I owe them more than I can tell. And Yale owes you everything for creating its Medical School and its Institute. In the long term, that will never be forgotten. In the short term, it is never forgotten by me! Or by Anne.
>
> Affectionately,
> "Charlie"

In a typwritten letter labeled "confidential," Angell wrote on Jan. 2, 1935: "If you are still disposed to withdraw your name from consideration in connection with the Deanship of the School of Medicine, I think it would be helpful if, at your convenience, you would write me a note setting forth your disposition to give all your time and energy for the present to your departmental work." Another letter from Angell, dated Jan. 4, 1935, is handwritten on stationery from the Office of the President:

Dear Dr. Winternitz:

Your personal note of this date is at hand.

I had in mind a little more explicit reference to your purpose and desire to give yourself more completely to your work in pathology and therefore your decision to withdraw, for a time anyhow, from administrative work. My whole purpose in suggesting such a note was to protect you as far as possible from unkind and unfair comment. I think that what you have written will perhaps serve the purpose.

My own attitude I think you must know. It is one of profound regret at the turn things have taken and of no little [illegible] and foreboding for the immediate future. No one, no matter how able, can step in and [run?] things as you have done. I shall turn to you constantly for counsel and advice. You have built for yourself a monument which will stand as long as the University endures and nothing can change that fact. I think your position would be so uncomfortable if you went on as Dean, that you could not wisely subject yourself to the kind of opposition which you would encounter. Sheer differences of opinion on educational issues can be objectively and dispassionately dealt with and an administrative officer can serve effectively against a considerable opposition in such matters. But the personal elements in the present situation, unreasonable and unjust as they seem to me, create quite another kind of case. If it were merely a matter of a fight, the Corporation would stand behind you and let nature take its course. But things being as they are, it seems to me that a dignified declination on your part to permit the use of your name at present as a candidate to succeed yourself as dean is the judicious course to pursue. You have carried yourself in the finest possible way and left the opposition looking a bit guilty.

How well B-J will do the job, if he goes in, I am far from sure. His greatest assurance is that he seems to be sympathetic to your policies and desirous of continuing them.

Faithfully yours,
James R. Angell

A handwritten letter from John Fulton dated Dec. 21, 1934, is of interest:

My dear Winter:

Dr. Cushing came in last evening and told me of the Wednesday meeting, and of his subsequent conference with you, B-J and the members of the Committee. I am grieved, and I keenly regret your decision to withdraw without first having a Board Meeting attended by the central university administration. There has been no open discussion of the issues involved. Harrison and I were absent from the meeting, and Cushing's breath was taken away by the closely premeditated and precipitate character of the proceedings. Cushing, Harrison, Winslow, [Busser?]

> and I–and undoubtedly others–wish open discussion and we are ready to fight for it and for you. Through agitation of an unpleasant character, there is a majority against you on the Board, but I believe that majority would dwindle and become insignificant if there were open discussion with a fair presentation of the facts in the case.
>
> I am sad, Winter, very sad, and I especially regret that a blow such as this should have come now when the school has just commenced to flower–all as a direct result of your unremitting and utterly unselfish devotion. I am fond of B-J and I am convinced that, in doing what he has done, he was sincerely assured that he was acting in your and the School's best interest, but for me, the School will never be the same if not directed by the man who made it what it is.
>
> Yours ever devotedly,
> John Fulton

Fulton had been offered a job at Oxford, but so great was the admiration for him at Yale that B-J and Winter worked together to persuade him to stay. A letter of June 13, 1935, from Winternitz (who was still dean) ran partly as follows:

> By the use of every known means of transportation and communication B.J. and I have canvassed the sentiments of the members of our Prudential Committee concerning the possibility of your leaving us

> for Oxford. . . . This morning after my conference with you I saw B.J. again and conferred with President Angell and I am now sure that you will hear from him directly that the increase in budget necessary for secretarial work and a librarian will be guaranteed by the President. . . . You are giving us all a great joy in the knowledge that you are going to continue your fine work at Yale.

Winter was not giving up his job until the very last day.

Part 3.

Life After Yale

Chapter 11. Wandering in the Wilderness

The years 1935 to 1940 saw the national economy slowly recovering. Although much of the country was in an isolationist mood, prudent observers knew there was trouble–and war–ahead. Winter was among those who were ready to dust off their old wartime skills. One of the very few refugee scientists for whom he had found a berth, Ernst Mylon, was set to work on chemical burns. As Winter reread his book on war gases, he started to think about where he fit into the picture. On the radio he discovered newscasts, which he found of great interest as he searched for a new focus for his ruined ambition. For Winter, 1935 was a year to be endured, a year of bewildering disappointment, depression masking outrage.

Fondness After the Fall

Even the effusive letters he received must have increased his bitterness at losing the chance to do more. And there were lots of them, sincere and flattering, but hardly consoling.

On January 28, 1935, Robert Maynard Hutchins wrote:

> What I want to know is did the stuffed-shirts get you at last? If they did may they be blasted eternally to hell, with them Mr. Angell + the whole sorry Yale Corporation.
>
> You must know, I know, and they know that you are the only intelligent, courageous, far-sighted man in the whole bunch.

In an undated response on his official dean's stationery, Winter replied that the was to have an office in a "rather neat but small compartment" that had been Robert Yerkes' monkey-chimpanzee station for

> the impotent and senile members of his colony. This I think must have been in anticipation for it is uninhabited and there I shall sojourn after July 1,'35.
>
> As an experiment it will be interesting for with the peace + quiet of the roof abode and the associations available through the wire screening that separates the compartments perhaps I like the simian will get inspiration from my unrestricted gaze at the many architectural beauties that have sprung up around the masterpiece the Harkness 1st quad and its magnificent Tower during this remarkable period since the Great War when your Alma Mater has engraved herself with structural steel on the educational world. . . .
>
> The King is dead, Long live the King.

In a letter dated January 25, 1935, Winter wrote John Fulton in response to what he called Fulton's "inspirational expression":

> Everything goes through its own cycle–life itself–and this I believe is fortunate. Influences live and grow or atrophy, and it may well be that the planting of the seed without too much cultivation is all that is desirable. Ultimate survival of an influence depends upon so many conditions. It may prove more effective for a plan to be lost and rediscovered if it is correct than to be grown further in an ultimately impossible medium. Time alone will tell and in the interim there is much to do.

On July 5, 1935, Anson Phelps Stokes, an old Yale ally, wrote:

> Personally I should think that with your scientific interest it would be a great relief not to have to carry longer the heavy administrative burden. At least you can feel that you have done a great piece of constructive work, not only for Yale but for the cause of Medicine in this country, and I am glad to think that it was started in an administration with which I had the privilege of being connected.

John Paul, a man remote to many, had changed his opinion of the dean. On January 21, 1935, he wrote:

I am sorry that you are not going to drive that fiery chariot which is to blaze the way along which the Yale Medical School is to trundle. I am sorry not for sentimental reasons, nor for reasons of policy, nor for reasons of politesse. I am sorry because I know that something (what shall I say) dynamic is sure to drop out of the life of the school when you step out of the carriage–or the driver's seat–which I have just mentioned. . . .

You know, for the first three years I was here you were a complete mystery to me–which was my loss, and I don't have to say how I have come to respect you, for you know all that any way.

From Robert Yerkes came a note dated May 10, 1936:

Give your genius a fair chance and a square deal. Return the idea of the Institute of Human Relations and Human Welfare Center to the incubator, and while it is maturing go ahead with something in which you can make first-rate progress.

Years later a man signed only as "Dan," who lived on Peck Road in Bethany wrote a sympathy letter to Bill Winternitz that is still pertinent:

Am still completely lost in admiration for a man who could get such outstanding people to come to Yale when he had nothing to offer but himself. Raising

> money, buildings and so forth can be done by lesser men, but to gather together the faculty he did took vision and warmth which few people can offer.

On April 25, 1949, after President James Angell's death, his widow, Kay, wrote to Polly Winternitz:

> Jim was simply superb. Winter never had a better friend. The night he told me of Winter's retirement as Dean there were tears in his eyes of grief and frustration. He said, "I would have gladly given up my own job–in fact I may have lost it by now–to prevent such an outrageous thing." He talked all evening of Winter's ability, his brilliancy, his courage and vision. When he was ill Winter's opinion was the one that always meant most.

After Abraham Flexner and Winter had their serious falling out over the Institute for Human Relations, it was some years before they were able to sit down again quietly and talk about the issues. In a predictably elegant letter to Winter, Flexner wrote:

> : All the real distinction of the Medical School began when a certain Dr. Winternitz became Dean about 1920 and his daddy [Hadley] had awfully little to do with the improvements. The fellows who did the work were Winternitz and Dean Stokes.

At the bottom of the letter ran a note, apparently in Flexner's handwriting: "I saw Hadley only once: when he warned me about Co. Ullman because he was a Jew and manufactured corsets!"

Wallace Nordstein, professor of English history at Yale, spoke for those who only knew Winter by his achievement:

> I know little about the Yale Medical School save your annual reports which I have long admired. Their high imagination, their clear headedness mark them out among reports. . . . It was refreshing and unusual. Here seemed to me to be an academic statesman. . . . I hope that your influence is still powerful here and all through medical circles in the country.

Dr. David Lyman, founder of the Gaylord Sanatarium, wrote:

> You think about twenty years in advance of most of us and I know it has made the going hard for you. I hope and trust that you will live to see many of us wake up—.

Polly's advice was, "Never let them know you care." Winter listened and tried not to show his bitterness.

A RETIREMENT PARTY

The students wanted to let Winter know they cared, so Philip Le Compte and Levin Waters called at 210 Prospect Street to invite him to a dinner in his honor. When word of the party reached the new dean's ears, approaches were made to persuade the students to invite Bayne-Jones and a few other professors, but they refused, for it was to be Winter's party.[1]

The dinner, attended by more than two hundred students, was held on February 14, 1935 in the new recreation hall at the Medical School. What a Valentine! Much later, Le Compte wrote, "The main speech of the evening was given by our classmate Rafael Arrilaga-Torrens whose eloquence was such that some of us suggested that some day he would be Speaker of the House in his native Puerto Rico"–a prophecy that came true. The students gave Winter a watch, which still keeps good time seventy-five years later!

TRYING TO FIND HIS WAY

The family gathered at Treetops for the summer, as usual. A gathering of that size made for plenty of distraction, but chances are nothing was right as far as Winter was concerned. Life went on, nevertheless. Courtships and romances were flourishing: Polly and Louise Whitney were planning the first of eight family weddings in September; Frank Griswold was the lucky man. Winter wrote to Mrs. Watson early in the fall.

> September 17, 1935
> Dear Grandma:
> There is so much to tell you that I hardly know where to begin, but the Clinical Congress is starting today and I must get over to the Law School where our first sessions are to be held. . . .
>
> As I wrote you Sunday I was entirely unaware of what was going on in New Haven concerning where I was to be located in the Medical School. Polly, however, seemed to be interested and after supper we came over here to find that she and Freddy and Miss Bishop together had provided me with an excellent secretary and had decorated several rooms with all the things that I liked the best at 210 and at my old office, the little one. So I am really very comfortable in my pleasant surroundings and seem very happy about the coming year's work.

Winter was trying to figure out what to do with the rest of his life. John Paul wrote how despondent he became as he realized that "during his 15 years as Dean, he had been so busy that he had neglected to keep up with the science of pathology to the extent that he felt himself practically unable to go back to its teaching or even to the running of the department." Paul noted, nevertheless, that he hid his bitterness. Winter spent many hours in the laboratory with an eye to finishing his book, *The Biology of Arteriosclerosis,* which was published in 1937. He remained director of the Institute of Human Relations until 1950, and focused more than ever on teaching and his broad view of medical education and administration. William Wiedemayer recorded that he

> brought in experts, active in the fields they discussed. We learned about T.B. from Bruno Gerstel, pathologist to a T.B. sanitarium. Syphilis was discussed by a practicing syphilologist. Best of all for neoplasia we had three lectures, the first by Dr. Strong whose work with inbred strains of mice demonstrated the genetic factor in carcinogenesis. Second we had Dr. Durand-Reynals on the viral etiology of neoplasia (in animals). On the third day Harry Greene, after slyly poking fun at the research of the two previous speakers, expounded his, at that time revolutionary, views on the unique anatomy of malignant cells as demonstrated by their survival after heterologous transplant. To really impress us he produced from the pocket of his lab coat a live guinea pig with human cancer–wow!

Winter couldn't give up his habit of cruising the corridors of the Medical School and the hospital dressed in a lab coat to find out what was going on. He knew that "the boys" had a running crap game in the cellar, but as long as it didn't interfere with their work and they didn't get caught, he let it go. He saw what needed painting, what needed cleaning, and reported on it. Coughing repeatedly, he often scowled at those he met, slamming doors shut with his heel because they should not have been left part-open. He was as angry outside as inside.[2]

Winter had the time to read newspapers. A letter to Jane dated January 17, 1936:

> The next shock was the increase in the national debt . . . from five and a half billion to eleven billion. What's a billion more or less to say nothing of half a dozen of them. Certainly the situation is getting complex. What with Japan pulling out of the naval parley, Italy claiming a victory on a forty mile front in Ethiopia and continuing its bombing of hospitals, and the crash of the transcontinental passenger plane. . . . Think what a bombing plane could do to our metropolis if all action was converted into static by the destruction of powerplants! It would be worse than when the well goes dry at Treetops.

ELIZABETH'S ILLNESS

Elizabeth (Buff), struggling with mental illness, had to drop out of Vassar for treatment at Silver Hill, a sanitarium in western Connecticut. Winter went to see her after she had been there a week and wrote the rest of the family: "It is just too bad to be sick, and it is such an unusual thing for us to have one of the children incapacitated that it is hard to know how to act. I . . . lack the understanding of illness in spite of the fact that I am theoretically a doctor."

After she left Silver Hill, Elizabeth was treated at the Henry Phipps Psychiatric Clinic in Baltimore. Winter planned frequent trips with stopovers there and wrote to her nearly every day. When, unsure of himself, he told his children that "it is hard to know how to act," he was being unusually open with them. Buff's illness was a humbling experience that made him wonder if he had contributed to her condition, for she was the most like him of all his children. He had remained both passionate and remote, but he finally learned to control his rages pretty well in public, even if less well at home.

By mid-November 1936, Elizabeth's doctors thought she was well enough to consider sending her home, but Winter didn't think it was advisable and vetoed the idea.

> Perhaps I can make myself clearer if you realize that New Haven is a reasonably small community, and that no definite program has been developed for Elizabeth when she returns here, and that our household is an extremely complicated one. It will be very hard for us to assume responsibility for Elizabeth until there is reasonable security and a well organized program for her to carry out.

On the surface, Winter's decision seems harsh. Quite possibly he was remembering the years when Helen was an invalid and the household revolved around her care and comfort. More likely, he felt that the environment at "210" would not allow for the healing atmosphere that Buff needed. Lately the front hall had seemed more like a busy hotel lobby. Winter and Polly had extended their hospitality to the Corning family for weeks at a time when Mr. Corning was undergoing treatment at the New Haven Hospital. Winter visited him there every day, occasionally complaining that attention to Corning was cutting into his time. He no doubt expected a handsome endowment for the Medical School, but there is no record of such a gift.

SURVEY OF SPELMAN COLLEGE

In the winter of 1936 Winter was asked by the Roosevelt Administration to consult on a project in Georgia that took him away from New Haven. He described the trip in a letter to his daughter Mary:

> There is a large federal development going on down there in association with Atlanta University and involves some half dozen city blocks between Spelman and Morehouse Colleges which have been cleared and are being improved now by a federal grant of something over two million dollars as a housing project. My job is to try to institute a health program in this experimental development and it will be interesting to see what the possibilities are.

As mentioned in Chapter 8, Winter stopped off in Baltimore on his way south to visit Buff and his mother. After an "uneventful" train ride to Atlanta, he was "met on the platform by a distinguished looking mulatto gentleman" who "drove me up through the campuses of the colleges and University to an exquisite building."

> The colleges . . . constitute a group built on three hills adjacent to each other just on the outskirts of Atlanta. I think my memory is correct that these take in some seventeen odd acres, about the size of the big field above the garage: lovely rolling country, beautiful landscape, and with exquisite buildings by Gamble Rogers, much simpler than the Yale buildings and made after the design of the divinity school group here. So that the setting is delightful, a very beautiful chapel, a very satisfactory library, good science buildings, etc. etc. . . .
>
> Within this setting, there is the new development which I went down to aid, the huge federal development that has arisen on the cleared land lying immediately adjacent to Atlanta University. The houses are almost complete and will accommodate 2500 people in some six hundred and fifty odd single entry, two story apartments with many common facilities. . . .
>
> The three days were extremely interesting. I spent two and a half of them making observations and interviews, and the other half in writing a detailed report of a social engineering scheme for the housing

> project and its utilization as an exploratory laboratory for the University, then . . . took the night train back [to Baltimore]. I saw Elizabeth and Dr. Meyer again. She is fine, and Dr. Meyer feels she is doing very well indeed. . . . [After a] three-hour session in New York with the General Education board, on the Atlanta situation, [I] got the ten o'clock train to New Haven. . . . I wanted you to have a little bit of the bloom of this very pleasant interim experience of mine.

WHY WERE THERE NO OFFERS?

Where were Winter's allies and friends were when he needed them for support and solace, and a new career, after his fall? Harvey Cushing had contacts in Boston and Washington, yet we found no evidence that he smoothed the way for the man who brought him back to New Haven. One can only conjecture why Winter's career reached its peak as dean, and why he never found another academic position of equal authority, although he was still relatively young.

Some thought Winter's marriage to Pauline Whitney made him content with his new life, as the letters quoted in Chapter 10 suggest. However, we find this explanation unconvincing, given Winter's singleminded quest for authority and his dedication to changing the world of medicine. Indeed, his annual reports testify to his increasing interest in university policy rather than in the

Medical School alone. The expected progress of such a hard-nosed administrator would have been to move on to some other deanship or university presidency, but it never happened. It seems probable, as we have already suggested, that Winter would have loved to have become a university president, like his younger colleague Robert Maynard Hutchins. Whether university presidencies were open to Jews at that time is an open question.

In any event, the question why Winter did not receive an offer at least equal to the position he had lost–to him it was a great loss, despite his silence on the subject–suggests other answers. Everyone was aware of Winter's difficult personality, the antagonism he aroused by his contempt for the ideas of others, and his frequent failure to keep his word. So his fall must have elicited more than a little of the malicious satisfaction that the Germans call Schadenfreude. That the Prudential Committee voted not to reappoint him for a fourth term says something about his lack of popularity at Yale. Another factor may have been his heart attack, which must have been the last straw.

CHEST PAIN, REST, AND RECOVERY

Sometime in the early spring of 1936, Winter developed chest pain. The last week in April Bob Hutchins came to town for a few days, and Winter reported: "He is the same delightful, upstanding, outspoken personality, and we do seem to understand each other pretty well. It is a tremendous pleasure to discuss things with him." Nevertheless, for the first time Winter had to admit that anticipation of stress gave him pain and that he was very tired after a long meeting with people from the Carnegie Corporation. A nap followed by relaxation at an "amusing farce," *Three Men on a Horse,* and a good night's sleep temporarily revived him. Yet a month later, he still did not have his strength back. Witness the following letter to Bill, who was not particularly happy at Andover and would have preferred to continue his education in Switzerland. Bill was feeling predictably rebellious and wrote home as little as possible. Winter's sarcasm often came out in his speech, but it was uncommon in his writing before 1935. He could not contain his bitterness.

> May 23, 1936
> Dear Bill:
> I suppose you are still at Andover, but it is far away and as it requires more than two days for the Graf Hindenburg to bring mail from the German port to the New Jersey station it is obvious that we can not expect to hear from you very frequently. Moreover you are undoubtedly an extremely busy man and your effort to make up for any deficiency that crowded in on your scholastic work during the year makes your time reasonably unavailable for writing.

REGAINING HIS STRIDE

Not all the news was bad, however. One night after the lights were out at 210 Prospect, Freddie rapped on the bedroom door and handed Winter a telegram from Jane telling him that she had won the prize for the senior who had done the best work in physiology and zoology during her four years at Vassar. Winter's fatherly pride was equaled by his pleasure that his daughter couldn't wait to share the good news with him–and he couldn't wait to crow about it!

As Winter began to recover and regain his resilience, his letters show that he could not long–at that stage, at least–remain depressed.

> October 12, 1936
> Dear Buff:
> . . . Friday night we had a party at 210. Dr. Mendel's successor, a very charming man from England, who also held some important positions in Canada and Philadelphia, has arrived in New Haven and we felt we wanted to have Dr. Long, for that is his name, and his wife meet some of the people in the Medical School and the rest of the University. Polly, in her inimitable fashion, arranged a party a week or two ahead but the epidemic of respiratory and alimentary upsets that come in the fall caused one and

> then another of the first group to drop out, so that on Friday at noon Polly had to find four new guests: but of course she did . . . and we had a charming party. Mrs. Cushing and Mrs. Day were there . . . [as well as] Dr. Thompson and his wife. Dr. Thompson is a very delightful person who is working with Dr. Cushing. He is a Harvard medical man, and told us a funny story. One night while he was a resident at the Brigham he went out for a walk. It was rather dark, and he thought he heard the burr of an auto starter. Finally, after listening a while he felt the driver was having trouble . . . and offered to help. The driver consented and asked him to get in and try himself. So he got in, and thought the first thing was to see if the switch was turned on. He lit a match and saw not only that the switch was not turned on, but also that the driver was President Lowell of Harvard University. Perhaps this is the reason they denied him a driver's license recently.

He ended the letter with the news that Freddy had found his métier as an antique dealer, and a very successful one at that. Freddy was always good copy, and extremely thoughtful besides.

Winter was trying to regain the laboratory skills that he had allowed to atrophy during his tenure as dean.

> October 19, 1936
> Dear Tom:
> . . . Saturday and Sunday we had remarkable success over here. We uncovered one of the important links in our investigation, and now it seems as though a good deal of the problem that we started with originally was unraveled. . . . I think we were all hyper excited, so much so that we will have to make a very definite effort to come back to earth. The thrill of investigation certainly is much more stimulating than any other I know anything about.

210 Prospect Street may not have been the best place for Elizabeth to convalesce, but it provided a nurturing environment for Levin Waters when he fell sick with tuberculosis. After receiving his M.D. from Yale, Waters had applied to Johns Hopkins, planning to become a family doctor in the Green Spring Valley outside of his native Baltimore. Winter asked him why he wanted to do that, when he could stay in New Haven and become a pathologist. Waters was thrilled. He still would have no money, but room, board, uniforms, and laundry would be free. What is money, he asked himself, compared with the privilege of working for the Great Man? And work he did, day and night, finally becoming resident in pathology.

The cumulative effects of working his way through medical school and up through the ranks from intern to resident, took its toll in the form of tuberculosis, a common occurrence among the junior staff in those days.

Winter brought Waters home to 210 Prospect Street and put him to bed. He personally climbed the long flight of stairs to bring his patient eggnogs and ice cream to start the cure while a bed was being found for him at Gaylord Sanitarium in nearby Wallingford. Winter and Polly drove out to Wallingford to see Waters almost every week, bringing wine jelly, books, news of the department, and sometimes other visitors, preferably young and female.[3]

WINTER AND HIS FAMILY

Winter had an unusual relationship with his parents, and consequently with his children. Once Helen died, the strains within the family quickly became apparent. Winter's children were now his main concern, or at least the major focus of his attention and ambition, while he himself was at loose ends.

In any case, close relationships with kin were never Winter's passion. We have noted earlier that as a young boy he was not particularly close to his mother. Once or twice in his letters Winter refers to something they did together, but overall their relationship hardly resembles the legendary devotion of the Jewish boy to his mother, whom Freud praised as the font of self-confidence. A letter of June 1, 1932, addressed to Tom, contains a rare mention of visiting Mrs. Winternitz:

> When I got to Baltimore I went to see my mother. She seemed really quite aged since I had seen her last which was a year ago, but on the whole she appeared cheerful and well. Ruth was home. She did not go with the rest of the family to the country because she was not feeling well, but being Memorial Day and a holiday all the others took advantage of it and went to their summer place to get it ready for occupancy, which I suppose will be in the near future.

A letter of March 31, 1933, records another brief visit: "I went then to see my mother. She is well and I spent a pleasant hour with her and my sister and her children, who are growing up to be nice youngsters."

Of Winter's father, Carl Winternitz, we know no more than is related in Chapter 1. Winter's apparent lack of interest in his early medical background is surprising. One would have expected the dean of a medical school and the teacher of medical students to speak of his father-the-doctor, the way Lewis Thomas did in his essays. It is all the more surprising that Winter remains so silent about his father's career as an insurance physician. Indeed, we find no references whatsoever to his father in his files, apart from a lone recollection that he taught his son Milton to play chess.

We know of one postcard of a Jewish cemetery somewhere in Eastern Europe, which Mary Cheever described as presumably the grave of a relative. Mary, who never knew her father's father, was told that he came to America along with a brother named Felix, who had been with the Vienna Symphony Orchestra. She had the impression that her father despised her grandfather's medicine because it was nonscientific and "homeopathic." Winter had very little, if any, religious education; we do not even know if he had a bar mitzvah.

Winter's sister Irene married into the Bachrach clan, who describe her as dull, prudish, and cold, confirming Winter's only known comment about her. They recall, however, that she worshipped her brother and was much hurt that Winter never picked up the phone to talk with her. He is said, nevertheless, to have done his duty by her. One story sounds typical: that he would send Irene a poinsettia at Christmastime, although she and her family were practicing Jews. "Here it comes again," the family would laugh. In general, surviving relatives describe Winternitz as niggardly, cold, and largely uncaring, which they ascribe to his bitterness at being passed over at Johns Hopkins because he was Jewish.

In letters to his children, Winter refers to his mother as "*my* mother," never as "*your* grandmother," whom the Bachrachs remember as delightful and fun, with a great sense of humor. He is far more inclusive in referring to the Watson grandparents as "Grandpa and Grandma" Watson, but there is no mention of "Grandma Winternitz." In fact, his children recall nothing at all about their paternal grandparents and have little, if any, memory of the paternal side of the family. Mary vaguely remembered a shadowy little person dressed in black visiting at 210 Prospect

Street. Harry Zimmerman, who claimed to be very close to the family, stated that Winter kept his children from seeing his relatives in Baltimore and did not encourage them to know much about the Jewish side of the family. While Helen was alive, she corresponded with her mother-in-law, keeping her informed about family news. There is a reference to the senior Mrs. Winternitz visiting before Helen became ill. After Helen's death, it was up to Winter to maintain what ties there were.

One is forced to conclude that Winter was neither a good nor a dutiful son. He went alone to his mother's funeral, without his children. Even there, he is described by the Baltimore relatives as brusque and impatient, saying, "Let's get the show on the road." The senior Winternitzes are said to be buried in the Hebrew cemetery on Belair Road in Baltimore.

WINTER AS A FATHER

Winter had few role models to help him become a father. His own father played little or no role in his conscious reminiscences. Curiously, although Winter is said to have been very close to "Popsy" Welch, there is no evidence, in the archives at Yale at least, of close or frequent conversation or correspondence between them once Winter left Baltimore. Winter, like Erik Erikson, was his own creation, in a sense his own son. Although his relationship to Levin Waters is largely unrecorded, because they worked so closely together, it was Waters who filled in for Bill, serving as number-one son when Bill couldn't be there.

That Winter was a distant and forbidding father there can be little doubt. The letters he began to dictate to his children after Helen's death are full of formal, command-like instructions, along with advice and reflections that sometimes mirror his own career. One of the daughters remarked that she destroyed her letters from Winternitz because she found them so hateful. Dictated to his secretary and carbon-copied to each child, those "bulletins" were impersonal accounts of such banal topics as the flowers on Prospect Street. Most astounding of all, when Winter decided to marry Polly Whitney, their proposed marriage came as a surprise to his children, who had had no inkling of how far the relationship had developed.

Except for his first letter to the children after Helen's death, quoted in Chapter 6, it is hard to find much fondness remembered or expressed. More concerned with their achievements than with their personal lives, Winter regarded his children as trophies. He expected them to get high marks in school and succeed in life, and they did. Nor did Winter's children return very much in the way of love. One daughter flatly stated that she hated her father, while the others give the impression that although they respected what Winter did, theirs was far from a close family..

Mary Cheever felt that her father was a stranger to his children, a distant man who almost never discussed anything personal. As an example, when she complained to him about a boyfriend whom she didn't like, his only response was, "Well he got three good meals from us anyway." Mary was the rebel of the family, and the letters she wrote as a young woman were the most exuberant of all.

Elizabeth (Buff) was remembered as "overweight and strange" in college, although friends describe the mature Buff as a warm, friendly, blond woman. Winter was crushed when she developed schizophrenia; her mental illness occasioned considerable discussion about whether she should be sterilized, given her apparently great sexual appetite. Winter favored that course, which for uncertain reasons was never carried out. In commenting on this, Susan Cheever, Mary's daughter, noted that Buff's two children both became doctors. "She fought for the right to decide her own fate, she fought for the right to have children, and she won." Susan also evidences some of the anger that the Winternitz children have passed on to their own children:

Much of Winter's abrasive manner in public and his temper tantrums carried over into his private life. Susan Cheever, who has wrestled with her Winternitz heritage, describes her grandfather's "terrifying didactic methods," which at times reduced the grandchildren to tears. An ambitious and distant man who cut himself off from most intimate emotional contact, Winter did not mellow with age. As the children matured, they experienced the same kind of strained relationships with their father as he had with the medical faculty at Yale.

"Winter's increasing influences started to appear as a malignant power on my mother and on the chemistry of our family," Susan writes. John Cheever stopped going to Treetops, she adds, and by the time Winter died, "there was nothing left of his friendship with my father except disappointment." (What a sad parallel to Winter's professional disappointments between 1930 and 1935.) Even now, Treetops arouses only mixed feelings in the Winternitz children. After Winter and Polly's deaths, it became a kind of "temple" for them and the grandchildren, one they maintain despite the unhappy memories of Polly that keep them from going there very often.

One son believes that Winter "didn't have a childhood": he was a little guy who played football either as guard or quarterback, and took to "spitting at the guy on the other side." Never particularly well coordinated, he was awkward in sports and was not a good tennis player. Winter really didn't do many things "for fun," around his own family at least. Everything had to have some purpose, from improving the Prospect Street house or organizing affairs at Treetops to running the chicken farm at Treetops in a businesslike manner. He bought Yale football tickets regularly, but rarely went to a game. As one son relates, "Just imagine him sitting through a football game!" The "steam engine in pants" never stopped chugging along.

Chapter 12. The War Years

In these more cynical times, it is not easy to conceive of men going to work for the government for a dollar a year when there is no war on, out of patriotic zeal. In the 1930s, however, many were so motivated, because Washington was the place to be for idealistic liberals.

National Academy of Science

Even before the war, Winter seized every chance to dash off to Washington, particularly to the National Academy of Science, where he found the life of authority and excitement he loved so well. Chartered by Congress in 1863, the academy advised on scientific investigation during the Civil War: one of its committees worked on the "iron-clad" vessels, the *Monitor* and the *Merrimack*. In 1916, just before the United States entered World War I, the federal government founded the National Research Council (NRC). Both the academy and council are still housed in a beautiful neoclassical "Temple of Science," dedicated in 1924 on the Mall, facing the Lincoln Memorial.

After World War I, the belligerents put chemical warfare behind them as rapidly as possible.[1] Great stocks of chemicals were dumped at sea, in a manner incomprehensible today. At the League of Nations, thirty-nine nations signed a treaty outlawing gas warfare, but the United States refused to sign, which made it legal for government agencies to reopen the investigation of war gases.

Until 1940, the Division of Medical Science, a subsection of the National Academy, acted in an advisory capacity to the surgeon general. In 1941, President Franklin Roosevelt created the Office of Scientific Research and Development. The Medical Science Division developed a series of committees to deal with medical problems arising from the war; one of the first was the Committee on the Treatment of Gas Casualties. The names of Harrison, Fulton, Blake, and others from Yale appear on the list. Winter had been lobbying for the chairmanship of the committee, convinced that he was the obvious choice. He accepted the offer quickly and agreed to serve for token compensation. Among his priorities were speeding up communication in research, treatment, and training, and establishing a permanent liaison with the Royal Society in Britain.

The NRC was fun for Winter, who loved the sense of urgency. Office space was provided for him at the Academy of Science building, and a suitable job category, technical aide, was already in place on the personnel roster, permitting Winter to immediately call on his protégé, Levin Waters, for help. Forty-eight hours after being summoned to Washington, Waters wrote that he was

> securely situated in an office–in Washington D.C.–as Technical Aide to the Committee on the Treatment of Gas Casualties. I was charged with the responsibility of knowing immediately, besides everything else on the subject, a language which belonged only to the military and whose nouns consisted almost entirely of such meaningful expressions as "H," "semi-H," "HS," "H-I," "CG," "Dick," "yperite," "yellow cross," "green cross," "lost," "Klop," "tabum," "1080," "1120," and so on. The Army did provide a sort of Rosetta stone to some of this in the form of a long poem of doggerel which contained such gems as:
>
> Never take some chances if
> Garlic you should strongly sniff
> Don't think Mussolini's passed
> Man, you're being mustard-gassed!
>
> Imagine the bigwigs of research having to deal with this sort of thing! But they did. That was how everyone learned in the early days. Chemical warfare medicine differed from other branches of military medicine in that there was no background in civilian medicine. Only a few scientists were still active who

> had witnessed the chemical warfare of 1915-1918, or had taken part in investigations on the subject. It was necessary in 1941 to take stock and then to prepare for the use of chemical agents old or new.

With Waters in place, Winter set out to tour the leading universities to see what was already being done. MIT faculty were eager for financial backing, and Ernest Lawrence of Harvard stopped by New Haven to assure Winter that Harvard's cyclotron was stronger than MIT's. Winternitz managed to work out a cooperative agreement between the two rival Cambridge institutions.

Once a team was engaged in war work, the first problem was security. Investigators had to be investigated and cleared "soonest" for top-secret access. The investigators were mostly already known to Winter and his colleagues, so security was largely a question of judgment. There were no obvious leaks, but plenty of paranoia. It was so easy to be suspicious of a coworker one didn't like.

The built-in differences between the military and civilians led to intense rivalry. The word *obey* carried weight with the servicemen, whereas *think* was the operative word for the scientists. Men and women who had chosen a life of academic freedom and independent thinking had an uneasy feeling that their inner thoughts were stamped "TOP SECRET." They had to lock up bench notes, and their research was directed and classified. Winter knew how they felt, having "been there" in the

First War, and proved effective in dealing with these problems. He had also learned much from his travails as dean.

Winter's interests rippled far from war gases; as usual, ideas spawned during the war would join the mainstream afterwards. He had foreseen the need to study chemical burns when he hired Ernst Mylon at Yale for his knowledge of the subject. Blood, plasma, blood substitutes, dried plasma, and reactions to blood substitutes were all investigated. Shock was another subject of vital importance. Experiments to protect the eye from gas sprays led to an interest in the cornea. Tangential studies grew out of the effects of war gases and their antidotes on disease processes. Indeed, the observations made on war gases, especially mustard gas, led to the basic research on chemotherapy for cancer.

Waters liked to tell about the day he drove Winter out from Washington to Edgewood Arsenal, a World War I relic in Maryland, to see what would be needed to reactivate the place for chemical warfare research. On the way back to Washington, Winter squeaked, "There is nothing there but a pair of mangy old goats and a desiccated Colonel!" Nevertheless, by the time they reached Washington Winter had a plan for rebuilding the arsenal.

Winternitz and Col. John Wood were responsible for setting up war gas research in the United States. Colonel Wood (not the "dessicated Colonel") was endowed with the sort of raw materials that Winter liked to polish into a smooth-running showpiece. He was accessible and, like

Bayne-Jones and Waters, a southerner. Winter outranked Wood on the organizational chart, but they treated each other as equals.

When the Gas Casualties Commission was being formed, it was proposed that Winter be given the rank of general in order to have authority, but he refused, commenting to his son Tom that he would lose all autonomy and would have to obey orders! But he could think of someone else admirably suitable to wear a star–Bayne- Jones.

TRAVEL TO WARTIME ENGLAND

The following summer, 1942, the British urgently requested a high-level team to consult on war gases, so Winternitz and Wood were assigned to go to England together.[2] Before leaving New Haven, Winter received a letter from John Fulton by campus mail, detailing the interpersonal relationships and personalities of the people he would be meeting, advising whom to contact and whom to avoid–a veritable road map through the mine field that led to the prime minister's ear. Fulton urged Winter to read the letter before leaving, "and for heaven's sake don't take it with you."

Winter kept a detailed journal of the trip. Starting with the red tape of leaving on a mission, it was "hurry up and wait." Crossing the Atlantic took three days by flying boat, in the discomfort of what appear to have been bucket seats, with stops in Newfoundland and Ireland. The latter gave Winter and Wood a chance to eat a good meal, rest, and clean up. By the time they reached London, the two men were refreshed and very excited. After they presented themselves at the American Embassy, a doctor took them back to his flat for a drink and then on to dinner at the English-Speaking Union, where they met more people they knew. Later that evening they attended a meeting of the Royal Medical Society. Winter and Wood felt welcome–and they had connected with their British and American colleagues.

When Winter tells about their accommodations in London, he nearly always comments on the food, soap, towels, and the person who is serving him.[3] A typical comment: "These breakfasts and the environment are not attractive (the luetic osteochondrotic waitress adds nothing)." In the evenings he and Wood walked the streets, looking for where the latest bombs had landed. Winter was invited out to dinner fairly often, the conversation running to war gases interspersed with reminiscences. He was impressed by the efficiency and practicality of the British, noting that tea was always served on schedule.

Wood and Winter began making the rounds of people and places. They discussed a projected *Medical Manual of Chemical Warfare* in detail, visited first-aid stations and hospitals, and gathered a lot of practical information for setting up Edgewood Arsenal. On July 29, 1942, Winter recorded, "To Guys Hospital with Col. Wood."

They observed how civilian casualties were handled, the special training of civilian doctors for gas emergencies, the decontamination center, and therapy after war-gas exposure. "Briefly the educational system for civilian physicians is of the simplest variety," he reported. The next day he mentioned experiencing his first air raid. "Another raid last night–our third alert and a few shots, then the 'all clear.' We were up at seven, packed overnight bags and had breakfast, elaborated by sugar and marmalade gotten yesterday on our ration cards at Selfridge's. We had a bit of cheese and biscuit and chocolate also. These supplement our diet and are very welcome."

Winter's journal is interspersed with such nuggets as meeting "a tall young man, Dr. Short." He recorded many details about the doctors' training courses that he believed could be copied in the United States. The British were also testing the physiological effects of altitude on aviators and experimenting with oxygen. They knew why protective clothing was important and which kind was most effective, and they had learned refined decontamination techniques.

A few days later, Winter and Wood spent a day at Mill Hill, a welcome intellectual stimulus between two very intense periods of work. At Porton, an important government research center in the Salisbury Plain, they met the director of the Physiology Section, Surgeon Captain Fairley, who made an impression "when he showed us a well worn copy of the War Gas Pathology book on his desk and admired the illustrations made, as he said, a quarter of a century ago and never surpassed. What a splendid way to greet a person. I felt at home at once."

Winter records a discussion of which gas should be used in the current war. More than fifty years later, it is disconcerting to read. The words *protection* and *decontamination* appear again and again. The need for better communication between the British and the Americans was underlined. (PWK, classified as "most secret in America," turned out to be the code for beeswax!) They agreed to share information freely, a spirit of cooperation that lasted throughout the war.

Apparently, Winter was not aware of the hunger for more protein during severe rationing, but Waters (who went to England in the summer of 1944) noted that the technicians repeatedly took experimental animals home to put into the stew. That section was working on all manner of ointments, washes, and experimental conditions to protect from contamination and to treat it. At Oxford they visited Dr. Solly Zuckerman, then a very young man, who was investigating a number of destructive agents, including "water blasts," which were just being set up in the United States. Zuckerman's laboratory was small, and he was studying a wide variety of problems. Afterward, Winter wrote,

> we went to Florey's home and were told something of pennecillium. It was so interesting that we asked to see the set up and made an appointment to go to the laboratory the next day. This in essence is the story.

> Some years ago Dr. Alexander Fleming, bacteriologist at London University, noted a pennecillium mold growing on one of his streptococcus plates. The strep did not grow in the vicinity of the mold. He cultured this mold and it is still one of the varieties used extensively. In the fall of 1938 Florey and one of his associates took up the problem rather by chance . . . .

Professor Florey promised to send Winter a resume of the cases treated. Winter wanted to find out all he could about penicillin. Before leaving for England, he had gone for a walk with his son Bill. Waiting until no one was near them, he said in a loud whisper, "Penicillium!" After one last stop at Dr. Florey's laboratory,[4]

> the ride back–late Sunday after Bank Holiday Monday–was what might have been expected. First Class tickets just didn't count and we stood from Oxford to London.–But everybody was cheerful whether it was their elbow in your side or your foot on their bunion.

Winter mentions groping about in the blackout with a flashlight and braving the crowds on the London Underground. At the ICI and the Sutton Oak plants, he and Wood investigated the medical effects and manufacture of HS, S, Lewisite, and HCN. They learned down-to-earth, practical information and visited the "ambulatory," a small clinic and infirmary in the plants. Winter reported every detail; he and Colonel Wood were getting what they came for

August 13 found them in Glasgow, where they were shown burns in various stages. Glasgow was a good place to observe the spread of infection because troop ships landed there, emptying their sick bays into the hospitals. They also saw treatment of mustard gas lesions, with either "penicillium" or a sulfonamide derivative, Albucid, in staphylococcus-infected eyes.

Back in London. Winter made his final round of calls, the most heartwarming of which was on Dr. Alexander Fleming.

> It should be recalled that he originally observed the antagonism of penicillium for streptococcus, etc., while working with Florey and that years later Florey picked up the work, as he says, selected as one of several possible problems. Fleming, I am told, has written the story during the past year as a letter to the Journal of Bacteriology. . . . He is much interested in antagonisms of bacteria, a field that looks very fruitful.— It was obvious that our visit pleased him, that his gruff Scottish mannerism covers a very sensitive disposition and that he, like all men, wants an occasional pat on the shoulder. He should be given a break, brought to the United States for a visit and a few talks.

Fulton saw to it that Dr. Fleming did visit Yale after the war.

On their last evening in England, Winter and Wood dined at 63 Harley Street with Sir Stewart and Lady Duke-Elder, both "charming and vital medical people." They talked shop and discussed mutual friends among the medical greats. "The good scotch and good food was exceptional even among the many pleasant ones we have had here in Great Britain." The following day Winter and his papers were ready to leave.

EDGEWOOD ARSENAL

Colonel Wood and Winter had been traveling together more than forty days, sometimes sharing a room, and apparently always sharing a point of view that had been well aired, since they both liked to talk.[5] This must have been one of the reasons they were able to build Edgewood Arsenal and set up the training program there so quickly and effectively. Among other lessons in England, Winter had learned to become a team player.

Judging from their correspondence, the two men were of one mind most of the time. They agreed on the need for (1) buildings for laboratories, training, and administration; (2) housing for students and some staff; (3) testing grounds; (4) an infirmary, and (5) housing for test animals. Winter and Wood had to design their training course, assemble their staff, and fight the classification battle, which they did right up to the dedication of the new "campus" less than two years later.

Their experiences in Britain had taught them that the closer one was to the front, the less one fussed with non-essentials. Research was to be focused on protection and treatment of gas casualties, with testing and training to follow. Their report stressed the need to compile all the literature related to warfare chemicals and make it available to those working in the field. They recommended that "centralization of medical work in proximity with other major aspects of Chemical Warfare be planned as an immediate and essential need." This would be Waters's chief assignment.

As a civilian, Winter could sprinkle his conversations with talk about the Blitz, blackouts, bombers, and other nonclassified experiences, while Colonel Wood could wear another star on his ETO ribbon. Whenever the opportunity arose, Winter enjoyed telling about rubbing elbows with "Sir This" and "Admiral That," staying in the Lodge at Trinity College, Oxford, mentioning a London club by name, and describing the occasional vintage port or memorable meal enjoyed in wartime–all of which testified to the importance the British placed on the pair and their mission.

Wood and Winternitz corresponded regularly, if circumspectly, in what turns out to be the richest source of information about Winter during the war years. The constraints of security in wartime made Winter limit his personal correspondence more than ever to general topics, though exchanges such as the following with I.S. Ravdin–who was stationed in Louisiana and a member of Winter's advisory board–illuminate the scene.

> My dear Winter–,
> It was good to get your letter. It has been a long time between drinks as far as we are concerned. I have no idea that we will go to England but if we do, I shall do my best to hold Elliott down. I think I can. My guess is that we will be shipped elsewhere. We are very "hot" at present and I hope you can "snoop" out our destination. What was the use of working in Washington for two years if I can't get a little dope.
> I am sure that when in Philadelphia, you will give Betty the cheer she will need. I know of no one who can do it better. You are at once the most provocative and loveable fellow I know.
> My best to you
> Rav

> September 25, 1942
> Dear Rav:
> . . . I certainly did enjoy getting your note when I reached New Haven this morning after two days in Washington and prior to leaving this evening for Washington–please note—it's the same Washington! But between you and me and the lamp-post, things are getting pretty well set now, so your Gas Officers will know something. Johnny Wood, who is in [Gen-

> eral] Magee's office, through a little conniving on the part of some of your friends, is a corker. The information we got abroad is being formulated into action, and classes are under way. They are going to be good too. We still have one little job to complete, it involves moving a fellow with spread eagles [Bayne-Jones] up and out of the way. I have got my fingers crossed, but I am hopeful. The crowd working with our committee is good and results are coming in. Your old friend Newt Richards is a rock of Gibraltar. He's playing ball in good style. . . . Yesterday I stopped by to see my young medico [Bill] in Baltimore. He seems to be taking it in his stride, but then being six feet, he's got quite a stride.

Bayne-Jones, who loved the formality and discipline of military life, had spent enough time in uniform to slip back easily into the mold. He was accepted by career officers far more easily than most civilians were. Winter worked to get him a commission as colonel and a quick promotion to general, reasoning that this plan would serve the country and himself best. Bayne-Jones had a military bearing and was comfortable with protocol. His manner of speaking was quiet, calm, and collected. In short, he made a good general.

One of the first teaching tools prepared primarily for training officers in the field was a filmstrip of slides and photos illustrating the cardinal features of chemical warfare. For training enlisted men, it was later adapted into a very graphic comic-book format. As for research, the question arose, Where to get the best rabbit cages and good breeding stock? They asked Harry Greene, Winter's colleague at Yale, who advised them to write to W.J. Seifried, but only if they addressed him as "Judge." Greene explained that Seifried was only a judge of rabbits!

Ground was broken at Edgewood for the laboratory and by August they were ready to work on treating the skin for Lewisite in temporary labs. Winter seems to have been removed from making moral decisions about experimenting on human beings. According to a recent publication of the National Academy Press, *Veterans at Risk,* the policy was set by the military: "The specific role of the Committee on Gas Casualties was to review and supervise 23 grants dealing with chemical warfare agents." Edgewood became the center for chemical warfare research, testing, teaching, and training. Winter lectured the officers about shock during their training period, and Wood wrote that the students loved him.

A report titled *Summary of the Committee on the Treatment of Gas Casualties,* dated April 16, 1943, has a full page of organization and two pages of accomplishments, showing that "we had brought together approximately ten thousand references, summaries of all important work made available to contracting teams, over seven hundred illustrations of the effect of chemical warfare agents assembled and being used for teaching, film strips prepared, also for teaching and the files were being updated on a daily basis." The last pages of the report focus on perfecting therapies. The fact that Walt Disney was tapped to design the gas masks for children to be made at Edgewood is nowhere mentioned.

As the gas studies and teaching hit a rhythm, Edgewood started to focus on insect and rodent control, which were particularly important in the Pacific theater. DDT was used with abandon. After the war, when Winter gave a radio talk about DDT, he received only one negative letter from a "Mr. Fink of the Duzmore Products Co." The letter blasted him, warning Winter that DDT was dangerous stuff.[6]

OTHER WARTIME TRAVEL

During the war years Winter traveled so much that he memorized the train schedule between Boston and Washington; he also knew the best trains to Chicago. His technical aide, C. Chester Stock, ran the Washington office. Winter was in his element, delighting in every detail. He wrote a note to Stock asking him to

> Please see Flexner on the two following points,
> 1. Fenn would like to study the influence of increased interalveolar pressure on the blood reservoir of the lung.— He says it will be simple to do but wants Flexner to know about it. Tell Flexner I said it's a very important contribution.

2. Ask Flexner to please give you the name of the deodorant he said made a remarkable difference in the happiness of the psychiatric staff by eliminating the disagreeable stimuli to the olfactory tract.

Winter was very precise:

October 5, 1942
Dear Stock:
. . . I shall go to Chicago, after a short visit with Rhoads and Waters, (in New York) and also one with Gasser on Wednesday. On Thursday and Friday I have the meeting with the men out there [Chicago], and will be in Washington on Saturday morning. You're going to see about my appointment with the Surgeon General of the Navy and with Mr. Merck? I'll want very much to see Dr. Weed, and if possible to see Mr. Bundy in the late afternoon, Saturday. . . . Ask his secretary whether he will be free any time Saturday afternoon? I'll also want to see Col. Wood, or at least talk with him on the telephone, and I will also look forward to seeing Dr. Andrus and discussing with him the Longcope proposal.

As I told you over the telephone I had a letter from Dr. Richards asking us to evaluate the Chicago projects sponsored by CTGC. This is going to be a big job but it will help me immensely to have you complete the project evaluations for me and to get them to me before I reach Chicago.

Another time Winter asked Stock to help him prepare a report over the Memorial Day weekend and to find him a room in Washington, costing "not more than $5.00 if possible." With a war going on, there was even less reason for Winter to expect his assistants to have lives of their own! A typical itinerary was: April 6, Boston; April 7, New Haven; Saturday, April 10, New York; Sunday to Chicago; east to Washington, DC by Thursday afternoon, April 15; all day Saturday, April 17, at Edgewood; then back to New Haven on Saturday evening. Freddy often met him at the train. He spent Sunday mornings across town at the office, and Sunday afternoon at home resting.

Winter's time in New Haven was mostly devoted to catching up with his department and his family. Polly had her own war work and her own women friends, and knew all the gossip of Yale and New Haven. Each day began with a telephone call to Hester Tyghe, whose husband was treasurer of Yale; war was no reason to upset that routine. Polly seemed never to be without her knitting, only now it was often coarse navy-blue wool instead of fine wool in pastel colors, worked into tiny garments for newborns. Instead of bringing Polly chocolates, Winter brought cigarettes–when he could get them, for cigarettes were even harder than sweets for civilians to find, although they were freely dispensed to military personnel.

Polly continued to be deeply involved in Planned Parenthood. She also ran the Blood Bank, conducting blood drives at the Winchester Arms plant and other factories. The ladies of New Haven got together to sew or make bandages for the British who had been bombed out of their homes, and for children who had been evacuated from London. They carried their knitting to meetings and lectures, so that a lecture hall sounded like a field of crickets clicking away.

Winter and Polly still enjoyed a good gossip when he came home, but time, like everything else, was rationed, for sleep and rest were essential to get the job done. Throughout the war Winter not only kept up his family bulletins, which were read by hardly anyone, but also corresponded with all the children individually and with Polly in letters that were typed by his secretary, destroying any intimacy.

COMMITTEE ON ATYPICAL GROWTH

With Edgewood Arsenal built and running, Winter spent most of his time administering contracts, overseeing the dissemination of information, and lecturing. In 1944 he resumed his teaching at Yale. That summer he shepherded his idea for a Committee on Atypical Growth into being, with himself as chairman. This project would occupy him for the rest of his career. The committee developed a nationwide program of voluntary coordination of research, which impressed the American Cancer Society so much that they requested the National Research Council to establish a similar Committee on Growth, to be the sole scientific adviser in research to the Cancer Society.

Chapter 13. After the War

Winter's postwar return to New Haven was short-lived. He remained a strong presence in the Yale Pathology Department long enough to impress his views and his methods on four more classes of students and house officers, and on the Medical School when the class size doubled to accommodate veterans returning from war. There was a new secretary to train and Winter pitched right in with more than his share of teaching, but he remained eager to dash down to Washington for committee meetings whenever possible.

Miss Barnes

The secretary, Miss Jean Barnes, was a newly minted graduate of Katherine Gibb's Secretarial School who was given a choice of positions when she applied to Yale: an easy job or a challenging job with a difficult boss. She chose the challenge and was the best secretary Winter ever had.[1] He assumed that anyone that young and cute couldn't know anything, so he was brutally demanding.

Jean infuriated him because there was nothing to correct. One day he threw the telephone at her and she threw it right back at him. That did it! What spunk! Winter fell in love with her. It wasn't long before the staff learned to knock before barging into his office.

Jean was so efficient that she could handle both the departmental and Winter's personal correspondence, correcting and typing the "weekly bores," running errands, finding plumbing parts for Treetops, and selecting silver for the new babies in the family. She even did secretarial work for Polly. Jean was a cheerful and engaging person, and the letters she saved illuminate Winter off-guard. After he retired, Jean stayed on as secretary to the chairman of Pathology, Harry S.N. Greene. They fell in love, married, and had two daughters, to whom we are most grateful for their unique contribution to Winternitziana.

In one undated letter to Jean, Winter wrote:

> The noon mail is welcome astounding and delightful. So I'll write at once hoping this letter will go this p.m. when I take Marie Noreen & Ella to the movies, and that it may arrive in New Haven on Friday. Please include me in the $ for Frank [Fusek] and give him my very sincere thanks for 25 years of superlative friendship loyalty and service. The younger men on the Staff will never be able to repay Frank.
>
> As for the green article by Greene–obviously you are coming definitely under his Messmer [sic] like

influence if you can understand that heteroplastic Brown by Greene.

Please—

1. Send checks enclosed
2. What outstanding vouchers are there from N.R.C.
3. Acknowledge Chalkley's letter & put date on yellow pad
4. Ask Mrs. Hollbrook or Miss Mester to find out facts–Gardner will be back shortly or from George M or then Meader & answer Cook letter.

You see I am lazy as ever.– Now lunch but its too hot even here to eat. I'll read your delightful letter again and then write more. Meantime many thanks & my best to the young ones in the sunshine of your office.–

Emeritus to be

THE CHILDS FUND

Best of all, 1947 was the year in which Winter succeeded Bayne-Jones as director of the Jane Coffin Childs Fund for Medical Research. Founded in 1937 by Starling W. Childs to support research into the causes, origins, and treatment of cancer, it was "the greatest gift ever made to Yale for work in the field of science," according to President James Angell. As the first private fund for cancer research, the Childs Fund was the forerunner of the American Cancer Society..

As the fund's first director, Bayne-Jones had wisely asked Winter to serve on the Board of Scientific Advisors. Winter, who served as director until his death, put into practice some ideas he had not been able to sell before, such as supporting research for a year after a Childs Fund Fellowship ended. Levin Waters became his assistant director, and William Welch's nephew, William Walcott, whom Winter had admitted to medical school out of loyalty, joined the Board of Managers in the 1950s, closing another circle for Winter.

Still, Winter must have felt "out of the loop." After the excitement of a world war, life at Yale had lost its glamour. One of his frequent visitors was Lewis Weed, still director of the National Research Council (NRC). After a few years, however, Weed developed tuberculosis, and a leave of absence at the Saranac Sanatorium led to his retirement. After some maneuvering, Winter was asked to be interim director of the NRC, with Weed's assistant, Phil Owen, as his associate. That appointment coincided with Winter's official retirement from Yale.

OFFICIAL RETIREMENT IN 1950

Born in 1885, Winter reached Yale's mandatory retirement age of sixty-five in 1950. A *Festschrift* seemed to be the most appropriate way to celebrate the event, and

Waters was duly asked to be guest editor for volume 22, number 6, of the *Yale Journal of Medicine,* the "Milton C. Winternitz Number." Joseph Fruton, Averill Liebow, and Max Taffel were among those listed on the editorial board of the journal, with Waters and Liebow the prime movers for that issue.

An informal gathering of the whole Department of Pathology (the "Christmas party list") preceded a dinner in Winter's honor in the Beaumont Room. We don't know if Winter was served his favorite foods–bay scallops, steak, and ice cream–that night, but the food was incidental as spirits flowed freely. Liebow presented Winter with the Samurai sword he had brought back from the Pacific five years before. When Winter pulled the sword out of its scabbard, he said, "By God, I'm going to leave my mark on this place!" He was lifted onto the shoulders of the tallest men in the room, Waters among them, to etch the initials "MCW" into the panel above the door. In the right light, his mark is still visible in the Palladian panel, although it was almost sanded away, inadvertently, in 2006.

Winter cherished the letter he received from President James Angell's successor, Charles Seymour, who wrote on April 29, 1950:

> My own conviction is that during that period [the preceding thirty-three years] there has been no one on the Yale faculty or in her administration who has contributed so much as yourself to the development

> of the university ideal and the translation of that ideal into fact. It is not merely that you made a great medical school; that was universally recognized. But in so doing you achieved something less obvious but perhaps even more important: you impressed upon the other divisions of the University a sense of unity of spirit and effort in a common devotion to scholarship, teaching, and community service. This you accomplished not only as Dean but through the power of your own personality during these past 15 years.
>
> My personal gratitude to you is beyond estimate. It was your judgment, and determination that enabled us to meet the crisis in medical affairs, bring George Darling here, and set us on the right course. I look back on that development as the most important event of my administration.
>
> Don't answer this. I wanted you to be sure of my feelings as you and I go out of active Yale service.
>
> With affection and appreciation,
>
> [signed]

A letter from John Peters, written on December 7, 1952, said in part:

> It has been a great adventure, that, I think, arose from a great idea–and there can never be any doubt whose idea it was. Sometimes it has been hard to keep it in mind, especially of late; but I still owe a great debt of gratitude to Winter that he elected me to be a participant.

After his retirement in 1950, and with a new job in Washington, Winter was emotionally free to sell 210 Prospect Street and rent a house just off Embassy Row in Washington.

CHAIRMAN OF THE DIVISION

After the disheartening interval at Yale, it must have come as a vindication for Winter to succeed to the chairmanship of the Division of Medical Sciences of the NRC, where diplomacy and tact were equated with vision and firmness as qualifications for the job. He was happy enough to "put on Dr. Weed's velvet slippers," but his joy was enhanced when he acquired a chauffeur. As he did not like driving in Washington, he enjoyed having the car waiting, and the door held for him, especially on cold mornings when he could wear his mink-lined coat that Freddy had picked up at an estate sale. Both the image and the thrift pleased him.

Marie de Grasse, who had been Polly's faithful "right hand" and who had helped her get settled inWashington, then retired after a lifetime of service. A young man from the National Gallery hung the pictures in their new house, and "Bernina and Garland" became their "custodians," as Winter called them. Bernina was an excellent cook and Garland was the houseman, butler, and chauffeur. Had Polly known just how much fun it would be to live in Washington, she would have moved there sooner, but it was a wrench to leave New Haven.

The annual spring meeting of the Board of Scientific Advisors of the Childs Fund was planned to coincide with the National Academy of Science meetings in Washington. They were congenial occasions, with Sunday supper afterwards at the Winternitzes'. Many of the men were Nobel laureates who found one another's company stimulating and enjoyed Washington at that lovely time of year.

Yet they were not above a bit of silliness. One time Dr. Salvador Luria, Nobel laureate, was explaining to one of the younger wives a difference between simians and humans that had to do with the ability to furl the tongue lengthwise. Soon they were making faces and sticking out their tongues while trying to furl them. At another dinner, when the Bayne-Joneses were present, the atmosphere was more staid and one would have thought Bayne-Jones was Winter's lifelong buddy. Winter put on a pose of hearty camaraderie and flattering good fellowship, which fooled all but those who knew him well

Winter's chairmanship of the Division of Medical Science lasted three years, form 1950 to 1953. After that, he and Polly moved into an apartment, spending half the year in Washington and the other half in New Hampshire. Winter remained a charter member of the Committee on Atypical Growth. At that same time, he served on the Atomic Casualties Commission, the Commission on Veterans' Medical Problems, and the Subcommittee of

Oncology, whose *Atlas of Tumor Pathology* was undertaken on his initiative. There is an excellent summary of Winter's accomplishments in the *National Academy of Science News* for September/October 1953.

As chairman of the Medical Sciences Division, Winter fostered mutual understanding and cooperation with the armed services and other agencies, and the research aspects of the National Blood Program were reorganized. The creation of the Medical Sciences Information Exchange bore witness to how much Winter valued scientific information, and that of the Committee on Cancer Diagnosis and Therapy to his belief in the social responsibility of science.

LAST YEARS

After his retirement, Winter remained a vital force in pathology, enlivening, or harassing, discussions by his outspoken criticism and his intolerance of complacency whenever he had the chance. He continued to try to break down the barriers separating the several sciences, but he no longer had a base of power, and that was hard on him.

Winter kept the directorship of the Childs Fund until he died. By then, his son Bill was working at the Yale Medical School and living in the rural suburb of Bethany. A harmonious rapport developed between father and son when medicine and maturity finally brought them back together. Retirement from the NRC had left Winter with only the Childs Fund to manage, and for that he relied on Waters, who remained in New Haven. The Childs Fund meetings brought Winter to New Haven, where he usually stayed at the Lawn Club. Bill and Levin Waters alternated having breakfast with him before driving him to the Childs Fund office. Bill said that he became almost as comfortable with Winter as Levin was. One morning, Winter was delighted to see Wilmarth Lewis having breakfast at the Lawn Club and, after a friendly chat, suggested they have dinner together sometime. Lewis replied, "Yes, some long Winter evening," giving Waters a sly wink.

But the emptiness of his new life depressed him: no one needed him, people rarely consulted him, and he was in poor health, all of which made him increasingly difficult to live with. Sadly for us, he was not interested in writing his memoirs, in late life as in earlier times preferring action to reflection. And he was sick. Polly was concerned, but "tender loving care" was not her style. As with some other elderly couples, their chief amusement became bickering.

Those on the scene thought Winter's dyspepsia was aggravated when he hired someone to write the history of the Childs Fund. The writer was a singularly difficult person, and Winter's great expectations for the history dwindled to desperation. He became more and more frustrated, ill, and difficult. Polly insisted he fire his bugbear, but the damage had been done, and Winter was never well again.

Before he died, Winter had been working on a plan for universal public service for all young men and women after high school, to train them just as they had been in the armed services during the war. He had seen how many servicemen and women reached unexpected potential through training, discipline, and a new environment. He believed the country would be better off getting its young people ready to work at jobs for which they were suitably trained. It was the Winternitz answer to welfare and warfare. He spent most of his time gathering statistics and writing letters promoting these ideas.

By the summer of 1959, Winter knew that he was ill and unlikely to recover. He went through all his papers at Treetops, discarding and organizing, throwing away a great deal in his preparation for final fame.

Early in September, Polly called Waters from Treetops to tell him she had summoned "the girls" because she could no longer handle Winter alone. When Mary Cheever and Jane reached New Hampshire, Winter agreed to go to the hospital, but first they must have some ice cream. So they sat in the kitchen, eating ice cream as they had so many times as children after coming home from the movies. Then they cleaned up the dishes before leaving for the Mary Hitchcock Clinic at Dartmouth, where Waters met them at the door.

Winter needed an operation on his stomach, and Waters stayed until it was over. He was with Winter when he came out of anesthesia. Since Winter had had a lesion on his tongue removed a few years before, one concern was the possibility of a recurrence of the tumor. As Winter woke up, Waters told him, "No cancer!" to which Winter gave a look that seemed to say, "You fool, I knew that."

Bill, who had just left for a year's fellowship in England, was called back, leaving his own young family in strange surroundings. He stayed with his father as long as he could, and when he had to return to England, Waters took over. Not being an M.D., Tom could only stand by.

Winter was not an easy patient, and postoperative infection in his belly overwhelmed him. He died on October 3, 1959, in the early evening. Almost twelve hours later he underwent an autopsy at the Dartmouth Medical School Department of Pathology.[2] According to the autopsy report,

> Apparently he had been well prior to the development, two days before, of fever and some shortness of breath. He had been known to have had a peptic ulcer for one year with anemia. On admission, his abdomen was soft and the liver was three to four fingers down. His white count was 23,000 with a shift to the left and his hematocrit was 34. A. medical consultant thought that he might have a silent cancer and suggested laparotomy or needle biopsy of the liver. Five days later, an operation discovered a perforated ulcer on the greater

> curve of the stomach with a large abscess between the stomach, the colon, and the liver. Winternitz died some 13 days later after a gradual downhill course.
>
> At autopsy some 12 hours later, his height was said to be 67 1/2 inches. He had false teeth on the upper jaw, a jejunostomy tube, a colostomy, and many abscess pockets. Despite his history, the heart showed no evidence of a myocardial infarction, he had a hiatus hernia and multiple ulcerations in the stomach and esophagus.

The autopsy showed nothing more than a perforated gastric ulcer and a chronic duodenal ulcer as well. Most of the other findings were incidental. Winter's insurance was noted as Connecticut Blue Cross and his occupation as "Retired Dean med School."

The family asked Waters to make the arrangements, and Winter's ashes remained in his closet until the graveside service in New Haven's Evergreen Cemetery one chilly, damp October day. Before the service, Polly had lunch upstairs at the Lawn Club, probably with one of her close friends, since she did not like to dine alone. The children, Steve and Ethel Whitney, Janie and Joe Hotchkiss, Louise and her son Robin Griswold, Mary and John Cheever, Jane and Bob Mellors, and Tom with Elizabeth (Buff) Thomson, ate together downstairs in a less formal dining room off the tennis courts. Bill, Freddy, and Buff's husband could not be there.

The only outsiders invited to join the family at the grave were Levin and Priscilla Waters. When they arrived, no one was in sight, but the grave was ready. Waters looked to the right and to the left, then placed Winter's ashes tenderly into the ground with a "Goodbye, Winter." Soon the family gathered, but there was still no clergyman in sight. Two women stood at a respectful distance—Molly, the maid, and her niece. A simple ivy wreath with a cluster of white camellias was the family's only floral tribute, making some other rather garish flower arrangements look out of place. Once the minister arrived, the service was simple, as Winter had wanted. He read the Episcopal Order for the Burial of the Dead, and there were brief exchanges among those present. Buff was the only one who hugged. Later that fall, a gathering was held at the Medical School to remember and honor Winter.

WHAT HAPPENED TO THE TWO FAMILIES?

Polly returned to New Haven, taking an apartment on Prospect Street, and carried on life as usual, always ready for a good gossip or a game of bridge, her manicured hands still knitting for a new generation of babies. She enjoyed visits and calls from her ever-expanding family. When John Cheever or his son Ben called, she particularly relished the lively repartee. Her namesake,

Polly Hotchkiss, was the most beautiful child ever in her grandmother's estimation, and Robin Griswold, now an Episcopal bishop, was the ultimate paragon.

Polly gave the impression of caring about all her grandchildren, if not always approving of the way they dressed or styled their hair, and enjoyed playing the role of matriarch to such a large brood. She died in 1978 in the elegant comfort of her own apartment, with private nurses and family in attendance.

Treetops is still in the family and shared by those who choose to go there. Winter was spared some of the tragedies that befell his children, but he would have taken great pride in his grandchildren. Buff's two children, Helen Thomson Morehouse and John Thomson, are both radiologists. John is married and has four children. When we interviewed Helen, she quipped that she was "Jewish enough for Hitler, but not Jewish enough for Mount Sinai." Bill assured us, however, that she made the grade at the Albert Einstein School of Medicine at Yeshiva University. Buff was killed by a train outside Philadelphia at age fifty-eight. Her husband has a Ph.D. in physical chemistry and does equations for fun!

Jane, the child who had had the most technical conversations with her father, the most giving child, earned a Ph.D. in physiological chemistry and married Bob Mellors while he was at Hopkins working on one or another of his graduate degrees, Ph.D. and M.D. He practiced medicine and they had four children: Robert, Jr. and John are internists, Alice is a radiologist, and William has a Ph.D. in biology. Robert Mellors, Jr. has become world renowned for his work on HIV. Jane was in her fifties when she died.

Tom–more formally, Thomas Watson Winternitz–earned his Ph.D. in engineering and worked for Bell Telephone all his life. He marred Elizabeth Austin, who had a Ph.D. in botany, and they had three children. Tom, Jr. majored in engineering and shared his father's and Great-Grandfather Watson's fascination with practical technology. Charles and Sally are both practicing physicians, Charles an internist and Sally a psychiatrist.

Priscilla Norton visited Tom, Sr. when he was living with his second wife in Virginia on the Chesapeake Bay. His physical resemblance to Winter was very apparent, and he moved in much the same way. A friendly black dog completed the familiar picture. Tom was growing oysters in mesh bags suspended off the dock, his unusual plants flourished in a sunroom, and he had a little fish hatchery in the house. Winter would have been as intrigued, as she was, at yet another most unusual and creative mind, nourished by native curiosity. Tom's radio call letters are on his license plate.

That the Winternitzes' daughter Mary is Mrs. John Cheever always gets people's attention. Two of her children, Susan and Ben, are well-known writers, while Frederico is a lawyer in Colorado, where he practices and teaches law. Mary has lived for years in Ossining, New York, with her dog in a charming old house surrounded by established gardens and woods. She enjoys foraging for mushrooms and knows a secret spot where she finds morels in the springtime. She still gardens, loves her dog, and loves being a grandmother.

William Welch Winternitz, the youngest child, was born in 1920. After teaching in Kentucky, Bill set up the Department of Medicine at the University of Alabama in Tuscaloosa. Now professor of medicine (retired) at the university, he works part-time and lives in Tuscaloosa with his third wife, Madeline Hill. Bill's first wife, Mary Primac, died in 1965 of cancer. He raised their three children by himself, choosing not to remarry until the children were out of the nest. His son Bill, Jr. is an orthopedic surgeon in practice in California, with two children of his own. Helen Watson Winternitz is a journalist and writer, and his other son, Paul, is a photographer.

The Winternitz home in Alabama was in the woods at the edge of a beautiful lake, where the mountain laurel blooms abundantly every spring. At the time of Priscilla's visit, Bill's landscaping was skillfully restrained. A path winds down to the lake, reminiscent of the paths at Treetops, with flowers and shrubs growing alongside as if by chance. Here, too, dogs are essential members of the family, and plants are everywhere.

The statistics say it all about Winter's influence: He had five children, fifteen grandchildren, and twenty-five great-grandchildren. Of the fifteen grandchildren, eight are physicians, three are writers, one is a lawyer, and one a Ph.D.

AFTERWORD

WINTERNITZ AND HIS LEGACY: A SUMMING UP

"But if anyone deserves to be done in bronze and placed in a prominent position on the campus of the Yale Medical School, it should be Dean M.C. Winternitz." As a student at Johns Hopkins, John Paul hated Winternitz. Later, as his colleague at Yale, Paul came to admire what Winter had accomplished, offering these words at Winter's retirement. Such praise must be very rare today, when so few at the Medical School even recognize Winternitz's name. Perhaps Paul's encomium can be read as a sly hope that a bronze bust would be both silent and movable–characteristics for which, as dean, Winter received little praise..

Sadly, suggestions that Winter be memorialized at the very least by naming an activity or lecture for him have been rebuffed on administrative levels, largely, we suspect, because of his reputation as an anti-Semitic Jew. Arrived now at the end of our tale, we remain convinced that his achievements outweigh the failings of this brilliant but difficult man. At Hopkins, Winter grasped the big ideas, but at Yale he lacked the personal qualities to see most of them to a successful conclusion. We hope that our account of his life and work will earn for his name at least a "study unit" or a "Winternitz Society" to foster goals that are as relevant in the twenty-first century as in the last.

One question to which we find no answer is whether Winternitz was the originator of the ideas which we so much admire or, more likely, the facilitator of their realization at Yale. Abraham Flexner, to whom he owed so much, was his friend and William Welch his mentor. The two of them may have played a more paternal role than his little-mentioned father.

CONTRAST WITH ABRAHAM FLEXNER

There are many parallels between Flexner and Winternitz. Both were young, ambitious Jews, born in the South and married to Christian wives, who moved away from their Jewish traditions. Both were short and little disposed to exercise, and both had the not uncommon Jewish social conscience.

Despite the similarity of their careers, however, Winter and Flexner were quite different people. Flexner seems to have been more hardheaded and independent. He was personally responsible for the study of American colleges that made his name and gave him the chance to work for the Carnegie Corporation. That he visited all the country's medical schools, good and bad, accounted for the effectiveness of his famous survey. His marriage would have been difficult for many men of that time, but he had good friends and somehow knew how to keep them.

Flexner may have begun as an acolyte to the rich and famous, but he found his level and knew how to give advice and remain sociable at the same time. Bonner's biography makes it clear that he was a very political and polite young man. Unlike Winternitz, Flexner did not allow himself to show pride in his achievements. While he clearly was stubborn and usually convinced that he was right, unlike Winternitz, he did not make a big thing of it.

Winter, by contrast, took credit for work whenever he could, and was hard on people around him. He was lucky in a good marriage to a physician wife who abandoned her own career to raise their children, but he had few friends and no cronies. Flexner had two children and his ambitious wife was away a lot; Bonner makes it clear that he took the responsibility for their education. Winter had five children, and although he was happy to direct them as long as his first wife was alive, Helen devoted her life to them while he was building his career at the Yale Medical School.

We conclude that Flexner had ideas and convictions. More important, he handed out the money to get things done. Who knows whether it was Flexner's largesse or Winter's determination that made Yale accept the full-time academic salary system that Flexner favored? Flexner was not successful everywhere he tried pushing the idea, so Winter deserves considerable credit. The famed Yale Plan, still honored in more than name, for medical education must have originated with Winternitz himself.

PATHOLOGY, MEDICAL EDUCATION, AND SOCIAL REFORM

Of the three fields that attracted Winternitz's attention, pathology remained his first love. In light of his lifelong fervor for social medicine, it might seem curious that Winter followed this route. Like molecular biology and genetics today, pathology back then provided the ticket to an academic career, which doubtless accounted for his choice. Winter was certainly ambitious enough to recognize that pathology was at the "cutting edge" of medicine and provided a foundation, as it does to this day, for clinical medicine.

Certainly, Winter made the most of pathology when he had lots of people to labor in the vineyard of his ideas. He was facile enough to look at big new problems when they popped up. War gases first provided him with material for a book, and then revived his career during World War II, when it was feared that the Nazis might revive germ warfare and poison gas. Winter had the good judgment to recognize that the effect of nitrogen mustards on tissues might prove therapeutic, as they have in the chemotherapy of cancer. When influenza struck in 1918, Winter was ready to take advantage of the pathology that came to the autopsy tables of the New Haven Hospital.

Pathology was always the center of his attention, whatever other activities he was engaged in. When his vistas widened, his ambitious plans for an ideal medical school curriculum called for pathology to remain focused on the human, but to encompass "comparative" pathology and plant pathology as well.

As dean, Winter reshaped the Yale Medical School into a research institution, while consistently fostering a view of the patient as a whole. That he had always been a social reformer at heart is manifest in his later projects, particularly the Institute for Human Relations. However fruitless it proved in the end, the institute promoted the concept that medical education should serve the general welfare of humankind.

After his forced retirement from the deanship, Winternitz remained a senior personality at the Medical School, chairing committees, advising whomever would listen, and inspiring more than twenty years of medical students. Always a doer rather than a deep thinker, he was in his element working in Washington during and after World War II.

Winter left few intellectual heirs, but there were many whose careers he fostered and cherished.

Foremost among them were Levin Waters and Harry Zimmerman. Averill Liebow, who most resembled him in stature and personality, chose pulmonary pathology at Winter's urging, and renowned hepatologist Gerald Klatskin became an expert on liver disease for the same reason. Most important, generations of Yale medical students have had Winternitz to thank for the Yale Plan, which gives them the chance to study without excessive academic constraint.

In an address to the alumni upon Winter's retirement in 1935, Winslow eulogized him for transforming and rebuilding the Medical School. Winter, he said, had brought about a rebirth of interest in the patient and the stimulation of scientific advances. He credited Winter with the construction of "an admirably designed and humanely administered hospital," not forgetting an endowment "never dreamed of" and a faculty to match. Generously finding no fault in his friend, Winslow went on to praise all that the institute stood for. In bolstering Winter's self-confidence at a time of despair, Winslow may have slighted George Blumer, the dean who had prepared the way for much that Winter accomplished. But Winter was the catalyst who brought about the major changes.

THE MEDICAL SCHOOL

Winternitz saved the Medical School in the 1920s, thanks to his determination, energy, enthusiasm, and conviction that he was always right. Crucial to that success was his close friendship with Abraham Flexner and other agents of the rich foundations. The endowments of Rockefeller and Carnegie made it possible for him, building on the plans of his predecessors, to renew the Medical School and hospital. Those who disliked Winter–and they were more than a few–found him "ruthless" in getting rid of people who did not do his bidding. Nevertheless, although a dedicated group of people were responsible for the changes in medical education at Yale, it was Winternitz who had the energy and drive to put the enterprise on the track to success.

It is easy to list the physical improvements at the Medical School that Winternitz brought about. A collection of new buildings, mostly still standing, shifted the physical center of the school from York Street, near the main college campus, to Cedar Street, conveniently adjacent to the New Haven Hospital. The construction of the Sterling Hall of Medicine stamped a marble seal on the move. The neoclassical edifice, with its blue-green dome, provided a counterpoint to the spires of Yale and its newly constructed "girder-Gothic" campus. It has remained a permanent and impressive hub for the Medical School, even as the school's center of gravity shifted eastward, with the huge, ten-story Anlyan Center for Medical Research and Education (the third-largest structure on the Yale campus) on Congress Avenue.

The hospital too has grown immensely. Spreading outward from its original block, it took over the lot where a Catholic church stood for more than a century and now extends all the way to South Frontage Road, where the new Smilow Cancer Hospital rises to the heavens. To old-timers, the growing remoteness of the Yale Medical School and the New Haven Hospital in years past reflected the changing objectives of the two institutions, which were probably most in sync when Winternitz was dean. Once sadly estranged, the school and hospital are now happily cooperating once again.

Although the move to Cedar Street entangled the Medical School with the New Haven Hospital, it also gave it an independence that might not have flourished in closer proximity to the central campus. Winternitz was free to expand the borders of his new duchy. He had money enough to buy up old buildings, tear them down, and erase streets that dated far back in New Haven's history. The university hierarchy showed little concern for what was happening four or five blocks from the undergraduate colleges, as long as they weren't paying the bills.

The partnership of Winternitz and President James Angell fostered the school's independence. Even after he retired, Angell attended an occasional Medical School function, a practice that his widow continued as long as she lived in New Haven. Later Medical School leaders, bolstered by the growing support for medical research by the National Institutes of Health in the 1950s, acted even more autonomous. Now that the Medical School accounts for more than a third of Yale's entire budget, university officials pay attention–and sometimes even tribute–to the school. The grand Anlyan Center, for example, was funded out of the central purse.

Proximity to the hospital gave the school the clinical gravitas it needed, students for "teaching material," and patients for clinical practice and study. At the same time, it frayed the bonds that might have tied the Medical School into the institutional life of Yale College. The freedom conferred by distance hindered the intellectual and scientific integration of the Medical School with the university. In particular, it prevented Winter from realizing his vision of uniting the medical campus with those of the Law and Divinity Schools. The Law School faculty and administration vetoed a proposal to move to the vicinity of Cedar Street, choosing to remain in the center of campus, while the Divinity School ultimately decided to move to a charming but remote new quadrangle much farther north.

Not even the shuttle bus that has operated since the 1990s has entirely overcome the psychic barrier of the five- or ten-minute walk from the Medical School to the central campus. For a few years after Winter's Institute for Human Relations was established, some college professors and teachers, particularly in the Psychology Department, trekked down to the Medical School, but by the 1960s the imposition of a six-lane highway and a behemoth parking garage separating the two domains erased any easy proximity. Had he not been so jubilant about his new empire,

Winternitz might have foreseen the "downside" of relocating the medical campus in the 1920s.

Winter's goal of integrating medical education into the general university curriculum was complicated by the disposition of midcentury Medical School professors to feel like second-class citizens. More than a few college teachers in the 1950s and 1960s expressed a fear that hordes of "Visigoths" from the Medical School were poised to invade the comfortable Gothic colleges. At the then-popular football games in the Yale Bowl, disparaging remarks could be heard about the number of medical doctors crowding into the section reserved for the faculty. By the 1990s, however, a renewed emphasis on cellular research made it agreeable for science departments like Molecular Biology to bridge the intellectual gap that Winter, and others of his time, so deplored.

Winter wanted to be more than just the dean of a medical school. His correspondence is sprinkled with clues to his growing ambition once his friend Robert Maynard Hutchins left the Law School for the presidency of the University of Chicago. In his later dean's reports, Winter seems to have dreamed of playing an administrative and less specifically medical role. Flexner was not wrong in remarking that his friend wanted to make the Institute of Human Relations into a "second" university. Winter was eager to play on a larger field, national or international. What he might have done had he continued as dean can only be conjectured.

Exile from the deanship in 1935 was a huge blow from which Winter never really recovered. He had so identified himself with the Medical School that losing his job, and with it the cadre of people necessary to carry out his ideas, led to a decline in his ambition, coupled with depression. His second wife, Polly, is said to have muted his disappointment by introducing him to a new social milieu that seemed to delight him, but the social whirl could have been no more than a poultice for his anguish. His work in Washington during World War II, with all its traveling and international talk, must have comforted him far more. After the war, an international stage and a class to teach at Edgewood Arsenal continued to raise his spirits as it polished his image. But his ambitious plans had all been thwarted.

THE HOSPITAL

Winternitz saw his duty to improve the New Haven Hospital and did so, again building on the collaborative efforts of the Yale administration, hospital officials, and many others who preceded him, like George Blumer and Ross Harrison. He presided over the erection of new facilities for the hospital (long before it was renamed Yale-New Haven Hospital) and its consolidation with the independent Grace Hospital (whose name was preserved for some three decades as Grace-New Haven Community Hospital). Those ideas and plans had been long in the making, but it was Winter who twisted the arms of the donors to make them a reality. Somewhere along the line, the new medical buildings (the Tompkins and Fitkin stacks), which provided open wards for the sick in the 1920s, were turned over to the hospital, as a kind of ransom, in a series of agreements by a university seemingly still fearful of too close involvement with patient care.

No one now remembers that the dean of the Medical School was responsible for the hospital buildings. That they were converted into offices for the Medical School in the 1990s in no way diminishes Winternitz's achievements in bringing the Medical School and hospital closer together. As he reminded his colleagues, "the hospital must also be regarded as the laboratory of the clinician."

The final union of the two institutions never took place, however, in part because the Medical School never controlled the hospital. Neither a university hospital focused on teaching and research, nor a city hospital that welcomes "unreimbursed" care for the sick, Yale-New Haven has never enjoyed a loyal constituency of any great size. Nor, despite the hospital's financial success in recent years, did it ever become the clinical academic enterprise that the Yale faculty has always wanted. As a result, the school and hospital continue to go their separate ways in the early twenty-first century, sometimes collaborating, but more often competing. Their disparate aims have inhibited the development of the grandiosely labeled Yale-New Haven Medical Center.

The Yale Plan

Easier to praise as a long-lasting legacy of Winternitz are the changes in medical education embodied in the so-called Yale Plan. That plan treated medical students as graduate students, motivating them to keep up their own education without the spur of repeated examinations. Required courses for students were reduced by a quarter as Winternitz eliminated many lectures and most examinations, replacing them with a required thesis for graduation, and corroded the iron wall between departments. He consolidated the Medical and Graduate School curricula in the biological sciences in the hope that the "most brilliant scholar will be more willing to spend longer periods in investigation and specialization." Although this policy is debatable, it persists to the present, because more than a few medical students, clinicians at heart, are discouraged by having to learn material in which neither they nor their clinical instructors can find any relevance to a future medical practice. Unfortunately, the Graduate School's criteria for Ph.D. candidates have goaded the research faculty at the Medical School to "keep up" standards by training would-be physicians in arcane science far more than they need.

Winternitz initiated the concept of "study units" to bring people together from disparate departments to look into specific clinical research topics. The first was the Neurology Study Unit, headed by John Fulton, out of which came the Atypical Growth Committee, the nucleus of the Childs Fund and its research. Study units stemmed from Winternitz's belief that departmental barriers impeded research advances. Abraham Flexner, on the other hand, was sure that departmental specialization was the best way for medical science to advance.

Although Winter recognized the importance of the student thesis, and even argued that not enough time was devoted to it, he cautioned that "while research is an aim of the school, it is not the only one." In tune with the times, he, like Osler, wanted the Medical School to become part of the university, but he never lost sight of the patient as the focus of the medical academic enterprise. This explains his otherwise paradoxical enthusiasm for the move to Cedar Street. Winter's insistence that students study the natural history of disease by frequent attendance in the out-patient clinics meant that they could follow patients through sickness and health. He hoped that research would follow, flowing from clinical problems.

Most important, Winter fostered the full-time professorial system at Yale by sheer will. The original plan had been Flexner's, supported by the Rockefeller money of the General Education Board. By hiring likeminded people, Winternitz made the full-time faculty a reality at the Yale Medical School until the end of the twentieth century. Indeed, full-time salaried clinicians remained almost unique at Yale after the defection of other schools at which the system had been tried. Winter's problems came with the new faculty, however; no longer independently wealthy practitioners, they were mostly dependent for their livelihoods on furthering their academic reputations. They were unhappy that Winter's innovative plans took money away from their research. Of Winternitz, Robert Yerkes said that he had a "constructive imagination," adding that some of his directives made the faculty "quite as often victimizer as aids." In the twenty-first century, the growing repute of entrepreneurial activities–and the money they generate–have almost entirely eliminated the full-time system for Yale physicians. As a result, the academic enterprise erected by Winternitz has been greatly altered.

SOCIAL MEDICINE

Winter never fulfilled his hope to redo medicine as a social science. Once he lost the dean's post, he never again had the chance to influence the general society from his old bully pulpit. Curiously, Harvey Cushing, whose daughter had married a Roosevelt son, was not helpful to Winter in realizing his desire to work in the Roosevelt Administration in the mid-1930s. Winter, who had so much to offer, wandered through such a wasteland between 1934 and 1936 that one wonders where his associates were when he needed them. His downfall was, as Winter once joked, like the overthrow of a monarch. Few follow kings into exile, or give them jobs.

Winter's influence on social medicine and the later "holistic" movement is hard to trace. To be sure, he enlarged on concepts already abroad in the United States and Europe: social medicine was in the air, as much in Britain as in Boston. But the group at Yale never linked up with the group at Harvard, where Dean David Edsall, from 1918 to 1935, espoused both preventive and social medicine. Other Harvard men like Lawrence Henderson and Richard Cabot also were strong proponents of enhancing the patient-physician relationship, but Winter never talked of them. Again, we can only wonder that Cushing, who bridged the two schools, did not do more to further a connection for the discomfited Winternitz, or that the Medical Advisory Committee of the Committee on the Costs of Medical Care, which made its final report to the president in 1933, did not snap him up on their own. The fault must have lain in Winter, not in his contacts.

Yet, to contemplate his ideas about what physicians should know and how they should approach patients as persons, makes it easy to conclude that Winternitz should be recognized as one of the forerunners of current "mind-body" medicine. His 1930 proposal for a "Graduate Department of Clinical Sociology" makes this clear.

> Few students have had the experiences so helpful for the training of the prospective physician; there is nothing in the curriculum of medical educa-

> tion, designed to bring to the student's consciousness of men and women as people with bodies and minds. . . .
>
> The proposed plan for filling this gap in the medical student's education, and restoring that interest in human beings which was largely lost when the old family doctor was replaced by the highly trained specialist, provides in the first place during the preclinical years certain courses in the fundamentals of psychology and sociology. The student will pursue these courses at the same time that he is mastering the essentials in biology. This is practicable at Yale, where the content of fundamental courses in biology has already been reduced so that the student has fifty percent of his time free for elective subjects.

One wishes that Winter had left more written reflections about such matters, not just "throw-away" speeches for ceremonial occasions, which praised social medicine but gave no detail.

AFTER THE FALL

Winter's children always believed that a cabal struck him down while he was away, a suggestion that has the ring of truth. Regardless, it became clear to him–and even more to his friends–that the shortest road to peace in the Medical School lay in his resignation. Too many of the faculty were outraged by the institute, which took money away from their favorite projects, and felt betrayed by his leadership, which someone described as "more despotic than autocratic." His faculty complained that Winter treated them like children; conversely, his children often felt like satellites of the Medical School. However worthy the institute was, it had to struggle with a general feeling that Winter had set it up as an alternative, if not an outright rival, to the university. Others have pointed to the resentment and anxiety that its creation incited among the faculty of both the college and the Medical School, noting that Winter made enemies at both ends of the campus. The idea that ambitious young scientists would work toward common goals in the confines of an institute that aspired to be a "community of scholars" was unrealistic.

If Abraham Flexner had not been so opposed, or if he had continued to channel money to it, the institute might have survived. But he had more faith in the many small epiphanies of independent genius, which made it certain that the big foundations would end their support. Flexner may have been right: research may flourish in a diaspora where many work independently better than in an institute that tries to control it. In our time, the frenzied search for a triumph over AIDS or the creation of stem cells suggests the virtues of competition as opposed to collaboration.

The Yale Medical School still benefits from other Winternitz legacies. The Psychiatry Department, the Dentistry Department as a postgraduate exercise, and the School of Nursing as a graduate school for nursing, are other activities that he saw through to fruition, although he did not originate them. The tripod of the Medical School, at least since the 1950s, has been research, teaching, and clinical medicine. Winternitz fully supported those ideas, although, like others of his time, he might have labeled them scholarship, teaching, and community service.

Community service won Winter's heart, to judge from the often unfinished plans that he proposed after the mid-1930s. Not many of the college or Medical School faculty would have found their duty in community service, which they regarded as far less important than research and generating new information and ideas. Yet before his death Winter was working on a plan to require two years of community service from every citizen. This "last idea" remained largely in his head, according to those close to him, who described the yellow sheets on which he had been figuring costs and other details.

In the political arena, Winternitz looks even now like a liberal. Like Welch, who supported a national health system as far back as 1891, Winternitz was a fervent admirer of FDR. Married to a physician, and with a daughter who became a physician, he would surely have supported the entry of more women into medicine, even if he might not have advanced that idea against opposition. Given his interest in social medicine, his earlier plan to bring the Law and Divinity Schools to Cedar Street, and his enthusiasm for psychiatry, we think it likely that he would be a supporter of what now would be called "single-payer" health insurance.

WINTERNITZ AS A TEACHER

In a letter to Elizabeth dated October 12, 1931, after Helen's death, Winter wrote, "I had my first class this morning. It is really quite a lot of fun to teach, and I enjoy it now that I am in it again." He was a teacher first and foremost.

At first Winter thought of himself as a researcher, but he was brought to Yale for his administrative promise and drive. Nevertheless, he was a superb teacher, which is how he is remembered by colleagues and students alike. His methods were not easy: like a fencing master, he terrorized students, both to get their adrenalin going and to inspire them to see, think, and correlate. Paul contrasted his "terrifying" teaching methods at Hopkins with Welch's far more benign approach.

Even after he left the dean's office, Winter continued to teach pathology. From students' reports, we know that his lecture style depended on the rough and tumble of confrontation. According to Ray Yesner, "Dr. Winternitz was a short, muscular man, proud of his physique. When lecturing, he would roll up his sleeves and flex his biceps. . . . His own lectures were anything but didactic. He might ruminate on the day's events, or toss a bear's kidney to some hapless student and ask him to discuss it. No one in the audience fell asleep."

Anecdotes about Winter's teaching in pathology are all very much of a piece: it could not have been easy for a student to catch a fresh animal organ thrown at him and, holding on to it gingerly, come up with answers to questions about diseased tissues and organs. Winter knew the ground he wanted to cover and tailored his lectures to the responses of each class, making it difficult for students to use last year's notes.

Beyond assuring students a knowledge of "the life history of disease," Winter expanded the medical curriculum from one concentrating on disease to one concerned with preventive medicine and health. He encouraged regular visits of patients to an ambulatory clinic, which he regarded as "not only a disease clinic but also a health clinic, and in part, a health center for its immediate environs." Very early, Winter urged psychiatrists to study the mind "not only from the standpoint of the insane and pre-insane, but also with the idea of analyzing the mental factors of safety in the individual," issues that continue to echo in the modern world of neurobiology. Winter often lamented that the new specialists in internal medicine and subspecialties had no "fundamental interest in the mental reaction of the individual."

Another objective was strengthening the Medical School Alumni Association. Winter hoped that regular teaching of practicing physicians at "clinical congresses" would bind the practitioners in town to the

Medical School and do away with town-gown rivalries. Such rivalry has remained a problem for Yale ever since. Although little discussed, it was rampant during the second half of the twentieth century, despite valiant efforts to bridge the gap between the university and the community.

WINTER AS A PERSON

Winternitz had grand ideas, but his personal failings hobbled their development. Therein lies his tragedy.

On March 6, 1932, In a newspaper article entitled *"Religio Medici Yalensis,"*_published on March 6, 1932, Winter summarized what he had done for the Medical School up to that time, at least as he saw it:

> Medicine is not looked upon at Yale as a self-sufficient entity, set apart by man and God as an independent realm into which only a chosen few may enter: it is considered rather that medicine can become enriched and significant to the extent that it fits into the scheme of a social organism as a whole and contributes to the well-being of a society. . . . Man is to be seen as a soul as well as a body. The aim of Yale University is to restore to medicine the point of view of the old family physician and at the same time to retain the benefit of concentration in special fields.

Winter had few cronies or close friends, rather like his colleague President Angell, of whom it was said, "Nobody beat a path to his kitchen door." Work was Winter's life; his passion lay neither in people nor even in the laboratory, but in the organization of ideas and people. He was good at spotting a new idea–"seizing" is probably a more appropriate word–and then running with it. That ability never left him: even late in life, his colleagues remarked on his interest in the adrenal, vitamin A and clotting, and drugs to control blood pressure, all new ideas. Even guests at Treetops were invited with an agenda and were expected to join in with the work.

Priscilla Norton is convinced that Winternitz had a sense of humor about himself. Although he could be ruthless, he went out of his way to show genuine concern for those around him, at least when they were not his tools for success. He took pleasure in helping anyone who was sick, especially family, friends, and servants, and was adept at explaining the problem and its treatment in an easily understandable way. He turned around more than a few relationships by a single act of kindness, something that people never forgot. When Helen Owsley Heard's mother was dying of cancer, he talked at length about what could be done, and she felt the better for it.

Winter had many faults, as we have seen. His terrible temper often made him lose self-control. Once he told a student in a fit of rage, "A medical student should be in medicine up to his knees. You are up to your ankles!"

Although he praised interconnection, collaboration, and cooperation, creative tension was more his style; he pitted one person against another, maybe unconsciously. But he was heard to state that a lot of good could come from response to conflict and criticism. Later Medical School deans have encouraged that same conflict, doubtless in the spirit of "divide and conquer." Winter believed that was the way to progress: "When dispute arises, progress happens" was a typical phrase

Curiously enough, when it came to his own health, Winternitz was something of a valetudinarian: he complained of neuralgia, myalgia, and recurrent disabling lumbago, which his wife Helen treated with heat from a flat-iron. He would tell anyone he could about his troubles with a peptic ulcer–but that was back in the days when an "ulcer" was a badge of hard work, not just an infection. His former secretary at the Childs Fund recalls the letters he wrote about his health problems. In later years, she relates, he was a "man of many moods," a "chameleon."

The Greeks had the word for it: *hubris*, pride that goes before the fall, the seeds of destruction within. Winter had the right ideas, he had the right training, and he had the power to reach the right goals. Whether he originated them or, more likely, facilitated them, his determination and, yes, his ruthlessness brought them to the fore. But the good manners he so admired and his hope for social medicine, enriched by the contributions of law and divinity, were swept away by his narcissism and ambition. Although his goals are memorialized in stone, they were lost along with his power. The "Yale Plan" thrives today, but it is different from the plan that Winter conceived.

Whenever we enter 333 Cedar Street, as we look up at the words "The Institute for Human Relations" boldly incised above the portal, we remember Shelley's Ozymandias, the long-forgotten "king of kings." This may be the lesson that Milton Winternitz has taught us. Yet, both of us, Priscilla and Howard alike, wish that his visionary project had been more than a dream. May it yet provide a goal for the medical profession?

NOTES

PREFACE

1. On the back of a framed letter, now in the hands of his son, Winternitz commented on the Greek legend above the door. He disagreed with the architect, Atterbury, that the torches symbolized cooperation "and are therefore especially applicable to the Institute of Human Relations. There was no exchange of torches in the race, and the runner received from someone else the torch that he lighted and passed on."

In "A Welcome to the Returning Alumni" (unpublished MS, June 8, 1996), Dr. Lycurgus Davey, a well-known neurological surgeon, recalled the origin of the Greek inscription and gave a new translation.

2. Kennan, G. Interview. *New York Review of Books,* circa 2000.

CHAPTER 1. THE EARLY YEARS

1. G. Sandler, *Jewish Baltimore* (Baltimore: Johns Hopkins University Press, 2000). Jews from Germany and Austria

had found their way to Maryland, thanks to the shipping routes of the North German Lloyd line, which brought immigrants to Maryland and returned with tobacco and lumber. Later the boats brought over Eastern European Jews shipping out from Bremen after their arduous overland trip from Russia.

Sandler tells how the German Jews, anxious at the influx of Russian Jews, started their own social clubs in the 1880s and abandoned East Baltimore for more northern areas of the town. Eutaw Place, built by rich men in the 1880s, gradually turned into a German-Jewish enclave, peopled by folks like the Friedenwalds, as Baltimore's "old families" moved on. The arrival of the German Jews (largely from Bavaria) in the 1840s gave them a head start of a generation or so, and although they encountered social anti-Semitism on their own, they preferred not to socialize with the Russians. This was more a matter of class than prejudice and disappeared in the 1930s.

In describing the baths that Jews frequented in East Baltimore–some on the same Lombard Street on which the Winternitzes lived–before the spread of indoor plumbing, Sandler tells that Welch liked to use them because, as he said, "They give you all the benefits of exercising without the nuisance of it."

2. Given the hierarchical nature of academic medicine and the Hebrew Bible's listing of who was fathered by whom, it is hard to understand Winter's repeated failure to refer to his father the doctor.

3. Interviews with members of the Bachrach family. According to Irene Bachrach, Winter's parents are buried in the Hebrew Cemetery on Belair Road in Baltimore. Rhona Bachrach Druck related that when Winternitz came to his mother's funeral, he hurried it along, saying, "Let's get the show on the road." He was unaccompanied by family.

4. *Annual Report of the Department of Pathology #1* (Baltimore, 1916). The contents page lists 17 papers, including 5 by Winter and his colleagues.

5. 1896 diary of Helen Watson. School lasted until June 23. The next day the family started for Vermont, their coachman driving up ahead with the trunks. The family traveled overnight by train, stopping at Milton, Vt., for breakfast at the hotel. They traveled 27 miles further to their house, Bow Arrow, on Lake Champlain. Their boat was a steam launch called the *Arrow*, and the nearest post office was Adams, which is no longer on the map. The next morning, Helen was up early, delighting in the freedom to go barefoot and wear bloomers. The boys caught 17 fish before breakfast, she noted. Another morning she went hunting for leeches and crayfish, which she gave to the boys to use for bait. (No sissy, she!) On July 30 she noted, "President McKinley is boarding at the Champlain House which is a hotel we can see from our house."

Helen and her sister Esther collected moss to make a moss garden, which they watered all summer. They occasionally played with their dolls in the glen, but more often

Helen was at the water's edge and in the water with the boys and involved with the natural world. She was observant, finding it worth reporting that the potatoes cooked slowly in boiling water and quickly in the ashes of their campfire, and that a man came with a bag of dynamite sticks that looked just like a bag of sausages. She trained a squirrel to eat out of her hand and reported her brothers' symptoms whenever they were sick–a harbinger of her later interest in medicine.

On the last day of vacation, Helen went with the boys to Pondlilly Bay, gathering large snails. They returned home just in time for school, taking the overnight train to Boston and the horse-drawn trolley cars to Weymouth. She mentions helping teach mathematics (certainly not spelling). At home the Watsons had a coachman who was also their driver, but no other household help is mentioned. Helen was pleased that she still led her class in algebra and mathematics, though she remained a poor speller. She mentions that she wore her best dress to school one day because her other dress was being mended. Reading aloud was very much a part of her life. Her father, the dominant person in the family, spent a good deal of time with his children when they were sick, reading to them or just sitting with them. Years later, when Helen became an invalid, she had readers for her while she rested.

Once Helen was back in school the diary stops, but a tantalizing handful of pages have been torn out of the book, by whom and why we do not know.

7. Helen Watson, letter to Winternitz, March 28, 1917. "Father Watson" quotes Welch as comparing Winter to Flexner.
8. J.M. Slemmons, letters to Winternitz, 1917, passim, assuring him he would get the job.
9. In January 1917, Bartlett ran the "Pathological Laboratory," but by 1919 it was called "Laboratory of Pathology and Bacteriology." Turf battles are nothing new.

2. THE YALE, HOPKINS, AND HARVARD MEDICAL SCHOOLS

1. In this chapter we have relied on several sources, including the Yale historians and K.M. Ludmerer, *Learning to Heal: The Development of American Medical Education* (New York: Basic Books, 1985).
2. C.S. Bryan, "Mr. Gates's Summer Vacation: A Centennial Remembrance,".*Ann. Intern. Med.* 127 (1997): 145-53. This is an account of how Frederick T. Gates, a Baptist minister, took on John D. Rockefeller as his "congregation of one" and directed his beneficence toward "scientific medicine." Gates credits Osler's textbook of medicine, which he claimed to have read straight through, as the impetus for that decision. Dr. Bryan relates some fascinating anecdotes—for example, that Gates and his wife were among the first to receive insulin for their diabetes, and that Gates died of appendicitis, presumably undiagnosed.

3. T.N. Bonner, *Iconoclast: Abraham Flexner and a Life in Learning* (Baltimore: Johns Hopkins University Press, 2002). The curious decline in Flexner's reputation in the late twentieth century, when he was, somewhat uncritically, blamed for the emphasis on science at the expense of "humanism," is changing again with a more realistic revival of interest in what he actually wrote. Bonner, whom we quote, writes that the decline in his reputation was due more to "change in historians than to changes in available knowledge."

4. C.S. Bryan and M.S. Stinson, "The Choice: Lewellys F. Barker and the Full-Time Plan," *Ann. Intern. Med.* 137 (2002): 525-31. The authors relate that Hopkins never came up with the $20,000 originally promised to Dr. Barker, and leave the impression that he was too much of a gentleman to raise specific complaints. He had an illustrious career anyway, and was widely honored in American medicine

5. Welch was a Yankee from Norfolk, Conn. His father was a doctor and there were many other physicians in his deeply religious family. At Yale, Welch had planned to become a professor of Greek, but after some disappointing ventures into teaching, he somewhat reluctantly attended the College of Physicians and Surgeons in New York. Abraham Jacobi, another German Jew, suggested that Welch study in Germany. During his European sojourn he turned increasingly to science. He was to remain a man of the "two cultures" throughout his life, his head with science but his heart with the humanities,

as witnessed by his lifelong interest in social medicine and libraries. In Germany he acquired a good knowledge of science and worked with Julius Cohnheim, whose influence brought him to pathologic physiology, and who later recommended him to the Johns Hopkins Medical School.

Returning to New York, Welch set up America's first pathology laboratory at Bellevue Hospital Medical College, after having been turned down for that task at the College of Physicians and Surgeons. Thanks to Billings, who had met Frederick Dennis, Welch's classmate and longtime friend, on a trip to Germany, he came to Hopkins in Baltimore in August 1885, as the first appointee to the faculty.

During the next few years a large building program immensely expanded Hopkins. By 1913, the Phipps Psychiatric Clinic (1909) and the Harriet Lane Home (1912) had been opened; in the same period came the Phipps Dispensary for Tuberculosis and a four-story surgical building with gynecological wards, given by Dr. Howard Kelly, one of the fabled four at Hopkins.

6. Winternitz, letter to Flexner, 1937.

7. H.K. Beecher and M.D. Altschule, *Medicine at Harvard: The First Three Hundred Years* (Hanover, N.H.: University Press of New England, 1977). This encomium by two Harvard professors has much of interest to one of the authors, but sadly we omit much that pertains to its glory. We paid attention mainly to Harvard's status in the years 1910-1920.

8. A colleague reported acidly, "It was in keeping with Cushing's nature, however, that when he left the Hopkins he took with him a bundle of Hospital histories of patients that had been under his care, and Dr. Smith once told me that it was no easy matter to recover those histories for the Hopkins file."

3. THE YALE MEDICAL SCHOOL BEFORE 1920

1. J.M. Prutkin, "Abraham Flexner and the Development of the Yale School of Medicine," *Yale J. Biol. Med.* 72 (1999): 269-79. A fourth-year medical student when this article appeared, Prutkin did the spadework when he was an undergraduate at Yale, using many of the same references that we have studied in the Yale archives.
2. J.A. Schiff, "Getting Yale on the Right Track," *Yale Alumni Bulletin*, November 1999: 88. The hope of uniting the management and the responsibilities of the Medical School and the hospital has never been realized. Howard Spiro recalls that when he came to the Medical School in 1955, the hospital was responsible for washing the outside of the office windows and the Medical School the inside, but the two could never coordinate the jobs, with the result that the faculty could only dimly glimpse the environs of New Haven. Whether that played a role in their insulation from the city can be argued.

3. M.D. Tilson, lecture notes, Feb. 2, 1981. This unpublished manuscript is a mine of information, on which we have relied.
4. Board of Permanent Officers, Notes 1920 (Medical-Historical Library files).
5. George Blumer is the man for whom the Blumer shelf was named. (This is the mass one feels in the rectal vault when a gastric cancer has spread to the pelvis.) He is also remembered for his aphorism exhorting physicians to carry out a routine rectal examination: "If you don't put your finger in it, you'll put your foot in it."
6. C.-E.A.Winslow, *Dean Winternitz and the Yale School of Medicine* (New Haven: Yale University Press, 1935). This paean to Winter originated as an address delivered before the Association of Yale Alumni in Medicine on June 17, 1935.
7. *Report of the Committee on the Relationship between the Hospital, the Dispensary and the Medical School* (1920), pp. 71-75.
8. John R. Paul, "Dean Winternitz and the Rebirth of the Yale Medical School in the 1920s," *Yale J. Biol. Med.*. 43 (1970): 110-19.
9. Winter wrote to Welch on Jan. 3, 1920, that "the medical school is in a rather precarious situation. The Corporation has neither decided its policy nor just how far it will support the Medical School, and the hospital, now on full-time, has been boycotted by the local physicians and has a deficit of over ten thousand dollars a month.

Needless to say, it will be unable to continue in the present year unless financial help is received."

Later letters from Flexner to Winter asked about the full-time system at Yale and how it was working out, as he was planning to write a book on the topic. In May 1921, Flexner wrote that Dean David Edsall of Harvard was appalled that Henry Christian, then the first head of Medicine at the old Peter Bent Brigham Hospital, wrote to a Dr. Holland that he could earn an extra $30,000 from his clinical practice, a substantial sum in those days. The letter was certainly calculated to extract support from the loyal Yale alumnus.

4. Professor Of Pathology

1. Her surname, given Winter's fun with names, must have provided a rare moment of levity that first year
2. Letter from Nelson Ordway, June 2, 1996. Ordway recalls the oft-told story about Winters's bike ride from the slaughterhouse where he had stopped to get some organs as happening at Hopkins, when Winter was younger.
3. Letter from William Wedemeyer, June 19, 1996. This letter is the source of many of the details in this chapter.
4. Frank Fusec, after whom the Pathology Department library was named, was the first department embalmer; he endeared himself to generations of medical students and pathologists. Winter hired him when he was a boy

with an eighth-grade education, and Frank never worked anywhere else. Just as Winter had sent Bayne-Jones to study with Hans Zinsser, on a totally different level he sent Frank to embalming school, figuring he had the man he wanted. He trained him for the job and Frank repaid him with unquestioning loyalty, learning his lessons well and training the students and interns. He kept the instruments sharp and set them out for the prosector who was to do the autopsy and whose responsibility it was to clean up and powder the reusable rubber gloves. He became Winter's errand boy and the staff's "banker." He played "the numbers" with apparent success because he always had a wad of bills in his pocket. Rumor has it that he charged the staff no interest, to tide them over the rough spots. Frank was smart, and he heard everything and repeated nothing, so everyone liked and trusted him.

Married to Frank, Millie Fusec was a very important part of the subculture of the hospital and Medical School, which in those days seemed to be one big family—as it was. Millie's whole family worked at the hospital. Living in the neighborhood, they started working there after school before they had even graduated. Millie's mother washed glassware "up on the third floor," and Millie started washing glassware in the clinical lab, while paying attention to the technical work being done in the lab. A quiet person, she trained on the job and became one of the finest technicians because she had a sixth sense about bacteriology and an excellent memory.

Frank did all sorts of personal errands for Winter. When a truckload of chickens came down from New Hampshire, the truck would drive into the morgue entrance, where it was met by Frank, who unloaded the chickens and put them in the morgue freezer! If no one else was available to drive to the station to meet a train, Frank was asked to do it, and never seemed to mind. He and Millie had no children. Like Winter's, their life centered around their work.

Jonnie Severo and Eddie Einucci were technicians who started out working for Winter and were inherited by the younger men in the department. Eddie became Levin Waters's man and anyone else had to ask Levin first, to get Eddie to help them. Eddie was a smart observer, understood research, and was good with animals. Peter Integlia was a handsome man with a sweet, even disposition and a quiet voice. The women all liked him, and he got along well with his coworkers. He married Gladys, who worked in the laundry, and it was said they had to marry after too many trips to the linen closet.

5. M.C. Winternitz, "The Yale School of Medicine in Wartime, 1917-1941" (unpublished MS).

6. M.C. Winternitz, *Collected Studies on the Pathology of War Gas Poisoning* (New Haven: Yale University Press, 1920).

7. M.C. Winternitz, I.M. Wason, and F.P. McNamara, *Pathology of Influenza* (New Haven: Yale University Press., 1920).

8. Interview with Wedemeyer and Yesner, June 7, 1996. While the CPCs and Grand Rounds were excellent teaching sessions, John Peters would walk out of the CPC after presenting the clinical material to avoid being harassed by Winter, and others did the same. Francis Blake was described as making long, leisurely clinical diagnoses, which were entirely wrong, as Winter announced in no uncertain manner. That frankness and arrogance won him few friends.

9. Soon after Priscilla Norton moved to New Haven in 1945, she joined a sewing circle that made clothes for Dutch children who had been bombed out or uprooted by the war. The leaders of the group were Mrs. George Parmelee Day, wife of the treasurer of Yale, and her good friend Mrs. Shepherd Stevens. Mrs. Stevens understood that this "child" who had managed to survive wartime Washington, London, and Paris could easily run aground in New Haven. The two women gently indoctrinated Priscilla into "the way we do things" without knowing that they were passing along living history, for the social mores of New Haven have changed more since World War II than they had in the preceding century. Mrs. Stevens towered over her protégée, and when she wore her cape, the effect of being tucked under her wing was graphic. Priscilla has drawn heavily on these recollections and more recently interviewed Mrs. Franklin Farrel, who came to New Haven as a bride in 1932. She is a perceptive observer with a worldly perspective. Mrs. Drayton Heard grew up in New Haven and called Polly

Whitney "Aunt Polly." She had illuminating and fair-minded insights and knowledge of the Whitney/Winternitz family. The photographic archives of the New Haven Colony Historical Society confirmed visual memories, and a history of the Fortnightly Club by Club by Catharine Barclay, illustrated by Jane Hooker, confirmed the rules of social behavior of the first half of the twentieth century.

10. Until it closed temporarily, a dinner at Mory's, with the voices of the Whiffenpoofs or the women of the New Blue filling the low-ceilinged, wood-paneled rooms hung with photographs, made one dream that things had not changed very much at Yale. But of course they have–and fortunately so.

11. Asians were treated somewhat better if they came from abroad. Since 1834, when Peter Parker, a graduate of both the Divinity School and the Medical School, with conditional degrees forbidding him–so legend has it–to practice either divinity or medicine in the United States, sailed for Canton as a medical missionary, Yale has had an interest in China, as it does to this day. In Parker's day, divinity was considered a more demanding and serious subject than medicine. So Asians from abroad were welcomed if they were well connected, had a proper introduction, and were only passing through. Europeans with titles were exciting, but European scholars and students–one had to know more about them before letting them into the house. New Haven society was not fond of foreign travel and not much interested in the outside world.

They found their comfort and inspiration in the past and in their home territory.

12. Winter would go out of his way for a delicacy such as crab, bay scallops, or a good loaf of bread, but he never sneaked anywhere–except possibly to preserve a lady's reputation.

13. Ross Harrison is given full credit by Hannah Landecker in her wonderful book *Culturing Life: How Cells Became Technologies* (Cambridge: Harvard University Press, 2007). Landecker emphasizes that Harrison's cell-culture techniques made it possible to study cells "in vitro" rather than "in vivo," and so facilitated the "immortal cell" advances of Alexis Carrell, who received the Nobel Prize. In her view, Harrison's signal advance paved the way to the victories of organ transplantation in the twenty-first century. He was a great man, personally as well as scientifically.

5. THE GLORY TRAIL

1. We have drawn heavily on Levin Waters's unpublished history of the Yale School of Medicine, 1920-1960, for the first part of this chapter.

2. Winternitz, letter to Dean Blumer, Jan. 2, 1920. Here he comments, as head of the "laboratory of pathology and bacteriology," about the importance of keeping bacteriology at the Medical School.

3.George Blumer, Memorandum of suggestions derived from meeting at Mr. Stokes's house, May 29, 1919. The original manuscript suggests a "shot across the bow" of the dean's ship, to which he responds with the terse series of comments.

4. Winternitz, Acceptance of Deanship, May 7, 1920, pp. 113-14 (2.

5. Winternitz, Dean's Reports, 1921-1935. These reports, available in a bound volume, are an invaluable guide to Winter's thoughts and accomplishments. They were usually "preprinted," but the last, his 1935 report, was "reprinted" from supplements to the *University Bulletin*. In it Winter regretted that his request for 15-year summaries "was not followed in all cases," a reflection of his rapidly shrinking authority.

6. Robert Hutchins was the "Wiz kid" of his time. A poor boy, he worked his way through Yale, achieving considerable intellectual celebrity that was not particularly valued at that time. After graduating in 1921, he went off to Florida to teach school, but was rescued from that job to become secretary of the university in 1923! After graduating from the Law School in 1927, while carrying on the duties of the secretary, he was made dean of the Law School almost immediately. He soon moved to the University of Chicago to become its president, but was to be disappointed in what he could do there.

7. Miss Dasey was the centerpiece of a skit in the 1946 student production that "brought down the house." Whoever played her role "caught" her vividly, and the

response of the students showed great warmth of feeling for her.

8. Winternitz kept the title of chairman of Pathology, Levin Waters believed, not so much because he wanted to do both jobs as because the chairmanship represented a "fall-back" refuge if he were not always dean, as indeed it did. In darker moments, Waters also wondered whether Winternitz might be drawing two salaries in these circumstances.

9. It was the same problem that he had later with the Institute for Human Relations–trusting in "propinquity" without planning for how it would come about. The easygoing approach at Harvard, in the English tradition of hospital clinicians without university appointments, may have been a more productive way: in the 1950s and 1960s, one striking contrast between the Massachusetts General Hospital and the Grace-New Haven Community Hospital was the abundance of important clinical reports by the so-called "part-timers" at Massachusetts General, in contrast to the relative reserve of similar physicians in New Haven. This changed in the last part of the twentieth century with the appearance, as if in recompense, of a number of talented surgeon-writers, all in private practice, among them Richard Selzer, Sherwin Nuland, and Bernie Siegel.

10. N.K. Ordway, letter, June 2, 1996.

11. "Dean Winternitz: Worcestershire Sauce in the Academic Bill of Fare,"
Yale Scientific Magazine 16 (Autumn 1932): 15-19.

12. By 1927, when Welch was president of Scientific Directors of the Rockefeller Foundation, Blake was its secretary.
13. Interview with Betty Harvey, Aug. 25, 1995. Betty Harvey was frank: her father saw himself as a WASP gentleman who never took credit for other people's work, whereas Winter, she had been told, often put his names on others' papers. Winter aroused a lot of antagonism by getting rid of those who did not do things his way, and relations between her father and Winter were so difficult that Winter never dined at Harvey's house. On the other hand, Betty emphasized the friendship between Harvey and Max Taffel, who often came to dinner there.

6. The Winter Years: Highs And Lows

1. Winter must have seen in Taffel something of the earnest young Jewish student he had once been.
2. J. Fulton, *Harvey Cushing: A Biography* (Springfield, Ill.: C.C. Thomas, 1947). Fulton skips over Winternitz almost completely in his account of Cushing at Yale, except to refer to him a few times as the "dynamic" dean.
Howard Spiro can vouch for the truth of the nickname Fulton acquired when he was admitted, regularly, for removal of ascitic fluid from his belly, though he has been criticized for perpetuating the story by those who want our heroes to have no faults.

3. Ray Yesner, a pathologist of many years' standing at Yale, and for whom a professorship has been named, accepts Susan Cheever's account of her grandmother's "follicular tonsillitis" after which she was never well, and notes that no autopsy was carried out.
4. F.T. Murphy, letter to President Angell, May 5, 1927. Murphy comments frankly to Angell about the insistence of Flexner that various appointments be made, but he goes on to mention Winternitz's financial problems and his own offer of help, which Winternitz had turned down.
5. Interview with Tom Winternitz, April 29, 1996. Among other matters, Winter's son Tom thinks that his father got the Department of Dentistry going because he was convinced that Helen's illness had its origin in her teeth. This was a popular idea in the early part of the last century, one that led in the 1920s to the wholesale extraction of innocent teeth for many different problems.
6. Helen's death is recorded in a death certificate dated April 25, 1930, and signed by Francis G. Blake, M.D. It gives the primary cause of death as "chronic nephritis" and the contributory causes as "acute pericarditis and pleurisy," usually inevitable complications in the days before dialysis. The duration of disease was recorded as four years. Helen was 45 years old.

7. Winter, Social Medicine, and Psychiatry

1. In their holistic approach to patients, this new breed regards mind and body as one, as they should, but their assuredness might be tempered by this cautionary tale.
2. Nick Spinelli as a medical student observed that Winternitz was happy and voluble one day, but the next found him depressed and withdrawn, all of which made Spinelli wonder whether Winter was manic-depressive, or as is said nowadays, bipolar. No one else has suggested this possibility, however.
3. J.W. Engel, "Early Psychiatry at Yale: Milton C. Winternitz and the Founding of the Department of Psychiatry and Mental Hygiene," *Yale J. Biol. Med.* 67 (1994): 33-47. Engel gives a full rendition of Winternitz's strong interest in psychiatry and discusses the misadventures that arose in recruiting a psychiatrist for Yale, which he ascribes to Angell's concern about spending too much money. There was considerable conflict over Kahn's interest in psychoses as against the concerns of Winter and his allies for the "normal" functioning of people, then called "mental hygiene."
4. The story has many times been repeated of how Harkness, rebuffed by the president, went up to Cambridge, where the president of Harvard greeted him warmly and accepted $10 million for the houses at Harvard. Thereafter, Harkness returned to New Haven, where a chastened

president of Yale greeted him more warmly and got another $10 million for the colleges at Yale.

5. Winternitz, "Summary of Observations on European Trip, April 24-June 14, 1929." This frank document , prepared for private circulation, is philosophical and seems intended to emphasize Winternitz's contempt for the tight compartmentalization that he found rampant in Europe. "Clinical psychiatry as we conceive it can only be done by a man with a long and stable experience in clinical psychiatry. . . . If he has training and experience in basic scientific branches so much more is gained, but the first is fundamental and without it no clinic will flourish." Of Eugen Kahn, Winter wrote, "I think Kahn is a Jew. He is married and has three children. He certainly has none of the disagreeable qualities personally of his race and seems like a fine chap." Incidentally, Ted Lidz said that Eugen Kahn was fired because he was growing paranoid and it was thought that he might have something even worse wrong with him. Lidz did not know that Kahn, at least ostensibly, was a Jew.

6. Later, under the leadership of Fritz Redlich, the Psychiatry Department went on to great success, despite its less than propitious beginnings. For many decades it was a home for psychoanalysis, but latterly it has become a center for first-rate neurobiology as the mind gives way before the images of the brain.

7. Winternitz, The Arthur Hiller Ruggles Oration (to the Rhode Island Society for Mental Hygiene), May 7, 1954. Winter was not one to recognize defeat very

readily. In this lecture honoring Ruggles, he referred in passing to the Institute for Human Relations and the defection of the Law and Divinity Schools. "The rest of the program, however, developed without delay. The central theme remained the behavior of the individual and of the group. Its approaches included the arts as expressed by medicine, law, sociology, religion, and also the sciences relating to biology and health." Winter went on to tell how the members of the institute paid more attention to their own quests, destroying his grand hopes, and lamented his own failure to provide "even a hypothetical pattern."

8. G. Rosen, "Approaches to a Concept of Social Medicine: A Historical Survey," *Milbank Memorial Fund Quarterly* 26 (1948): 7-21. One of the earlier papers from an important Yale historian of social medicine.

9. As they were to do again in the death camps there half a century later.

10. D. Porter, "Changing Disciplines: John Ryle and the Making of Social Medicine in Britain in the 1940's," *History Science* 30 (1992): 137-64.

11. J.A. Ryle, "Social Pathology and the New Era in Medicine," *Bull. NY Academy of Medicine*, June 1947: 312-29; *Changing Disciplines: Lectures on the History, Method and Motives of Social Pathology* (Oxford: Oxford University Press, 1948). The author, a hero to Howard Spiro since the 1940s, in these writings adopted statistical methods to bolster his teaching about social medicine. "We no longer believe that medical truths are only or chiefly to be

discovered under the microscope, by means of the test-tube and the animal experiment, or by clinical examination and the increasingly elaborate pathological studies at the bedside."

12. D. Porter, "John Ryle: Doctor of Revolution?" in D. Porter and R. Porter, eds., *Doctors, Politics, and Society: Historical Essays* (Amsterdam: Wellcome Institute, 1993).

13. This imbalance persists today. Lewis Thomas, the articulate champion of science, is enshrined as the saint of molecular medicine for stressing how molecular medicine makes superfluous what he derided as the "halfway measures" on which clinicians–and public health workers–have so long relied.

14. I. Galston, *The Meaning of Social Medicine* (Cambridge: Harvard University Press, 1954). With John Ryle, Galston stands as one of the great proponents of social medicine. This book is his masterpiece.

15. Sarah H. Tracy, "An Evolving Science of Man," in C. Lawrence and D. Weisz, eds., *Greater Than the Parts: Holism in Biomedicine, 1920-1950* (Oxford: Oxford University Press, 1998).

16. Priscilla Ellis, "The Institute of Human Relations at Yale: A Study in the Creation and Prehistory of a Setting" (M.A. thesis). Seymour Sarason, professor of psychology at Yale, gave us a copy of the dissertation of Priscilla Ellis, a Yale graduate student in the 1970s. Her 109-page typescript contains numerous references to archival material, much of which we have also reviewed. Ellis reports on interviews she carried out with people who had been active

in the IHR in its early years. Like our interviews, however, they took place 30-odd years later. Consequently, the conclusions drawn by the principals are subject to the usual caveats about the gloss of nostalgia.

17. J.B. Gordon, "Notes on the History of Clinical Sociology at Yale," *Clinical Sociological Review* 11 (1989): 42-51. Gordon discovered and printed a paper from memos in the Winternitz Papers dating from 1930. We are grateful for her generosity in sharing both her discovery and her paper with us. Also preserved in the Winternitz Papers (Box 90, folder 663) is a letter from Adolph Meyer dated Jan. 4, 1924. "Not all the 'pathos' can be expressed in terms of tissues and structures," Meyer writes. "The mind . . . is a function of the body; it is the individual in action."

18. A.J. Viseltear, "Milton Charles Winternitz and the Yale Institute of Human Relations: A Brief Chapter in the History of Social Medicine," *Yale J. Biol. Med.* 57 (1984): 869-89. This is an important document from one of Rosen's successors, unfortunately cut off early in life.

19. Later, when it was clear that clinical sociology was never to be at the Medical School, Winter began to compromise by suggesting the need for a "social physician" who would deal with crime and the courts, all under the umbrella of the IHR as the "great unifying agent." His faith in all the get-togethers, which were so characteristic of the Medical School in the 1920s, today seems somewhat naïve, when work alone is what counts and leisure has been lost.

20. E.D. Smith, "The Scientific School and Human Relations," *Yale Scientific Magazine* 1931.
21. J. Dollard, "Yale Institute of Human Relations: What Was It?" *Ventures* 1964: 32-40. In his memoir of gratitude to the institute a quarter-century later, Dollard praised the "passion to integrate," which he saw as the driving force, and not as formless as others have remembered. The institute failed, he believes, because the money ran out and because the institute was, as Flexner realized, a competitor to the university.
22. R. Lemov, *World as Laboratory* (New York: Hill & Wang, 2005). This very informative book came as a surprise to Howard Spiro in its disclosures of aspects of the institute that have gone unmentioned or unrecorded at the Medical School.
23. Seymour Sarason, *The Making of an American Psychologist: An Autobiography* (San Francisco: Jossey-Bass, 1988).
24. E. Shorter, *A History of Psychiatry* (New York: Wiley and Sons, 1997). In part relying on Sarason, Shorter reports that Eugen Kahn, who had been a student of Kraepelin, was ousted at Yale by a group of rebel psychoanalysts headed by Fritz Redlich, who succeeded him. Such a cycle of events cautions against too much certainty.

8. Winter And The Quota System

1. The research for this book, carried out when Oren was still a college student, was "vetted" by Prof. G.W. Pierson, the Yale historian on whom we have relied for many details of this period. It is a remarkably candid account of the restrictions that Jewish students endured during the first half of the twentieth century, made all the more forceful by Oren's free access to Yale's archives. Oren kindly made his research cards and notes available to us, for which we express our gratitude.

2. Harry Zimmerman claimed that Winternitz went to Baltimore to be with his father for the High Holy Days each year, keeping it a secret from everyone but Zimmerman. However, no one else, not even Winter's Baltimore relatives whom we have interviewed, has corroborated the story, which might have added a scintilla of loyalty to Winter's credit. Given the virtual absence of Winter's father and mother from his life in New Haven, we discount its reliability.

3. J. Cuddihy, *The Ordeal of Civility* (New York: Basic Books, 1974).

4. Polanyi migrated from Hungary to Germany and thence to England. His life was typical of the assimilated Jewish intelligentsia of the early 20th century. The passage of time has made his direct quotations no longer available to us, although reviews of his published work suggests his adherence to the larger society: "Jews who

were not satisfied to be Jews had made tremendous contributions to humanity," in contrast to the ghetto Jews, whom he described as a "somber, squalid mass."

5. Charles Angoff, *Journey to Dawn, The Morning Light, The Sun at Noon:* these are his "Polonsky stories," published by the Beechhurst Press in New York from 1957.

6. Incidentally, H.L. Mencken, whose reputation as an anti-Semite is as ill deserved as that of Nietzsche, is mentioned numerous times in Angoff's *The Sun at Noon*, while another character, favorably treated, strongly resembles a fictionalized Mencken.

7. S. Klingenstein. Jews in the American Academy, 1900–1940: The Dynamics of Intellectual Assimilation (New Haven: Yale University Press, 1991).

8. H. Horowitz, *Campus Life* (New York: Knopf, 1987).The daughter-in-law of the first Jewish trustee of Yale points out that even the most urbane and educated Jews suffered discrimination in the universities. When Felix Frankfurter was asked to speak at one of Harvard's exclusive clubs, a number of members boycotted the dinner because a Jew had been invited to speak. Horowitz contrasts the changes at Harvard: in the 1880s Bernard Berenson, a Lithuanian Jew by birth, was admitted to the "final" clubs, she relates, while Walter Lippmann was excluded from them and from many organization on campus despite his "assimilated" upbringing.

9. L. Kalman, *Abe Fortas: A Biography* (New Haven: Yale University Press, 1990). It seemed of interest to review the life of this oft-appointed favorite of Lyndon

Johnson because he was a nonreligious Jew at the Yale Law School and editor of its *Law Journal* in 1932. Regardless, Kalman paints an even more dismal picture of the profound if genteel anti-Semitism that pervaded the legal profession in those days, in the university as much as in the firms. She casts light on Winter's uneasy relationship with other Jews at Yale by describing an encounter between Fortas and another student: each circuitously tried to find out whether the other was a Jew before "admitting" that fact.

10. Sarason, *Making of an American Psychologist*. In his autobiography, definitively entitled "American," as it should be, this eminent clinical psychologist sharply recorded his own experiences in joining the faculty at Yale as the first Jewish member of the Psychology Department. Sarason explains the rapidity with which Yale and other colleges overcame the prejudices of their past.

11. Even now, it might seem almost ungracious to recall such unpleasant memories, were it not for the lessons they have to offer in the current world of growing diversity and the unhappiness that students of Asian origin, for example, though born in America, still feel. The sympathy we feel for the trials of the Jews in the last century should remind us of the difficulties that more recent immigrants and African-Americans still encounter.

12. Interview with Philip Sapir, Oct. 3, 1995.

13. Interview with H. Zimmerman, May 31, 1995. Zimmerman, born in New Haven, went to college at Yale with the class of 1924. He credited Colonel Ullman, who hired Jewish boys to work at his Strouse-Adler corset factory so they could earn money for medical school tuition, with getting him into the Yale Medical School. Zimmerman indicated that Winter was impressed by what Ullman was doing. He implicitly compared his relation to Winter with that of the famed Sidney Farber of Harvard to his mentor, S.B. Wolbach, allegedly also a Jew. Farber had told Zimmerman that Wolbach had always been kind to him. Incidentally, Zimmerman was convinced that despite their sojourn in Vienna, the Winternitz parents were "galitzianers."

Winter "picked up" Zimmerman when he was a student, nurtured him, and steered him toward neuropathology and neurophysiology, even sending him to Germany for a year. His kindness toward some Jewish boys, the bright and presentable ones, stands out over the years. Given the few Jews at the Yale Medical School in those days, we suspect that Winternitz thus showed a proverbial and statistically probable soft spot for men he perceived to be much like himself.

14. The unwillingness to record much of the polite anti-Semitism of the 1930s in America is paralleled by the difficulty Germans have nowadays in discussing the history of their country in that same era.

15. S.R. Kaufman, *The Healers' Tale: Transforming Medicine and Culture* (Madison: University of Wisconsin Press,

1993). This is a full and engaging account of what the medical world was like in the middle of the last century. We quote extensively from it in the text.

16. Patricia Norton feels that Winter wanted to hire more refugees, both for humanitarian reasons and because they were well trained. The "quota," she thinks, may have been cloaked in economic numbers.

17. Although Mary Cheever commented that her father did not regard himself as a Jew and considered him anti-Semitic, none of the Jewish doctors who were his students has ever suggested this to us. They regard him as helping out, within the limits of the system, those Jews he admitted. One might surmise that he regarded his children as Christian and therefore not people with whom he could be entirely honest

18. In the end, Winter can be seen as an ambitious Jewish boy, not so much forsaking his Jewish background as being attracted to the Protestant background of the people he most admired. He had convinced himself that he was a WASP and could therefore act as Jewish as he wanted, without fear of appearing (to himself) overly "Jewish" What we have learned suggests that he was fair at all times to the Jews who were lucky enough to get into the Medical School. Dr. Sam Ritvo's story, already related, bears some relevance here.

In *The Social Transformation of American Medicine* (New York: Basic Books, 1982), P. Starr notes the anti-Jewish atmosphere in American hospitals, but curiously does not emphasize the limitation of numbers in the medical schools. Bayne-Jones as dean is reported to have upheld the anti-Jewish restrictions wholeheartedly, certainly more enthusiastically than Winternitz. Indeed, Bayne-Jones, was unwilling to keep Louis Weinstein on as an instructor in immunology for more than one year. Weinstein related to Howard Spiro, with great bitterness, the strong stand that Bayne-Jones took against him in April 1938. He went on to a great career as a microbiologist and clinician, much beloved at the Tufts Medical School.

9. THE WIDOWER REMARRIES

1. The letters to Winter's children, dictated to his secretary, were long and quite impersonal. Filled with formulaic descriptions of flowers and other inconsequential information, they were of little interest to his children, we understand. On the other hand, Mary Cheever says that nothing personal was *ever* discussed at home or in the family. Letters to and from Mary, who was something of a rebel, seem the most exuberant of all.
2. The apartment in New York was not a unique alternative to boarding school. Such arrangements were fairly common, especially among parents who believed in progressive education. In fact, one of us shared an apartment in New York with an art student the last two years of high school. It was a kinder, gentler world then.
3. "Dean Winternitz Quietly Marries Pauline Whitney," *Waterbury Herald*, April 10, 1932: The newspaper went on

to note that Winternitz had been arrested three or four years before because he had failed to answer a summons on a motor vehicle charge, adding that Dean Charles Clark of Yale Law School was judge in the town court. The newspaper omitted to mention that Clark had been dead set against bringing the Law School down to Cedar Street, but it did describe the fight that ensued when the Yale-controlled New Haven Hospital tried to take over the Grace Hospital. The newspaper article closed by noting that the dean had been fined $25 and that after the trial he asked that the fine be remitted to him by the court.

4. Interview with Betty Harvey, Aug. 25, 1995. There were three Whitney families in New Haven: the "sporting" Whitneys, the "academic" Whitneys, and the "inventive" Whitneys. Polly was a New Yorker, and presumably from the first group. No one could believe that she would marry Winternitz.

10. Rebellion And Defeat

1. Parenthetically, this has been a common phenomenon in academic medicine over the past 50 years. The more intellectually oriented college students, it has seemed, often choose a course of study leading to a Ph.D., preferring the rigors of science or humanities to the easier rewards of clinical medicine. For the most part, those who choose medicine are more interested in people, and

eager for the nearer than the farther rewards. Regardless of whether that assertion is entirely valid, many students come to medical school wanting to help leave the world "a better place." They have had very little prior interest in science except for knowing that a scientific background is more likely than one in the social sciences to get them into medical school.

Once admitted, however, they run the risk of seduction by their elders into trying a scientific career. The argument runs something like the following: "You want to take care of patients and to teach. To do that you must establish your credentials by going into a laboratory for three to five years. Learn to do science, write some papers to establish your reputation as a research scientist, and then you can do what you want." Having bent to the will of another, the would-be medical teachers ("medical Marranos" they have been called, after the Jews who survived in newly all-Catholic Spain by accepting baptism but remaining Jews in their secret observances) turned academic physicians continue to "do" research and never really get back to patient care. How much Winter's career was influenced by similar considerations can be a matter for speculation only, but it is telling that after his long period as dean, his laboratory pursuits in pathology seemed always to run at a second or third remove.

2. Even if Gregg was not fostering the idea, but had simply sent around a memorandum, Winter's response would be as apt today as it was then. What would he think of the "technology transfer" of current times, with

its numerous patents and other profitable circumscriptions of academic freedom and academic conversation? Or of the "equity interests" of the medical faculty in the 21st century?

3. The BPO notes state that on Dec. 12, 1934, a group was constituted "to discuss the question of the Deanship." On Dec. 19, after Bayne-Jones was selected, "Harvey Cushing was informally delegated to wait upon the Dean and acquaint him with the situation. Signed, H.S. Burr."

4. It may not be anachronistic to suggest that this too has remained a characteristic flaw in the management of overall full-time medicine at Yale. The dean's office into the 21st century maintained total control over the allocation of clinical funds, which may be a legacy of Winternitz that has held back Yale's development of an international clinical reputation.

5. Sixty years later, in the 1990s, we noted that some of the collegial amenities so cherished by Winternitz had been lost once there was no forum for faculty to express or discuss their concerns. The Board of Permanent Officers had swollen to more than 250, which made it largely an innocuous gathering that few attended because nothing of consequence has ever been acted upon, and was rarely even discussed. In concert with department chairmen, the dean was believed to make all decisions; he controlled information about salaries. Matters of policy came down as pronouncements on which the faculty had no vote and little choice. A general faculty meeting had

been held only every several years, usually when a new dean came aboard to promise increased collegiality and more frequent faculty meetings, and then again, sometimes, when he announced his retirement. The rebellion against Winter's dictatorial rule may have succeeded, but the overall hierarchical approach has little changed at the Yale Medical School in the subsequent six decades. Indeed, at this writing, the regular meetings of the BPO have been suspended, apparently to no one's regret.

6. Albert E. Cowdrey, *War and Healing: Stanhope Bayne-Jones and the Maturing of American Medicine* (Baton Rouge: Louisiana State University Press, 1992); M.C. Leikind, "Stanhope Bayne-Jones: Physician, Teacher, Soldier, Scientist-administrator, Friend of Medical Libraries," *Bull. N.Y. Acad. Med.* 48 (1972): 584-95. Stanhope Bayne-Jones was the son and grandson of physicians. After his mother's death he was raised in relatively comfortable surroundings, secure in himself if sometimes disappointed in his own accomplishments. He became a war hero after volunteering to serve as a physician in the British Expeditionary Force during the First World War, as well as in the Second. Apparently a likable, elegant, and "clubbable" academic, he is revered by his biographers, however unlikely that seems to those who liked Winternitz.

Bayne-Jones's deanship was quite different from Winter's, as attested by Morris Wessel's experience as a medical student in 1941. Wessel came to Yale believing that Winternitz's philosophy of medical education still held firm. When Franz Goldman, the eminent German public health expert, was slated to give a seminar on finances and medical care, Wessel signed up for the course, only to receive a message from the dean to "stop going into sociology and stick to medicine." Wessel's solution was to ask Goldman if he might audit the course, which he did. Not a lot of correspondence exists, but what we have found corroborates much of the foregoing supposition.

7. Peter Dobkin Hall, personal communication, ca. 2006.

11. Wandering In The Wilderness

1. The party was held in the Beaumont Room above the library, a pine-paneled room with a very large table in the middle and long windows with window seats facing east. Now these handsomely draped windows look out over the roof of the library, but in the 1930s they overlooked the tennis courts. There are three chandeliers, wall sconces line the walls, and handsome portraits grace either end. William Beaumont is at the head, above the fireplace, with Peter Parker, graduate of Yale's Divinity and Medical Schools, and the Rev. Jared Eliot, the first physician in New Haven Colony, at the other. To use one of Winter's favorite words, it is a "splendid" room entered through glass doors over which is a semicircular panel, unadorned until the party.

In 1935 liquor was once again freely available and was served openly. Winter was not in a mood to worry about decorum, nor were the students. As the evening reached its climax, Winter said, "By God, I'm going to leave my mark on this place." The weapon of choice varies according to who is telling the story, but it was either a sword or a carving knife that he brandished as he was lifted on Waters's shoulders. He carved an *M* and a *W* over the door, a brand that is still there, however diminished by later error. As he did so, a loud cheer rang out for the dean.

2. Incidentally, Helen Angell much later wrote to Winter of her husband's anger at what he saw as Hutchins's "desertion" of Yale, predicting, if not hoping, that nothing good would come of his move to Chicago. According to Helen, Hutchins was so upset with Angell's attitude that he asserted he would move to Chicago even if he had to open a "peanut stand on the grounds."

3. After a while, Waters began to enjoy days that started with steak and baked potatoes for breakfast, a nap, a good book, and sometimes a lecture from one of the warmly clothed doctors, whose words of wisdom were wrapped in clouds of vapor. He tried to pick up the rhythm of those vapor puffs, but never could make it into a musical beat. Waters and his fellow patients watched spring come one day at a time. They watched one of their number weaken and be moved off the porch, never to be seen again. They watched most get well, graduating to ambulatory privileges, to being allowed to play bridge,

and finally to wandering about the grounds to see what was behind and beyond the field of vision from a stationary bed. Only his shoes and socks still fit him when he left Gaylord six months later, weighing 207 pounds. The treatment saved his life for a while, but cost him his life in the end. His arteries were loaded with fat, and by the time he was 35 he was suffering angina pains regularly.

12. THE WAR YEARS

1. L.L. Waters, "Chemical Warfare Medicine in Two Wars." We have relied extensively on this unpublished manuscript for many of the details in this chapter. It was given as a Beaumont Lecture.
2. Priscilla Norton has drawn heavily upon her own first-hand experiences during World War II, working for the Navy Department in Washington and with the OSS in England and France. "Most of us had been trained for something else. Just knowing how to do what we were assigned to do gave one great authority and believability. Those of us who were very young really thought we could make a difference in the outcome of the war. A man like Winter knew he was the right man for the job. Rivalries between the services, between career military men and '90 day wonders,' the rivalries between departments trying to cooperate on plans for production, all were fascinating to observe for someone who was just stepping into the adult world. Patriotism was easy to

understand, but the blindness of prejudice and the insecurity of paranoia were disheartening for someone who had observed Hitler's Germany first hand and knew what she was fighting for. In London she found the spirit, the civility and the gutsiness that deserve to be called 'their finest hour.'"

Priscilla Norton disembarked at Glasgow after waiting three days in the Firth of Clyde while the *Queen Mary* was unloaded. It was an endless procession of ships, filled with new arrivals. The sick bay was emptied first, then the men, and lastly whatever was in the hold. Then the sick bay was loaded with the seriously wounded amputees returning home. The *Queen Mary* and the *Isle de France* were fast enough to travel alone, as opposed to traveling in convoy. In New York they were able to load at the same time, and the *Queen Mary* set sail first, at night and only hours ahead of the *Isle de France*, loaded to capacity, bunks three deep with narrow aisles between, zigzagging our way to Scotland in hope of dodging the German submarines.

The term *disembarking* had been shortened to *debarking*. The sick bay was debarked first, transferring the patients to hospitals, then the men heavily laden with all their personal equipment. Each of our handful of civilian women carried one suitcase, with a musette bag and a handbag slung over our shoulders–all we were allowed for an indefinite period of duty. Last to be emptied was the hold. The return trip was a simpler operation: only those who were not fit for overseas duty or who were being transferred were shipped home, with enough rations for the trip. American ships were "dry," but British crews were issued rations of spirits. We found the Firth of Clyde a bone-chilling place to wait, and when we finally reached dry land our first destination was to sample the *vin du pays*, scotch. We were served the "weest dram" and the bar was closed!

3. The significance of the food and wines served to Winter should not be underestimated. Fifty plus years later, anyone who lived on British rations during the war will feel a twinge of envy at the VIP treatment that he and Woods received

4. Interview with Tom Winternitz, April 29, 1996.

5. Winter's longhand letter to Waters, undated but received on April 5 (1944?) at the NRC and enclosing a letter from Willard Machie, Lt. Col. Medical Corps, Commanding, on Fort Knox stationery. Winter tells of an air-line respirator that has proved to be a sound and efficient means of protecting men from airborne hazards. Machie's letter describes a tube and a face mask, commenting that it protects against all agents except those which can be absorbed through the skin. Characteristically, Winter's mind jumped ahead to visualize an envelope, and no time should be lost! Salter should be dispatched to Fort Knox "soonest" and the engineers should be available to discuss the practicality of an envelope. It should be tested at Knox, and Winter tells Waters to discuss it with General Helman and Colonel Langer.

6. V. DeVita and E. Chu, *A History of Cancer Chemotherapy* (Cancer Research, 2008, 68:8643-8653).

13. AFTER THE WAR

1. Interview with Elizabeth Ford, Oct. 31, 1995. She came to work for the Childs Fund shortly before Winternitz became its chief. She believes the previous woman had gotten in trouble by telling Winter, "This is how B.J. does it." In any event, word of Winter's reputation as a womanizer had reached her, and she quickly made her position clear, with the result that thereafter he called her "Mrs. Chevrolet" rather than "Mrs. Ford." Winter knew how to get his way and could be obsequious when the need arose. He was apparently a valetudinarian who loved to tell others about his ulcer symptoms. Betty Ford relates that when he was in the hospital in Dartmouth, he would send down "reams" of description of his vital signs and excretions. After his death, she discarded all this.
2. We are grateful to Alan R. Schned, of Dartmouth's Department of Pathology, who confirmed that the autopsy on Winter was carried out on Oct. 4, 1959. Dr. Schned, who was graduated from Yale College in 1971 as a member of Berkeley College, gave us access to the autopsy findings with the family's permission. Autopsy of Milton C. Winternitz, #A-59-244, by R.K. House, M.D., Dartmouth Medical School, Hosp Record 154800.

SOURCES

In writing this biography, we have used a number of primary and secondary sources. For the general history of Yale College and University, we have relied on the books listed below, as well as on several unpublished manuscripts that were kindly made available to us. Because of untoward gaps between writing and publishing, we have tried our best to ferret out details, but have not always succeeded. We ask forgiveness.

In addition, we have made extensive use of the Department of Manuscripts and Archives at Yale's Sterling Memorial Library, where are deposited personal letters and other material pertaining to Milton Winternitz, James Rowland Angell, and numerous other worthies. Although we have not always listed the specific box or reference, we have examined a large number of papers, letters, and manuscripts, including many from President Angell's files (boxes 133-135), as well as the Milton C. Winternitz Papers.

In general, we have tried to give references for quotations, but we have read more than we can remember or have annotated, so that in putting together our impressions we may not always have given credit where it belongs. We ask the reader to understand that we claim industry, if not always originality. Again, alas, the gap between the writing of the manuscript and its publication made it almost impossible to fit all the pieces of this jigsaw puzzle together. We have a 3′ x 3′ cardboard box of research material that is so daunting we cannot look within.

If we have inappropriately borrowed phrases from earlier authors without putting them inside quotation marks, we ask the reader to know that we have labored to put together a description of this great hero. The chief author, Priscilla Norton, knew Winternitz well, as her first husband was his protégé. The second author, Howard Spiro, assumes responsibility for comments made about the Yale Medical School, some of which may seem out of place, but which are meant to suggest that the more things seem to change, the more they remain the same.

We have relied on personal interviews with a great many people, including members of the Winternitz family, former colleagues, and friends. We have interviewed former Yale students from Winter's time and are fortunate in having received many written responses to our request for memorabilia and anecdotes. Their names are recorded in the appropriate chapters, but our gratitude is expressed here.

Susan Winternitz Cheever has described her grandfather in two of her books, *Home Before Dark* and *Treetops.* She told us about classified files with much blacked out in them that she had not seen. But no one who has recently been in the office of the dean of the Yale Medical School seems to recognize, or at least acknowledge, their existence.

We admit that this book is as much a memoir as it is a biography, and that Priscilla has been influenced not only by her experiences, but by her love for her first husband, Levin Waters, who for so long worked with–and very much admired–Milton Winternitz.

Howard recognizes that he was shaped, a generation later, by forces not very different from those that shaped Winternitz. His birth in Cambridge, Massachusetts, and his education and training in a Newton far less diverse than it is today contributed to his admiration for Winternitz and gave him an intuitive feeling for Winter's faults as well as his influence. He records his gratitude for the melting pot that shaped both their lives and made it possible for Winter to save the Yale Medical School.

Judith Schiff, chief research archivist at the Yale University Library, and memorable essayist and historian, made our lives easier and our brains fuller by her estimable help. Through her, we praise her staff, who happily brought the files to us and dutifully returned them to the archives.

Books

Bailey, Blake. *Cheever: A Life.* New York: Knopf, 2009.

Bernheim, Bertram M. *The Story of the Johns Hopkins: Four Great Doctors and the Medical School They Created.* New York: Whittlesey House, 1948. A colorful historical account of the early years at Hopkins by a contemporary of Winternitz. Dr. Bernheim was Hopkins A.B. 1901 and

M.D. 1905. His book has the same charm as that by J.M.T. Finney.

Cross, Wilbur. Connecticut Yankee: *An Autobiography.* New Haven: Yale University Press, 1943. Principal of a high school, professor of English and later dean of the Graduate School at Yale, and governor of Connecticut, Cross was a supporter of his young colleague deans at the Law and Medical Schools.

Cushing, H. *The Life of Sir William Osler.* London: Oxford University Press, 1940. One might have anticipated that the noted surgeon would have written a biography of William Halsted, but doubtless his interest in libraries and in bibliography provided Harvey Cushing with the impetus to write about the famously great clinician, still the most revered in the modern western world. More than that, Osler left so indelible an impression in his writings that his biography seems all the more necessary. In this volume, Welch's nickname is spelled "Popsey"; in Finney's it is "Popsie." It comes as a small surprise to find Winternitz not listed in the index of a book first published in 1925, given Cushing's continuing contact with Yale. The motives behind this omission, if any, remain unexplored by us.

Davenport, H.W. *Doctor Dock: Teaching and Learning Medicine at the Turn of the Century.* New Brunswick, N.J.: Rutgers University Press, 1987. Davenport, a noted gastrointestinal physiologist and a teacher of Howard Spiro, describes the life and teaching of George Dock at the University of Michigan from 1899 to 1908. Although only aficionados now remember him, and then mainly as a friend of Osler, Dock was a great clinician, a writer and teacher of surpassing empathy. The book relates anecdotes and examples from the times in which Winternitz was a student and young professor. Great background.

Donaldson, Scott. *John Cheever: A Biography.* New York: Random House, 1988.

Finney, J.M.T. *A Surgeon's Life: The Autobiography of J.M.T. Finney.* New York: Putnam, 1940. This is an account of fifty years of active surgical work by a well-known surgeon at the Johns Hopkins Medical School. Finney trained at the Harvard Medical School and the Massachusetts General Hospital, and then had the good fortune to work for many years at the Johns Hopkins Hospital from its very beginning. His delightful stories of the clinical ways and personalities of the hospitals at the turn of the century just ended helped us set the stage for Winternitz. One example comes in Finney's description of how madly busy Halsted was when he practiced surgery in New York City before his later, far more leisurely life at Hopkins. There are many other delightful passages in this book from another time.

Flexner, A. *I Remember: The Autobiography of Abraham Flexner.* New York: Simon and Schuster, 1940. Flexner is candid about his life and his abandonment of the Jewish religion of his observant parents, amply testifying to the attractions of a wider world. It is of interest that in his early years in Baltimore, he spent Sabbath evenings at the home of Julius Friedenwald, one of the early Jewish gastroenterologists, whom he later appointed to the Institute for Advanced Study at Princeton. Of his parents, Flexner wrote, "Our parents remained to the end of their lives pious Hebrews, attending the synagogue regularly and observing religious feasts. They saw us drift away into screens of thought and feeling that they did not understand. They interposed no resistance. . . . They knew where we were and where we were going, and they made our friends, from a world alien to them, welcome in our home at our table." Flexner's account is worth reading not only for a picture of the medical scene of the time, but for an entry into the mind of a man much like Winternitz, though far more politic. He relates many amusing stories from that more leisurely time.

Harvey, A M. *Adventures in Medical Research: A Century of Discovery at Johns Hopkins.* Baltimore: Johns Hopkins University Press, 1974.

Harvey, A.M., G. H. Brieger, S.L. Abrams, and B.A. McKusick. *A Model of Its Kind.* Vol. 1 of *A Centennial History of*

Medicine at Johns Hopkins. Baltimore: Johns Hopkins University Press, 1989.

Horowtiz, Helen Lefkowitz. *The Power and Passion of M. Carey Thomas.* New York: Knopf, 1994. Before becoming president of Bryn Mawr College, M. Carey Thomas led a group of high-minded, socially prominent Baltimore women interested in higher education who raised the $500,000 needed to complete the Hopkins Medical School and donated it with certain conditions. That women be admitted on an equal footing with men was accepted without objection from the doctors, but the women's insistence upon requirements for admission were thought to be too stringent; it was feared that too few women would qualify or apply. Bernheim thinks Mary Garret has been given credit for the high standards because she gave most of the money and handled the negotiations with the university, but Miss Thomas was the driving force. Through her influence upon Miss Garrett, she played a continuing role in the fortunes of Hopkins. Horowitz has much to say on this subject in her biography.

Kaufman, M. *American Medical Education: The Formative Years, 1765-1910.* Westport, Conn.: Greenwood, 1976.

Lemov, R. *World as Laboratory.* New York: Hill and Wang, 2005. This very informative book came as a surprise to Howard Spiro in its disclosures of aspects of the

Institute of Human Relations that have gone unmentioned or unrecorded at the Yale Medical School.

Ludmerer, K.M. *Learning to Heal: The Development of American Medical Education.* New York: Basic Books, 1985. A learned account that makes plain the growing and widespread urge to improve medical education in the United States. The implication we derive is that both Blumer and Winternitz were part of the zeitgeist that was to bring American medicine up to–and then ahead of–the scientific medicine of Germany and Austro-Hungary.

Miller, Anita. *Uncollecting Cheever.* Lanham, Md.: Rowman and Littlefield, 1998.

Nuland, Sherwin. *The Doctors.* New York: Knopf, 1988.

Pierson, G.W. *Yale: The University College, 1921-1937.* New Haven: Yale University Press, 1955. This history of Yale during the Angell administration is adorned by its author, a professor of history at Yale, with numerous classical allusions, rhetorical niceties of all varieties, and a great love of Yale. The facts are doubtless all correct, but the judgments may be biased. We note with admiration that in the 1970s Pierson helped Daniel Oren with his book about Jews at Yale, opening doors that might have remained shut without the help of an "Old Blue" so much the insider.

Sandler, G. *Jewish Baltimore.* Baltimore: Johns Hopkins University Press, 2000. A loving account of the Russian-Jewish community of Baltimore after 1880, this book offers glimpses of the members of the older German-Jewish community who looked down on the *Ostjuden* as diminishing their status as Americans. Nevertheless, they loyally set up many charitable organizations to help their coreligionists become Americans. The book largely celebrates the triumphs of the mercantile Jews and ignores their progeny of doctors and professors, although there is an account of Henrietta Szold, the Baltimore-born founder of Hadassah, the Jewish women's organization. Julius Friedenwald, the physician-friend of Flexner, is mentioned only in connection with his family's residence.

ARTICLES

Fritz, Jay M. "Dean Winternitz, Clinical Sociology and the Julius Rosenwald Fund." *Clinical Sociology Review* 11 (1989): 17-27.

Fulton, John F. "Some Notes on the Yale University School of Medicine, with Special Reference to Milton Winternitz." *Yale Journal of Biology and Medicine* 22 (1950): 589-94.

Gordon, Judith B. "Notes on the History of Clinical Sociology at Yale." *Clinical Sociology Review* 11 (1989): 42-51.

Liebow, Averill A., and Levin L. Waters. "Milton Charles Winternitz, February 19, 1885-October 3, 1959." *Yale Journal of Biology and Medicine* 32 (1959):
143-72.

Viseltear, Arthur J. "Milton C. Winternitz and the Yale Institute of Human Relations: A Brief Chapter in the History of Social Medicine." *Yale Journal of Biology and Medicine* 57 (1984): 869-89. This is a closely researched piece by a medical historian in love with Yale but never quite rewarded by it before his untimely death. Viseltear was a grand and knowledgeable friend. We have relied heavily on his documents and published papers.

Winternitz, Milton C. "Documents and Correspondence on the Founding of Clinical Sociology at Yale, 1930-31." *Clinical Sociology Review* 11 (1989): 28-41.

Yesner, Raymond. "A Century of Pathology at Yale: Personal Reflections," *Yale Journal of Biology and Medicine* 71 (1998): 397-408

MANUSCRIPTS

Smith, G. "Yale and the External World: The Shaping of the University in the Twentieth Century." The DeVane Lectures, Yale University, 1998. We have consulted these lectures to find material that our own searches may not have turned up—and find it we did, of course. We are grateful for the advice and counsel of their author, Yale professor Gaddis Smith.

Waters, L.L. "The Yale University School of Medicine (1920-1960}."

9969146R0032

Made in the USA
Charleston, SC
28 October 2011